PLEASURE PARTY

by

Hugh O. Smith

UNCLE DONALD,

THANK YOU FOR ALWAYS BELIEVING IN ME + FOR YOUR ENCOURAGEMENT! IT MEANS A LOT!!

[illegible signature]

III

"She was a ghost in a strange house that overnight had become immense and solitary and through which she wandered without purpose, asking herself in anguish which one of them was deader: the man who had died or the woman he had left behind."

GABRIEL GARCÍA MÁRQUEZ, LOVE IN THE TIME OF CHOLERA

CONTENTS

CHAPTER ONE

It started with an angry voice that caused hands occupied with wine glasses and finger foods to freeze midway to waiting mouths. The small group of women turned and stared wide-eyed at the source of the commotion, an angry, dark-haired woman standing by the open door. Her hands were clenched into tight fists like smoking grenades at her sides, and her mouth was set in a grim line. She spoke once more, and her Brooklyn-accented, cigarette-roughened voice pulled apart the words and reconstructed them with drawn-out vowels and hard G's.

"What the hell are you doing here, you whore?"

The party was thirty minutes old and gathering steam slowly. Strangers gathered and chatted amiably among themselves. As the minutes passed and they grew more comfortable, they nonchalantly picked up the catalogs their hosts strategically placed around the room, leafing through them together and whispering conspiratorially, giggling like schoolgirls.

The new arrival's voice was a knife in the heart of the party. Conversation died, and those holding the catalogs put them down guiltily and looked around to see who the recipient of the furious woman's wrath was.

"I know you heard me, bitch," Laura Green said through gritted teeth. "What the fuck are you doing here? Shouldn't you be somewhere wrecking another home?"

The kitchen door swung open, and a curvy redhead, Kristin Zbornak, one of the hosts of the party and owner of the home, emerged. Her ample rear held the swinging door open, and, smiling, she walked carefully into the room, a pitcher in each hand.

"Okay, ladies, I've got homemade sangria. Come get it while . . ." Kristin stopped in mid-sentence upon seeing the enraged Laura standing in her doorway. Her smile disappeared, and she looked around the room, confused.

A tall and pretty Black woman used her hip to open the kitchen door a moment later and backed into the room, laden with yet another pitcher and a large tray of finger foods.

"Ahhhh yeah, ladies, it's on! You're about to taste my famous crab cakes. It's time to get this party started."

She looked around at the silent guests, and her smile also disappeared, replaced by the same uncomprehending look her best friend wore.

"Um, Kristin, what's going on?" she asked the redhead.

"I have no idea, Bianca."

"Wanna know what's going on?" the woman shouted, pulling on the hem of her too-short and too-tight dress, wobbling from foot to foot drunkenly. A few stray hairs covered her eyes, and she brushed them out of the way.

"That bitch over there on your couch is a fucking whore!" She pointed, and the accusation flew from her finger like a lightning bolt, landing directly on an attractive young brunette seated on the tasteful couch in the middle of the room.

One of the last to arrive, Veronica Castillo entered hesitantly and helped herself to a bottle of sparkling water. She chatted with the other attendees, and soon her face lost its anxious look and she relaxed, sipping her sparkling water contentedly as if she'd just then made up her mind to stay.

Veronica was the first to notice Laura's arrival. She saw the doorknob turn with no result, as if someone on the other side pulled instead of pushed. A moment later, the door fell open and Laura staggered in. Veronica's blood ran cold, and she fought the instinct to find the back door and run far and fast, away from the new arrival. She wasn't frightened, but she knew how and when to pick her battles, and this was not one worth fighting. Not here and most definitely not now. She averted her eyes, praying Laura would pass by without recognizing her, thus providing the opportunity to slip out unnoticed.

Laura lurched into the house, glaring at the doorknob as if it had somehow mistreated her as she tugged on the hem of her dress. She glanced around at the décor, the comfortable but tasteful furniture, a couple of framed Edward Hopper prints and a large landscape painting that looked like something her six-year-old twin grandsons might have painted in kindergarten and smirked as if she'd judged the home and found it not up to her standards.

Veronica sat motionless, awaiting the inevitable explosion. Before long, Laura's dark eyes landed on her, but barely stayed a moment or two before they darted off again. Veronica lowered her head, and the hope flared that Laura hadn't recognized her and she could make her escape. But when she lifted her head again, Laura's eyes were firmly fixed on her, burning with an intense fury.

"What the hell are you doing here, you whore?"

"Hello, Laura," she said.

"You slut! I knew I would find you sooner or later."

"Ladies, what the hell is going on?" Bianca asked. She put down the food she carried and stepped between the two women.

"Who the fuck are you?" Laura asked.

"Bitch, watch your tone with me. Who the fuck are *you*?"

"Who am I? I'm the bitch who got her husband stolen by that whore over there!" She said, pointing at Veronica.

Veronica lowered her head, mortified. This was a battle she didn't want to fight, but now she had no choice. "It's good to have someone to blame, isn't it, Laura?" She said. Her voice was low and lyrical, sweetened with a slight Spanish accent that lent extra strength to her words.

"Who else should I blame? Who broke up my home? Who killed my husband? You did it, you whore! You!" Laura screamed, underscoring her words with jabs of her bright red fingernails.

"You can call me whatever you like, but I'd rather be a whore and a slut than a sick, degenerate, alcoholic bitch."

Veronica drew the phrase out, as if doing so gave each word extra power.

Sick!

Degenerate!

Alcoholic!

Bitch!

Bianca still stood between the two women and held up her hands. "Let's just calm down, okay?"

"Fuck you and fuck your calm!" Laura shouted. "I'm gonna beat that bitch's ass!"

Laura dropped her Hermès purse, pushed Bianca out of the way, and stepped toward the younger woman. For all their murderous intent, the steps were unsteady, and she stumbled. Just then, one of the guests, a large African American woman, broke off from the group and moved in between the combatants.

"Laura is it? Laura, can we take a minute?" the woman said.

Laura scowled. "Who the fuck are you, you fat bitch?"

The woman's smile faded but only for a moment. "I'm Jessica, the party planner. I met you at the school, remember? You were picking up those adorable twin grandsons of yours, and I invited—"

"Get the fuck away from me."

Laura pushed past Jessica and took another unsteady step. Almost as one, the women closest to Veronica hastily shifted to the other side of the room.

Bianca rushed to get in front of Laura, and Kristin moved quickly to intercept Veronica.

"Ladies," Kristin said, "we're supposed to be having fun. This is a party, after all."

"Some party," Laura said. "I never would've come if I'd known you invited that no-good slut."

"Like I said, I'd rather be a slut than a degenerate alcoholic," Veronica shot back.

"Oh, how the worm has turned," Laura said. "You used to be quiet as a mouse when you worked for us. Oh, well, I guess you don't talk so much when you're scheming to *fuck someone's husband*!"

"That's not what happened," Veronica said.

"That's exactly how it happened, bitch. You weaseled your way into our office, then into my husband's pants."

"I loved him, and he loved me."

"Yeah right, bitch. You loved his money."

"I didn't care about money. I loved him."

"And what about me?" Laura screamed. "I was his wife! I helped him build that business. I raised his kids. Then you come along and convinced him to divorce me. Next thing I know, he's dead!"

"Convince him? Please! He finally opened his eyes and saw you for what you are."

Laura's face tightened. "That's it, bitch. I'm gonna kill you!"

Laura stepped forward, fists clenched tightly and murder in her eyes. Her step was unsteady and the next even more so. She would have fallen if Bianca hadn't held onto her arm.

"Ladies, ladies, it's a pleasure party, not a UFC fight party. That's next week," Bianca said, trying to lighten the mood.

Laura scowled, and Bianca quickly released the grip on her arm. No one as much as grinned at her joke, and she continued in a sterner tone. "Remember this is Kristin's home, so let's show some respect please."

Veronica's face reddened and she stayed seated, but Laura kept standing, staring at the younger woman with undisguised hatred.

"You killed him," she said, her voice cracking with emotion. "You killed my husband. I hate you."

"No," Veronica said. "I brought Dave back to life. For years you tortured him every damn day with your anger and your insecurity and your evil ways!"

Laura's face became even redder. "You had no right! He was my husband! *Mine!* And you killed him!" she screamed, tears burning trails through her makeup. "You killed my David!"

"Your David? What did you ever do for that poor, sweet, man besides tell him how useless he was? He wasn't your David anymore. He stopped being your David a long time ago."

"You . . . fucking . . . whore . . . I . . . I . . ." Laura stammered, her face a mask of rage and pain. "You think this is over, bitch? It isn't! This isn't over!"

Laura shot Veronica one last, murderous look before she stalked out, slamming the door behind her.

CHAPTER TWO

Kristin and Bianca - One Month Earlier

Kristin arrived at her son's school and searched in vain for a parking space. She was early, school wouldn't let out for another forty-five minutes, but as usual, there were no spaces anywhere close to the Oak Street Academy. She cruised around for a few minutes more before finding a space a few blocks away. She walked back to the school and took a seat on a faded green bench under a huge oak tree that spread gnarled branches over the street. Her seat gave her a clear view of the playground, and she watched the school's only male instructor, Mr. Hector, play a raucous game of tag with a group of screaming first graders. Hector was the school's newest teacher, a twenty-something ex-Marine who seemed to have more muscles than brains, but he was gentle and patient and quickly became a favorite with the children. A favorite with the mothers, too, Kristin thought as she watched other mothers ogle Hector with undisguised lust. She quickly grew tired of watching them and dug in her purse for her iPhone and opened its e-book application. She'd bookmarked her page in the latest Shaun Harmon novel and couldn't put it down. The bestselling author recently moved to their town, and his daughter had become fast friends with her son, Lucas. His new book was said to reveal explosive secrets about their town. She didn't know if all that was true or not, but the man certainly could write an exciting novel.

"You're not fooling anyone, you know," Kristin's best friend, Bianca, said when she arrived a few minutes later.

"Huh?"

"Oh please," Bianca said. "I see you, sitting here, pretending to mess with your phone when it's obvious you're checking out Hector's fine ass."

"Um, no. I was reading the new Shaun Harmon book." She held up the phone so Bianca could see.

"Whatever, girl. Denial's not only a river in Egypt."

Kristin rolled her eyes at her friend, who was now staring at the handsome teacher.

"You're talking about me. You're the one checking him out, hard!"

"I sure am. I mean, look at those arms! OMG! Can't you feel him manhandling you, throwing you down, and just taking it?" Her eyes took on a faraway look. "Using those big-ass hands to choke you and pull your hair and smack your ass until it's all red . . ."

She stopped talking when she noticed her friend staring at her.

"What?" Bianca asked.

"Choke you? Smack your ass?"

"Hey, ain't nothing wrong with a little slap and tickle. Don't knock it until you try it."

"No thanks. I like my sex a little more . . . civilized."

"Booooring. The rougher the better."

"I had no idea my best friend was such a freak. This is a new side of you."

"Freaky deaky," Bianca responded.

"Well, he is hot," Kristin conceded. "Maybe I would have a chance with him. Hispanic men like a woman with a few curves and booty. God knows my ex sure didn't."

"Oh please! There are plenty of guys who would love to date you. You're a thick white girl with curves and booty, and a natural redhead at that. You're damn near an endangered species! We should make a website for you or something," Bianca said, laughing.

"Yeah, www.myexcouldnthandleallthis.com. I bet that'd

get a lot of hits."

"Yeah, but you're not bitter, right?"

"Screw you," Kristin said, laughing.

"Such language," a voice said from behind them.

Kristin and Bianca smiled at the new arrival and scooted over to make room for her on the bench.

"Have a seat, Jessica. I was trying to counsel Kristin about her obsession with Mr. Hector over there."

"What? We were not," Kristin said, laughing. "Don't pay her any mind, Jessica. Come sit down."

"No thanks. I'll stand," Jessica said.

"There's plenty of room," Bianca said.

Jessica eyed the bench as if doing mental calculations involving the space on the bench and the proportions of her big backside.

"No, I'm okay," she said, looking uncomfortable.

"Hey," Kristin said, changing the subject, "we have the invitations." She dug a stack of envelopes from her purse and handed them to Jessica. "I handed some out at the gym before I got here."

"They look great," Jessica said. "Now who do you guys think we should hand them out to?"

"You're the party planner," Bianca said. "You tell us."

"Well," she said, "the thing about this kind of party is you never know who might come. The woman who looks like a freak might be a total prude and vice versa, so don't go by looks alone. Hand them out to whomever and see what happens." Jessica glanced at her watch. "If we're gonna do it, we better hurry before the bell rings."

She divided the invitations into three equal stacks and gave one each to Kristin and Bianca, keeping one for herself.

A few minutes later, they returned to the bench just before the bell rang and the children poured outside like ants from an anthill.

"How'd we do, ladies?" Jessica asked above the joyful screams of the children. "I gave out all of mine."

"So did I."

"Me too."

"Do you think they'll come?" Kristin asked.

"They'll come," Jessica said. "A girl's night out with food, a little alcohol, and sex toys is a winning combo, watch and see. Oh, there's Brianne. Her ballet class starts soon. I have to run."

After Jessica left, Kristin shot a look to Bianca. "I wish I could be as confident about this as she is," she said.

"It'll be fine. Like she said, liquor, sex toys, and food. What could go wrong? If someone invited me to a party like that, I'd be there in a hot minute."

Kristin grinned at her friend. She loved how Bianca could see the bright side of anything. She, on the other hand, could always cloud up a sunny day, as her ex-husband, Stan, always said.

"Hey, don't look so depressed," Bianca said. "Wasn't it you who had this idea? Have a pleasure party, you said. Let's make a little extra money, you said. It'll be fun, you said."

Kristin frowned. "You're my best friend. You should know I don't have any damn sense. Why would you listen to me?"

"Girl, you're so full of it. You're a psychiatrist, for God's sake. You're the smartest person I know!"

"Psychologist. I didn't go to medical school, as Stan was fond of reminding."

"See, there you go again, putting yourself down. You need to stop it, girl."

"It's hard when someone put you down for the last ten years," Kristin said sadly. "Stan never had anything good to say. I was too fat, I was only a psychologist, I was . . ."

"Forget that fool, Kristin! You've been divorced for almost two years. It's about time you put it behind you, and this party is just the thing."

Across the street, Bianca's younger son, Christopher, spotted them and made a beeline for the bench. He grudgingly accepted a kiss and hug from his mother, said hello to Kristin, then sat on the bench and immediately became engrossed in his handheld video game.

"Even if it doesn't work out, you can play with the toys yourself," Bianca spoke under her breath so her son wouldn't hear. "You haven't been with a man since forever. I know you could use a good um, you know."

"Toys?" Christopher asked. He paused the game and looked up curiously.

"That he hears," Bianca said. "I scream for him to clean his room and he's deaf, but for this, he develops super hearing. No, honey," she said to her son. "Not kids' toys. Toys for, uh, adults."

"Oh, boring," Christopher said.

Kristin shook with silent laughter and Bianca punched her shoulder playfully.

"I'm glad you think this is funny," Bianca whispered.

"Don't worry about it. You know how kids are. He's probably forgotten about it already."

"Mommy, what kind of toys do adults play with?" Christopher asked suddenly. Kristin and Bianca looked at one another, then went into fresh gales of laughter while a puzzled Christopher shook his head and resumed his game.

"Mom, are you guys okay?"

Kristin and Bianca looked up from their laughing fit to see both their fourth graders standing in front of them. Kristin's son, Lucas, and Bianca's son, Max, stared at their mothers as if they had six heads.

"Are you okay, Mom?" Lucas asked again.

"I'm okay, honey."

"What's so funny?" Max asked.

"The adult toys," Christopher said without looking up from his Nintendo.

At another mention of toys, Bianca and Kristin broke out into yet another gale of laughter.

"I blame you for this," Bianca said once their laughter subsided and they walked to their cars.

"Oh please, he's already forgotten about it."

"Right. Until Thanksgiving dinner when he tells my in-laws Mommy plays with 'adult' toys."

"Oh, speaking of in-laws, I saved an invitation for Gloria." Kristin dipped her hand in her purse and handed the invitation to Bianca.

Bianca scowled. "Keep it. Ed already told his mother about the party."

"Are you ever going to tell me what's up with you and your mother-in-law?" Kristin asked. "I thought you guys got along great."

Bianca sighed. "We used to, but . . ."

"But?"

"Nothing . . . it's nothing."

"So, you're okay with bonding with your mother-in-law, who you don't get along with, over giant dildos and cock rings?"

Bianca made a face but remained silent as she stared at the boys running and playing ahead of them.

"It's okay if you don't want to tell me. Forget I asked," Kristin said.

"No, it's not that."

"It's fine, Bianca. I'm sorry I brought it up."

"I cheated on Ed," Bianca blurted out.

"What?"

"I cheated on Ed. With his father."

Kristin stopped dead in her tracks.

"What? I don't think I heard you right."

"You did. I slept with my father-in-law."

Kristin's mouth fell open. "Damn. I mean . . . holy crap."

Their sons scampered almost a block ahead of them, and they began walking again to catch up.

"You must think I'm a huge whore," Bianca said.

"Nah, I always thought you were a huge whore. This just confirms it."

The two friends walked together, chuckling nervously.

"Okay, so I get why you would be uncomfortable around Will, but why Gloria? Does she know?"

"I don't know. I don't think so."

"Bianca, I have to ask. How on Earth did it happen? I mean, did you, um, have a thing for Will?"

"No way! He's sexy for an older man, I guess, but no, not really."

"Then how?"

"Remember last summer when I told you Ed and I were having problems?"

"I remember."

They arrived at their cars and Bianca used her key fob to open the doors.

"Get in the car, boys. We'll be leaving in a minute."

The boys piled into the car, all too happy to have a few more minutes to spend together while their moms continued to talk.

"This was about the time Ed made partner at the law firm. He was working so much that even when he was home, he was so preoccupied it was like he wasn't there," Bianca said. "Our guest bathroom needed a lot of work which Ed planned to do himself. I told him we should just hire a contractor, but he loves to do that handyman stuff, but because of his caseload, he had no time. Anyway, his parents came to visit one weekend, and Will realized the bathroom wasn't getting done, so he volunteered to do it. He's pretty good at that kind of stuff, I think he did construction or something when he was younger, so we were glad to have his help. The plan was for him to stay with us during the week, while he worked on the bathroom and go back home to New York on the weekends. Honestly, I was so lonely I glad to have him around. Ed was busy, and the boys were about to leave for sleep-away camp, so I figured it would be nice to have a little company for a while."

Bianca teared up and she paused.

"Bianca, you don't have to tell me the details, honey. It's okay."

"No, I want to." Bianca wiped her eyes and continued, "I swear something was different about Will that day. He was always a bit of a flirt, but before this, it seemed, you know, harmless. I would catch him staring at my chest sometimes, but he always looked away. Men have been staring at my boobs since I was twelve years old, so it wasn't that big of a deal."

Kristin nodded. "Uh-huh. I know the feeling."

"Right? Anyway, it was a little creepy—he was my father-in-law and all—but I let it go. Like I said, he always looked away, but that morning, he didn't. Something was . . . different. There was tension in the air. Ed left early for New York, and the boys were already at camp, so we were all alone. He was like a predator, and he was hunting me, you know?" She shook her head. "No, it was like he already caught me, only I didn't know it. All morning he stared at my chest. I caught him looking a bunch of times, and he didn't even look away like he usually did. He just smiled."

Bianca sighed and leaned against the car. "It was kinda uncomfortable, but I tried to ignore it. Later on, I made lunch, and he suggested we should eat out by the pool and said he would make us some rum punch. The rum punch was delicious and super strong, and he just kept on refilling my glass. Before I knew it, I'd had too many drinks. It was a hot day, so he suggested we go swimming, and I said okay." She paused to wipe the tears that were quickly forming. "So we were in the pool, just cooling off, you know, and things get *weird*."

"Weird how?" Kristin asked, almost in a whisper.

"I was in the water, and he kept walking around me, circling me like a shark, telling me how sexy I was. He said when he was younger, he had a girlfriend who looked just like me. He told me how hot she was and how much he enjoyed fucking her."

"He said that?"

"He sure did. And the whole time, he's still walking in circles in the water around me. Then he told me to guess what he liked most about his old girlfriend. It's like I was hypnotized. I couldn't say a word. Then he said he liked her because she loved to take it in the ass."

"No! Way! He said that?"

"He did. Right there in our pool, Judge Will Truman, one of the most respected judges on the whole East Coast, hell, in the whole damn country, went into explicit detail about how he used to have anal sex with an old girlfriend."

"Wow. I mean . . . wow!"

"As he's talking, something floated up to me in the water, and I realized it was his damn swim trunks, Kristin. He was butt naked. I couldn't help it, I looked down and, well, you know how when you look at something underwater it looks kinda distorted?"

Kristin nodded, repulsed but at the same time entranced by the story.

Bianca looked around guiltily to make sure no one could hear her. "He was *hard*," she whispered. "I swear it was about to pop out of the water like a telescope. He took my hand and put it down there, and it was no distortion, let me tell you. I know I should have stopped it then. I should have run out of the damn pool and cursed his old ass out."

"What did you do?"

"I stroked it. I stroked it, and it got even harder, Kristin. And God help me, I swear I never wanted something so bad in all my life."

She paused, closed her eyes, and took a deep breath.

"Then he made me get out of the water and lay down on the side of the pool, and he started kissing my thighs."

Bianca's eyes were still closed, and a slight smile appeared on her face.

"Kristin, I was so shocked, but I didn't stop him because it felt so damn good to have someone want me. We did it right there by the side of the pool, and I knew it was wrong, but I loved it. I've never had so many orgasms in all my life. He treated me like some whore off the street. He pulled my hair and choked me and slapped my face and spanked me. He fucked me to within an inch of my damn life, and, Kristin, I loved it. I. Could. Not. Get. Enough."

"Jesus Christ," Kristin said, her eyes wide. "So then what?"

"Then nothing. He got dressed and continued hanging drywall and cutting tiles. Me, I felt so guilty and confused I went inside and cried. I tried to fool myself into believing it was the alcohol that made us do it. Then I tried to blame Ed, since he was working so much and I was lonely, but the truth was I wanted it. That's the worst part, Kristin," she said. "I knew what I was doing."

Kristin hung her head and nodded. She knew all too well what her friend meant.

"Will went home a couple of weeks after, but I still felt guilty, and I guess Ed could tell something was up. One night he confronted me, and we had a huge argument. He said I'd been acting strange and asked point-blank if I was having an affair."

Bianca pushed off of the car and stomped her foot.

"I should have lied to him, but I didn't. I confessed. Kinda. How could I tell my husband I'd slept with his father? I told him an ex-boyfriend was in town, we met for lunch, and one thing led to another. I said it didn't mean anything. I was lonely and vulnerable and it just . . . happened."

"What did he say?"

"I'd never seen him so mad, Kristin. The look on his face was pure rage! For a minute I was sure he was going to hit me. And you know what? I wanted him to. I did! I craved the punishment."

"You what?"

Bianca continued as if she hadn't heard the question. "I swear to you, I would have been happy for him to choke me then fuck me to within an inch of my life. I wanted it, just like his daddy gave it to me."

Kristin couldn't believe what she was hearing. Suddenly the remarks Bianca made earlier about getting treated roughly made sense.

When Bianca spoke again, the glazed look was gone, and her voice returned to normal.

"He didn't do any of those things. He calmed down and just kinda looked at me like I was some poor soul, then walked out the front door."

"Did you ever find out where he went?" Kristin asked, looking down at her feet.

"No. He didn't come back until after midnight, but when he got home, he was so calm it was almost scary. No—more than calm, he seemed *happy*. He said he loved me and forgave me and we needed to find a counselor and work some things out. I'd just made a mistake, but things were going to be okay, he told me. Then he kissed me on the cheek, and in about a minute flat, he was asleep. I don't understand it. His wife told him she'd slept with another man, and he just fell asleep."

"That was a good thing, right?"

"He and his mother are close, so I think he drove to New York and told Gloria everything."

"Ahh . . . so that's why you have such a thing about her. You think she knows what you did? Did she ever say anything?"

"Not a word. We saw them a bunch of times after that, and she was the same robotic Stepford Wife she always is. Everything was normal—even Will acted like nothing happened. But I'm pretty sure she knows."

"Don't you think if she knew her husband slept with her daughter-in-law she would have said something by now?"

"I guess," Bianca conceded. "But I just can't shake the feeling something is going on. Call it woman's intuition."

"Or paranoia?"

"It's more than that. Something's up. I can feel it. Ed's been different. He seems, I don't know, happier."

"What's so bad about that?" Kristin asked, trying to sound nonchalant.

"Nothing, I guess."

"I would leave it alone. It sounds like you dodged a bullet. Things could have turned out a lot worse."

"I don't know. Ed's been 'working late' an awful lot lately. Maybe he found himself some floozy to run around with like Stan did."

Kristin gritted her teeth and said nothing.

"Oh God, Kristin, I shouldn't have mentioned your ex. I'm sorry."

"It's okay," Kristin said. "Bianca, the truth is you're super guilty about what you did and you're projecting that guilt onto Ed. It's making you see things that just aren't there."

"There's that psychology degree of yours at work," Bianca said. "I'm sure you're right, but you should have seen him when he came home that night. There was no anger in him at all. I mean zero. Something happened when he went out, I'm sure of it. There's something I don't know, and it drives me crazy. I know I need to just let it go, but—"

"But nothing. My advice is to quit obsessing over some imaginary girlfriend and process what's going on in your head. You did a bad thing, Bianca, and you feel terrible about it, so finding out Ed did the same thing would make you feel less guilty, but it doesn't work like that. Ed probably had a couple of drinks and thought things through. Maybe he owned his part of the blame for what happened and came to terms with it. You should be grateful; most marriages wouldn't have survived. Mine sure didn't."

"You're right," Bianca agreed. "But how do I let it go?"

"You made a terrible mistake, girl," Kristin said. "But it's not unforgivable. Nothing is. Sleeping with Will was a mistake you made. It's not who you are."

"What do you mean?"

"What people do, especially we women, is take our mistakes and make them a part of who we are, our identity. So instead of saying, 'I'm a person who stole,' we say, 'I'm a thief.' Or instead of saying, 'I'm a person who cheated,' we say, 'I'm a cheater.' Understand?"

Bianca nodded, fighting tears.

"But our mistakes are just that, mistakes. They're not who we are. So remember that and forgive yourself. That's how you move on."

"I'll try," Bianca said. Just then, the boys began a loud argument in the car, and she knocked on a window to quiet them.

"Let's get these boys home before they kill each other," Bianca said, wiping her eyes.

"I think you're right," Kristin replied. She opened Bianca's car door and motioned her son out.

"I'm glad I told you, Kristin," Bianca said once Lucas was in Kristin's car. "I needed to get that off my chest. So, do you want to hang out later? I'll bring the boys over for a playdate. Ed's working late again." She rolled her eyes.

"Ah, n-no," Kristin stammered. "Lucas is spending the weekend with his dad, and I, uh . . . have a client this evening. Then I'm going to stay at the office and catch up on my notes."

"I thought you didn't see clients on Fridays?"

"I don't usually, but this one is in crisis, and since Lucas will be with Stan, I figured I'd make an exception," Kristin said, surprised at how smoothly the lie slid from her mouth.

"We're a couple of high rollers, aren't we? Such big plans on a Friday night. Well, girl, thanks for listening and not judging me, and thank you for the advice. I love you, Kristin. I don't know what I'd do without you."

Kristin smiled. "I love you too."

The friends hugged goodbye. Then Bianca started her car and took off down the street, shouting at her warring sons.

Kristin made sure Lucas was securely buckled in then started her car, but tears blurred her vision. She wondered if she would ever have the courage to confess to Bianca she knew exactly where Ed went that fateful night, but she knew she never would. She didn't have the courage. Kristin wiped away her tears as she checked the rearview mirror to make sure her son hadn't noticed her crying. Then she started the car again and headed home.

CHAPTER THREE

"You killed my husband, bitch! Trust me, this isn't over!"

Laura's words hung in the air like a terrible smell while the women listened to her unsteady footsteps as she stomped down the driveway, slammed her car door, then burned rubber and sped away.

As the sound of Laura's car faded, all eyes turned to the young woman to whom her toxic words were directed, but Veronica, red-faced and crying, fled from the room, leaving behind a stunned silence.

"Ladies, I swear we're not shooting a reality show," Jessica joked a moment later, trying to clear the air. No one laughed.

Bianca and Kristin glanced at one another. Then Bianca forced a smile and faced her guests, who were still standing around, shocked.

"Okay, girls, that happened, but we have a ton of good food, plenty of liquor, and lots of fun toys, so let's get this party back on track." She filled glasses with sangria and handed them to the subdued guests.

Kristin left Bianca to try to salvage the party and hurried out to the deck, where Veronica sat, crying silently.

"I'm sorry," Kristin said as she sat down. "We didn't know . . ."

"It's not your fault," Veronica said. "Willows is a small town. I knew I was bound to run into Laura sooner or later. I thought I would be better prepared when it happened, you know? I had so many things I wanted to say, but . . ."

"It's okay, Veronica. It's not your fault."

"I swore I would never mess with a married man, then I met Dave. He was the nicest, most generous human being I've ever known, but inside he was so sad. Laura just beat him down. She treated him like shit, and he didn't deserve it."

She began to cry again, and Kristin offered her a tissue.

"God, what these women must think of me," Veronica said. "God, what must *you* think of me?"

"I don't know about them, but I sure don't think any less of you."

"Riiight."

"It's true," Kristin said, thinking of her own secret and what would happen if it were made public. "No one's perfect. We've all got our skeletons."

"Not like this," Veronica said.

"Oh, you'd be surprised. Anyway, I'm not judging you, and neither is Bianca."

"Then you're the only ones. They're all probably wondering which one of their husbands I'm going to steal next."

"Hey, maybe a few of them are hoping you will."

Veronica smiled. "Thanks, Kristin. You're being very nice about this, but I think I'm gonna go."

"You're not going anyplace except to the bathroom to fix your makeup. Then you're getting your butt back inside and buying so many toys you won't need a man anytime soon."

Veronica shook her head. "I'm going, Kristin. If I stay, your party will be ruined." She sighed. "Who am I kidding? It probably already is."

"I wish you would stay."

"Kristin, would you stay if you were me?"

"No, I guess I wouldn't. Come with me. I'll show you where the bathroom is."

Kristin showed Veronica to the restroom then returned to the party, happy to see their guests looked much less stunned as they talked among themselves. Bianca and Jessica pulled her into the kitchen and huddled at the kitchen table.

"Is she okay?" Bianca asked.

"Okay as she can be, I guess. She just got called a slut and a whore in front of a room full of strangers."

"She deserved it because that's what she is," Jessica said. "I feel terrible for Laura. My mother went through the same thing. One day my dad suddenly up and got himself some young whore, divorced her, and—poof—he was gone."

"Are you kidding me right now? Bianca asked. "It's Laura's fault. She's a psycho. Who wouldn't leave her crazy ass?"

Jessica shook her head. "How would you feel if you showed up somewhere and your husband's side chick was there? You might go a little psycho too."

"You might have a point there," Bianca admitted.

Kristin turned red and quickly changed the subject. "That's neither here nor there. The drama is over, so let's figure out a way to salvage this party before everyone leaves."

"They're not going anywhere now," Jessica said. "A little drama is a good thing. I guarantee this is a party they will never forget." She picked up a pitcher of margaritas and put on a big smile. "Okay, ladies, let's get this party started," she said as she walked back into the living room, holding the pitcher high.

As the kitchen door swung shut, Kristin gave Bianca a side-eye, hands on her hips. "Let's throw a pleasure party, you said," she called in a high, mocking voice. "We'll make a little money, you said. It'll be fun, you said."

Bianca laughed. "You worry too much. You heard Jessica. She's right—a little drama will be good for sales."

"Oh really? I wonder what she'll say when they start slamming each other across the head with my furniture like Hulk Hogan and the Macho Man in the WWF."

"Hulk Hogan? WWF? Girl, you need to get up on your wrestlers. That was like a hundred years ago. It's the WWE now."

"You get the point. It's gonna be a disaster. I just know it."

Bianca rolled her eyes as she removed trays of appetizers from the oven. "You're my best friend, Kristin, but you can be a real Debbie Downer sometimes."

"Maybe," Kristin said. "But you have to admit what just happened was reality-show level crazy. And did you see your mother-in-law's face? She looked mortified!"

Bianca's face fell. "Yeah, well, she's the one who invited herself along. I didn't tell her to bring her happy hips from New York to crash our party."

As if on cue, the kitchen door opened, and Gloria walked in.

"Well, that was an auspicious start," she joked. "I felt like I was in a scene from *Days of Our Lives*."

Kristin smiled at the older lady's joke, but Bianca said nothing. She continued to pile appetizers on trays, looking uncomfortable.

"Do need any help?" Gloria asked after a moment's awkward silence.

"No," Bianca began.

"Thanks, Gloria," Kristin interrupted. "We would love some help." She pointed to the tray of coconut shrimp Bianca prepared. "Could you take these out to the ladies, please?"

"Certainly, honey," Gloria said as she took the tray and disappeared into the living room.

"Do you need any help?" Bianca mimicked after her mother-in-law was safely out of earshot.

"Will you stop."

"She knows," Bianca said. "I can feel it."

"No, she doesn't. Don't you think if she did she would have said something? What kind of woman attends a party with the woman who screwed her husband and—"

"Kristin! Shhhhhh!" Bianca opened the kitchen door a

sliver and peeked out to ensure no one was within earshot.

"See, now you're acting guilty," Kristin said. "Stop being so paranoid. If Gloria knew about you and Will, we would have another Laura-type situation."

"No way. That's not her style. She keeps that crazy smile on her face and pretends everything is okay no matter what. Ed's the same way, the two of them are buttoned up so damn tight. God, I'm so sick of them."

"Maybe you're right about Gloria's personality," Kristin said, bristling at Bianca's insult of Ed. "But think about it. This situation is completely different from anything in the past. Her daughter-in-law fucked her husband—that might get a rise out of her if she knew, don't you think?"

Bianca stamped her foot, then peeked out into the living room once again. "Kristin!" she hissed. "Will you stop saying that? OMG, it's like you *want* someone to hear you."

"Will you relax. No one can hear us. Anyway, Gloria doesn't know. You have nothing to worry about."

Bianca exhaled. "I guess you're right. A minute ago, I was lecturing you about being a downer; now look at me."

"It's okay, hon. You're just stressed. Listen, remember when we met Jessica a couple of months ago and decided to throw this crazy party? What did we say we were going to do, no matter what?"

"Have fun," Bianca replied unenthusiastically.

"Have fun," Kristin repeated. "If we're not going to have fun, we might as well tell everyone to go home."

"You're right," Bianca said. "I'm sorry."

"Don't be sorry. Let's go out there, drink some alcohol, and sell some big ol' dongs."

"To hell with that," Bianca said, laughing and raising her glass. "Let's go out there, drink *all* the alcohol, and buy some big ol' dongs."

"I'll drink to that," Kristin said, raising her glass in agreement.

They returned to the living room, where their guests

seemed to have recovered from the shock of Laura's appearance and were busy discussing the drama they witnessed.

"So the husband died while in bed with her?" Asked a pretty blond, chuckling. "Damn, she must have some killer pussy. Get it? Killer pussy?"

Gloria looked aghast. "Really, young lady? Is that appropriate?"

The blond chuckled again. "The name's not *young lady*, it's Brooke. And that was a pretty funny joke."

"Cheating is not funny," Jessica said. "I feel for that poor woman."

"You feel sorry for that lunatic?" a tall, thin, woman asked, rolling her eyes. "That bitch is obviously—"

"Maya!" a fit-looking older woman with stylish short hair said. "Judge much?"

Maya smiled. "Maybe you're right, Tina, but you have to admit the chick was mental. Thank God she left."

"You might be mental too if your husband died in his young girlfriend's bed," Gloria said.

Bianca rolled her eyes at her mother-in-law's comment. "I'm with Maya. That bitch looked crazy. If I were her husband, I might have found me a side chick too."

Gloria scowled. "There is never an excuse for infidelity, Bianca. They took vows, and he broke them. Period, end of story."

"Life is too short to be unhappy," Bianca said. "Her husband went out and found happiness. I say good for him."

"Amen," Maya said, looking lovingly at Tina.

Gloria was about to respond when a petite Indian woman spoke up. "Excuse me, but wasn't he the wealthy real-estate person? With the ads on the bus stops?"

"I think you're right, Dr. Dee," Tina said. "My husband and I bought our first house from his company."

"Have we met?" the Indian woman asked.

Tina smiled. "I think I've read every magazine in your waiting room. You were my daughter's OB/GYN. I took her to your office a bunch of times before she was old enough to go on her own."

"Ahhhh shit, we have a gynecologist in the house. I bet you can tell us about killer pussy. Right, doc?" Brooke asked the embarrassed doctor.

No one laughed, and Brooke made a face. "Y'all are a bunch of squares. That's still a funny-ass joke."

"I think my son and daughter-in-law bought their home from his company too," Gloria said. She held out her hand to the woman who'd spoken. "I'm Gloria, by the way."

The woman shook her hand. "I'm Tina, and this is my, uh, friend, Maya," she said, gesturing to the tall, thin woman.

Maya nodded hello to Gloria.

"Since we're making introductions, I'm Brooke," the blond woman said.

Kristin smiled. "I think you're going to be the life of this party, Brooke."

"Hell yeah! C'mon, it's time to get this party started."

Just then an embarrassed-looking Veronica entered the room and all conversation ceased.

"Thanks for inviting me, ladies, but I'm going to go. I hope you have a great time. I'm sorry for all the drama," she said.

"Bye, Felicia," Jessica said under her breath.

Kristin shot Jessica a nasty look. "Veronica, I meant what I said earlier. You're welcome to stay," she said.

"Thanks, but I'm going. I'm sorry this happened, I didn't mean to—"

Just then the front door flew open with a bang, startling them. "Going somewhere, whore?" a familiar voice said.

"Oh, hell nah," Bianca said under her breath.

"Laura. I'm happy you decided to rejoin us." Jessica said in a cheerful tone. "Veronica is just leaving, so if you want to take a seat, we'll . . ."

Laura glared at Jessica as if she were something distasteful on the bottom of her shoe.

"She ain't going nowhere," Laura said.

Veronica shook her head in disbelief. "Get out of my way. Your bullying won't work on me. I refuse to take it."

"Refuse nothing, bitch. You'll take whatever the fuck I tell you to take," Laura said as she pulled a shiny revolver from her purse and pointed it at Veronica's chest.

Veronica's olive complexion went deathly pale.

"Yeah, I thought so," Laura said with a smirk, gesturing toward the couch with the pistol. "Now sit the fuck down! I told you this wasn't over."

#

CHAPTER FOUR

Bianca - One Month Earlier

Bianca hugged Kristin and started her car, shouting at her warring sons.

Two minutes later, they were at peace occupied with their video games, but Bianca's mind was still in turmoil. She felt better now she'd finally revealed her secret, but a part of her wished she could confess the whole truth.

The boys began arguing again, and she glanced in the rearview mirror. "Boys, take it easy," she said. They calmed down, but two minutes later, were at it again.

"Boys!" she said, more sternly. "Cut it out!"

"He started it!" Christopher shouted, pointing his finger at his brother.

"No, Mom, he did it. He keeps on touching me."

Bianca suddenly swerved to the side of the road and whirled around to face her shocked sons.

"I said shut the hell up!"

The boys' eyes went wide, and they sat back, quiet as church mice. Bianca pulled the car back onto the road, mentally kicking herself for losing it.

They arrived home a few minutes later, and the boys ran up to their rooms, still subdued. Bianca poured herself a glass of wine, brought it outside by the pool, and thought about the lie she was living.

What the hell is wrong with you, Bianca? she asked herself. But she needn't have asked because she knew the answer.

It was Will.

The affair didn't begin quite the way she told Kristin. She'd caught Will staring at her body—that was true—but they weren't the shy glances she'd told Kristin about. Will ogled her constantly. He hid it well when Ed and the boys were around, but once Ed went back to work and the boys were away at camp, Will made no attempt whatsoever to hide his true feelings. His stares usually began at her feet and moved up to her thighs, traveled up to her stomach, and lingered for a while on her breasts before he looked her right in the eye, his thoughts crystal clear. Will's stares made her uncomfortable at first, but very quickly she came to enjoy his stares and soon met his lustful gaze without looking away. It wasn't long before she jumped into the flirtation with both feet, bending over to pick something up way longer than was necessary when she knew he was watching or going braless every day. She was very well endowed, and Will practically salivated at the sight of her large, full breasts rolling free and her nipples trying to poke holes through the fabric of her thin T-shirts.

Their affair began in the morning, not at lunch over rum punch. She swam laps in their pool every day in her usual swimming attire, a hideous one-piece thing for triathletes made for comfort and function, but that fateful morning, she dug up a sexy two-piece number that barely covered her breasts or anything else. Will sat by the pool, sipping his coffee, and his eyes widened as his daughter-in-law sashayed out of the house and dropped her towel onto a chair.

"Morning, Will," she said with a coy smile.

"Morning B," he said. She stretched in front of him, bending over to give him a good view, then walked into the shallow end. Will sat poolside, taking her in. Their eyes met as he drained the last of his coffee then removed his shirt then shorts to reveal a long, thick manhood that stopped Bianca's swimming cold. Her father-in-law was almost seventy years old, but he had the solid, muscular build of a much younger man. Will's smile showed his teeth, like the fox who successfully infiltrated the henhouse, and he walked slow circles around her in the warm water. She felt like prey, mesmerized by a predator who had her well and truly trapped.

"You know who you remind me of?" he asked.

She shook her head.

"You remind me of an ex-girlfriend from back in the day. A sexy ass chick named Joanna. Well, she wasn't an ex-girlfriend. She was . . . what do the kids call it nowadays? A hookup. A fuck buddy. She looked a lot like you. Cute face, little waist, big, juicy titties, and a fat ass. Man, she loved to fuck. And she loved to suck dick too. I mean, loved it! Trust me, that was like finding gold! Ain't many chicks sucking dick in those days. Unless you paid for it."

The profanity startled Bianca. She had never heard him curse before. He circled in front of her again, and she glanced down again to see his erection was long and strong and showed no signs of going down. If anything, it looked even larger and stronger.

"I fucked her everywhere. In the shed, out in the woods, in the root cellar, even snuck into the church and did it there a time or two . . . I gave her this fat dick every chance she got, and I never pulled out. It was a miracle I never knocked her up."

He smiled his sly predator smile.

"I was dating Gloria the whole time I was fucking Joanna." He put a finger up to his lips. "Shhh . . . don't tell her. God knows I love her, but she would not give up the pussy at all. Not even a taste. So Joanna got all this good, long dick."

The day was hot and the water warm, but Bianca's blood was ice cold and she trembled at his gaze.

"Know what I liked about Joanna the most?" he asked, stopping in front of her.

"What?" she asked, her voice barely audible.

"She looked innocent," he said. "You should have seen her, sitting in the front pew of church next to her momma and daddy, praying and singing like a sweet angel. But I'd sit in church, remembering how the night before she was butt nekkid on her knees sucking this fat dick. Man oh man, I sat in church many a Sunday right next to Gloria, thinking of all the nasty things Joanna and I did."

Will resumed walking circles around her.

"Then one day she was just gone. Didn't even get a chance to say goodbye. Her parents shipped her off down south. Last I heard, she got married to some preacher, some hick who probably doesn't know the first thing about how to please that pussy. Anyway, the first time I saw you, that's what I thought about. You're just like her, with your big titties and fat ass. Same kind of innocent look, too, but ain't a thing innocent about you. I can tell."

He grabbed her hand and thrust it between his legs.

"Will, what are you doing?"

"This is what you want, isn't it?"

Without waiting for her reply, he roughly ripped off her bathing suit top and tossed it into the deep end of the pool. His actions rendered her speechless, and he took advantage of her shock and thrust his hand roughly between her legs. Involuntarily, she opened her legs wider to grant him better access, and he smiled cruelly. *I knew you wanted it, bitch*, his smile seemed to say. He led her from the pool, lay her down on the hard concrete, and quickly removed her swimsuit bottom. She lay naked and soaking wet under him, and he smiled again as he placed the head of his penis between her legs. Then with one hard, brutal, thrust, he plunged its full, thick length inside of her.

"Will . . . what . . ."

"Cut the shit, bitch. You know you want it," he said. He put a hand on her neck and expertly squeezed, hard enough for her to struggle for breath but not enough to cut it off entirely.

God help her, she did want it.

She quickly stopped struggling as the feeling of his strong hand on her neck and the sensation of his insistent, rhythmic strokes overcame her, and she spread her legs wider.

"Yes," she said. "Take it, take it!"

And he obliged.

When multiple orgasms made her weak as a kitten, Will turned her over and entered her in a way she'd never experienced. He went slowly, but it was still painful. And she reveled in the pain, almost blacking out from sheer pleasure.

She'd loved Will's rough handling of her body, the feel of his lips and tongue in places his son long neglected. She'd loved how Will didn't treat her like some precious breakable object like her husband did.

No.

He hadn't cared if she was ready. He simply spread her legs and took what he wanted while saying the filthiest, most degrading, most amazing things anyone ever said to her. He saw past the false suburban wife facade and told her the things he saw so clearly inside her head. He said he recognized her for the dirty whore she was the moment his son brought her home. He'd been thinking of this for years, and now her entire body belonged to him, and he could have it any time he wanted. She wouldn't say a word about it, ever. If she did, the world would see past her facade, too, and finally realize how dirty she truly was, inside and out.

He read her like a book. And God help her, he was right. He was *so* right!

She was freshly violated in the backyard of their dream home, where their children played, where they made a life together, and she didn't care. Her vagina and ass throbbed painfully, but she didn't care. She lay naked and exposed, her father-in-law's seed drying to a hard crust on her body, and she simply did not care. She had faithlessly betrayed her loving husband with his father.

She. Did. Not. Care.

After a while, she tried to dress herself, but her mind could not make sense of whether she should put the swimsuit back on before the T-shirt or which foot each flip-flop went on.

Finally, she abandoned her clothes and stumbled naked into the house, her mind a blank, the better to enjoy the bewildering, amazing, terrifying new sensations.

In the days and weeks following, Will took her whenever he wanted. And he wanted her a lot, multiple times per day. Every morning after taking Ed to the train station, she sped home to Will. She parked the car in the garage, shedding her clothes as she went. He was always naked and ready for her and she for him. They did it everywhere. In the bedroom, in the children's rooms, in the garage, on top of the washing machine. Will's drive and stamina were amazing for a man his age. Hell, it was amazing for a man of any age.

Each time was better than the last. He knew of countless ways to bring her to quick and devastating orgasms, leaving her weak and useless for hours. He used his lips, tongue, and even his teeth to make her scream his name as climax after earth-shattering climax possessed her body. The rough, taboo sex that hurt the first time became rougher and still painful, but she didn't care. She was addicted and didn't give a damn about the pain. She only wanted him inside her, and it didn't matter where he entered so long as he did, and the rougher the better.

When she and Ed made love, it was slow and gentle, and he took pains to hold and caress her afterward, telling her how much he loved her. If he only knew this treatment only made her feel so much more unworthy, so much more unlike the queen he held her up to be. She hated it, but she tolerated it because she knew it was his way of showing her love and affection.

Will, on the other hand, took what he wanted, slow and gentle be damned. He continued to call her filthy names and treat her like a slut and did it with a smile that said he was one hundred percent sure of his control over her. When he was done, he shot his seed wherever he wanted, whether inside her body or anywhere on it, then he pulled his clothes back on without even offering a towel to clean her up. To him, she was only a collection of holes for his pleasure, and God help her, she simply could not get enough.

Bianca's dread grew as the day drew closer to Will completing the work on the house and returning home. She had grown addicted to the sex and could not imagine living without being violated daily. She cried the day he returned home and continued crying every day for a week, until her husband, suspicious at his wife's sadness and sudden mood swings, confronted her. That was when she lied and claimed the affair with a nonexistent ex.

Part of her felt better at the false confession, hoping his fury would be the catalyst for him to manhandle and punish her. She hoped he would grab her neck and choke her as his father did so expertly; she hoped the anger would overwhelm him and he would throw her around the room before roughly taking her by force, reclaiming what was his. Her heart beat with anticipation as she lied about what she had done, and she watched with glee as his face grew darker and his body become tense. The story grew more salacious by the second, and she reveled in the telling of the lies, adding embellishments and obscenely graphic details designed to stoke his rage and provoke the inevitable explosion. When she finished, veins stood out on Ed's temples, his fists were clenched, and his breath came in short, angry bursts. She watched his hands carefully, waiting for the inevitable flare of temper that would surely result in her man using his big, strong hands to give her the punishment she richly deserved.

It never came.

"Is that all?" he asked.

"Yes."

"Are you sure?"

"Yes."

His fists were still clenched, but he closed his eyes and took several deep breaths until the veins pulsing at his temples subsided. He unclenched his fists, which had been clamped so hard his fingernails left deep, crescent-shaped marks in his palms. As Bianca watched with dismay, his breathing returned to normal, and his eyes regained their gentle look. He sighed. Then without another word, he left their home.

A shocked and disappointed Bianca watched as he drove away. She hoped to bear the brunt of Ed's anger, but she knew her husband was a calm man who, like his mother, prided himself on his control over his emotions. Control or not, she reasoned, no husband in the world would stay calm for long after hearing the filthy things his wife did with another man.

She hoped against hope the time apart would serve to fuel the fires of her husband's anger. She fantasized about him storming home in a rage, kicking the door open, and grabbing her by the neck with his big, strong hands, choking her until she struggled for breath. She would try to move his hands from her throat, but he would be much too strong. Once she was weak from lack of oxygen, he would lift her skirt and rip her panties cruelly off her body before bending her over and roughly violating her, leaving marks and bruises for her to treasure. It wouldn't be long before he would finish, leaving the evidence of his violation on her face, her chest. Then he would walk away and leave her where she lay, bruised and battered and violated.

And happy.

Like father. Like son.

She hoped, she prayed, but no such luck.

When he returned hours later, he seemed like his old self. Ed was completely calm and reasonable and assured her he'd forgiven her, and they would quickly move past the indiscretion and regain their lost happiness. He resolved to be a better husband and spend more time with her and the boys so her mind would be at ease. He would be such an attentive, loving, and dedicated husband she would never again be tempted to stray.

Bianca forced a smile as she thanked him for forgiving her, then she hugged her sweet and gentle husband while shedding crocodile tears and mouthing the right lies.

Inside, she wanted to scream.

An hour later, she still lay wide awake in the dark beside Ed, confused by this new person she'd become. No, not new. She had mentally cast off the disguise she'd worn for so long to reveal the person she always was, she now realized. All her life she believed she was strong and confident and capable, an independent woman with the power to change the world.

Lies.

Lies of the worst kind, because they were lies she told herself.

She wasn't any of those things, not even close.

Will opened her eyes to her truth. All she was was a body that craved punishment and subjugation, with absolutely nothing to offer but a collection of orifices that, God help her, she would gladly offer up to anyone, anyone at all, who could give her what she wanted and treat her the way she needed to be treated.

At that moment, her life changed irrevocably, for she knew with certainty she was damaged. She knew she could never get what she so desperately needed from her gentle and oh-so-loving husband happily snoring next to her. She could never go back to slow, romantic, weak, lovemaking or live each day treated like a delicate queen.

She didn't want that life. Not anymore.

She wasn't worthy of that kind of love.

She wept silently as she imagined being held tenderly in her husband's arms, subject to his sweet, pathetic words of love falling like burning acid onto her. Ed's love once comforted her, but now those days were over.

They were over forever.

She knew that now.

She was ruined.

#

CHAPTER FIVE

"What did I say, bitch? Sit the fuck down! Didn't I tell you this wasn't over?"

Veronica's eyes went wide with shock and fear, but she did as Laura ordered.

The rest of the women stood still as statues, all eyes locked on the woman with the gun.

"Now what, bitch?" Laura asked with an evil grin. "Not so chatty now, huh?"

"Laura, this is crazy," Veronica said. "You can't just—"

"Oh? I can't what? I think I can, bitch, and I sure as hell am. I told you this shit wasn't over."

Just then the muted ring of a cell phone sounded.

"Whose phone is that?" Laura asked, waving the gun around wildly.

There was no answer, and she pointed the gun at each of the women in turn.

"Whose fucking phone is that?" she asked again.

"It's m-mine," Kristin stammered.

"Turn it the fuck off," Laura ordered. "Matter of fact, all you bitches, get your phones out and turn them off."

The women hesitated, no one willing to make the first move.

"Now!" Laura screamed.

Slowly, they all reached into purses and pockets to get

their mobile phones.

"Turn them off," Laura ordered.

There was a series of beeps and buzzes as the devices powered down. A large, decorative bowl of potpourri sat near Laura, and she grabbed it and emptied it, causing dried flowers, cedar wood shavings and mint leaves to fall in a pile onto the floor. She then gestured toward the empty bowl with the gun.

"Put them in the bowl."

One by one, the women filed past her and dropped their phones into the bowl then stood as far away from Laura as they could get.

"You, too, whore," Laura said to Veronica.

Veronica reached for her purse, removed her phone, and began to walk over to the bowl, but Laura stopped her.

"No, bitch. Stay right here. Gimme your phone."

Veronica returned to the spot she had vacated and handed Laura her device.

Suddenly, Laura took the phone and smashed it against Veronica's head. It fell to the floor, miraculously undamaged, unlike Veronica, who held onto the arm of a couch to keep from falling, the side of her face rapidly swelling where she had been struck. For a moment, no one spoke. Then Maya approached Laura, anger on her pretty features.

"Wanna be a hero, bitch?" Laura said, pointing the revolver at her. "Go ahead. Do something. I dare you!"

"Maya, just do what she says," Tina said, pulling her back.

"Believe me, bitch, I don't have a problem blowing your goddamn brains out, so do what the fuck I say," Laura said.

She moved closer to the immobile Veronica and pressed the gun into her forehead, moving her manicured finger toward the trigger.

"I knew I would catch up to you one day and give you what you deserved. Just one bullet is all it will take. Quick and clean," she said, smiling.

A soft voice came from the corner of the room. "If you

shoot her, it will be quick," it said, "but not clean at all."

"Who said that?" Laura asked, waving the gun toward the group of cowering women.

No one answered for a moment, then Deepa stepped forward.

"I did. I said it," the Indian woman said softly, holding up her hand.

"Dr. Dee, don't," said Kristin.

"Shut up, bitch," said Laura, swiftly turning the gun in Kristin's direction. Kristin paled and quickly stopped speaking.

"You're a doctor?" Laura asked Deepa.

"Yes," Deepa said. "If you shoot her, it won't be—"

"Shut the hell up. I didn't ask you for your opinion. Go sit the fuck down."

Deepa's face reddened, but she remained standing.

Brooke spoke up. "She's right. It's gonna be messy as fuck."

"Brooke, don't antagonize her," Gloria said.

"I didn't ask your fucking opinion either," Laura shouted, pointing the gun at Brooke.

Brooke glanced at the weapon pointed at her chest and chuckled.

"Oh, you think this is funny?" Laura asked.

"Listen, lady," Brooke said, "this ain't some movie. There ain't no special effects. This is real! If you shoot that chick in the head, they'll be scrubbin' brains out of the furniture for weeks."

"I don't give a shit," Laura said.

Deepa took a small, hesitant step forward. "Please, don't hurt her," she pleaded, tears starting to run down her face.

"Goddamn it, didn't I tell you to sit down?"

Deepa ignored the order and took another step forward toward the bleeding Veronica. "Please just let me look at her head. She is bleeding, she might have a—"

Laura threw her hands up in exasperation. "Why are these bitches so concerned about you?" she asked Veronica.

"Are they your friends? Did you tell these bitches all the juicy details when you were fucking my husband!"

"He *was* your husband," Veronica said. "Then he divorced you and married me."

"It wasn't hard, was it?" Laura asked, ignoring Veronica's statement. "David was, what, twenty-five years older than you? Easiest thing in the world to bat those big Latin eyes and twitch that fat Latin ass and show him them big, juicy Latin tits. It probably wasn't long before you had that weak asshole by the balls."

Veronica began to cry and Laura grinned, happy to see her words were having an effect.

"I bet you put it on him reallllll good," Laura continued. "I can see it now, David's skinny ass with you in bed. Pathetic! I bet he got himself some little blue pills, and you did all the nasty things whores like you know how to do. Then when he shot his pitiful little load, I bet you told him he was the best you ever had, didn't you?"

"That is not the way it happened," Veronica said, her eyes red with tears.

"And you kept on giving it to him real good, I bet. As much as he wanted, whenever he wanted. Did he fuck you in the office? In our house? Did you hide underneath his desk on your knees and service him while he was on the phone telling me lies about working late?"

"That is not what happened," Veronica said again.

"I bet it wasn't long before you had the old man exactly where you wanted him. You got him addicted to hot young pussy, then you convinced him to divorce his wife of thirty years. Then one day you gave it to him extra, extra good, and his old heart just couldn't take it. I have to hand it to you, you had a plan and you stuck to it."

Veronica wiped her tears and composed herself. "You have one thing right," she said. "He had a plan. The plan was to get away from you as soon as possible. He finally woke up and realized you were poison, Laura. Toxic. He could not wait to get away from you."

"You shut up, bitch. David loved me. He did."

"No, he didn't. Not anymore. He used to love you, but one day he saw you for what you really are, and he just felt sorry for you."

"You shut up. He loved me!" Laura bellowed. "He loved me!"

Laura grabbed a handful of Veronica's long hair, yanked her head back, then placed the revolver's stubby muzzle flush against her forehead. The cylinder had five identical holes drilled into the shiny steel, holes that seemed small until you saw them up close. Then, they looked like huge caves from which death emerged at subsonic speed. Bullets peeked out from the darkness of the holes like deadly eels poking their heads ever so slightly from their dens.

"Laura, please," Kristin said. She took a hesitant step toward the woman with the gun, her eyes filling with tears. "Please don't hurt her."

"You're so concerned about her, but this slut could have done it to any of you. Any of you! One day my husband was perfect then out of the blue, BAM! D-I-V-O-R-C-E. No explanation, just some stranger giving me papers and meetings with lawyers. Didn't take me long to figure out there was a little Latin whore whispering in his ear."

"Please, Laura," Kristin implored. "You don't have to kill her."

The angry look on Laura's face faded, replaced by one of confusion. She released her death grip on Veronica's hair and unlocked the gun.

"I don't have to kill her? What the fuck do you know about me or what I have to do?" she asked, waving the gun in Kristin's face.

Kristin opened her mouth to speak, but the gun just inches away from her face, made her speechless. All she could think about was Lucas, her son, coming home to find dead bodies in their living room.

"I . . . I . . . have a son . . . please . . ."

"So what, bitch? So fucking what? I have kids too. Or I did. I had a whole goddamn family. I was happy," she said as she lifted the gun and pointed it at Veronica's head. "I was happy!"

"Please . . . you don't have to hurt her," Kristin pleaded once again. She wiped her tears and tried to fight the fear that threatened to overwhelm her. "You don't have to hurt anybody. We can talk about—"

"I was happy!" Laura screamed again. "And now I have nothing! All because of this whore!" she screamed, waving the gun around and pacing the room frantically, never taking her eyes off of Veronica.

Kristin swallowed hard and tried to find her voice.

"I'm really sorry that happened to you," she said. "I can see that you're in pain, but I don't think she deserves to die for what she did. Look what you did to her face. Isn't that enough?"

Laura laughed.

"No, bitch, it's not enough! It's not nearly enough."

"Please, Laura, don't do this."

Laura raised the gun and pointed it at Veronica.

"Please, Laura," Kristin said again. "Shooting her isn't going to bring your husband back."

"No, it won't," Laura agreed. "But she took my life away from me. She took my family away from me. She's gonna get what she deserves."

She turned her attention to Veronica and raised the gun again, her hand shaking visibly.

"Laura don't," Kristin said. "You don't really want to do this. It's just the anger talking. But if we just take a minute to —"

"Why the fuck do you care what happens to her anyway, huh?" Laura asked. "Why do any of you care what happens to her?"

"I-I just don't think she deserves to die for what she did."

"Are you a whore too? Is that it? You fucking someone's else man like this whore did?"

Kristin's eyes went wide and her heart skipped a beat. She didn't think it was possible to be more terrified than she was, but at the question her blood ran cold, and for a second she believed with all her soul that Laura somehow knew her secret.

"Is that it, bitch?" Laura asked again, looking at Kristin through narrowed eyes. "Then you deserve one of these bullets too."

She drew the hammer back with a murderous click that caused each woman's heart to beat a little bit faster. Two things happened simultaneously: the trigger moved backward almost as far as it could go, and the cylinder's action revolved precisely and smoothly, placing a bullet directly in the path of the poised hammer. Laura smiled, then pointed the gun directly at Kristin's face.

#

CHAPTER SIX

Kristin

"Kris, I gotta go, honey."

Kristin knew this was coming but dreaded it all the same.

"I know, baby. Just five more minutes?"

Ed smiled. "Okay. Five minutes."

Kristin lay her head on his chest, savoring their last minutes together. For the hundredth time in the two hours since Ed had been in her bed, she was tempted to reveal his wife's secret. It had taken her a few hours to process Bianca's confession, and to her surprise, her reaction had been anger. Anger not for what Bianca did—after all, who was she to judge—but for who she'd done it with. She couldn't believe Bianca would sleep with her husband's father. Disgusting!

There were some things you just didn't do. It was unforgivable.

After much thought, she resolved to tell Ed everything. After all, both his wife *and* his father had betrayed him. The entire foundation of Ed's family structure was rotten, and it was up to her to let him know it. Wasn't it? After all, Ed was fast becoming much more than just a lover and she had an obligation to him. Or so she tried to convince herself before her training as a psychologist kicked in and she questioned her motives for wanting to tell Ed. She had no moral ground whatsoever to stand on. After all, earlier that day she'd lied to her best friend about having to see a patient, and now she lay naked with that same best friend's husband after making love to him for the past two hours. She knew she was being a hypocrite; her betrayal was just as bad.

But still . . .

She thought often of how she came to this, in bed with her best friend's husband every chance she got. She loved being with Ed, despite the guilt she felt when she thought about the lies they both told in order to be together. Since their affair began, guilt was ever present, but it evaporated the moment Ed climbed into her bed, only to reappear again with a vengeance the moment he left. The only way of dealing with it was to recall how it felt when he held her, when they made love, when they looked into each other's eyes. It wasn't only the sex. That was part of it, but the best part of being with Ed was how much he needed her. She felt his body melt when she hugged him and when he kissed her . . . My God, when he kissed her, he meant it. He was happy when he was with her, and she loved that, needed that, guilt be damned. Even so, every time she saw Bianca, the guilt reared up like a wild stallion, and she was forced to beat it back into submission.

She put the guilty thoughts out of her head, she didn't have much time left with Ed tonight, so she hugged him closer and tried to enjoy the few moments they had left, but her mind couldn't help but replay how their affair began.

That first night began horribly.

Her ex-husband, Stan, promised to take their son, Lucas, to a hockey game, but at the last minute, he decided to cancel. Instead of calling with the bad news, he came by to give it in person. Not because he wanted to apologize in person, but because he wanted to see the rise he got out of her. She knew because he had done it a thousand times. She'd let him in, but one look at his smug face, and she knew he was going to disappoint Lucas. Again.

"Stan, you're going to break your son's heart. You know that, right?" she'd said to him.

"Don't overreact, Kristin. Lucas will be fine. He's a big boy."

"He's only ten years old, Stan, and you promised to take him to the Devils game weeks ago. You have no idea how much he's looked forward to this. He's upstairs getting ready right now."

"This isn't the only hockey game they'll play. It's a long season. I'll make it up to him. Stop making everything such a big fucking deal!"

Stan picked up a banana from the fruit bowl on the counter and began to peel it, but Kristin slapped it from his hand.

"Ow! What the hell?"

"This isn't your house anymore, and this isn't your food."

Stan grinned.

"C'mon, hon, be nice to me. What's the matter?" He put one arm around her waist, and the other hand snaked around to rub her ample backside.

"The fruit isn't the only thing you don't get to sample anymore in this house," she said as she grabbed his hand and squeezed his long, thin fingers. She knew Stan had a thing about his precious hands. He was a plastic surgeon, and his career depended on them.

"That's not funny, Kristin . . . c'mon . . .ow, ow, what the hell?"

"Don't ever touch me again, Stan. Next time, I'll break them." She gave his fingers one last vicious squeeze then released him.

"I didn't want to touch your fat ass anyway," Stan whined as he massaged his hand.

Kristin rolled her eyes. Same old Stan. If he didn't get what he wanted, he immediately got nasty. There was a time when his remark would have caused her to run crying from the room, but those days were long gone. Being with him forced her to develop a thick skin.

"It might be fat," she shot back, "but Bruce enjoyed it. He enjoyed it a whole lot."

"Didn't we agree to never bring that up again?" Stan asked, turning red.

"I never agreed to that," she said, grinning.

Stan looked on the verge of tears, and she couldn't help but twist the knife.

"And for your information, my ass isn't too fat. Your hand is too tiny. And that's not the only thing too small to handle me."

Stan's eyes got the fake hurt puppy dog look that used to touch her heart and make her do stupid things in the name of love. "Fuck you, Kristin."

"What are you going to tell our son, Stan?" she asked. "Your new girlfriend got tickets to Ariana Grande so you're going with her instead of taking him to the game?"

"Hey, for your information, Ariana Grande is very talented. Those tickets were super expensive."

Kristin threw up her hands. "Are you being serious right now? You are forty-two years old. What the hell are you gonna do at an Ariana Grande concert? You'll be the only one there with hair plugs."

"See, that's why we're not married anymore. You're an emasculator. Energon says your emotional insecurity causes you to try and emotionally castrate me, but—"

"Come again? Megatron said what?"

"Energon! My energy coach. He's helping me to grow my aura."

Kristin rolled her eyes. "Megatron," she repeated. "Good grief. Is Optimus Prime there too?"

"I said his name is Energon and that's exactly the type of thing he warned me about. My energy is all over the place because of you. He said if you would quit putting shame in my pride bucket, then maybe I could get over my fear of intimacy and be a better partner in my new relationship."

"Hang on! So the fact you're a shit boyfriend is my fault? Please let Megatron know you were a shit husband, fast becoming a shit father."

Stan hung his head, and Kristin knew she had struck a nerve.

"Are you finished?" he asked.

"No, I'm not, you delusional, narcissistic, little worm! Tell Galvatron—"

"Energon!"

"Whatever! Tell your energy being it has nothing to do with your aura or filling your damn pride mug. We're not married anymore because *you* shoved your pathetic little prick into your nurse. Oh, pardon me, you shoved your pathetic little prick into your bimbo nurse *after* she made you gift her a new set of tits. Not your best work, by the way."

"Screw you. I did a great job on Flossie's boobs," Stan said, pouting.

"Maybe you're right. Soon as she got them, she found herself a bigger sugar daddy. He's enjoying the hell outta them, I bet."

"That's not true!"

"Didn't she meet some rich old guy and move to Venice?"

"Milan. And she didn't ditch me. We . . . grew apart."

Kristin rolled her eyes. "Yeah, right. Stan, you want to be a better person? Fine. Tell Megatron to teach you how to be a father to your son."

"Energon," Stan said in a sad, defeated tone. "I have to go. Your negative vibe is sending me down a shame spiral right now. Energon said when you target me with your anger arrows, I should get away from your toxicity and do something to fill my emotional bucket."

"What am I supposed to tell our son, Stan?" she asked his back as he walked out the door.

"Tell him I'll make it up to him," he shouted. She heard the door slam on his midlife-crisis Tesla before he peeled away.

"Fuck!" she said, pounding the dining room table in

frustration just as Lucas ran down the stairs wearing his New Jersey Devils jersey, looking around for his father. He didn't see him, and the look of disappointment on his face broke her heart.

"I thought I heard Dad. Did he leave?"

"I'm sorry, honey. He said he'd . . ."

"Make it up to me?"

"I'm sorry, honey," she said again as she put her arm around him.

"It's okay," Lucas replied. "It was going to be weird anyway. Brandy was coming to the game, too, and Dad acts like a stupid teenager when he's around her."

Lucas acted like he didn't care, but she could tell he was disappointed. He took his beloved jersey off and threw it in a crumpled heap on the couch.

"Can I spend the night at Bobby's house, Mom?" he asked. "I can watch the game with him and his dad."

"Sure, if his mom says it's okay."

After a phone call to her neighbor to confirm it was okay for him to spend the night, Lucas packed his handheld video game and his pj's into his backpack, hugged his mom, and ran out the door. Kristin watched from the window as he ran down the block and into his friend Bobby's house. Once he was safely inside, she dropped onto the couch next to Lucas's jersey and let the tears flow freely. Stan's self-centeredness ruined their marriage, and now it would probably ruin his relationship with his son too.

The doorbell rang, and she quickly wiped her tears and answered it.

"Hey, Lucas, did you forget . . ." she began but stopped when she saw it wasn't her son at the door. It was Ed, her friend Bianca's husband, looking flustered and confused.

"Ed," she said, surprised. "Is everything okay?" She looked behind him into the driveway. "Where's Bianca?"

"She's . . . she's not here. She's at home. Hey, do you think I could come in for a minute?"

"Of course, come on in."

"What's the matter, Ed? What's going on?" she asked after he dropped wearily onto her couch.

"I'm sorry, Kristin," he said. "I shouldn't have come here. It's just . . .something happened with Bianca, and I was hoping . . . I mean, I know you guys are close, I was hoping . . ."

"Ed, it's okay. Just tell me what happened. Is Bianca okay? The boys? What happened?"

At the mention of his wife's name, Ed's eyes flashed with rage.

"Apparently . . ." He sighed and tried to compose himself. "She's been . . ." He made a face as if saying the words physically hurt. "She's been having an affair. Did you know anything about it?"

Kristin recoiled in shock.

"That cannot be true, Ed. There is no affair! Bianca loves you. She wouldn't do that!"

"She confessed, Kristin."

"She what?"

"You heard me. She confessed. She told me the whole disgusting story. She met up with an ex, and they had sex in some dirty motel."

"I don't believe it. Bianca would never."

"She told me everything," Ed repeated. "You should have seen her. She told me the guy practically assaulted her and how much she loved it!"

"What the? Assaulted? She said that?"

"Yes. In detail." He closed his eyes, but a tear squeezed out. "She said—"

"Ed, you don't have to tell me. It's okay."

"No, I want to," he said. "I know . . . I know you know how it feels since Stan cheated too. I guess I just wanted to talk to someone who's been through this, you know? Someone who could relate."

She nodded. She sure could.

Kristin held his hand and was alarmed at the tension

in his body. His muscular forearm was knotted and hard and every vein was visible.

"She said he . . . he grabbed her and pulled her hair," he continued. "He ripped her panties off and he—God, I can't even say it—he took all her clothes off, then he smacked her on her ass. No, not just smacked. He spanked her. That's the way she put it. She got spanked like she was a disobedient child."

Kristin could not believe what she was hearing. If anyone other than Ed was telling her this, she would be laughing in disbelief.

"He spanked her, until her ass was red. That's what my whore of a wife said to her *fucking husband*!" He put his face in his hands.

"Ed, you don't have to tell me any more. Really."

"No, I want. You haven't heard the best part. Then she said . . . he . . . fucked her. That's just the way she said it. Not *had sex*, not *made love*, no, they *fucked*. Like two disgusting animals. Then he choked her. He choked her while they were . . . fucking," Ed spat the words out as if they made a rotten taste. He stopped talking, and Kristin offered him a Kleenex.

"Then she said . . . God, I can't believe this. Then she said he . . ."

"What did he do?" Kristin asked in a whisper.

"They had . . . anal sex. He made her beg for it. She literally got on her knees and begged."

Kristin didn't think she could be more surprised, but this bit of the story almost made her fall off the couch in shock. "She did *what*?"

Ed cried again, his body deflated.

"I don't know the person you told me about," Kristin said. "It sounds like you're talking about a stranger."

"That's what I thought too. It's like my wife transformed into another person overnight."

Kristin wished there was something she could say. The story Ed told had left her speechless. She *had* noticed a change in Bianca over the past few weeks. She'd become withdrawn and distant, and her mind always seemed to be elsewhere.

"You know what the worst thing was?" Ed asked.

She shook her head.

"Her face. It lit up when she told me about the disgusting things she did. I actually think she expected me to do the same things. How could she betray me like this, Kristin? I do everything for her and our boys. I work hard to give her a good life and she . . ."

He hung his head, and his eyes teared up once again. He tried to turn away so Kristin wouldn't see his tears, but the emotion got the better of him and he broke down.

She knew all too well what he meant, having herself felt the sharp sting of betrayal. For years she, too, had worked hard for her spouse. She'd stood by his side as he built his plastic surgery practice, putting her own career on hold while the practice grew. She'd been a maid, nanny, secretary, bookkeeper, cook, and janitor for him, and in the end, it hadn't been enough. She was surprised to find she was furious at Bianca. Too many times to count Kristin had confided in her about Stan's betrayal and how much it hurt her then and still did, and then Bianca went ahead and did the very same thing to her husband.

That damn fool, she thought. *She has everything, and she throws it away.*

She put her arm around Ed's shoulders and drew him closer. The tears were still wet on his cheeks, and she wiped them away. He looked at her face, also wet with tears, and his eyes opened wide with concern.

"Kristin, you're crying? What's going on?"

"I know how you feel," she said. She began crying again, and now it was his turn to wipe her tears away, caressing her cheek as he did so.

"I'm sorry I upset you," he said. "I shouldn't have come here. I thought maybe . . . I don't know what I thought. I should go."

"No. It's okay. Stay. Please."

He caressed her cheek again, and she closed her eyes and leaned into his large hand, savoring his gentle touch on her skin. She wasn't surprised when she felt his lips on hers, and she kissed him back with a passion she never expected to feel again. Ed pulled her onto him, but she resisted. The one time she'd straddled her husband, he'd complained she weighed too much. The disgusted look on his face made her so self-conscious and humiliated she'd vowed never, ever, to make that embarrassing mistake again.

"What?" Ed asked.

"I'm too . . . heavy," she whispered, ashamed.

"No. No you're not!" he said as he easily pulled her up onto him and kissed her passionately. She gasped in pleasure as he gently ran his hand over her curves, then pulled her blouse up over her head before he reached around and gently used both hands to unhook her bra. Her breasts dropped heavily from the constricting garment, and he caressed them gently and ran her large, erect nipples between his fingers. She threw her head back and let herself enjoy his touch, then, wild with desire, she took his hand and led him upstairs to her bedroom.

Once there, he hesitated, as if the sight of the bed cemented in his mind the thing they were about to do. Kristin hesitated, as well. This was the moment of truth. They could stop now with little damage done, but she resisted the thought and quickly undressed him. Then she slipped off what was left of her clothes while he watched and joined him on the bed. Ed was a big man, but in bed, he seemed like a little boy waiting for her to take charge. That was okay with her. She took her time with him, smiling as she felt the tension draining from his body. His lovemaking was slow and sweet and steady. Nothing was rushed. He took his time exploring every inch of her. Her climax wasn't earth-shattering. It, too, was slow and gentle, but she didn't mind. She didn't scream or shout, just gasped and held him tightly as it gently washed over her body.

"Kristin, just so you know, I didn't come over here intending for this to happen," Ed said a minute later when their rapid breathing had slowed, and they lay on the sweat-soaked sheets.

"I know."

"I don't want you to think I came over here to—"

"Ed, let's not think," she'd said.

She meant it. She didn't want to think. Thinking meant she would have to acknowledge how she had just betrayed her best friend.

"This was great," Ed said after a minute's silence. "I mean, really, really, amazing. But we can't do it again. I mean, never."

"I know," she admitted. "I ... I loved it ... but I think we made a mistake."

He agreed, and they both comforted themselves by resolving not to compound the mistake by repeating it.

One week later, Ed was back at her door, and Kristin led him upstairs to her bedroom without a word. As she undressed him, she knew she'd been deluding herself. The week since their "mistake" had been torture. She'd spent it reliving their time together over and over again, wishing with all her soul they could be together, even if it were just one more time. Now that Ed was here, she knew there was no way they would stop. Their supposed one-time mistake would blossom into a full-blown affair. She kissed his lips, then his chest, then moved lower. *If you don't want him, Bianca,* Kristin had thought as she felt him grow even harder in her mouth, *then I'll gladly have him.*

"I'm gonna go now, baby," Ed said.

Kristin mentally kicked herself. The last few minutes they had together, and she had spent it thinking about the past. Time never meant so much, she now realized, as when you don't have enough to spend with someone you cared about. The two or three hours she got to spend with Ed once or twice a week flew by too much too quickly.

"When will I see you again?" she asked.

"I don't know. Soon I hope. The senator's trial begins next week, so I'll be going 24–7 until it's over."

"I'm sorry," she said, rubbing his shoulders.

He shrugged. "I'll live." He turned a bedside light on and found his socks.

"But you know what kills me about the senator?" Ed asked. "What absolutely kills me is just because he's a buddy of my father's, he expects me to wave some kind of magic wand and get him off."

That's it, Kristin thought at Ed's mention of his father. *I'm going to tell him. I have to.*

"Ed, I have something to tell—"

"You know, Kris, sometimes I really hate being a lawyer. I don't know how my father did it for so many years. He's just so good at handling people, you know? He makes it seem so effortless. The man has a talent for getting people to do what he wants them to do. I wish I were more like him," he said, looking defeated. "Anyway, I'm sorry I interrupted. What did you want to tell me?"

The words she was so eager to say a minute ago died in Kristin's throat, and she knew for certain she would never, ever tell Ed what she knew. Ed loved and respected his father, and if he were to find out what he did, his world would explode and he may never recover. Maybe one day Ed would find out how rotten his family had become, but not from her.

"I wanted to say good luck with the trial. I know you're stressed out about it, but you'll do great."

"Thanks, baby. That means a lot."

"Can you do me a favor, Ed?"

What's that?"

"Stop comparing yourself to your dad. I know he was a great lawyer, but you're not him. You're your own man. And you're great too."

Ed smiled and hugged her tightly. "Thanks, Kris. I needed that."

A few minutes later, Ed was gone, and Kristin waited for the crushing guilt that always settled in whenever Ed sneaked out her back door under cover of darkness to return to his family. Bianca had the type of man Kristin dreamed about: a good, kind, gentle, loving, hardworking man who she threw away without a second thought so she could get slapped, choked, and abused. And by her father-in-law no less. Still, that was no excuse. Kristin knew she was violating the most ironclad rule in the BFF rule book—never ever mess with your friend's man. But now she didn't care.

No, that wasn't exactly true.

She did care.

But she was trying hard not to.

As much as Kristin tried to justify her actions, she knew she was wrong. The guilt might never go away, but for now, right this second, she had it under control. And for now, right this second, she would hold onto Ed. She would trace her fingers along his chest to memorize the contours of his body, she would inhale the scent of him and commit it to memory, she would meditate and quiet her mind using the rhythm of his breaths because when he was gone, the memories would be all she had until the next time he stole away to be with her.

CHAPTER SEVEN

Kristin turned cold as Laura pointed the gun at her face. Whatever horror she felt before paled in comparison to this overwhelming new terror. She tried to speak, but fear stole her voice.

"I asked you a question. Are you a whore too? Is that why you're standing up for her?"

Kristin swallowed hard. Her house, the women in the room, everything disappeared. Her whole world became the weapon inches from her face.

"Answer me, bitch," Laura screamed.

Kristin wanted nothing more than to say something to make this terrifying woman get far away from her. She would tell Laura about her and Ed, about the love they had made in this house, all of it in front of her lover's wife and his mother if only Laura would take the gun away.

Suddenly there was someone between her and the gun. Now that she couldn't see it, the spell of her terror-induced tunnel vision broke, and she blinked her eyes, momentarily confused as to who it was shielding her with their body. Her vision cleared. It was Bianca.

"Laura, stop! Why are you doing this to her? Leave her alone!" Bianca shouted. "She's got nothing to do with this. None of us do."

Laura shook her head, incredulous. "Is this house full of heroes? What the hell?"

"She's my best friend!" Bianca said. "I'm not gonna stand here and let you hurt her."

Bianca found Kristin's hand and squeezed it tightly while Laura pointed the gun at them. Finally, after a long, tense moment, Laura uncocked the gun and lowered it.

"No," she said, looking Kristin up and down. "I doubt you're the type to fuck someone's husband. You look like one of those boring, goody-goody type of bitches. Either that or you're a dyke. Are you a dyke?"

"No," Kristin said. "I'm not gay." Now that the gun was no longer pointed at her face, the worst of the terror was over, and she found her voice. The gears of her brain were slowly beginning to turn again, and she realized Bianca had probably saved her life. With that realization came a crushing guilt almost worse than the terror of a few moments ago.

"Then why are you bitches standing up for her?"

"Maybe she shouldn't have had an affair with your husband, but she doesn't deserve to die for it," Bianca said.

"What do you know about what this slut deserves?" Laura asked. "It wasn't just my husband she stole—it was my whole family! It was my life! So, yes, this bitch deserves to die. I'm gonna kill her dead, just one bullet, quick and clean."

"I told you, that shit ain't gonna be clean. It's gon' be real messy," Brooke said.

"She's right," Maya agreed.

"Maya, what the hell are you doing?" Tina asked, alarmed.

"This has gone far enough," Maya said. "Someone needs to do something."

"Maya, no," Tina said, holding onto Maya's arm.

"It's okay, baby," Maya said.

Kristin and Bianca glanced at one another.

"I knew they were together!" Kristin whispered to Bianca.

"Stop that damn whispering over there!" Laura screamed.

"Don't worry about them. Talk to me," Maya said.

"Why the fuck should I talk to you?"

"I'm a detective," Maya said with authority. She lifted her shirt to reveal a gold shield clipped to her belt. "And this ends now!"

CHAPTER EIGHT

Maya and Tina

Tina's phone rang, jolting her out of a deep sleep. Then it rang again, and she picked it up to see the caller ID displaying her husband's name. She pressed Ignore and sprang out of bed.

Clothes littered the floor, but she quickly located her bra then her blouse and her pants. Her panties were nowhere in sight, and she looked around frantically, trying to find them.

"Maya, where the hell are my panties?"

Maya peeked out from under the covers. "Don't leave, baby," she said in a sleepy voice.

Despite her frantic rush, Tina couldn't help but stop and stare at her young lover. Maya's long dark hair was a tousled mess, but she still managed to look incredibly sexy. With effort, Tina looked away and continued the frenzied search for her underwear.

"Come on, baby," Maya pleaded, kicking off the covers. "Stay. We have a few minutes before I have to get ready for work."

"That was Ted on the phone, Maya. I have to go. Mary's flight lands in an hour, and I was supposed to pick him up ten minutes ago to go to the airport. We shouldn't have fallen asleep," she said as she quickly fastened her bra. "I'm so mad at myself."

Maya twisted a lock of hair between her fingers guiltily.

"I wasn't sleeping," she said.

Tina did a double take.

"You weren't sleeping? And you didn't wake me up? You knew I had to . . . Come on, Maya. What the hell?"

Maya pouted. "I'm sorry, babe. I just didn't want you to leave. I mean, how often do we get the chance to spend time together? Between you working so much and being on this board and that board, we almost never get quality time."

Tina silenced her with a "talk to the hand" gesture and continued her search.

"Looking for these?" Maya asked, holding up Tina's missing panties.

"Give them here," Tina said.

Maya quickly pulled them away, her long arms keeping them just out of Tina's reach.

"I don't have time for games, Maya. I said give them to me!"

"Did I get you these? They're beautiful." Maya balled the panties in her fist, put them to her face and inhaled deeply. "OMG, I love the smell of you."

Good Lord, Tina thought as she snatched her underwear from Maya, hoping her face didn't betray how turned on she was. That was the thing about Maya. She was whiny, annoying, needy, and just a little unbalanced, but she was burning hot and sexy as hell. *What is it about the crazy ones that makes the sex so incredibly good?* Tina thought. As she pulled her pants on, Maya wrapped her long arms around her.

"Forgive me, babe? Please?" Maya kissed Tina lightly on the neck, snaked a hand down under the waistband of her lover's panties, and rested it between Tina's legs.

Despite her anger, Tina gave in to Maya's caresses. Her young lover had a way of touching her that she was utterly powerless to resist. She'd tried to break the affair off numerous times, but each time, it hadn't been long before she returned to Maya's apartment, cursing herself for returning, but returning all the same. She didn't know what Maya saw in her. She was gorgeous, much younger, much leaner, her face fresh and unlined. But, for some reason, Maya didn't care Tina was almost twenty years older; she was in love. Tina, for her part, wasn't sure she could be in love with a woman, but she sure as hell could get into bed with one.

Maya kissed her neck again, and Tina felt her legs turning to water. She was tempted to get undressed again, husband and time crunch be damned. A part of her mind protested mightily, telling her she should hurry up and get out of there, but Maya had a way of making her ignore her good sense. As if sensing Tina's internal battle, Maya loosened Tina's bra, kissed her breasts, and lightly bit her nipples, something she knew Tina loved.

"You know what we need?" Maya asked as she used her tongue to trace the contours of Tina's breast.

"What's that?"

"Toys. We need toys."

Tina arched her back as Maya's tongue traveled from the space between her breasts down her stomach.

"We don't need a thing long as you keep doing that."

"I got an invitation to a pleasure party from some chick at the gym. Wanna go? It'll be fun."

The part of Tina that would usually say absolutely not was currently occupied with the way Maya's mouth and tongue played over her body.

"Sure," she said breathlessly. "Okay."

"Great. We'll have so much fun."

Maya bit Tina's nipples lightly and placed her long, slim fingers between Tina's legs.

"So, um . . . did you think any more about staying the night sometime, or going away together for the weekend?"

And with that, the spell was broken. Tina pulled away, annoyed at Maya, but mostly at herself for falling under Maya's trance yet again.

"You know that's impossible. I can't get away for that long," she said as she retrieved her bra.

"Sure you can."

"And what do I tell my husband and my children? How do I explain it at the bank?"

"You'll think of something."

"You think it's that easy? So, tell me what happens when my husband finds out about us?"

"Jesus Christ, Tina, your husband is fucking his personal trainer! You know, sometimes I wish to God he would find out about us."

"Don't even joke like that."

"You don't think I know how you feel? I was married for five years before I faced who I really was. I just want the same for you."

"I've been married for twenty-five years, Maya. I have two kids, and I'm the CFO of a bank. I think it's a little different. I can't lose my family or my career. Not even for you."

Maya lit a cigarette from the pack on her dresser, took a deep drag, and blew the smoke toward the ceiling.

"But you can come over and fuck me, right?"

Tina said nothing.

"Don't you feel like a fucking fraud?" Maya asked, pointing the cigarette at Tina. "You make love to a woman, then you put your disguise on and go back to your big house in your suburb or your office on Wall Street, all the time with the taste of my pussy in your mouth." She took another drag of the cigarette and blew the smoke in Tina's direction.

"Your husband doesn't give a shit about you, Tina. He's fucking around, and you know it."

"You said that already."

"I'm saying it again, and I'll say it until you get it. You've known about the affair for a while, so why put up with it?"

"I don't care about Ted's affair, Maya. That's just what busy men do. My dad had affairs, and so do my brothers. I don't love it, but that's life."

"That's a really cynical way of looking at things, isn't it?"

"Maybe. But it's reality."

"Well, my reality is our relationship," Maya said. "I've never loved anyone as much as I love you. We should be together." She crossed her arms over her naked breasts, hugging herself tightly, looking like a lost and helpless little girl.

Tina sighed. Her heart went out to Maya, but she was so over this conversation. It came up almost every time they were together, and she dreaded it. The affair began as a fun thing to do, a stress reliever. *No matter how much I try to explain, Maya will not understand that what we have can never be more. It certainly isn't a relationship, and it's not a prelude to me coming out,* she thought.

It was fun. End of story! It was daring and dangerous, and she could indulge the fantasies she'd had since she was a teenager. But that's all they were, fantasies come to life. *My life, my* real *life, is at 227 Oak Street with my family and in my Wall Street office, and there's no room for anyone or anything else*, she told herself.

At times like this, she understood why most men only slept with someone a few times before moving on—because emotions *always* got in the way. She'd had affairs with men before, and while they were nowhere as satisfying to her as being with a woman, they were definitely easier. Men handled affairs like a business transaction. If it wasn't working, they cut it off. Easy-peasy. She sighed. She should have dropped Maya the moment she started to display feelings, but she hadn't, and now these annoying conversations were the price she paid.

"Maya, we talked about this, remember? I won't leave my family or endanger my career. We agreed this would be a casual thing, and when either of us thought it didn't work, we would end it."

"Things change, Tina," Maya said, tears running down her face. "I didn't think I would fall in love with you, okay! I didn't plan on it, but it happened. I love you. I want us to be together."

"That's not going to happen," Tina said gently.

"So just play my position, is that what you're saying? Just

take what little time you can give me and shut up?"

That's exactly *what I want you to do*, Tina thought, wishing there was a diplomatic way to say it.

Tina's phone rang. She didn't have to look at it to know it was Ted calling again.

"It's Ted again. I'll call you tomorrow, okay? You should get dressed and get to work."

"Fine," she said. "Go."

Tina tried to hug her, but Maya pushed her away.

"Just go," she said.

Tina walked out the door and hurried to her car. She called her husband and lied about Manhattan traffic and terrible phone reception in the Holland Tunnel. She ended the call and considered calling Maya to try to make peace but decided against it. She'd known Maya was going to be trouble when their affair started, and she slept with her anyway. Maya wasn't her first affair, but she was only her third female lover —the first was her college roommate, the second a quick fling during a business trip, and now Maya. The way it was going now, Tina doubted there would be a fourth. Oh, there were times she fantasized about she and Maya jetting to some far-off island where they could lay naked on their own private beach, but invariably reality intruded in the form of a text from one of her kids, or an email from work, shattering the fantasy and reminding her there was no room in her life, in her *real* life, for a female lover.

Out of the question.

Ten minutes later, she got a text from Maya just as she pulled up in front of the Willows Township Police Department.

Hey, baby. I'm sorry. I always seem to ruin what little time we have together. I know you won't go away with me, but will you still go with me to the pleasure party.

Please?

Tina sighed. The only place she wanted to go with Maya was to bed, and she was tempted to text back a strong *hell no*, but thought better of it.

Hopefully if I go with her to this one thing, it will stop her nagging for a while, she reasoned.

I'll go, she texted back. Then she called her husband, Police Chief Ted Brown, to let him know she had arrived. A few minutes later, Ted emerged from the building at almost the same time Maya's Mustang pulled to a stop in the parking lot. Maya got out and walked toward the building's entrance, the detective's shield at her belt flashing in the sun.

"Afternoon, Chief," Maya said as she passed Ted.

"Afternoon, Detective," Ted replied as he got into Tina's car.

Tina kissed her husband's cheek, then sped off toward the airport, watching Maya's reflection as it grew smaller in her rearview mirror.

CHAPTER NINE

"You're a cop?" Laura asked.

"I'm a detective. That's how I know what Brooke said is right. If you shoot, it'll be quick, but it it'll far from clean. Trust me."

"I told you," Brooke said.

"So what's your plan? You gonna whip out your gun and shoot me?"

"I don't have my weapon on me," Maya said. She lifted her shirt and did a slow 360-degree turn so Laura could see she wasn't carrying a concealed weapon.

"You tell me you're a cop like I give a damn," Laura said, pointing the gun at Maya. "You could be the governor for all I care. I'm still gonna kill this bitch."

Maya ignored the weapon. "Do you know how that works?"

"What?"

"The revolver. Do you know how it works?"

"What kind of stupid question is that? I put it to the whore's head, pull the trigger, and—bam—one less whore! That's all I need to know."

"It's not like the movies. There's more to it. If you think you'll murder her, then freshen up your makeup and sashay out of here. You're wrong."

"I'll be fine," Laura said confidently.

"No, you won't. Here's what's gonna happen. You put the weapon to her head, right, and pull the trigger. The round goes in the front of her head and comes out the back, along with most of her brains and a good-sized chunk of her skull. But what most people don't know is from close range, the gas propels the round out of the gun and goes in right behind it and expands under the skin. That'll cause the gas to either expand the exit wound or lift her skin clean off her skull, kinda like peeling a banana. If you're the shooter, you'll have blood and skin and disgusting little bits of skull and brain all over you. Very messy and very, very nasty. It'll be worse for them," she motioned to the women standing behind Veronica. "The bullet's gonna blow out the back of her head and brain matter, and sharp little needles of bone, will fly out of the back of her skull and paint the walls, and all these fine ladies along with it."

Almost as one, the women grouped behind Veronica took a step backward.

"She'll be dead"—Maya snapped her fingers—"like that. And you'll be scrubbing blood and brains out of your skin and hair for weeks."

"Nothing a good spa day can't fix," Laura said, grinning.

Maya chuckled. "Spa day? That's funny. Shoot her, and you won't see the light of day for a long time, if ever. There's no spa day after you murder someone."

"Bullshit! I got the best lawyers in the state on retainer. Two hours after this bitch is dead, I'll be getting a mani-pedi."

"You didn't think this through, did you?" Maya asked. "I think you came in here earlier and saw Veronica, and you were so angry you couldn't see past your rage. You ran home, got your pistol, then came back here with no thought of what would happen after." Maya cocked an eyebrow. "Or maybe you did. Is one of those bullets for you?"

Laura seemed taken aback by the question. "Is that what you think?"

"I do. I think you have no intention of walking out of here alive."

"You're wrong, cop."

"I know you're angry, Laura. I know you're hurt. A lot of unfair things have happened to you, and we all see your pain. But things *can* get better."

"They will be when I kill this bitch."

"No, they won't. They'll get a lot worse. Killing her will start a series of events you won't be able to control. Right now, you're in control, but that ends the moment you pull the trigger. Give me the gun and we'll—"

Veronica's laughter stopped Maya in mid-sentence.

"What the hell is so funny?" Tina asked, annoyed.

"Don't you see she's a monster?" Veronica said. "Monsters don't talk."

"No, I'll talk," Laura said. "I'll talk about killing you. That's what I'll talk about. Then I'll shoot you in the face and spit on your corpse."

The hate and venom in her voice made Veronica recoil in horror.

"Are you convinced now?" Veronica asked Maya. "Don't you see the type of person she is?"

"Nah," Brooke said. "We ain't got shit to worry about. She's all talk. She ain't killing nobody."

"Oh really? How do you know that?" Maya asked.

"Yeah, bitch, how do you know that?" Laura asked.

Until that moment, Brooke sat on the arm of a couch, absently chewing on her nails. At Laura's words, her body language transformed, and her face grew serious.

"Check it out," she said, pointing a ragged fingernail at Laura. "You can talk to these chicks any way you fucking want, but call me a bitch again, and I *will* beat your ass."

"All right, all right, everybody just calm down," Maya said. She pointed at Brooke. "You, sit the hell down."

"Whatever, cop. I came to buy some sex toys, and it don't look like that shit is happening anytime soon, so I need to get the hell on up outta here. But we ain't goin' nowhere until Ms. Angry Housewife of New Jersey over there catches a body, so . . ."

"Brooke, will you just sit down please?" Maya asked.

Brooke sat down and continued to mangle her fingernails.

"Laura, let me tell you exactly how this is gonna play out," Maya said. "You're holding a revolver in your hand and they are loud. Shoot Veronica, and everyone for a half-mile is gonna hear it, and two minutes later, this place will be surrounded by cops. Five minutes after that, a SWAT team will be in position out front. They'll see my car and figure out a cop is a hostage, which will make things that much worse. So, there is no way in hell you're just walking out of here. But I think you know that. So, I'll ask you again. What was your plan? Were you saving one of those bullets for yourself?"

Laura said nothing.

"Give me the gun, Laura," Maya demanded. "And we can all walk out of here safe and sound."

Laura lowered the gun slowly. "Maybe you're right."

"I know I'm right," Maya said. "Nobody needs to die today. Give me the gun, and let's end this."

Laura glared at Veronica as if weighing the pros and cons of what Maya told her. She breathed heavily, and her knuckles whitened as her hand tightened its grip on the handle. This action wasn't lost on the women in the room, and each held her breath, not daring to move or speak. Laura took one last angry glance at Veronica, exhaled, then lowered the gun.

"That's good, Laura," Maya said. "I'm going to take a couple of steps toward you, okay? What I'd like you to do is to turn the gun so the grip is pointed toward me, then hand it over to me slowly. Understand?"

Laura nodded.

Behind Maya, Brooke shook her head. "No, don't trust her!"

The tension in the room was thick, and the sudden, loud utterance caused Laura to flinch and look away from Maya.

Maya held up her hand to silence Brooke without taking

her eye off Laura.

"Ignore her, Laura. I'm the one talking to you, not her. Look at me, okay? Turn the weapon around, please."

Laura did as Maya asked.

"Thank you, Laura," Maya said. "You're doing great. Now I'm going to take another step toward you, and you're going to raise the gun slowly and hand it to me. Do you understand?"

Laura nodded again.

"Don't trust that bitch," Brooke muttered under her breath.

"Shut the hell up, Brooke," Bianca said.

"Yes, shut up, Brooke. Maya has it under control," Tina whispered.

If she heard the whispering, Laura gave no sign. She kept her eyes on Maya as she raised the revolver slowly.

"You're doing really well, Laura," Maya said. "Okay, now hand the weapon over to me, please." She was less than an arm's length away from Laura and held out her hand to receive the pistol.

Laura hesitated, then stepped closer to Maya as she raised the hand holding the gun. Maya's eyes were fixed on the weapon, but she raised them for a moment to make eye contact and give Laura an encouraging smile. Laura saw this, and before Maya could react, she lunged toward her and hit her hard across the side of the head with the heavy revolver. Maya's eyes rolled back in her head, and she dropped to the ground, senseless.

Laura stood over the unconscious and bleeding Maya, triumphant. "Who the fuck do you think you are, you stupid cop? Did you really think I would fall for that?"

No one moved as Maya lay motionless on the floor. Then a distraught Tina rushed to her lover's side. Laura smiled in triumph, lowered the gun, and glared at Veronica.

"I told you not to trust that bitch," Brooke said as Tina grabbed a napkin and tried in vain to stem the blood already gushing from Maya's head onto her starched white shirt.

CHAPTER TEN

Laura

"Bye, Grandma," the twins called as they exited the car. "Bye, Paris. Bye, London," they said to the Yorkies squirming in the passenger seat.

At the mention of their names, both dogs jumped up on hind legs and rested their paws on the window, yapping loudly as they watched the boys run.

"Bye, guys," Laura said, waving at the boys as they ran up the driveway at full speed, colorful backpacks flashing in the intense afternoon sun.

"Stop that damn noise," Laura snapped. The dogs knew that tone well and immediately stopped barking. Laura loved her grandsons, but the few minutes she spent with them each day as she drove them home from school were exhausting. The twins never seemed to wind down. It was like they were on a perpetual sugar high—and the dogs, sensing the boy's energy, were no better. As happy as Laura was to see them after school, she was equally happy once she dropped them off. She rummaged in her purse for her cigarettes until, frustrated, she emptied its contents onto the passenger seat, startling the dogs, who jumped down off the seat and onto the floor to avoid the cascade. Something fell from the purse, bounced off the seat, and hit the floor with a heavy thud, narrowly missing London's furry head.

"Shit," Laura said, looking around guiltily to see if anyone had seen. There was no one even close to her car, and even if there had been, the person would have had to practically be in the car to see what had fallen, but she was taking no chances. She pushed the dogs out of the way, picked up the shiny revolver that had fallen out of the purse and admired it. She loved everything about the weapon—it's heft, it's shine, but most of all, she loved the sense of power it gave her. The pistol was a holdover from the days when her husband, David, would transport large amounts of cash from their real-estate business to the bank. As more and more transactions took place online, the gun was relegated to a dresser drawer and forgotten until Laura came upon it during the divorce. Now it was hers. A forgotten relic of their years together, kind of like she was. Quickly, she stuffed it back into the purse and located the cigarettes, the pack crumpled and the cigarettes a little bent out of shape but otherwise sound.

She lit one and took a long, hungry drag, savoring the nicotine rush as she watched her daughter, Lily, open the door to let her rambunctious twins into the house. Lily kissed her boys then stepped outside and shaded her eyes against the sun, gazing out at her mother. Laura took another drag of the cigarette and held the sweet smoke in her lungs for a moment before she let it escape from her nostrils in slow, lazy wisps that followed the contours of her face before curling upward to become trapped in the plush ceiling upholstery of the Mercedes. Lily stepped from the doorway and began to cross the lawn toward her mother, a concerned look on her face. Laura took a last, hard drag on the cigarette then flicked the half-smoked butt out the window toward her daughter before putting the Mercedes in drive and stomping on the gas pedal. The sudden acceleration flung the dogs hard against the glove compartment and they crashed, whimpering, onto the floor. The car sped away from the curb and rocketed down the leafy residential street, leaving Lily motionless on her lawn, watching it disappear. Before she'd gone a mile, Laura's phone rang, and she glanced at the caller ID.

Lily.

She pressed the Ignore button. *If David were alive, he wouldn't have driven away; he'd be with Lily right now,* she thought. *They'd be sitting on the floor, drinking ridiculously expensive, piss-tasting tea while he listened to her whine.* He was that way with both their kids, the favorite parent, the one they ran to with their bullshit problems.

Laura and David didn't see eye to eye on many things, but David rarely argued, preferring more often than not to let Laura have her way. In their twenty-eight years of marriage, Laura could remember David putting his foot down on only two issues, starting his business and raising their children. On the first, she had to admit his instincts were correct because the company he'd founded with every penny of their savings blossomed into one of the largest private real-estate firms in New Jersey. On the other, she wasn't so sure. She was an old-school, spare-the-rod-and-spoil-the-child type of parent, exactly as her parents were, and David's too. They were both children of immigrants, her parents from northern Italy, his, persecuted Jews from Poland. Tough people from tough places who raised tough children. Although her father had been horribly abusive, she still appreciated the toughness he instilled in her and tried to do the same for her children, but David would have none of it. He was a sensitive child who grew into a sensitive man and resented his parents and his old-school upbringing. The scalding rebukes and frequent beatings that were as much a part of his childhood as stickball and the Brooklyn Dodgers left an indelible mark, a mark he steadfastly refused to pass down. Good enough for me, good enough for them, Laura argued, but David, usually eager to find compromise, was immovable and uncharacteristically tough when it came to his children.

The phone beeped and the screen lit up again, this time with a text message.

Mom we need to talk. I wish you could . . .

Laura didn't read any further, she deleted the message and looked up from the phone just in time to screech to a stop at a red light, once again flinging the traumatized Yorkies up against the dash. The shell-shocked dogs whimpered, but Laura ignored them. She sat at the light, fuming, and dialed Lily's number. Lily answered on the first ring, her voice precise and cultured, trained by the expensive private-school education David had insisted on. Laura's voice was rough by comparison, Brooklyn sandpaper to her daughter's prep-school silk.

"Mom," Lily began, "thanks for calling. There's something I—"

"Shut your fuckin' mouth," Laura said. The light turned green and she sped through the intersection, phone in one hand, the other holding her cigarette and the wheel.

"Listen, if I want to talk to you, I'll call you, understand? Don't call me or text me. I don't want to hear your shit."

"Mom, please. I just want to talk. Before Dad died—"

"I got nothin' to say to you or your brother, and I definitely don't want to talk about your father."

"My God, Mom, when will you let the anger go?"

"I ain't letting shit go. Not ever. You know what your asshole father did to me."

They had had this conversation in one form or another many times, and at this point Lily usually gave her some new age bullshit about forgiveness, but this time she was having none of it.

"Oh please, Mom. Stop playing the victim. You were no saint. You think we don't know—"

"You don't know shit, you fucking brat."

Lily chuckled. "We know a lot more than you think. But Dad . . . Dad always saw the good in you. No matter what you did, he forgave you. And you did nothing but make his life hell."

Laura flinched as if Lily had slapped her. Her daughter had never spoken to her like this.

"Listen to me. You don't know shit about me and your father, okay? He cheated on me with that whore, and you're defending him? What about what he did, huh? What about that?"

"If I were him, I would have done the same thing. You didn't deserve that man."

"If I was so bad, why didn't he say something? If he had anything on me, the lawyers would have—"

Lily sighed. "Mom, Dad was still looking out for you. If he had put all the stuff he knew about you in the divorce papers, it would have been public, and everyone would know. He didn't want that for you."

Laura said nothing. David had served her with divorce papers out of the blue, but he never gave a reason besides irreconcilable differences. There was nothing to contest during the divorce. The kids were grown, and David didn't fight the division of their very considerable assets, so the divorce had gone quickly and quietly.

Laura heard her daughter sob, and something in her heart stirred, but she killed the feeling as soon as she felt it.

"Before Dad died, he made me promise to try to reach out to you, Mom," she said, her voice softening. "He always thought there was something about you worth saving, but he was wrong. I'm done trying."

"Good, because I got nothin' to say to you."

"Okay, Mom. I tried."

Laura's heart skipped a beat. "What about the boys? You're gonna use them against me? What are you saying? I can't see my grandchildren now?"

"No, Mom, I'm not going to do that. I should. But I'm not. The boys love you picking them up from school. I wouldn't change that. Dad made me promise—"

"I don't give a fuck about your father or his goddamn promises. He promised to be faithful to me and he wasn't, so fuck him! I'm glad he's dead. I just wish I was the one who killed him!"

Laura hung up, threw the phone onto the passenger seat,

and stared into the distance as she drove, the tears in her eyes making the world blurry. "I'm glad he's dead," she said again.

She said it. But it was a lie.

It was at times like this she missed David the most. She knew the whole world, her children included, thought she was a raving bitch, and she certainly could be, but David's superpower had been the ability to see past her bitchiness and love her anyway. Over the years, she'd said terrible things to him during her rages. Nasty, disgusting things she regretted the moment they left her lips, but he never retaliated. He simply let her rant. Then when she was spent, he would open his arms to her. She would try to tap into her deep well of anger to stay mad at him, but she never could. He wore down her rage with the force of his love. David was a victim of the same kind of medieval child-rearing she was, filled with beatings and constant verbal abuse, so he understood where her anger came from. She marveled that her anger and resentment came from the exact same well of hurt and abuse David drew from for his love and patience. She had been grateful for him, even though she almost never showed it. Her anger didn't allow her to. It was that same anger that drove her to do the things she knew would one day finally exhaust his reserve of patience and forgiveness.

During their marriage, she often thought any other man would have long tired of her terrible temper and argumentative nature and simply divorced her or retaliated with abuse and beatings, and she expressed as much to David more than once. At those times, he'd held her close—she hated hugs, refusing them even from her children—but on those rare occasions, she melted in her husband's arms, and he'd simply said, "You're my Laura. I love you."

That corny line always melted her, and she silently thanked God for the one person in the world who truly loved her without reservation.

She missed him.

Ten minutes later, Laura turned into her driveway going

much too fast and braked hard, sending a cascade of crushed gravel spewing from beneath the wheels. She grabbed her purse from the passenger seat and opened the door to let the dogs run out, then she stalked past the massive columns framing the front door and walked into her house, slamming the door behind her. The Yorkies, happy to be out of the car, ran around her legs, begging for attention, panting and yapping ecstatically. Laura ignored their pleas and made a beeline for the bar, heels echoing hollowly on the marble floor. It wasn't that long ago she couldn't hear herself think in this house. The twins were constantly underfoot, and David Jr.'s college friends were always around lounging by the pool or with Lily and her husband as they grilled steaks on the enormous barbecue pit. There was always something going on, and David was the center of it.

Fuckin' David.

She made the drink a double, gulped it down, then made another and drank that one down in two large swallows. The liquor hit her system hard, but it wasn't enough, so she made a third and dropped heavily onto a love seat.

Fuckin' David.

She took a sip of her drink and groped in her pocketbook for cigarettes. As she pulled them out, the invitation she'd received while waiting at the school for the twins fell from the bag.

"Hope you can make it," the absurdly cheerful Black woman said as she'd handed it to her. Laura barely acknowledged her as she snatched the invitation from the fat cow's hand and slammed it into her bag with every intention of chucking into the nearest garbage can, but now she was glad she hadn't thrown it out.

This might be just the thing I need, she thought, *a night out with girls.* Girls she didn't know. Girls who wouldn't surreptitiously point and whisper about the woman whose husband divorced her then had a heart attack in his young girlfriend's bed.

"I'm gonna fucking go," she said to herself as she drained the last of the alcohol. She needed another drink, but her legs were rubber, and she couldn't find the strength to rise.

"I'm fucking going, David," she said, eyes heavy.

As they closed, she thought she saw David standing over her. She tried to open her eyes again, but they were heavy as rocks.

"I'm fucking going, David," she repeated.

She used the last of her waning strength to lift her hand to her dead husband, smiling as she felt him take it.

"David . . . I miss you. I'm sorry, I'm . . ."

"My Laura. I love you. I forgive you."

She smiled at the sound of his voice, then her chin dropped to her chest and she snored, the invitation still clutched tightly in her fist. Lupe, Laura's longtime maid, stood over her, shaking her head sadly. She let go of her employer's clammy hand, removed Laura's shoes, and placed them neatly on the floor. She knew it would most likely be the next morning before Laura awoke, so she walked and fed the dogs. When she returned, Laura still snored loudly, so Lupe covered her with a blanket before she walked outside to where her husband sat patiently in his truck, waiting to take her home.

CHAPTER ELEVEN

Blood ran in a steady stream down Maya's face as she tried to rise, but fell back, still stunned.

"Damn, bitch, what did you do?" Brooke asked.

Deepa quickly retrieved a linen napkin from the dining table and pressed it to Maya's wound.

"My God, Laura, that was uncalled for," Gloria said.

Laura watched the blood flow from Maya's wound and said nothing.

Jessica snapped her fingers to get Laura's attention. "Didn't you hear her? Why on Earth did you do that?"

"I knocked a nosy bitch out. Keep talking, and I might have to knock a fat bitch out too. Now waddle your fat ass away from me!"

"You just assaulted a police officer," Jessica said, ignoring the insult. "Don't you think this has gone far enough?"

"No, not even close. We're just starting this journey."

"Please, Laura," Jessica pleaded, "put the gun down. We can talk this out."

"Get the fuck away from me," Laura shouted, raising the revolver.

Jessica paled and started walking backward. Only Brooke remained where she was, biting her nails and looking agitated.

"What the hell is your problem?" Tina asked. "Just what

do you hope to accomplish here?"

"What do you hope to accomplish here?" Laura mimicked. "You think this is a fucking board meeting?"

"She hopes to accomplish bustin' a cap in this bitch's ass," Brooke said, pointing at Veronica.

"Exactly," Laura agreed.

"Do it then, so we can go the fuck home," Brooke said.

"I'll do it when I'm good and ready. And didn't I tell you to get back?"

Brooke stayed where she was.

"I said get back. Now!" Laura pointed the revolver at Brooke.

Brooke chuckled and flipped her hair. "Bitch, you don't scare me. You think this is the first time I had a pistol in my face?"

"It might be the last."

Brooke rolled her eyes. "Oh please! You're full of it. If you really wanted to kill her, you would already have put two in her head. You just wanna vent. You ain't gonna do shit."

"Brooke has a death wish," Kristin whispered.

"No," Bianca said, "I think . . . I think she's . . . she's high."

"High or not, we can't stand by and let her get shot," Kristin said. She grabbed Brooke by the arm and yanked her away from Laura.

Laura scowled at the still-smiling Brooke and lowered the gun.

"Ladies, Maya is still bleeding," Deepa said.

"I have a first aid kit in the bathroom," Kristin said. "I'll go get—"

"No!" Laura shouted. "You're not getting a damn thing."

"Laura, I have a huge first aid kit in the bathroom right over there," she said, pointing to a door a few yards away. "My ex-husband was a surgeon. He insisted on having every medical supply you can imagine, so there's everything Dr. Dee needs in that kit. It won't take a minute for me to go get it."

"I said no."

"Do you think I keep my spare shotgun in there?" Kristin asked. "It's a bathroom, for God's sake."

Laura was about to respond when Deepa rose up to her full five-foot two. In her hand was the napkin dyed red with Maya's blood. "Laura, she is bleeding a lot and is still unconscious. That's not a good sign. I need to clean her wound so I can see how bad it is. Kristin said there are medical supplies in the bathroom, and I am going in there. If you don't want me to get them, you are going to have to shoot me."

With that, Deepa dropped the bloody napkin and took one terrified step, then another, and another. Her bravery threatened to evaporate with each step, but she reached the bathroom door and put her hand on the knob.

The unmistakable sound of the revolver's click behind her made her mouth go dry and her knees threaten to give out. Deepa said a silent prayer as she waited for the impact of the bullet that would end her life.

CHAPTER TWELVE

Deepa

"Can we get McDonald's, Ammi, pleeeease?"

Dr. Deepa Singh glanced in the rearview mirror at her daughter's pleading face and couldn't help but smile. Anima, Annie to her friends at school, was as American as apple pie. Both her parents were Indian immigrants, but Anima had been born in Willows, New Jersey, and weaned on an American diet of *Sesame Street*, Barbie, and *SpongeBob*. At any other time, Deepa was *Mom*, but when Anima wanted something, suddenly *Mom* became *Ammi*, *Dad* became *Baba*, and *Grandpa* became *Dada*. It never failed to work on Anima's father and grandfather, both traditional men who puffed with pride when a word or two of their native language fell from Anima's Americanized mouth. Deepa knew better than to fall for it.

"No, darling, not today. We'll have dinner at home soon."

Anima pouted but didn't argue. Deepa would have liked to take her daughter to McDonald's. Anima was a good child and deserved an occasional treat. But her father, Hanif, and grandfather, Anuj, shared a disdain for all food not prepared in their kitchen. Still, she occasionally braved their ire and took Anima anyway. It was worth it to see her daughter smiling and happy as she devoured her favorite chicken nuggets and french fries. Deepa didn't particularly care for McDonald's, but she loved their sweet tea, even if she never finished even half of the enormous portion they served.

Anima soon forgot her disappointment and chatted happily about her day. Deepa half-listened to her stories, nodding and interjecting a "really" or a "my goodness" every now and then. She came to a red light, stopped, then picked the invitation up from the passenger seat and read it again. She'd read it several times in the few minutes since one of the other mothers, a pretty African American woman who introduced herself as Bianca, gave it to her while she waited for Anima at school. The invitation showed a group of women standing together, wide eyed and staring down at the contents of a gift-wrapped box. One of them had her hand over her mouth in shock and all looked guilty, as if looking at something they shouldn't but having a good time doing it. *PLEASURE PARTY*, it said in large, bold lettering.

"What is a . . . pleasure party?" Deepa had naively asked when a smiling Bianca handed her the invitation.

"Oh . . . you've never . . . well, it's only women. We get together and um . . . discuss . . . toys and maybe buy one or two."

"Toys? For the children?"

"No . . . ah . . . you know . . . for adults."

"Adults? I don't . . . ohhhhh." The realization dawned on her, and she covered her mouth with her hand and giggled like a schoolgirl, in a near-perfect imitation of the woman on the invitation. "I didn't know there were such parties."

"Oh yes. They're a lot of fun. I really hope you can come."

"Thank you. I will try to make it."

She said it to be polite, but now a seed of a thought began forming in her mind. Would she? Could she? The cars behind Deepa honked impatiently and she quickly accelerated. She envied American women and their ability to discuss such personal things as sex and its many accessories. Patients in her gynecology practice frequently confided things about their sex lives (most of which had nothing to do with their health) that still made her blush, even after years as a physician. It was as if some of them wanted to confess all the unusual things they did in the bedroom. It was better than keeping it inside, she supposed, but even so, there were some things better kept private.

A few minutes later, she turned into their driveway and parked, stuffing the invitation in her purse when she saw Hanif had already arrived home just moments ahead of her. He looked up as he heard her car, and she smiled and waved at him in greeting. He looked away without acknowledging her and walked into the house.

He can't even say hello, she thought to herself. *Not as much as a smile or a wave for his wife or his daughter*. A cold resentment at his callousness surged in her unexpectedly, and she shook with anger, the invitation crumpled in her fist.

"Mom, are we going inside?" Anima asked.

Deepa exhaled.

"Yes, darling, let's go."

They walked inside to find Hanif already comfortably ensconced in his recliner, he and his father engrossed in a cricket match. Anima kissed both her dad and grandfather, and Deepa greeted them with a practiced courtesy but wasn't surprised when neither man so much as glanced in her direction.

Ingrates, she thought. *Now they not only expect a home-cooked meal but expect to be served, as well, and not so much as put a dish in the sink when they are done.*

This was the worst part of her day, coming home to men who treated her like some faceless drone operating in the background strictly for their convenience. It was at times like this she wished she had the courage to actually have an affair. Living in a house with no love would be much more bearable if there were some passion in her life.

Her receptionist often pointed out how Steven, the strapping drug company representative with the New Yawk accent, loved to flirt with her. Deepa denied it, of course, but knew she was right. Or there was the beautifully muscled young man who owned the yoga studio she went to three times a week. He was Indian like her but born and raised in America. Very flirtatious, he took extra time with her, leaving his hand on her body just a second or two longer than necessary when working on her poses. Then there was Winston, the gorgeous older Jamaican man with the beautiful teeth and playful smile who owned the local car repair shop and who, no matter how busy he was, always made time to sit with her. All three men were possibilities. She wasn't blind to the way their eyes took her in when she was around them, but she didn't possess the courage to flirt back, much less initiate an affair.

She shot her husband one last contemptuous look and retreated upstairs to her bathroom, locked the door, and began to draw a bath, then stripped and gazed at her naked body in the mirror. She saw women's bodies every day of her life and knew she looked damn good, so it was a mystery why her husband hadn't the slightest interest in her. Early in their relationship, she blamed herself for Hanif's neglect. Was she too thin? Not thin enough? Was she a bad wife? Did her education, and then her medical practice, take too much time away from her husband?

She tortured herself with these questions, but in time she realized Hanif had room in his heart only for his engineering career. Steel fractures and load tolerances were his passion; loving and sexually satisfying his wife were of little consequence. He behaved as if sex were a duty and an unpleasant one at that, like cleaning the gutters or fixing a clogged toilet. On the rare occasions they copulated, it was passionless and over quickly. He deposited his seed inside her with his uninterested penis before turning his back and quickly falling asleep, while she lay beside him wide awake, consumed by a raging desire. Her father-in-law spoke often to her and Hanif of his desire to have a grandson, and she knew that the times they had sex were Hanif's half-hearted attempts to get her pregnant with a boy. What Hanif didn't know was that Deepa gave herself a birth control shot every three months; she would bear him no more children. Hanif denied her the love and affection a good wife deserved; it was only fair she deny him a son.

Despite Hanif's less-than-impressive lovemaking prowess, she would have been content if only he displayed an iota of passion. She prayed for kisses on the mouth, on her small and eager breasts, on her neck and back. Her nipples grew taut and hard at the thought of lips and tongue on her stomach and between her legs. She would be his forever if only he would run his hands over her body and touch her in the way she longed to be touched. But he never had and never would, and that was all there was to it. After facing that sad reality, self-blame and guilt evaporated, leaving only sharp resentment and the dull persistent ache of desire. She could live with the resentment, but desire, however, was not so easily dismissed. She tried to suppress it, tried to forget it, tried to ease it with work, but it remained constant.

It consumed her.

Invariably, after their brief and unsatisfying sex, she waited until Hanif was in a deep sleep before sneaking into the bathroom with her phone (she had chosen a device with a ludicrously large screen especially for this purpose) to surf to her favorite pornography websites and pleasure herself in a way her husband had no interest in doing.

She loved pornography. It was her only outlet.

She loved watching men with amazingly large *cocks* as they called them in the videos, expertly pleasuring their partners in every conceivable way. Fat or thin, short or tall, any color under the rainbow, it didn't matter. They pleased them with equal vigor and skill. She saved her favorite videos on her phone, secured by an app with an encrypted password. She even downloaded pictures of men with large penises. She had her favorites, the large, beautifully tattooed, and muscled African American man who wore a baseball cap and never took his shoes off, or the white man with the Spanish accent and the most beautiful penis. Both men ravaged their partners with a dominant energy that made Deepa almost faint with longing.

As she gazed at her reflection, she ran her hands over her tight stomach and small, pert breasts, fantasizing it was a man touching her, a large man with big hands and an even bigger penis. The thought made her shiver, and she desperately needed release, so she pulled her phone from her purse, the balled-up invitation falling onto the floor as she did so. She sat the phone on the sink, and moments later, a video began. In it, one of her favorites, the big, dark-skinned man covered in tattoos, lay on a bed, while his lover, a stunning Indian woman with enormous breasts, greedily took him into her mouth. This was an act Deepa had never performed, but as she watched the action on the screen, she felt the man in her mouth, she tasted the sweet-salty taste of him, finding it hard to breathe, but loving it anyway. Soon, the woman in the video straddled her lover, her long, dark, hair falling onto his chest. The man closed his eyes as the woman kissed him and put his hand around her waist and pulled himself deeper inside her, as he kept up a slow, steady stroke. Deepa closed her eyes, dreaming it was she on top of this stallion of a man. She felt his hands on her buttocks, pulling her as he thrust roughly into her; she felt his enormous manhood pulsing inside, almost ready to shoot his seed to depths her husband could never reach. The thought brought her to a massive climax, and she struggled to keep from screaming as her body shuddered in pleasure.

Her knees went weak, and she stumbled to the tub and lowered herself into the water, still shaking from the aftershocks of her orgasm. She tried to make her mind a blank as she luxuriated in the warm bath, but her eye caught sight of the invitation that had fallen from her purse. As she stared at it, the seed of the thought she'd had in the car now bloomed.

Yes, I'm going, she thought to herself as she soaked. Her mind was made up: soon she would attend her first pleasure party.

CHAPTER THIRTEEN

"Fine, bitch. Hurry up."

Deepa opened her eyes and turned her head slowly, expecting to see Laura in a shooting stance, gun pointed at her and finger on the trigger. In reality, the sound she'd heard was Laura uncocking the pistol, which she now held at her side.

"Go!" she ordered. "Hurry the hell up before I change my mind."

Relieved, Deepa quickly entered the bathroom and leaned on the sink, heart beating wildly. "You idiot! What were you thinking?" she asked herself.

Until this moment, she had lived a life of complete safety. Her schooling, her career, where she lived, none of it had been her choice; everything was decided for her. She had never had a chance to be brave even once in her life. Until now.

But her bravery had been foolish. *I had no part in the argument between these stupid, mentally deranged women. Inserting myself in their drama could have cost me my life*, she realized. But even as she thought this, she knew if she had to, she would do it again. She was a doctor. A healer. It was in her very nature to take care of the sick and hurt, and she had to be true to herself, no matter the cost.

Her reflection in the mirror was blurred by tears, and she wiped them away, surprised to feel an unexpected emotion.

Pride.

She did a brave thing. She stood up in the face of fear and did what was right.

Despite the terror she'd felt only moments ago, despite her still wildly beating heart, despite the desperate situation she still found herself in, a newfound feeling infused her body, a strength and empowerment she had never felt before. She faced death and came out the other side. To be sure, the danger was not over. She still might leave her daughter motherless today, but for now, she was alive and braver than she had ever been.

"Hurry up in there!" Laura shouted.

"I'm just looking for the supplies!" Deepa shouted back.

She looked in the cabinet under the sink and saw an enormous first aid kit. She wondered why Kristin would have such a professional kit in the house, but remembered she'd said her ex-husband was a surgeon. She understood, since she had a very similar one in her own home. The kit had everything from bandages of all types and sizes of bandages to nitrile exam gloves, to cold packs and sterile pads. She closed the kit, but something in it caught her eye, and with shaking hands, she opened it again. Fitting neatly in their respective spaces were a set of trauma shears next to a small pair of bandage scissors. The shears had blunt tips and sharp edges used mostly for cutting clothes or thick, heavy bandages. The bandage scissors were small, only around four or five inches long, and their cutting blades were short, designed to fit between bandages and skin and cut them efficiently, but unlike the trauma shears, they came to a small, but wicked-looking, point. She took the scissors from their space in the kit and held them in her hand, a thought forming that the old, scared Deepa of a minute ago would never have considered.

"Don't let me have to come get you in there," Laura shouted.

"I'm just coming," Deepa said. Quickly, she put the scissors in her pocket, closed the kit, and returned to the living room, where she was happy to see that Maya was coming around. She opened the first aid kit, making sure to quickly move its contents around so no one could tell the scissors were missing, then began to clean Maya's wound.

"Well? Is she going to be okay?" Tina asked.

Deepa leaned over Maya, inspecting her scalp as she cleaned the wound. "Fortunately, it's not as bad as I thought. Head wounds bleed a lot. She's lost some blood and might have a slight concussion that will need to be checked out, but I think she will be all right."

"Thanks, doc," Maya slurred. She tried to stand but was quickly restrained by both Deepa and Tina.

"See, the cop is gonna live," Laura said, grinning. "I told you."

"You fucking psycho, look what you did to her!" Tina said. "If you didn't have that fucking gun, I would beat your ass."

"It's not my fault!" Laura said. She pointed at Veronica. "Blame her! Blame this whore."

"Blame her for what?" Tina asked.

"She'd didn't hit Maya! She's not holding the gun! You are!"

Laura began to pace. "Blame her!" she said, pointing at Veronica. "You should have left him alone. Why didn't you just leave him alone?"

Veronica said nothing. She sat quietly, head down, lips moving almost imperceptibly.

"Praying, bitch? Is that what you and my weak ass David did? Did you pray before he tried to fuck you with his limp cock?"

"Don't you talk about Dave like that," Veronica said.

"*Dave* now is it?"

"That's right. Dave. He liked Dave. If you paid half the attention to him as you do those ugly little inbred dogs, you might have known that."

"I knew him! I. Knew. Him. He was my husband! *Mine!*

Not yours!"

"He wasn't yours!" Veronica shouted back. "You didn't love him."

"I loved him," Laura said, pounding her chest. "I did! He was mine for twenty-eight years until you came along." Her tears carved ragged trails through her makeup.

Veronica seemed taken aback by Laura's show of emotion. "Did you really love him, Laura? Then why did you treat him so badly?"

Laura paced the room, as if thinking about the question. "He was the only person," she began, overcome by emotion. "He was the only person in the world who loved me."

The women said nothing, shocked into silence by Laura's surprisingly calm tone of voice and the sadness and vulnerability on her face.

"You think I don't know what I am? I'm not stupid. I know I'm a bitch, but he loved me anyway. Nobody else gave a shit about me."

Even after he died and his affair became common knowledge, it made no difference. They still loved him—friends, relatives, clients, everyone. No one comforted her. Oh no, it was all about David. Poor fuckin', cheating David. Well, now he was dead and even more sainted in their eyes than he was in life.

Laura wiped a tear and continued, "My father used to beat the shit outta me when we were kids. I mean he really beat me. He had a special leather belt just for whipping my ass. My mother never lifted a finger to help me, even when I lay in bed with busted lips and black eyes and welts and bruises all over my body. David was the only one who cared. He used to climb up the fire escape of our building and sneak in with ice for my bruises or some treat he stole from the grocery store he worked at. David was always there for me. When Papa found out I was hanging out with this Jewish boy, he went ballistic." Laura winced as if reliving the memory. "I wasn't even David's girl or nothing. He was just a friend from the neighborhood, but Papa didn't believe me."

Laura's voice got lower and the women listening to her leaned forward to hear her better. "Papa was so mad one night that he didn't use the belt like every other time. This time . . . this time he used his fists. David found out what happened, and when Papa went to work that night, he snuck in and took me out of there. He couldn't take me to his apartment, his folks were just as bad as mine, so he begged his cousin and her husband to let me stay on their couch for a few days. The next day I was in and out of consciousness, I had a fever, and my eyes were swollen so bad I couldn't see. I was in real bad shape. I needed a doctor, but we barely had money for food much less a doctor."

She began openly crying, not bothering to wipe the tears obscuring her sight. "David had a baseball card collection. It was his pride and joy. He'd been collecting those stupid cards since he was a little kid. That morning, he took the subway into the city, and he sold it. He sold his collection. For me. He got enough for the doctor and for a couple of weeks' worth of food and medicine, but it ran out quick. But somehow he got more. I asked him where he got it, but he never told me. I found out later that the fool sold his blood. That man literally gave his blood for me. And I wasn't even his girl, can you imagine? He was just a friend from the neighborhood. He sold his blood and used it to buy me food and medicine, and little by little, I got better."

She stopped talking for a moment, looking as if she were about to start sobbing, but she took a breath and continued. "I was free from my parents, but not in my head. I would wake up sometimes feeling like Papa was standing over me with that belt. Drinking was the only way to kill the nightmares, so that's what I did. It only took a couple of years for me to hit rock bottom, I-I was doing real bad, and once again, David rescued me. I was drunk, I smelled, I had thrown up all over myself, but here was this man." Laura choked up, the tears running down her cheeks. "Here was David, telling me it was going to be all right. And I believed him. I would have killed myself if David hadn't convinced me there was something to live for. He took me to his crappy little room, and he locked us in, and he held me for four days while I went through withdrawal. I punched and kicked and scratched him and called him every name in the book, then I slept for almost forty-eight hours straight. The first thing I saw when I woke up was him looking down at me, smiling. He looked like he was in a fight with a wolverine —he was all scratched up and bruised up, but he was smiling anyway. Up until then, he was just a good friend, but he gave me something to live for during those four days because it was then I fell in love with him."

Veronica stood with arms crossed tight across her chest and rolled her eyes.

"I fought him like a wildcat, and he just held me until I was better. I wouldn't be alive today if not for David. He saved my life more than once. Yes, I was a bitch to him, I know I was. But I loved him."

No one said anything for a long moment, then Gloria spoke up.

"So if you loved David, if he did all that for you, then why didn't you treat him better? Why couldn't you show him how you felt?"

"I did. In my own way," Laura said. She wiped her tears, and her face began to take on the angry look again. "I'm damaged. I know that. But David knew that too, and he loved me anyway. It was fucked up, okay? But it worked. Until she came along."

"It might have worked for you, but it doesn't seem like it worked for him," Gloria said. "A little love and affection would have gone a long way."

"I tried to be all loving and sweet, but it just . . . I just couldn't. We didn't grow up that way."

"The way you were raised has absolutely nothing to do with it," Gloria said.

"Lady, you don't know shit. My father used to—"

"What? You think you were the only one who got beatings?" Gloria said, hands on hips. "I got my share, too, believe me. My father was an old-fashioned spare-the-rod-and-spoil-the-child, fire-and-brimstone type of Baptist preacher."

"Then you should know what I mean," Laura said.

"No, Laura, I don't. My papa beat me because he loved me and wanted the best for me. His punishments were his way of correcting my mistakes and showing me love."

Kristin gasped. "Gloria, that makes no sense."

Laura sneered. "My father never showed me love. He beat me because he was a mean, angry son of a bitch."

Gloria shook her head. "Maybe that's what it seemed like to you. But I'll bet he did what he did to teach you the difference between right and wrong. There are better ways to teach a lesson, but men often don't tackle problems in the best of ways. They're weak. My father certainly was. He was a womanizer, too, but he always came home, and he took care of his family."

Deepa made a face. "I am sure your mother was of a different opinion," she said.

"Not at all. Mother was . . . pragmatic. She recognized her husband was a good man, but like all men, he had certain weaknesses. So rather than fight against them, she managed them for the good of the family."

Tina rolled her eyes. "Lady, you have got to be kidding."

Maya was still on the floor, but she sat up, wincing at the pain in her head. "Managed them? What the hell does that even mean?"

"It's not hard to understand. Most of us are mothers here. Did we get upset at our babies for crying? Or at a toddler for spilling milk? No. It's just what they do. The same thing applies to men. It's just *what they do*."

"So we condone their bad behavior?" Kristin asked.

"Not condone it. We manage it," Gloria said. She answered Kristin's question, but looked Bianca in the eye as she did. "We manage it because men will take what they want, never mind the consequences."

"No, you're so wrong," Veronica said. "Some men may be like that, but Dave wasn't. He was a good man."

"So good he broke his vows and took up with you?" Gloria asked.

"It's not that simple, and you know it."

"I don't know any such thing, young lady. Vows are meant to be kept. He broke his vows, with your help. How do you live with the guilt?"

"I never felt guilty," Veronica said defiantly. "Not for a second."

"You never felt guilty?" Kristin asked, shocked. "Not even once? How is that possible? I mean, doesn't sleeping with another woman's husband make you feel terrible?"

"She doesn't feel shit," Laura said, "because she's a whore, and whores don't have feelings."

Veronica ignored her. "To answer your question, Kristin, no, I really didn't feel any guilt, and I never regretted one second I spent with Dave. Laura threw him away, and he needed someone to love him."

"Two wrongs don't make a right," Gloria said, her arms crossed.

"Like I said, she's a whore," said Laura.

Veronica shook her head, exasperated. "It's still so easy to place the blame somewhere else, isn't it, Laura? Yes, I was wrong for having an affair with a married man. But what about what you did? Dave would never have even looked in my direction if you'd been a better wife to him."

Laura's face turned beet red, and she raised the gun again as if to hit Veronica.

"Go ahead, hit me," Veronica dared. "Isn't that what bullies do? Lash out?"

The room fell silent.

"You stupid, stupid woman," Veronica said. "You had everything, and you didn't even see it. And now you have no—"

Without warning, Laura punched Veronica in the face. The blow was solid, and the younger woman staggered and fell in a heap onto the floor.

The women huddled behind Veronica gasped and took a step back. Only the still-groggy Maya moved forward to try to intervene, but Tina held her back.

"What the fuck is wrong with you?" Maya said. "That was . . ."

"Well deserved," a grim-faced Gloria finished.

"Gloria! What are you doing? Shut up!" Bianca hissed.

Gloria ignored her daughter-in-law, walked up to a stunned Veronica, who was on the floor struggling to get up, and pointed an accusing finger at her.

"You deserved that. Whether she was a bad wife or not doesn't matter. They had vows, and you helped her husband to break them. Shame on you, young lady."

"That's right," Laura said.

"And you," Gloria said, pointing the finger at Laura, "you're old enough to know better. What the hell is this? So your husband cheated on you. Is that any excuse to hold a whole houseful of people hostage? This is between you, your dead husband, and her," she said, pointing at Veronica, still splayed on the floor.

"Sh-she took my husband from me," Laura said weakly.

"So what if your man betrayed you? That's not important. He's gone now, so remember the good times. Remember the family and the home you built. Remember we women are the backbone of society, and we have to be better than them. If your man doesn't want to look out for your family, then the responsibility for the family is yours!"

She looked around the room and her gaze fell on Bianca.

"Even if a man is good, he's still only a man. They try to hide their fear and insecurity, but it's in their nature. They can't help it. They chase other women for something to conquer because if they didn't, their insecurities would turn them into puddles of jelly. Every time he's with another woman, he's trying to fill a hole inside him that no one—not you, not any whore, or ten whores—can ever fill."

Bianca tried to keep a straight face at her mother-in-law's words, but her mind was screaming. *Jesus Christ,* she thought. *She's talking to me! Gloria knows about me and Will.* A tear slipped down her face and her knees went weak.

Kristin felt Bianca stumble and held onto her, even as an icicle of fear stabbed her heart at Gloria's words. *My God, she's talking to me!* Kristin thought. *She knows about me and Ed!*

CHAPTER FOURTEEN

Gloria

By Gloria's calculations, Will had slept with almost two hundred women during their marriage. One hundred and eighty-eight to be exact. One hundred and eighty-eight women over forty-eight years of marriage equaled around four a year. And those were only the ones she knew about.

She glanced over at her husband as he drove the Jaguar across the George Washington Bridge. The Jag was a 1982 XJ6 she bought for him when he made partner at the firm. The car was almost forty years old, but still in excellent working condition, and it looked damn good, much like her husband.

That was the problem. Will was too handsome, too well-preserved, too damn charming. Women of all ages adored him. It took little or no effort on his part to induce them into bed.

And he was good at it. To the tune of one hundred and eighty-eight sluts, whores, and home-wrecking hussies.

Despite his cheating nature, Gloria knew Will loved her, and she did truly love him in return. But he was a man, and men were weak and would do as their undeniable nature compelled. So, over the years, she learned how not to entertain the thoughts of his incessant betrayals. But occasionally, when her mind slipped and the thoughts broke free of their mental bonds and bubbled up to the surface of her consciousness, she wrestled them, held them down, and chained them up again by turning her mind to other, more pleasant subjects like redecorating their homes, planning dinners and cocktail parties, arranging Will's calendar of speaking engagements, and scheduling vacations with their son and his family.

It was an exhausting fight but one she had to win because when she thought about the decades of lies, she felt the self-control painstakingly constructed over a lifetime slipping, and she would not, *could not*, let that happen.

There was a time when it was difficult for her to restrain her emotions. Early on in their marriage, the anger simply would not let her rest. It kept her awake in their marriage bed, listening to her faithless husband snore. It was during those times she began to feel an increasing empathy for her long-dead mother, who had also lived with betrayal courtesy of Gloria's father, the town pastor, a good-looking and very charismatic man, much like Will. And like Will, a serial cheater. He never frolicked in their town—he at least knew better than that—but he had women he "ministered" to in his travels throughout neighboring counties.

Gloria never knew how Mother found out about his indiscretions, but when she did, her priority became keeping their good name intact by ensuring knowledge of what her husband did never got out. Sure, there were whispers here and there about the handsome pastor, but nothing ever came of them, so their family name and reputation remained unsullied. Remembering her mother's example gave Gloria the courage she needed to endure Will's treachery. Thus empowered, she slowly made peace with her rage. It didn't go away. Oh no, it would never disappear. It was always there, like an apparition glimpsed from your peripheral vision. Over the years she'd thought about seeing a professional to vent her feelings, or maybe joining one of those silly support groups, but she never did. They would have tried to get her to release her anger, and that she would never do.

She wanted it close. That was how she kept it under control.

That was her secret.

She was always angry.

Still, there were times when it was almost comforting to stop fighting and allow the emotions to have their way. She did so now and quickly slipped into a rage as easily as one would slide into a warm bath in a familiar tub.

"What's the matter, Glo? Everything all right?"

Gloria opened her eyes to see they had crossed the bridge and were now on the New Jersey Turnpike. She had no concept of the minutes passing, so all-encompassing was her fury. She silently scolded herself for giving in to it and tried to recall what he said to her.

"Glo, you okay, baby?" Will asked again, saving Gloria the embarrassment of asking him to repeat himself.

"Yes, sweetheart. I'm fine. Just a slight headache, that's all."

"I think I have some aspirin in here somewhere," he said, rummaging through the Jaguar's armrest.

"Hey, I forgot this was here," Will said a moment later as he pulled a gigantic Cohiba cigar from the armrest. The search for aspirin forgotten, he reached for the Jaguar's cigarette lighter.

"You don't mind if I smoke this, do you, honey?"

"No, darling, go right ahead," Gloria said with a well-practiced smile, mentally shedding the anger like a winter coat and storing it away.

She opened the glove compartment, searching for the gold cigar cutter, one of the numerous gifts she'd bought Will upon his retirement from the bench. She found it, took the Cohiba, clipped it, then handed it back.

"Thanks, honey." He lit the cigar, sucked in the first mouthful of smoke, and smiled in satisfaction.

Gloria detested smell of cigars, but she tolerated the odor. The Jaguar was Will's, and she believed a man should do as he pleased in his own car.

Within reason.

Gloria glanced at her husband again as they passed through one of the many New Jersey tollbooths on the way to their son Edward's home.

"Why smoke it now?" she asked, pointing at the cigar. "Celebrating because I'm going to be out of your hair for a couple of days?"

"Of course not, honey," he said, blowing out a huge billow of smoke. "What's not to smile about? I'm alive on a fine day, smoking this fine cigar, driving a fine car, sitting next to my even finer wife. I'm the luckiest man in the world."

Gloria smiled and blushed at her husband's compliment. Even after decades of marriage, Will still had that effect on her, despite his numerous deceptions and her ever-present anger. God help her, the man was better looking at sixty-eight years old than the seventeen-year-old high-school basketball star she'd met all those years ago, and God knows he'd been absolutely gorgeous then.

Will had been the boy almost all her friends had shamelessly pursued. He used his charm and killer smile to good effect, hopping from bed to bed with impunity. Everyone knew he was a player, but he was the type of charming rogue everyone loved. She wasn't one of those who pursued him, however, even though she could never deny her strong attraction. But it wasn't long before he noticed the pretty, but shy, girl who never seemed to give him a second look. His invitation to a walk on the beach turned into lunches on the boardwalk, and soon they were dating.

"I'll work on a road crew for a couple of years, then I'll make foreman. That's where the big money is!" Will said one day when they were talking about plans for the future.

She nodded and smiled. By then Gloria knew they would be married, even if Will didn't yet, and she'd be damned if she would end up the wife of a construction worker. Gloria was no snob, far from it. There was no shame in an honest day's work, but she knew Will was capable of much more than he let on. Getting to know him made her realize he was more than just a beautiful body and a killer smile. Will was scary smart. He made A's and B's in school with little effort, his memory was razor sharp, and he soaked up knowledge easily. No, there would be no construction work in their future if she had anything to say about it.

That decided, she spent hours in the library researching the profession that would best suit her husband-to-be. Medicine? No. Even though the civil rights movement had made great strides, the medical profession was still hard for Blacks to get into, even light-skinned ones who could pass the paper bag test. Anyway, Will almost passed out at the sight of blood when she cut her finger once, so that was out. Politics? Maybe. More and more Black politicians were emerging every day, and he was certainly good looking and charismatic enough, but she quickly rejected that career. Women would always be Will's weakness, so the potential for scandal was plain. No, politics wouldn't do. She continued her research and finally settled on a career in law. True, there weren't many successful Black lawyers, but the writing was on the wall. The civil rights movement had transformed the country and would continue to do so, and it required good men. Good, educated, charismatic Black men like her Will to advance the Cause.

It was decided. Her Will would become a lawyer.

Will's future determined, Gloria gradually steered him in that direction, helping to apply for scholarships and fill out the reams of paperwork it took to get into a good school. Her efforts paid off, and Will won a basketball scholarship to Hillman University, where he excelled, easily graduating at the top of his class and winning yet another scholarship, this time to Hillman School of Law. They were married soon after graduation, and if you'd asked him, he'd have proudly informed you both the marriage and law school were his ideas, which was fine with Gloria.

Gloria chose wisely. Will took to the law like a fish to water, and by the time their first child was born, he graduated with honors and quickly landed a job with the small, but prestigious, New York City firm of Diamond, Horovitz, and Yauch. He was the first Black lawyer at the firm, and ten years and two more children later, he was the first Black partner. Then around the time their oldest began college, Judge William Edward Truman, Esq. was sworn in as a New York State Supreme Court justice, at that time one of only two Black men to ever be in that role. Will served on the bench with distinction for over twenty years before retiring as one of the most respected jurists in the state.

Not bad for a kid whose ambition was to lay asphalt on the New Jersey Turnpike, Gloria frequently thought. She knew without a shadow of a doubt none of it—not the education, not the firm, not the partnership, not the huge home in Westchester County around the corner from Bill and Hilary—would have been possible were it not for her. She made him what he was and worked hard to keep him there. There hadn't been a hint of scandal attached to his name in all the years he practiced law. Not one harassment claim or incriminating photograph, and best of all, no little green-eyed bastards running around trying to claim his name. Oh sure, everyone knew the very handsome Judge Truman could be a flirt, but that was as far as it went. Thanks to Gloria.

She recognized very early on Will's potential for disaster and encouraged him to hire her friend, Deidre, as his secretary at the firm. With every promotion, Gloria made certain he took Deidre along with him, thus ensuring she had a contact supplying her with inside information. She also made friends with the other firm wives, who kept her abreast of all the firm gossip so she was always informed. Years later when personal computers, then the internet and cell phones, became a part of daily life, Gloria quickly realized there was nothing you couldn't find out about online and quickly became an expert at ferreting out information. Thus armed, she quietly staved off disaster without Will ever suspecting her involvement. Over the years, keeping track of Will's dalliances became a full-time career, starting early on during their courtship with a floozy named Joanna, who worked in her father's grocery store and looked and acted like an innocent angel, but shared Will's love of sexual perversions. As soon as Gloria found out her beau and the whore, Joanna, were having sex every chance they got, she had a quiet word with Joanna's very strict mother, after which Joanna was promptly sent to live with relatives down south.

That was the start of her career of keeping her Will out of trouble. Very discreetly over the years, she paid for three abortions and got rid of a handful of other homewreckers who might have become a danger to them, but for Gloria's timely intervention. One of the brazen hussies had actually thought Will would divorce Gloria and run away with her, but Gloria put a stop to those ambitions tout suite. Her plan was to pay the woman off, but before she could, the hussy killed herself. Regrettable, but necessary. All told, Will's indiscretions over the years had cost her over $250,000, more than a few sleepless nights, and part of her heart and soul each time, but it was money well spent. Thanks to her, Will's career and their family's excellent name and reputation were one hundred percent clean and scandal-free.

Her mother would have been proud.

"Earth to Gloria," Will said.

"Sorry, dear, I was just thinking."

"So, are you looking forward to Bianca's party?"

Gloria grimaced and said nothing.

"Come on, Glo, lighten up. Who knows, you might have fun."

"William, what on Earth am I going to do at a, what did they call it? Pleasure party? I'm supposed to go ahead and buy those . . . those . . ."

"Sex toys, Gloria. You can say it. Sex. Sex toys."

"I know I can say it, William. I'm not a prude."

"I love you, honey, but you are. You're very much a prude."

"No, I'm not! Far from it."

Will rolled his eyes.

"I saw that eye roll, William. I'm not going to argue with you. I'm entitled to my opinion. For the life of me, I don't understand why anyone needs those . . . accessories. And what I really don't get is why buying them became a social occasion. I mean, does everybody have to know your business? I think those kinds of things should be, you know, personal. Don't you?" She continued without waiting for an answer. "Plus, it's probably going to be a little uncomfortable with me and Bianca."

"Really? Why is that? Did you have a falling out?"

"No. I just don't think Bianca cares for me very much nowadays."

"Oh, come on, Glo, that's nonsense. Why would you say that?"

Gloria sighed.

"Maybe it's only in my head, but she's been distant since last summer. I have no idea why."

Out of the corner of her eye she noticed Will tense and his eyes narrow. It was only for a second, and he recovered almost instantly, but Gloria knew him well enough to tell something had struck a nerve.

Then it was her turn to tense in her seat.

Wait a second, she thought. *There's no way that he . . . Will would never . . . Would he*?

Then, just like that, the puzzle pieces clicked into place, and the running mental tally of Will's affairs increased by one.

One
hundred
and
eighty
nine.

Gloria's blood ran cold as the cigar's thick, blue smoke swirled around Will's handsome head like a fragrant halo. Then an unimaginable tidal wave of rage filled her entire being because she knew, she *knew*, what he had done, and God help her, in that moment, if she owned a gun, driving or not, she would have shot her handsome, stupid, cheating, evil husband stone dead.

CHAPTER FIFTEEN

"Do you really believe that Dr. Phil bullshit?" Laura asked Gloria. "Your man is insecure and just trying to find himself? Please. These young bitches probably buy that crap, but you're old enough to know better."

"I could say the same about you," Gloria said. "You're the one holding the gun."

Laura laughed and pointed the gun at Veronica.

"Wasn't she old enough to know better? There's no question about what hole she tried to fill. She got David to fill it for her. That's the problem. She's got no idea what me and David went through together, what we did to build our life, start our business, raise our kids. Then one day she comes in and . . . and . . ."

"Oh, grow up," Tina said.

"What did you say?"

"I said grow the hell up. Do you think you're the only woman in history whose husband had an affair with a younger woman? Who do you think you are?"

"I'm the pissed-off bitch who's going to get back at the whore who ruined my marriage, that's who I am."

"Have you ever considered there are other ways to deal with this that don't involve a SWAT team showing up outside?" Tina said.

"I don't care," Laura said with conviction she did not feel. "I'm gonna pay this whore back for ruining my life."

Brooke chuckled. “Lady, you keep on saying that. Are you gonna do it or what?”

Tina shot Brooke a nasty look. “Shut up. You’re not helping.”

Brooke grinned and held up her hands in surrender.

“I agree with Brooke. I don’t think she will,” Gloria said.

“Oh, really? How the fuck do you know what I’m gonna do?” Laura asked.

Gloria thought back to the day before when she realized what her husband had done. David betrayed his family the same way Will had many, many times. Yesterday, if she had had a gun, there was no doubt she would have killed him without any debate or discussion. Brooke was right, Gloria reasoned. If Laura wanted to kill Veronica, she would have already shot her dead.

“You said she ruined your life,” Tina said. “But it takes two to tango. Your husband is just as guilty.”

“Oh, trust me, if that limp dick asshole were alive. I would have shot him a long time ago, But he isn’t, so I guess I have to settle for his whore.”

“Why the hell do you care what your husband did and who he did it with?” Tina asked. “If a man doesn’t want you, then fine. Have your own fun. Get your own . . . diversion.”

Maya tried to sit up but Tina held her hand to keep her lying down, but Maya pushed her hand away.

“Wait, what did you say?” asked Maya.

Tina rolled her eyes. “Not now, Maya.”

“Yes now.”

With a mighty effort, Maya tried to rise, but Tina gently pushed her back down again.

“Don’t touch me. Don’t you fucking touch me!” Maya shouted, slapping Tina’s hand away. She shook her head, trying to clear the cobwebs. “Is that all I am to you? A diversion?”

“I said not now, Maya.”

“That’s what you always say,” Maya said as she rose unsteadily to her feet. “Not now, Maya. I have to go to a board meeting. Not now, Maya. I'm too busy trying to convince people I'm the perfect suburban wife and mother while pretending I'm not a lesbian. Not now, Maya. I have to go live my life!"

"For God's sake, will you shut the hell up!" Tina said, her face red with embarrassment. "This isn't the place or the time."

"I'm tired of shutting up for you. I'm tired of pretending I don't feel anything for you." Maya began to cry. "I'm just tired."

"This cannot be happening," Jessica said. "Ladies, we have a situation here. This is not the time for a . . ."

"Lovers' quarrel," Gloria said, finishing her sentence. She faced Tina, hands on her hips. "Is this your advice to this woman?" she asked, pointing to Laura. "Get a 'diversion?' Like who? Like this young woman who's obviously in love with you?"

Tina's face reddened even more. "Excuse me, Saint . . . what's your name again?"

"You know my name. It's Gloria. And I'm no saint."

"Well, you sure as hell act like one, so excuse me, Saint Gloria. I'm so sorry if I don't measure up to your perfect standards."

"Perfect? You don't know the first thing about me."

Tina grinned. "I know *everything* about you. Look at you, perfectly put together. I bet you go to the same beauty salon you've gone to for thirty years. You buy your outfits at the same boutique where the same saleswoman helps you every time, and you have lunch with the girls twice a month at the same restaurant. You went to college, but you didn't do a damn thing with your degree except to pack it away, so you could support your man and his career. Or at least that's the excuse you used. You stayed home and wiped noses and asses, packed oranges slices for the Little League, and had dinner parties for the other wives in the neighborhood. Did I get any of that right?"

"You don't know me," Gloria said again.

"You stay-at-home types kill me," Tina said. "You hang out at home, make lunches, go to a few soccer games and PTA meetings, and suddenly you're the glue holding fucking society together. Well, unlike you, I didn't hide from the big, bad world. I went out into it and made things happen."

"That's where you're wrong, Gloria said. "My husband went out into the world and made things happen. Big things. And there's no way he could have done those things if I didn't have his back. Anyway, maybe if you made your husband a lunch once in a while, he wouldn't be sleeping around."

Tina looked Gloria up and down. "You look like you made a few lunches in your time. Didn't stop your man from straying, did it? Oh, I'm sorry. It's not that he can't keep his dick in his pants, he just has an emotional hole to fill, and we must understand him. Please!"

Gloria was about to respond when Jessica stepped in between her and Tina.

"Ladies, is this really the right time to debate this?" she asked.

"Is there a preferred list of subjects one might discuss while held hostage?" Tina asked.

Jessica said nothing.

"I'm sick of being judged by you stay-at-home mothers," Tina continued, staring daggers at Gloria. "You have no idea about my life or what I've been through. I worked damn hard to be where I'm at and I'm proud of it. I've been married twenty-five years to a man as obsessed about his career as I am with mine, and now he's obsessed with his young girlfriend. Unlike you, *mother of the year*, I'm not here making excuses for him, or crying about how I feel. I do what I have to do to make my life bearable."

"Don't sing me that song. I wrote the tune, the lyrics, and the melody, and I've been singing it for almost as twice as long as you have," Gloria said. "It's not easy, but if you made up your mind to stay, then stay and be better than he is. Two wrongs don't make a right!"

"What did you say?" Kristin asked, incredulous. "You want women to what? Stay in a marriage where you know your husband is sleeping around? With all due respect, Gloria, are you crazy? Why on Earth would anyone do that?"

"You want to know why?" Gloria asked. She took a step over to an end table that had a photo of Kristin's son in a frame. She held it up to Kristin's face. "That's why," she said.

"Bullshit!" Kristin said as she snatched the picture from Gloria. "He's exactly why I ended my marriage. I didn't want him to see his mother being disrespected every day!"

"That's not why you left. You left because you thought he was all yours, and when you found out you were sharing him, your fragile ego couldn't handle it."

Brooke snickered. "Damn, this bitch is gangsta!"

"I cannot believe you just said that to me," Kristin said.

"That was mean, Gloria," Bianca said to her mother-in-law.

Gloria shook her head. "Truth hurts, doesn't it?"

"Here's the truth for you, Gloria," Kristin said, her face reddening. "I met a man I believed in and I married him. My friends told me he was no good, he was a jerk, he didn't treat me well, but I didn't listen. I made excuses for him all day, every day. When he graduated med school, I delayed my career to help him with his. I was bookkeeper, janitor, receptionist for his practice. Whatever he needed, whenever he needed it, I was there. I did all the things you say we should do: I supported my man and I overlooked his faults." She lovingly placed the picture of her son back on the end table. "Then one evening, I went to the office when he said he was seeing patients late. Like a good little wife, I made dinner for him, packed it up, put our toddler in his stroller, and went to his office. When I got there, there were no patients, but the doctor was in all right. Inside his bimbo nurse. They didn't even notice me. He was too busy trying to get his tiny dick inside her, and she was too busy trying to pretend she enjoyed it."

"And then, let me guess—your hurt ego took over, and

you went and found you a divorce lawyer right away?" Gloria asked sarcastically.

Kristin smiled through tears.

"No, Gloria. I didn't. Not just then. I stood there and watched them. I was so disgusted I almost vomited, but I just couldn't move. They didn't even know I was there. I might have been invisible for all they knew. I watched them for a little while, but I had to go when he put his head between her legs. I went home and put his dinner in the oven to keep warm."

Maya gasped. "You did what?"

"I kept his dinner warm, then I fed our son and put him to bed. When Stan finally came home with some lie about why he was late, I didn't question him. I just made him a plate. Do you know what he said to me? He said, 'No thanks. I'm full. I already ate.' He laughed in my face then watched a basketball game."

"Oh, honey," Bianca said. "I'm sorry."

I don't know what's more pathetic, the fact you did that or that you told us about it," Laura said with a grin.

Kristin ignored her remark and continued.

"I wanted to kill them. I wanted to pick up something heavy and cave their skulls in. But good wives don't do that, do they? So I tiptoed out of there. I'd never felt so invisible and so insignificant in my whole life. I snuck out of the business I helped to build while my husband screwed another woman, and I said nothing. Like a good wife. I went home and fed our son and made my husband his dinner. Like a good wife. I did his laundry, and I wanted to scream because I could smell her on his clothes, but I kept it all inside. Like a good wife. At nine in the morning the next day, I went to see a divorce lawyer. Then by one in the afternoon, I was in bed with Stan's friend, Bruce. I set up a hidden camera, and then I fucked his best friend. Like a good whore. I did all the things I've ever wanted to do with a man who didn't think my breasts were too big or my butt was too flabby. We did it in the bed me and my husband slept in, and I recorded it all."

"Good for you!" Tina said.

"See, I told you there was more. It's always them quiet ones," Brooke said.

Gloria shook her head. "Oh, Kristin, I'm so disappointed in you."

"Later I fixed Stan's dinner, made him a plate, and brought it out to him. He was about to watch another game, but his regularly scheduled program was interrupted when I played the video of me fucking his best friend."

Gloria folded her arms, a scowl on her face. "I'm so disappointed in you," she said again.

"What was she supposed to do, Gloria?" Bianca asked.

"Yes, Gloria, what was I supposed to do? You said your husband is unfaithful, right? How do you handle it?"

"Yes, Saint Gloria, please enlighten us," Tina said.

"Unfaithful is too pretty a word for the ugly things my husband does," Gloria said, glancing at Bianca.

"But did you see him do them?" Kristin asked again. "Did you ever catch him in the act?"

"I don't see what that has to do with anything."

"Answer the question. Did you see him with another woman? Did you see his face buried between her legs? Did you see her ass get red where he smacked her? Did you watch as she spread her legs for him? Did you smell the odor of sex in the air, Gloria?"

"No, I didn't, but what did you accomplish with your little . . . video besides breaking up your family and making your son a child of divorce?" Gloria asked.

"She got her power back," Tina said.

Gloria rolled her eyes. "Are you joking? That is the stupidest thing I ever heard. Take what power back? You only lose your power if you give it away in the first place."

"You're right. That's exactly what I did. I gave up my power and made him think I was weak. Every time he called me fat or put me down, I just took it. Soon, I had no power left. And then I took it back," Kristin said.

"My God, you women are stupider that I thought. So by that same reasoning, I guess you have no problem with Laura holding us hostage because she's mad?" Gloria asked. "It's okay, right? She's only taking her power back."

"Damn right," Laura said. "That's exactly what I'm doing."

"You can take your power back without hurting anyone," Tina said. "If you have to hurt someone to do it, then you're not taking it back. All you're doing is passing on the hurt to someone else."

"You mean like you did with me?" Maya asked.

"What are you talking about?"

"You started a relationship with me to take your power back, since your husband was cheating on you, right? You might feel better, but all you did was pass on the hurt to me."

"Maya, I didn't mean . . ."

"See what I'm saying?" Gloria said to Kristin. "You and your hurt ego marched into the divorce lawyer's office. Then you came home and seduced your husband's best friend, recorded it, and you think you did something. You must feel like you're the heroine in the soap opera in your head, don't you? You got your power back. Whoop-de-do. All you did, my dear, was pass on the pain. Just like Tina did to Maya. Now your husband feels it, and your son feels it too. And what about the guy you seduced and recorded without him knowing it? Did he have a wife or a significant other? Did they have big fun, too, or did you just pass the pain on to them?"

"Why are you so scornful of her?" Deepa asked angrily. "She was unhappy, and she went out and made her own happiness. Maybe it was the wrong way, but she had to do something."

"She broke her sacred vows," Gloria said. "She made promises she didn't keep."

Deepa put her hands on her hips. "And what of the promises the men made? What of them? They don't have to keep them, but we do?"

"Amen, sister," Bianca agreed.

"We have to be—"

"I know, better than them, because they are babies who can't think for themselves," Deepa said. "Gloria, excuse me, but don't you hear how absolutely ridiculous that sounds?"

Gloria crossed her arms. "I see. So I guess you have a 'diversion' too?"

"My husband gives me no loyalty, no love, not even the respect to say good morning or good evening. Why should I stay true to him? Why should any of us stay true to any man who doesn't treat us like we deserve?"

"So it's yes, then," Gloria said, staring daggers at Deepa.

Deepa's eyes burned with anger, and she wrapped her hand around the handle of the tiny scissors still hidden in her pocket. "I only wish I had the courage to find a lover. The only diversion I have are . . . videos."

"Videos? What kind of videos? Like Bollywood?" Bianca asked.

Brooke chuckled. "Hell no. Homegirl's talking about porn. Right?"

Deepa blushed.

"What's your favorite type?" Brooke asked. "I love me some BBC. That's my favorite."

"BBC? What's BBC?" Gloria asked.

"Big black—"

"Brooke!" Bianca said.

"What?"

"I'm sorry I asked," Gloria replied, rolling her eyes.

"There goes Saint Gloria, judging us from on high again," Tina said. "Lady, you just don't stop, do you?"

"I'm not a saint, but I must look like one to someone like you."

"What the hell do you mean, someone like me?" Tina asked. She approached Gloria, eyes flashing.

"I shouldn't single you out. You're far from the only guilty one here."

"Guilty? What are we guilty of?"

"You have got to be kidding," Gloria said. She pointed at Veronica. "This one had an affair and broke up a home. This one"—she pointed to Deepa—"is addicted to pornography. By the way, doctor, there's help for people like you, you know."

Deepa turned deep red with embarrassment.

"You"—she pointed to Brooke—"are a drug user and an obvious degenerate. And you"—she pointed to Tina—"are an adulterer. And with another woman, no less. And you"—she gestured to Kristin—"I don't know what to say about you. I thought you were better. Shame on you. Shame on you all."

"You forgot about me," Bianca said. "What am I? What sins do I have on my conscience?"

Gloria stared at her for a long moment as if deciding what to say. "I don't know," she said. "Do you have anything to confess?"

Bianca stared at her mother-in-law, tears forming in her eyes.

"No, you're the one who should be ashamed of yourself," Kristin said quickly, getting in between Bianca and her mother-in-law.

"Why is that?"

"For being so goddamned judgmental. Who the fuck do you think you are? You don't know what any of us have been through, so how dare you judge?"

Gloria gave her a smug smile. "Weak excuses like that are precisely the reason we're here with this woman holding a gun on us. You all are weak. All of this could be avoided with a little mental toughness and some personal responsibility."

"Not everyone is a Stepford Wife robot," Bianca said. "We can't all suppress our feelings like you do."

"Another weak excuse."

"No, it's not an excuse," Bianca said. "Maybe . . . maybe there are some things we could do better, but that's our lesson to learn, not yours to teach!"

"Then who, Bianca? Who should teach it? If someone

had taught it to the lot of you, then maybe we wouldn't be in this predicament. Your generation has no idea what it means to be mentally tough."

"You're so wrong," Kristin said. "Our generation had it much harder than yours. You were expected to just find a man, get married, and have children. We have to do all that and hold down a career."

"Oh, Kristin, and here I thought you were the smart one," Gloria said, shaking her head. "That's just another excuse, dear."

"Gloria, right now I really don't give a shit how you feel about me or how weak or strong you think I am. If you're so much better than us, please give us a clue to how you handle your husband's cheating."

"I handle it, dear, by living in the real world. When we're little girls, we're told some prince is going to come and take us away to some happily ever after. Lies!"

"And you know the truth?" Tina asked.

"Yes. I do."

"Please enlighten us," Kristin said.

"I said it before. The truth is men are weak. Maybe God made them that way, maybe it's society, maybe it's our fault. After all, we're the mothers who raise them. I don't know. The fact is they are weak and it's up to us to be the strong ones."

"Not all men are like that," Kristin said, thinking of Ed, Gloria's son and Bianca's husband, making love to her in this very room. Ed was gentle, yes, soft spoken, undeniably, but the man was anything but weak.

"All of them. Every single one. If a man leaves his family to lay with another woman, he's weak."

My God, she knows, Kristin thought.

At the same moment Bianca's blood ran cold. *She knows about me and Will.*

"That's bullshit," Tina said. "Men aren't the only ones who step outside a marriage."

"Ah, that brings me to you, the woman who has a 'diversion.'"

"Say what you want," Tina said. "You might be a saint, lady, but I'm not. Why should I go to work day after day then come home to an empty bed because he's out with some girl half my age?"

"Yes, why should she?" Deepa spoke up. "Why should she be lonely? Why shouldn't she find someone to make her feel like . . . a woman?"

"Because we don't need men to make us feel like women. We are women and we are better than them," Gloria said.

"Oh no we're not. We're no better. Trust me," Brooke spoke up. "We're no better. Shit, we just might be worse."

"We're worse? What do you mean *worse*?" Bianca asked.

"Are you serious? You know we are. Shit, I really need a cigarette. Anybody got a cigarette?"

No one responded, and Brooke continued.

"Exhibit A: Ms. Thing over there all bent out of shape holding us fucking hostage because her man got some on the side. Then there's Veronica over here, saying, 'Oh, I didn't mean to fuck your man until he had a heart attack and died, but he needed some looooove.'"

Brooke laughed, pointing at Gloria. "This one is saying, 'Let your man do whatever he wants—we have to manage them, we have to take the high ground. But look at her. You can tell she's so goddamn angry she doesn't know what to do with herself. Thank God she's not the one holding the gun. I'd be really scared. Then this one"—she pointed at Tina—"is having a gay lesbian affair with a younger woman who's obviously in love with her but, guess what, she doesn't care 'cause she's just having a diversion."

"What about you?" Tina asked angrily. "You seem to have the rest of us all figured out. I guess you're the only innocent one in the room."

Brooke grinned.

"Innocent? Hell no, lady. That word don't apply to me. I got more sins than all you bitches put together."

CHAPTER SIXTEEN

Brooke

"Want anything to eat, Ms. Brooke?" Portia asked in the exasperated tone that said she hoped Brooke would say no.

Brooke glared at the maid, annoyed. *I swear*, she thought, *bitch does that just to piss me off.*

"Portia, you know what I want," she snapped. "The same fucking thing I eat every day. Egg whites and toast."

Portia gave her employer an insolent look as she removed a pan from its hook on the wall.

"And don't put too much salt on my damn eggs."

"I been makin' the same t'ing for you for years, Mrs. Brooke Kowalski. You t'ink I don' know how to do it?"

"Whatever. And stop calling me out by my name. You know I hate it when you do that shit."

Portia sucked her teeth in response as she cracked an egg and began to separate the white from the yolk.

We should fire that damn Jamaican voodoo bitch, Brooke thought as she angrily rummaged through the kitchen cabinets for some Tylenol. It was nowhere to be found, and she slammed the cabinet doors and drawers, getting increasingly agitated as her headache worsened. Annoyed, she turned to Portia.

"Portia, where the hell is . . ."

She stopped short because the maid stood behind her with the Tylenol in her hand. Brooke grabbed the bottle as Portia mumbled something in Jamaican patois under her breath. Brooke ignored her and sat down, glad to be off her feet. She hadn't meant to be out all night. Usually she tried to get home long before the kids went to school and her husband went to work, but she'd been either too drunk or too high to drive. She couldn't remember. Probably both. Either way, by the time she slept off the worst of it in the parking lot of her favorite bar and rushed home, the kids already left. Part of her regretted staying out all night. She enjoyed seeing the twins in the morning, even though she suspected the days of them believing she had been home all night instead of sneaking back in at the crack of dawn were long gone. She opened the Tylenol bottle and shook three of them into her hand and was about to yell to Portia for water when the maid, anticipating her need, placed a glass on the table.

"What time is it?" she asked.

"It's one thirty. You been sleeping 'bout five hours."

"Did I ask you all that, Portia? Damn, I know how long I slept. I don't need a report from you."

The truth was Brooke had no idea how long she'd been sleeping. She remembered arriving home, parking her car in the driveway, and stumbling into the house, then waking up a few minutes ago with the afternoon sun streaming through the window into her eyes.

We really should fire that bitch, Brooke thought again as she downed the pills. She had, in fact, raised the subject of firing Portia with her husband, Nick, many times over the years, but neither he nor their twins, Amy and Alex, would hear of it. Brooke had to admit Portia was a great housekeeper and she could cook her ass off, even if most of the meals she made were highly-seasoned Caribbean shit, but none of that mattered if the bitch didn't know her damn place.

Portia placed the breakfast on the table and Brooke took a forkful of the bland eggs. As she chewed, her iPhone rang.

The words on the caller ID, *unknown number*, caused the eggs to turn to sawdust in her mouth. She swallowed with difficulty and nervously stared at the phone for a moment before answering.

"Hello? Who's this?"

"You know who this is, Brooke."

"Oh, hi, D," she said, trying to stop her voice from betraying the excitement she felt.

"Come by the buildin'. I got some people waitin' for you."

Icy fear combined with a cold thrill of excitement made Brooke shiver.

"Now? I don't know if I can make it. Maybe later tonight? I think I can move some things around and . . ."

Portia raised an eyebrow.

"Brooke, stop playing. Get over here now, girl."

Brooke closed her eyes, enjoying the thrill of excitement that began between her legs and made her body weak.

"You know what, now that I think of it, I remember I had something cancel. I think I can make it."

"Yeah, that's what I thought."

"Thank you so much for calling. I'm looking forward to our meeting."

"Yeah, whatever, just hurry up. You know where we at."

The line went dead, and she placed the phone on the table.

"Portia, I have to go out. Will you let Nick and the kids know I'll be back sometime later?"

"Sure, Ms. Brooke. Sometime layta. No problem."

Brooke ran upstairs to her bathroom and locked herself in. *Calm down, Brooke,* she said to herself, her heart beating wildly, knowing what D had in store for her. Brooke had known Damien "D-Mo" Morris since high school. They were both freshmen together, both of them outcasts. She was the white trash trailer park slut, and he was the short-fused project-bred weed dealer. D was a loner who everyone stayed away from. He had no friends, but for some reason, Brooke was drawn to him.

She and D soon became unlikely friends. They stood up for one another, confided in each other, and knew each other's secrets. Brooke knew that the fearsome D-Mo was gay, and he knew about the abuse she'd endured at the hands of her father and the particular sexual proclivities she had. There was no one she trusted more in the world, and he trusted her in return.

Almost twenty years later, she was now married, the respectable wife of a very well-off business owner, and D-Mo and his crew controlled the drug trade in their part of the state, but the friendship they formed as kids had grown. D-Mo knew Brooke's history, and therefore knew she needed to be used and abused. As a victim of abuse himself, D-Mo didn't judge her or look down on her because he knew firsthand the things a life of abuse could compel you to do. He knew full well that without an outlet, Brooke's self-destructive tendencies would eventually get her killed, so he made sure she got what she needed under his strict supervision. It was a sick relationship, but Brooke knew D-Mo did it because he loved her in his own way, and in her own way, she loved him back.

Flushed with excitement at what awaited her, she quickly undressed and leaned against the door with one hand between her legs and the other pinching a nipple as hard as she could. She raised her hand and brought it down hard between her legs with a loud smacking of skin on tender skin, stifling her cry of pleasure with a mighty effort. She raised her hand and brought it down again, much harder, and this time didn't even attempt to contain her loud moan. She rubbed herself slowly, enjoying the sensation, then suddenly moved her hand away as if it burned. Timidly, she moved her hand back, but the part of her that felt compelled to obey pulled it away again.

There was no time, she had to go. She splashed cold water onto her face, hoping to quench the raging heat inside her, but the water didn't do a thing to help, so she sighed and quickly stepped into the shower.

As many times as she'd cruised the streets of South Willows,

Brooke still felt out of place. She'd put her long blond hair up in a simple ponytail and ditched her designer clothes for a cheap pair of sweats and an old T-shirt, but for all that, she still might as well have had a neon sign shining over her head. Brooke had been coming here far too long to be scared about getting robbed or hurt, but she still felt the unease of being in a place where she did not belong. Her trips to the hood usually took place at night. And at night, the streets were mostly deserted, except for dealers, hookers, and their customers. The dealers used to solicit her but had long since stopped, knowing whose business she was about. She supposed she'd become an urban legend of sorts. The rich white woman coming on the regular to the hood to . . .

The light changed, and she accelerated as she thought about her life and why she did what she did. Vivid memories came of her trailer-park upbringing and severe beatings from her father, followed by late-night visits to her bedroom. With a mighty effort, Brooke pushed the memories aside and tried to concentrate on where she was going and what would happen once she arrived. She enjoyed the trips to the hood, needed them, craved them, but to think about exactly why that was so would lead to painful memories, and those she absolutely wouldn't allow herself to have. At least not now.

Minutes later, she arrived at her destination and turned onto a narrow, dead-end block, gloomy even under the afternoon sun. She parked her car in front of an abandoned apartment building, tires crunching under crumbling mortar and decomposing garbage. Two shadows detached themselves from the murk in front of the building and walked toward her. As they moved closer, Brooke saw they were barely sixteen, but slim and sinewy with the hard, world-weary look of a lifetime spent in the hood. One was dark skinned with shoulder-length dreads, the other lighter skinned and sporting a short afro. But for the hair and skin tone, they could have been twins, dressed similarly in white T-shirts, designer jeans, and brand-new Timberlands.

"Let's go, bitch," Dreadlocks said while Afro tapped a text message into his cell phone.

She dropped her head and meekly followed them into the crumbling building, her new Uggs crunching over discarded bits of drywall and splashing into puddles of dark, dirty liquid. The building seemed abandoned, except for her and her escorts, and they led her up two flights of stairs then down a dirty hall, stopping in front of an imposing-looking, shiny new metal door, glaringly out of place in the decrepit structure. Afro knocked once before he opened the door and peeked in.

"Yo, D," he said. "She's here."

Afro motioned Brooke in then closed the door behind her, leaving her alone with the men standing in a room heavy with fragrant smoke. Several pairs of dark, hostile eyes regarded her coldly, and she stood unmoving, head down, awaiting an order.

"Well," D-Mo said, "didn't I tell you ya'll?"

"Yo, you was right."

"That bitch finer than a mothafucka."

"Damn she got a phat ass."

One of the men ran his large, calloused hands roughly over her breasts and ass.

"This my man, Black. He jus' come home from . . . college," D-Mo said to Brooke. "But he ain't get no degree."

This earned a laugh from the others present.

"We been waitin' for your ass," the man called Black said. "Take them clothes off."

Brooke quickly did as ordered then climbed onto a surprisingly clean mattress on the shaky metal bed in a corner of the room. The men, their faces lit up with lust, passed an enormous blunt between them, and she watched it hungrily as it went from mouth to mouth. It finally got passed to her, and she grabbed it and sucked in the white smoke greedily as one of the men removed his pants, his penis already incredibly large and hard. She moved to the edge of the bed, noticing as she did all the other men except D-Mo had also removed their pants and stroked their erections in anticipation of their turn. D-Mo watched them, a sad look on his handsome face. The drug was already working in her system, but she took another huge hit, and a shiver of excitement ran through her body. She smiled at D-Mo. She knew he was disappointed in her, but this was the only time she felt anything approaching good. At any other time, she felt exactly like what she knew herself in her heart to be.

Damaged goods.

It was only in these moments that the crushing, heavy sadness that pressed down on her like a weight every moment of her life lifted. It was only in these moments that she felt worthy. It was only in these moments she felt alive.

The man called Black grabbed a clump of her hair and yanked her face up. He stared down at her, like a big cat staring at its prey just before consuming it alive. He had evil eyes, empty and devoid of feeling, but she didn't care. He slapped her hard, and her face immediately reddened and her eyes teared up, but she smiled because she felt a sensation she only felt at these times, a sensation she might describe as love.

A twisted sort of love, not for the evil man who grinned as he administered pain, but love of the pain itself and for what it meant. She closed her eyes and savored the exquisite sensations that told her Daddy cared and only wanted the best for her. The pain told her she was broken and unworthy and unlovable, but that's why Daddy did what he did—he was only trying to make her better. The pain told her Daddy was the only one in the world who could care for her, and he would come into her room after dark so he could show her just how much he loved his little girl.

The man was so close she could smell his strong, musky body odor, but in her mind, she smelled Old Spice and Marlboro Reds with a hint of the grain alcohol Daddy and her Uncle Jack made in the hills behind the trailer park. The man yanked savagely on her head again, bringing her face closer to his crotch, but he needn't have. She was already reaching for him, smiling as she closed her eyes and hungrily took Daddy into her mouth.

Brooke heard the metal door creak open then footsteps move closer, tensing as she felt hands on her. The men were gone, and Afro and Dreadlocks were in the room with her, one freeing her from the blindfold and gag while the other undid the handcuffs that bound her spread-eagled to the bed. Freed from her bonds, Brooke slowly sat up, wincing at the pain in her buttocks and back. Her scalp throbbed and ached from the savage hair-pulling, and her neck was sore where strong hands had brutally squeezed. She took a wobbly step, stumbling and almost crying out from the pain in her ass and vagina. After the first man took his turn, they'd gagged and blindfolded her and took turns using her so many times she lost count.

She bent over to retrieve her clothes, and when she stood up again, she saw Afro going through her purse, pocketing the few dollars in cash she'd brought with her. He grinned when he saw her looking, then dropped the purse, spilling the contents onto the dirty floor. She picked up her shoes, but Dreadlocks stopped her.

"Yo, gimme them," he ordered. "Them Uggs? My girl been asking for them."

Brooke meekly handed him her brand-new shoes, then got on her hands and knees to pick up her belongings and put them back in the purse. There was a card under the bed, and she stretched her hand to retrieve it. It was an invitation, and she squinted at it, for a moment forgetting where she'd got it. *PLEASURE PARTY* it said in a fancy font. As she read it, she remembered the curvy redhead who had given it to her at her gym. She returned it to her purse and was about to rise when a rough hand yanked her to her feet.

"Yo, Imma get me some of this freaky bitch. You want some?" Afro asked his companion. He held Brooke's hair in a vice grip with one hand and ran the other roughly over her still-exposed breasts, savagely squeezing her nipple.

"Hell yeah, mothafucka," said Dreadlocks, rubbing his crotch. "I'm down!"

Afro threw her back onto the bed, then hesitated, stopped, and looked over at Dreadlocks as if unsure. Brooke, already aroused again despite her pain, smiled broadly and opened her legs wide, staring at the two nervous young men, erections already visible even in their loose-fitting jeans.

"Well," she said, the first she'd spoken since leaving home hours before, "what are you waiting for?"

They glanced at one another then nervously approached, already beginning to undo their pants, but before they could reach their target, the door opened and D-Mo stepped in. Startled, Afro and Dreadlocks hurriedly pulled their pants back up.

"Out," D-Mo said.

Dreadlocks picked up Brooke's Uggs and followed Afro on his way out the door, but D-Mo put a large hand on his bony shoulder and squeezed.

"Leave the shoes," he ordered.

"Yeah D, my bad, sorry, sorry," Dreadlocks mumbled as he quickly dropped the Uggs and scurried out of the room.

D-Mo locked the door then slowly walked over to the bed. He took a large blunt from his pocket, lit it, and took a hit, then handed it to Brooke. His face was a mask, displaying none of the emotion she knew he always felt at witnessing her violation. She took a hit, savoring the sensation of the sweet smoke, then handed it back to D-Mo.

She was still naked but made no attempt to cover herself. She'd been naked before D-Mo many, many, times over the years and was comfortable with him. In fact, if she were honest, there was no one in the world she was more comfortable with than this notorious drug dealer.

"You okay?" D asked, tenderly brushing the hair from her face.

Brooke closed her eyes, savoring the feel of his touch.

"I'm good," she said, smiling.

"Did they hurt you?" he asked, examining the bruises on her breasts and thighs.

"Yes. Yes, they did. Thank you."

D-Mo's face lost its calm look, and he threw his hands up in exasperation.

"Don't fucking thank me, Brooke! That shit is fucked up, man."

D-Mo handed her the blunt, and she took another hit then handed it back.

"Maybe," she said. She didn't want to do this with D-Mo. Not now. Not again. All she wanted was to enjoy the lingering pain and get high.

"No maybe about it. It's fucked up, girl. Real fucked up."

"It is fucked up, but it's what I need. You know that more than anybody."

He sighed. "Yeah. I know," he said. "I know."

Brooke handed the depleted blunt back to him, and he took a last hit before he threw the remnants on the floor and stamped it out. He took a small sandwich bag of pills and a wad of cash from his pocket and handed them to her.

"Here, this is for you."

"Thanks, D."

"These fools outside will make sure you get home okay. Do you need anything else?" he asked.

"Just for you to let them back in so they can fuck me before I go."

D-Mo nodded, gave her one last sad look, then walked out the door. She heard him bark an order, then moments later, Afro and Dreadlocks were back in the room.

She was still naked, still bruised and battered, but she felt much better now the blunt was working in her system. Once again, she opened her legs wide and smiled at the two young men.

"Welcome back, fellas," she said. "Now where were we?"

CHAPTER SEVENTEEN

"I'm damaged, ladies," Brooke said. "Fucked up. Broken."

"That ain't nothing to be proud of sweetheart," Laura said.

"Bitch, please. The only difference between you and me is I know I'm damaged. I own it."

"So boo-hoo. Big deal, you got a beating once in a while?" Laura said. "Pain makes us tougher."

"There's a lot worse things you can do to a little girl than hit them," Brooke said. "Let's just say my daddy, um, loved me a little too much."

Kristin put her hand over her mouth in shock. "Brooke, honey, I'm so sorry," she said. "Did you ever talk to someone?"

"No. I didn't need to."

"You should. Unresolved trauma can—"

"Make you stronger," Brooke said.

"See?" Laura replied. "You're proving my point."

"Sure, pain can make you stronger," Brooke said. "It also fucks you up. But as long as you know you're fucked up, then you're ahead of the game. And trust me, I know I'm fucked up."

"You experienced trauma, Brooke. It isn't your fault," Kristin said.

"That's true," Brooke said. "And what Laura's father did to her wasn't her fault, neither, but it sure don't give her permission to do what she's doing."

"This doesn't have a goddamn thing to do with my

father. Leave him out of this," Laura said.

"Lady, pretty much everything we do has to do with our fathers. What my father did changed me. I can't love the way other people do. I try, but something in me just isn't right. The only time I feel anything is when things get . . . rough."

"Rough?" Deepa asked.

"Rough," Brooke repeated. "As in getting choked and slapped around. Rough."

"Oh," Deepa said. "Oh my."

Bianca's ears perked up. "You like that? Really?"

Kristin shot Bianca a sideways glance but said nothing.

"I don't know if I like it exactly, but I need it."

"What do you mean?" Bianca asked.

"I saw this documentary once about this crazy fool who climbs mountains without safety equipment. When they asked him why he did it, he said it's the only time he feels alive. I guess it's kinda like that. It's the only time I feel alive. The rest of the time I'm just kinda here."

"Why on Earth do we need to know this?" Gloria asked. "What you do with your husband is private."

"Who said anything about my husband?"

"This therapy session is great, but what does that have to do with me?" Laura asked. "Your daddy was a damn pedophile, mine wasn't."

"Watch your mouth, bitch," Brooke said.

"Whatever. You got some nerve comparing yourself to me. Your daddy was a dirty pervert, and now you are too."

"Bitch, you better take that back," Brooke said. Her hands shook and tears welled up in her eyes.

"I ain't taking shit back. I'm nothing like you!"

"I said take that back," Brooke demanded as she took another step.

"Get the hell back," Laura ordered, raising the revolver. "Now!"

Brooke took another step forward until she was only inches away from the gun pointed at her head.

"You think I'm afraid to kill you?" Laura asked.

"Bitch, do you think I'm afraid to die?"

The two women stared each other down for a long moment before Bianca and Kristin stepped forward and pulled Brooke back.

"I promise you this ain't over," Brooke said. "I'm gonna fuck you up for talking about my dad."

Laura grinned. "You ain't gonna do shit. Sit your ass down and—"

"Laura!" Kristen interrupted. "What your father did has got everything to do with what's happening here. You have a lot of unresolved anger, and you're taking it out on Veronica. And us."

Laura rolled her eyes. "I'm not angry. I'm fucking furious, and it's this whore's fault," she said, pointing at Veronica.

"That's just the trauma talking," Kristin said.

"No, it's not," said Veronica. "Don't give her any excuses. She's not the only one who had a shit childhood. Matter of fact, I'm positive I'm the winner in the screwed-up upbringing department."

"Is that why you became a whore? Daddy didn't give you hugs?"

Veronica chuckled.

"You think this is funny?" Laura asked.

"What's funny is you trying to play the victim after all you did," Veronica said.

"I am the victim!" Laura said. "I am. You—"

"Stole your husband, ruined your life and blah, blah. Maybe you can fool these women into thinking you were innocent. They don't know you. I do. I saw how you treated your family. It was so bad your kids cut you out of their lives after they found out exactly who you were. Thank God they had Dave. At least they had one loving parent."

"David?" Laura scoffed. "All he did was make them soft. I wanted to raise them to be hard and take no shit from anyone! Those ungrateful brats should thank me! I gave them what they needed to survive in this world. I made them tough. I gave them heart!"

"All you gave them was pain and trauma," Veronica said. "And they hate you for it."

"That's a lie!" Laura said through gritted teeth.

"You came her to murder me, right? Then what do you have to lose by telling the truth to me? Admit it—you were a terrible wife and an even worse mother. You never cared about your husband and your kids. You did what you wanted to do, family be damned."

"You don't know shit about me or my family, you stupid bitch."

"I know you're not capable of loving your children. Maybe at one time you tried to fake it, but you stopped trying a long time ago. Your son couldn't wait to go away to college to get away from you, and your daughter would be very happy to never see you again."

"See, now I know you're full of shit. Lily loves me! I see her boys almost every day."

"The only time you're around the twins is to pick them up from school, and she only allows that because David made her promise she would let you have a relationship with them. He insisted on it. Don't you get it? The only reason you see those boys is because Lily is keeping a promise to her dad. David was convinced being around your grandsons would be good for you."

"You're lying!"

Veronica looked at Laura as if she were speaking to a small child. "Do you see your kids for the holidays? Did you know Lily took over the business? Do you know David Jr. was valedictorian of his college class? Do you know anything at all about them?"

"I-I do," Laura said.

"No," Veronica said, shaking her head. "No, you don't. You've never even been in your daughter's home. You weren't invited to your son's graduation. You know nothing about the people you claim to love."

"Shut up, bitch. I'm warning you!"

"You never had a family, Laura, what you had was a bunch of people you inflicted pain on. Now you have nothing and no one except your ugly little dogs, and even they liked David better than you."

"Leave Paris and London out of this."

"Veronica, that's enough. You're just making it worse," Jessica said, wringing her hands.

Veronica ignored her. "Now that everyone sees you for the monster you are, you have to have someone to blame. Me. But I'm just a convenient target for your hate."

"I don't hate anyone. Except you!"

"You hate everyone! Especially yourself. And everyone hates you right back! You're a vile excuse for a human being. So blame me all you want, Laura, but everyone here knows the truth."

"Veronica, be quiet," Bianca piped up. "Just stop it. Jessica is right. You're just making the situation worse. Maybe if we all just calm down, Laura will—"

"No, Bianca! I won't stop. I won't."

"So you're going to keep on talking and get her so riled up she kills all of us. Is that the plan?" Gloria asked. "That's the same type of selfishness that made you sleep with her husband in the first place."

"There's Saint Gloria again, gifting us with her wisdom from on high," Tina said.

"No, she's right," Maya replied, giving Tina a nasty look. "We need to de-escalate the situation, not make it worse."

Veronica threw up her hands. "You don't get it, do you? There is no de-escalation. She said she wants to kill me, and she means it. You think if we'll have a nice chat, maybe we'll all have a good cry, and talk Laura through her issues, I promise you, that will never happen. She wants to kill me, and that's what she'll do sooner or later, but I won't go quietly."

"I don't want to hear anything you have to say," Laura

said.

"Oh, but you will. I won't stop talking until you shoot me, and even then I'll bet you'll still hear my voice in your head because you know I'm telling the truth."

"What truth do you think you know?"

"I know Dave loved you and he forgave a lot. At least he did until he found out about all your . . . activities."

"What the hell are you talking about?"

"You know perfectly well what I'm talking about."

"No, I really don't."

Veronica rolled her eyes.

"Yes, what are you talking about?" Tina asked.

"I'm talking about things she did behind her husband's back. David knew everything. Who you were with, when and where. And he had the pictures to prove it."

"What pictures? Where did he . . ."

"From the last place he expected, your kids. They knew he would never leave you unless something drastic happened."

"My kids would never do that."

"Oh, but they did, Laura. They hired a private detective. He got everything."

Laura shuffled her feet and turned her head away, her discomfort plain. "I have no idea what you're talking about," she insisted.

"I'm talking about the young male escort you kept in Florida and saw every month."

Gloria crossed her arms. "My God, it just gets more and more scandalous, doesn't it?"

"It sure does," Brooke said. "I wish I had some popcorn."

Laura turned a deep red. "Shut up, bitch. Nobody wants to hear your lies."

"Fuck that, let her talk," Brooke said. "I want to hear it."

"He found out about the secret apartment in Manhattan."

"I said shut up."

"The one you used a couple of times a month to screw

Dave's best friend behind his back."

"Good Lord," Gloria exclaimed, clutching her pearls.

"I swear, bitch, if you don't shut the hell up."

"He found out about the bartender in Brooklyn whose rent you pay. Oh, I'm sorry, the young bartender *and* his roommate."

"Okay, bitch," Laura said, turning a deeper red as she shook with rage, "that's just more made-up bullshit."

"And he found out about the parties."

Laura flinched as if she'd been slapped. "What did you say?"

"You heard me. He knew about the sex parties you and your rich friends throw."

"Hold up! Those parties are really a thing?" Brooke asked. "I heard some of you rich fuckers got freaky on the regular, but I thought it was just an urban legend."

"What are you talking about?" Gloria asked. "What parties?"

"There's been rumors for a while that some of the wealthy assholes in this town have a sex club," Brooke said. "The author who moved to town a couple of years ago wrote about them. What's his name again?"

"Shaun Harmon," Kristin said.

"Yeah, him. He wrote a book about it."

Veronica shook her head. "Dave thought those parties were a rumor, too, and he told the kids as much. So Lily and David Jr. did something they didn't want to do. They showed him the video."

Laura turned pale and for a moment her legs went unsteady. "Video? Impossible. They don't allow cameras."

"He had video, Laura. Of you."

"That's enough!" Laura shouted. "I'm not going to warn you again!"

"You were naked on a bed with three men."

"Shut the hell up!"

"Three very young men, probably only a couple of years

older than your son."

"I swear, bitch, I'm going to—"

"And they were . . . with you . . . all at the same time. In front of an audience."

Laura lifted the gun as if to hit Veronica again, but Veronica looked her in the eye, unflinching.

"David forgave a lot, but that was the last straw."

"And you saw an opening and you took it!"

"Seeing that video broke his heart. That's why he divorced you. It had nothing to do with me. All the damage to your marriage and family that you blame on me, *you* did yourself. I was just there after to pick up the pieces."

"Now I know for sure you're lying. If he had all that evidence, why didn't he give it to the lawyers, huh? They never brought any of this up during the divorce."

"Because Dave felt sorry for you, Laura. He looked at the photos and the video, and he saw a sad, tired, angry, old woman trying her best to feel something. It wasn't anger he felt, it was pity. He didn't say anything during the divorce because divorce records are public, and he didn't want the world to see the person you truly are. That was his last gift to you."

"I've known bitches like you all my life," Laura said. "So don't try to sell me the hooker with the heart of gold. You saw your chance and you took it. And now my husband is dead thanks to you."

"You're a real piece of work, lady," Brooke said. "You had a gigolo on retainer, hoes in different area codes, fucked your husbands' friends, *and* had orgies, and you have the nerve to call her a whore?"

"Fuck you," Laura said. "What I did or didn't do is none of her business. Or yours."

"Call me what you want, but you know the truth," Veronica said. "You broke Dave's heart. You abandoned your family, screwed his friends, and made a spectacle of yourself. And now you're threating me because of what I did when you've done far, far worse. All I did was give a good man a little love and make his life a little better."

"How was it better, huh? How? He's dead. You took him away from me! You took him away from his children! He died sleeping with you in your bed. He should have been with his family."

"He was with family. I was his family. He was in my bed . . . our bed. That night we made love, and then he kissed me and told me he loved me. I told him I loved him back, then I kissed that sweet man on his lips, and he fell asleep smiling and he never woke up. I'm so proud the last thing he heard in this life was me telling him I loved him."

"He should have been with his children and with me."

"They were there. When I woke up and saw he was gone, I called the kids, and they came and sat with him. With us."

"Wait . . . us?"

"Yes. With me and with their brother."

There was a collective gasp from the women as they realized what Veronica meant.

Laura's eyes filled with tears, and she leaned on the back of a chair for support.

"You had David's baby?" she asked.

Veronica nodded. "Yes, I did. He looks just like his dad. He was born just a couple of months before David died."

A locket hung from a thin gold chain around her neck, and she opened it, gazing lovingly at the two tiny pictures nestled inside: one of an infant and the other of a smiling older man.

Laura snatched the locket from Veronica's hand, causing the chain to pop. She looked at the picture of the baby, and her hands began to shake.

"I'm going to kill you," Laura whispered as the tears streamed down her face.

"Laura, you can't," Bianca said. "She has a baby . . . Please don't hurt her."

"She's right," Gloria said. "That poor child doesn't have a father. Don't leave him without a mother too."

Laura glanced from the picture of the baby to Veronica and back again. Laura's voice grew louder, but Veronica tuned it out and closed her eyes. She was sure she would soon die and felt something inside her shift, as if her soul unshackled itself from her body. She was sad she wouldn't get to see her son grow up, but he would be well taken care of by his sister, Lily. If these were to be her last moments of life, she wouldn't spend them in panic or useless pleading. She would spend them in peace, thinking about the love of her life.

CHAPTER EIGHTEEN

Veronica

Her attraction to David came as a shock to Veronica. After a lifetime of abuse at the hands of men, men linked to her by the bonds of blood and family no less, she was surprised to feel anything for any man, much less one almost thirty years older and who happened to be her married boss.

She was careful to keep tight control over those emotions because she liked her job and also because David showed no signs whatsoever of the attraction being mutual. He was an old-school gentleman who treated her with the utmost courtesy and respect, the same as he treated all his employees. She loved working for him, and actually looked forward to the many nights when they had to work late. Those were happy times for her. They would order pizza and work until well into the night.

Their love affair began on such a night over a large pepperoni pizza with extra cheese. Veronica had already eaten a slice, but David's slice sat on his plate, untouched.

"Not hungry?" she'd asked him.

"Not really," he'd said, looking up from the contract he was trying in vain to concentrate on.

"Are you okay?"

"I'm good," he said, but the look of total sadness in his eyes gave away the lie. "No, I'm not," he confessed. "This divorce is hard."

"I'm sorry," she said.

"No, you're not," he said with a chuckle. "No one is. Not even the kids. I've forgiven Laura for a lot over the years, but this—this is too much. And the worst part is how I found out. The kids told me."

Veronica gasped. "The kids?"

He nodded. "Right here in this office. A few months ago, they hired a private eye and . . . and . . ."

Holding back tears, he told her how his children had recently broke the news to him of his wife's many betrayals. When the telling was over, he wiped his eyes, embarrassed.

There was silence for a minute. Some invisible wall between them was down, and they both felt it. It should have been awkward, but it wasn't for either of them, as if something that was supposed to happen had finally come to pass.

Touched by the way he had shared his pain, she felt compelled to confide her own. David listened intently as she told him the story of Veronica Castillo who'd been born Christina Hernandez, a young woman who knew there would be no happy ending to her story. Her father, uncles, and brothers were all violent, unhinged drug dealers, and the only way out for them, and for her, was death. She had to make a plan, or else become another painful East LA statistic.

The point was driven home one evening when her uncle, Tito, visited the house while her father and brothers were away, having driven over the border to Mexico on one of their frequent drug business trips. For as long as she could remember, Christina recognized the lust in Tito's eyes and was careful not to ever be alone with him.

She wouldn't let him in when he showed up at the door that night, but he insisted her father wanted him to get something from the house, and, scared of repercussions, she opened the door. Once inside, Tito, high and drunk, quickly forced himself on her. She fought him, but he punched her in the face, stunning her, then dragged her into her bedroom. When she came to, her uncle's full weight bore down on her, and he breathed hard in her ear as he forced himself inside her. The act didn't take long. When he was done, he saw the virgin blood staining the sheets and smiled a predatory smile, then fell asleep next to her, as if they were a loving couple and not a rapist and his terrified victim.

As she watched him peacefully snoring, she thought about the many indignities and molestations she had endured over the years. Her drunken father wasn't above bursting into the bathroom as she showered or into her bedroom as she got dressed, ogling her body as he told her how much she looked like her whore mother. It wasn't only her father who had no respect for the bonds of family and blood. A few of the many cousins who worked with her father in the drug trade and drifted constantly in and out of their house had tried to assault her, as well, but she had always managed to fight them off. The disgusting comments, often accompanied by pats on the backside or groping of her breasts, had become just another part of life, but this . . . this was very different. Christina had managed to keep her virginity intact and harbored the romantic hope that it was a gift she would one day give to a man she loved, since in her mind her virginity and her love were all she had to offer. Christina had fiercely held onto that dream, but now it was dead. She'd become damaged goods, with nothing, less than nothing, to offer anyone.

Something inside of her broke as she lay next to her uncle. She mourned for the dream murdered by her uncle, but along with the mourning came a realization. If she stayed in that house, the treatment would only get worse, and she would end up dead or become another soulless zombie dependent on the poison her father peddled to dull the pain of existence.

She knew what she had to do, but first she had to rid herself of Tito's stink and wash the virgin blood drying on her thighs. In the shower, she turned the water on as hot as she could stand and wept as she watched her blood stain the water and flow down the drain. When her sobbing subsided, she dried herself, put on an old T-shirt, and walked quietly into the kitchen to search for her abuela's knives. Before she died, Christina's abuela would bring a live chicken over every Sunday to cook for the family's dinner. The old woman taught Christina how to hone a knife to such a razor-sharp edge the unlucky bird felt no pain, only a light kiss of steel as the blade opened the vein in its neck.

It took her a little while, but she finally found the long, unused knives and the old leather bag she kept her sharpening stone in. Just holding them in her hand made Christina feel better, and she turned on the radio to the same Mexican station Abuela loved listening to as she cooked. Christina hummed along to the same old Mexican songs as she worked, imagining Abuela smiling her beautiful toothless smile and guiding her hand as she sharpened the blade. Before long, the knife was sharp enough to cut paper, and she returned to the bedroom, where her uncle still snored loudly.

The sight of the blood-stained sheets almost killed her resolve, but she composed herself, then removed the old T-shirt she wore and stood naked at the foot of the bed, knife in her hand. She straddled Tito, gently caressing his face until he began to stir. Tito awoke slowly to see his naked niece on top of him. His eyes shone with lust, and he smiled at the sight of her large, full breasts.

"Want some more, huh puta?" he said.

She said nothing, just nodded as he adjusted himself so he could slip inside her.

The feel of him inside her, the smell of his disgusting breath, the sound of his rapid, piglike grunting, and her awareness of his thick, calloused fingers groping her breasts combined to make her stomach heave, but she endured, waiting until he closed his eyes in pleasure before she retrieved the knife from its hiding place under a pillow and put it to his throat. His smile quickly died when he registered the sensation of the cold steel. Before he could say a word, Christina ran the blade lightly across his throat from ear to ear. The knife did its deadly work to perfection. Tito's lifeblood sprayed in a fine mist across her face and chest, then flowed like a thick, red waterfall from his severed jugular. Eyes wide in panic, he tried to buck her off, but she was too strong, and he'd already become weak from blood loss. Christina calmly stayed on top of him, feeling his dying penis wither inside her as the flow of blood from his neck slowed then stopped altogether as the light of life left his eyes.

Blood was everywhere. Her face and chest were covered in it. It was painted on the walls, but most of it soaked into the mattress, completely covering the stain of her own blood. She left the blood-soaked room and stepped into the shower again to cleanse herself, amazed at how calm she was. Once again, she watched blood swirl down the drain, but this time it was not hers and there were no tears.

Christina knew she had to run. Tito, for all his depravity, was a good earner and valuable to her father's drug business. Once it was known what had befallen him, there would be hell to pay. She knew where her father and brothers kept their cache of drugs and money, so she waited until after dark, then snuck out to the garage and pried open the false wall of their hiding place. She expected to find a few thousand dollars at most, enough for a plane ticket to somewhere far away and to live on for a few weeks, but she was shocked to see there was more, much more. She packed all of it, the drugs and the money, into a large rolling duffel bag and a few items of clothing into a backpack. This was the perfect time to leave. Her father and brothers' trips to Mexico usually lasted for at least a week, and they had only left that morning, so she had a few days' head start. When they returned home and discovered Tito's body and saw that Christina, the drugs, and the money were gone, they would likely surmise some rival gang had killed Tito and taken her. They would quietly dispose of Tito's body as they had so many others, then the search would be on for their drugs and money. There was no time to waste.

Tito's pride and joy, his very distinctive purple lowrider,

was parked in the driveway, so she waited until about three in the morning when the neighborhood slept, then out of sight of prying eyes, she loaded the car and drove away from the house of horrors she had lived in all her life without a backward glance.

Her brother was excellent with technology and knew how to track people via their phones, so she left her phone in the house. She drove for an hour until she was sure she was in a neighborhood where no one knew her or her murderous family and bought a burner cell phone in a twenty-four-hour Walmart. She rummaged through Tito's glove compartment for any paperwork that could be used to identify the owner of the car, ripped it to shreds, and threw the scraps in a sewer, then left the keys in the ignition and walked away. She used her burner phone to call a cab and had it take her to the bus station in downtown Los Angeles, where she bought a ticket for the first bus of the morning, a Greyhound to Austin, Texas. An hour later, the bus arrived, and she joined the line of passengers as if intending to board the bus, but slipped away in the crowd just before boarding and quickly exited the station. Christina was taking no chances. One of her father's former business associates in the drug trade had once tried to steal from him and run away, but her father had tracked him down because a bus-station ticket clerk, who happened to be from their neighborhood, had seen the man and given her father the clue he needed to track him down and ensure he died a grisly death.

She used her burner phone to search for the nearest used car lot, where she bought a cheap, but serviceable, car for cash and immediately began driving to Las Vegas, only stopping twice: once to put gas in the tank and buy an energy drink to keep her awake and another time along a desert road to dispose of the stolen drugs in a drainage ditch. She thought about trying to sell the drugs when she got to Las Vegas, but quickly discarded the idea as much too dangerous.

When she arrived in Las Vegas six hours later, her first

order of business was to quickly get rid of the car, so she cruised around until she found an area where the homeless congregated, parked the car in the McDonald's parking lot next door, and walked away, leaving the windows open and the keys clearly visible in the ignition. The car fairly screamed STEAL ME, and she was confident by evening it would be long gone.

She wanted badly to use some of the stolen money to get a room in one of the big, fancy hotels and live like a movie star in an enormous suite, complete with plush robes and room service, even for just one night. She knew, however, that was an excellent way to get caught. She needed identification to stay in any of the big hotels, and that would leave a trail for her father and brothers to follow. Instead, she used cash at a cheap hotel that didn't ask questions, where she spent a mostly sleepless night counting the stolen money and planning the rest of her life.

Christina had estimated that she had maybe one hundred thousand dollars of her father's drug money, but there was more. Much more. There was almost three hundred and fifty thousand dollars in the bag. So the next day she paid six months' rent in advance for a storage space, took out enough cash to live on for a month and stashed the rest. Her next order of business was to find a small room to rent, then a hairdresser, who cut her long, dark hair short and dyed it a drab brown. She asked around, and after a day or two, she found work in a seedy diner working for minimum wage and tips. The diner was far from the glitz and glamor of the Vegas strip and so were its regulars, mostly Vegas residents who worked in the casinos and small-time criminals always on the lookout for some big score. With that kind of clientele, it wasn't long before she was able to locate the kind of person who could provide her with a new license, social security card, and birth certificate. She opened a bank account and applied for credit cards under her new identity. and two months after arriving in Las Vegas, Christina became Veronica, with the papers to prove it.

New identity intact, she quit her job, left her rented

room, put the stolen drug money in several bank accounts, then caught the first flight out of Las Vegas. The flight was headed to Newark, New Jersey, a place she had barely heard of, but it was almost three thousand miles away from her family, which was good enough for her. She landed in Newark Airport, unprepared for the frigid cold. She had never owned a winter coat and knew no one on the entire East Coast, but still she was happy. She was far, far away from the terror her life had been. She was a new woman with a new name about to begin her new life in a new place where no one would ever find her. She bought a map of New Jersey at the airport, closed her eyes, and poked a finger on it, then hailed a cab and told the driver to take her to a hotel in the town she had randomly selected. A month later, she had an apartment, a job, and a new life in Willows, New Jersey.

When she was done telling her story, over an hour had passed, and David listened to her, saying nothing, for the entire time. Telling the story was a relief. She felt as if a weight had been lifted and suddenly began to cry. David tenderly dried her tears with his handkerchief, and they kissed for the first time. The kiss was long and sweet. There was no lust in it, no physical need, just a connection between two people who desperately needed someone else to lean on. There was no awkwardness or embarrassment as they undressed one another. They giggled together like schoolchildren. When she was down to bra and panties, his eyes took in the sight, drinking it in like a thirsty man.

"You are so beautiful," he said.

And she knew he meant it. If she weren't in love with him before, she would have been in that moment, because she knew he said it because he truly meant it and not as some ploy to sleep with her. No one had said that to her before. They'd only taken what they wanted, regardless of what she thought. It would have been more bearable if occasionally she'd heard that they thought she was beautiful, but she never had. The compliment, although welcome, made her feel naked and vulnerable, and she moved her hands over her breasts in embarrassment, but he gently moved them away and removed her bra, then her panties, and placed them neatly next to her dress.

He took her body in, smiling, his eyes shining with happiness. "You are beautiful," he said again.

If someone were to see them, their first response might have been amusement at the sight of the older, gray-haired man with the slight paunch and thick glasses making love to the beautiful younger woman with the curvy body, her long hair wrapped around them both and her moans accented with Spanish. They might have been mocked, or else mistaken for a prostitute and her paying customer. Those with eyes to see, however, would have known these two were in love.

They made love twice, and when they were done, they helped one another get dressed. It took three times as long as it should have, because they stopped often to kiss and caress one another, smiling and giggling, ecstatic in the moment. Soon they were dressed and shared one last deep kiss before going to their separate homes, floating on air.

The next morning, Veronica was awake for an hour before she realized for the first time in many months, she hadn't had nightmares and now felt something she'd felt very few times in her life.

She felt safe.

CHAPTER NINETEEN

"What's his name?" she asked, staring at the locket in her trembling hand.

Veronica sat unresponsive, eyes closed.

"I said what's his name?"

Veronica opened her eyes, her expression one of surprise as if shocked she were still alive.

"His name is . . ."

"Ethan. Ethan Isaac. Right?"

"Yes. How did you know?"

"David wanted a big family," Laura said as a tear trailed through her makeup. "That idiot wanted a house filled with kids. Remember that stupid eighties TV show *Eight Is Enough*? That's what he wanted. Chaos! Happy chaos, he called it. He had names picked out already, Ethan Isaac or Esther Rachel. I laughed and asked him if those were baby names or a couple of senior citizens. He was so hurt, but I didn't care, there was no way I was having more children . . ."

"Because you were more concerned about your weight," Veronica said. "David told me."

"Yes, I was, and so fucking what? I was looking out for me. It took me years to lose that weight! I wasn't going to go through that again. I told him if he wanted more kids he could damn well have them yourself." Laura stared at the images in the locket then back to Veronica. "But you knew that, didn't you? I'll bet you couldn't wait to get knocked up."

"We were happy when we found out, but it wasn't planned . . ."

"Just when I thought you couldn't sink any lower," Gloria said to Veronica.

"We never planned for it," Veronica said, looking hurt. "It just . . . happened."

Gloria chuckled. "If I had a dollar for every hussy who said that . . ."

"Hold up. Are you blaming Veronica for what happened?" Bianca asked.

"Who else should I blame? She opened her legs for a married man didn't she?"

"Are you deaf woman?" Tina asked. She pointed a finger at Laura. "She's a monster! Didn't you hear the way she treated her family?"

"Oh, I heard. But piling mistake on top of mistake doesn't fix anything."

"Oh, that's right. I forgot, Saint Gloria is perfect. She doesn't make mistakes," Tina said.

"I make plenty. But when I do, I try to fix them."

"Things are not always black and white, Gloria," Tina said.

"When it comes to my marriage . . . I mean *marriages*, yes they are."

"For you maybe, but for the rest of us regular humans, not so much."

"How could you excuse her behavior? Not only did she seduce another woman's husband, but she brought a child into this sordid mess."

"This 'sordid mess' is my life," Veronica shot back.

Gloria chuckled. "What kind of life can it be when you had to break up a family to have it?"

"So she deserves to die?" Kristin asked.

"Maybe not, but she deserves to suffer!" Gloria said, pounding her fist on an end table.

Tina rolled her eyes. "Once again, there's Saint Gloria handing out judgment."

"Woman, if you call me Saint Gloria *one more time*, I swear . . ."

"You'll what?" Tina said, rising to her feet. "What will you do?"

"Ladies, please," Jessica pleaded.

"No, I want to hear what Saint Gloria will do. Tell me, Saint Gloria."

Gloria's eyes narrowed, but she said nothing.

"You pretend to be so high and mighty, but you're no different from Laura," Tina said.

"Tina, what the hell?" Maya said. She took Tina's arm and tried to pull her back down, but Tina shrugged her off.

"You think you're so much better than us, but I bet you're a shit wife."

Gloria recoiled as if she were struck.

"My husband is running around town with his personal trainer, and it sucks, but I know what I did to contribute to that situation, and I take ownership of it. But not you. Oh no, you just judge and judge and judge. Well, I have news for you. I'm not perfect, and neither are you."

"We have to be perfect!" Gloria shot back. "We have to at least try! Don't you get it? It's the trying that makes us better than them. Perfection is my goal, and I won't apologize for it. I won't."

"I hate that word," Jessica said.

"What word?" Gloria asked.

"The P word. Perfect. Why do we have to be perfect? Why can't we just be—"

"Be what? Weak? Flawed? Inferior?" Gloria asked.

"What? No! Why can't we just be who we are and not be judged every moment of every day?" Jessica's hands shook and she fiddled with the ends of her scarf. "Doesn't it get too much sometimes? Doesn't it feel like things should be easier?"

"Yes," Tina said. "It does. That's called life."

Jessica's lip trembled and her face grew red. "No, it's not just life. It's not! And if it is, it shouldn't be."

"What are you talking about, Jessica?" Kristin asked.

"Didn't Veronica say everyone loved David, how he was a great guy, and blah blah blah?"

"So?"

"So how are you supposed to live up to that? Don't you get it? You have to be damn near perfect when you have a man like that, and if you're not, well, you might as well pack it in. You're just some fat blob holding this perfect person back from all he could be."

"What the hell are you talking about?" Kristin asked again.

"No, she's right," Laura said. For a moment the ever-present anger was gone from her eyes to be replaced by a profound sadness. "Everyone loved David. He was the good one, the perfect one. I was just . . ."

"You were just the complete bitch he was married to," Veronica finished her sentence. "The fact that no one likes you is because you a terrible human being. It had nothing to do with David."

"And you," Veronica said, turning to Jessica before Laura had a chance to respond. "Shame on you. Shame on you for trying to give her an excuse for her awful ways."

Jessica's eyes flashed. "It's not an excuse, it's the truth."

Tina chuckled. "That's such bullshit."

"No it's not," Jessica said. "My husband is like that too. Do you know how much pressure that is to live up to that?"

"No, I don't. Tina said. "And you know why? It's because I'm grown! I'm not a fucking child with low self-esteem who can't deal with the world. It sounds like you have a good man who loves you, and you can't deal because he's too perfect? Poor baby, I wish I had your type of problems."

"She's right," Brooke said. "What are you complaining about? Your man is all over you. What's wrong with that? He's a brotha, ain't he? Brothas love them some thick chicks."

"My husband's Jamaican," Jessica said.

"Ohhhhh shit!" Brooke exclaimed. "Girl, you hit the jackpot. You got you a yardie! I bet he got him a huge—"

"Brooke!" Gloria exclaimed. "That's enough."

"Okay, mom," Brooke said in a snide tone. "I'm just sayin', she ain't got shit to complain about. Her man loves her and wants her just the goddamn way she is, and she's up in here crying and complaining."

"They're right," Gloria said. "You should count your blessings. I would love to have a man like yours."

"Me too," Tina said. "It sounds like your husband loves you exactly the way you are. What I think is you're the one who doesn't love yourself, but you're pushing that on your husband."

"That's so easy for you to say," Jessica said. "I bet you can go into a store and buy anything you want, right? What are you, a size eight?"

"So what? What does my weight or size have to do with a damn thing?" Tina asked. "And I'm a six."

"I'm with her," Bianca agreed. "What does that have to do with anything?"

Jessica rolled her eyes. "Spoken like two skinny chicks."

Bianca laughed. "Skinny? I'm almost six foot tall and weigh . . . well, I ain't skinny."

"Hey, curvy bitches are in nowadays," Brooke said. Look at Kim K. Thick thighs save lives, bitches."

They all gave Brooke a nasty look.

"Curvy is one thing," Jessica said. "Fat is another! You wouldn't understand."

"That's crazy. Don't use weight as an excuse. Look at you, you're gorgeous," Bianca said.

"You're so beautiful!" Kristin agreed. "I would kill for eyes like yours."

"Oh really? Would you kill for my ass? My hips? My thighs?"

Kristin raised an eyebrow. "Are you blind? In case you

didn't notice, I'm not exactly a swimsuit model. I'm a curvy woman who was married to a plastic surgeon. He reminded me every day how flawed I was. You're preaching to the choir."

"You're curvy, not fat. And you're white. Sorry, but it's different."

"Really?" Kristin asked, looking annoyed. "Tell that to my ex-husband, who informed me I was too heavy to be on top when we had sex. Or when he complained about my ass being too big. Or when he told me—while I was pregnant mind you—that my boobs were too big. It's not different. It's not different at all!"

"I'm telling you, girl, you need to get you a brotha," Brooke said to Kristin.

Kristin suppressed a smile and said nothing.

"Please help me to understand why you put so much importance on anyone's opinion of your body parts?" Deepa asked. "I understand losing weight for health, but of what importance is anyone's opinion of how you look? If your husband loves you and desires you, then why do you care what anyone else thinks?"

Jessica looked taken aback by the questions. "Because it's a lot of pressure."

"Pressure? From who?"

"Pressure from my husband. He's all over me all the time. He would have sex every day and night if I let him."

Deepa chuckled.

"You think that's funny?"

"Your husband desires you, and you find that to be a cause for stress in your life. Ridiculous!"

"What? How dare you?" Jessica said.

"I pray every day to have the kind of 'problem' that you have," Deepa said. "I would be happy if my husband wanted me once a month, much less every day."

"I guess Mom and Dad chose the wrong dude for you, huh?" Brooke said.

"Wow, Brooke. That was a bit racist, don't you think?"

asked Bianca.

Brooke made a face. "No way, I watched that *Indian Matchmaking* show."

Deepa gave her a withering glance. "Not all Indian marriages are arranged, Brooke. This is the twenty-first century, after all. My parents didn't choose Hanif, I did. I chose wrong. I chose a man who cares about his career much more than he cares about his wife. But the choice was mine."

"It's not your fault," Gloria said. "Men are just babies. They don't know how to—"

"No, it is my fault," Deepa interrupted. "I was well aware of his personality while we dated. He complained about everything. I was too affectionate, medical school kept me too busy, my hair was too long, then when I cut it, it was too short, on and on. I married him anyway, dreaming things would change. They did. He found even more things to criticize. My practice took up too much time, my cooking wasn't good enough, I wanted sex too much, complaint after complaint."

"Don't blame yourself, dear. That's all on him," Gloria said.

Deepa shook her head. "His actions are his own fault, but I take responsibility for the husband I chose."

"You had control over that. It's not my choice to look like this," Jessica said. "My mother looks like this, my grandmother looked like this."

"Then embrace it. Love yourself. And give thanks you have a man who loves you the way you are," Deepa said.

"No!" Jessica shouted, slamming a fist on an end table. "It's too much . . . it's too much pressure."

"Jessica, relax," Kristin pleaded.

"Relax? Relax? How am I supposed to relax."

"I know," Kristin said in a soothing tone. "But if you—"

"If I what, Kristin? What should I do?"

Brooke grinned. "This chick is trippin'."

"I'm. Not. Tripping." Jessica said through gritted teeth.

"Sure looks like it to me. Just calm down."

"What did you say to me?" Jessica asked.

"You deaf? I said calm d—"

Brooke ducked just in time to avoid the vase that went sailing past her head.

CHAPTER TWENTY

Jessica

"Mommy, I can't find my dance shoes?"

"Look in your dance bag, Brianne. C'mon honey, hurry up or we'll be late."

They hurried out to the car, where Brianne fidgeted and squirmed as Jessica buckled her in.

"Sit still Bri," she said. "We're running late."

"I went to dance yesterday, Mommy," Brianne whined. "Why do I have to go again today?"

"It's good exercise. It helps you stay skinny."

"I'm not skinny. My friend Brandon called me chunky," Brianne said.

"Some friend," Jessica muttered under her breath as she pulled out of the driveway. "Don't listen to Brandon. You're not chunky."

"I am. Daddy calls me a chunky monkey."

Jessica sighed. Jessica hated that her husband Duane had all sorts of "cute" nicknames for Brianne. She didn't mind them now, but Jessica knew as Brianne got older, she wouldn't find them quite so endearing.

All throughout her pregnancy, Jessica prayed Duane's tall, athletic genes would win out over her curvy heavy ones, but no such luck. Brianne was the spitting image of her as a child. Very cute, but short and chubby. In an attempt to counteract what nature wrought, Jessica arranged an intense itinerary of physical activities for her daughter. Duane hated the schedule. He thought it much too rigorous, but Jessica fought him tooth and nail. He didn't understand what she'd experienced and had no idea of what Brianne faced. He filled their daughter with wild ideas, telling her she was beautiful and gorgeous every single day. Brianne adored her father and swallowed his lies hook, line, and sinker, but Jessica knew the ugly truth. Oh, people might think she was pretty—for a fat girl—but no one, absolutely no one, would think her daughter was *truly* beautiful if she were overweight. This Jessica knew firsthand. No amount of self-esteem or self-love would change the fact she was a fat chick who wanted nothing more than to be skinny.

The Bluetooth headset jingled in Jessica's ear, and she glanced at her phone then answered the call.

"Hello, Jessica Walter's party planning. This is Jessica speaking . . . Oh hi, Bianca . . . You gave them all out . . . That's great . . . Sure, sangria is okay . . . Oh please, tell Kristin not to worry so much. Do you want me to call her? Okay, I'll give her a ring later. I have to go. I'm rushing to get Brianne to dance class . . . Okay, no problem. Talk to you later, bye."

She ended the call as they pulled into the ballet studio's parking lot and, a few minutes later, Jessica watched with pride and a twinge of sadness as Brianne ran up to the barre with the other students and the instructor put them through their paces. She was proud because Brianne showed as much or more talent than the other students, but she knew if Brianne didn't lose weight, her ballet career would be short lived. She watched her daughter for a minute more, then hurried back to the car. She pulled out her planner, checking off items on her to-do list and calling clients to make sure they were happy and their functions on track. Party planning was an exhausting business, but Jessica loved everything about it.

With the economy the way it was, people weren't having celebrations like they used to, so she had to find creative ways to keep her business afloat and pleasure parties proved to be a godsend. Women might be feeling the pinch as much as men. They would cut coupons and wear Payless when they really wanted Prada, but damned if they wouldn't break out their credit card to get the latest toy. She didn't understand the fascination with them herself. She had little or no desire for sex with Duane at all, much less some construct made of wires and silicone, but they sold like hotcakes. Duane thought it was sexy and called her the sex toy pimp and offered, only half-jokingly, to help her "test" them out. She knew he would do it, too. If he had his way, they would be in bed three times every day and four on Sunday.

Last night was a perfect example. After her shower, she toweled off in the bathroom then put on her favorite robe. An ugly purple number, it was her favorite because it covered everything up, turning her into a shapeless terrycloth blob. Duane detested it for the same reason. She wrapped her hair and looked at herself in the mirror. As usual, she hated her reflection, but was pleased that the combo of the ugly robe and her hair wrapped up in a headscarf would most likely deter him from bothering her for sex.

She entered their bedroom, where Duane was working on his laptop, so she'd foraged in her dresser for an old T-shirt and some sweatpants to wear to bed, praying he would concentrate on his work, but no such luck. He quickly abandoned the laptop and put his long arms around her. Duane was a big man, still built like the star college basketball player he'd once been, so he was able to quickly get his arms around her thick waist, undo the belt on the robe, and pull it to the ground. He pressed up against her, and she felt him instantly harden.

She'd tried for years to understand why on Earth he would want her so much. There were way, way, more attractive women out there, skinny, toned women without the huge breasts, stretch marks, and a fat, jiggly ass that wouldn't get smaller or firmer no matter how much she ran or how many hours she spent in downward dog. Duane didn't seem to care, his eyes lit up at the sight of her breasts, and his hands were constantly running all over her ass. His obvious desire should have aroused her but all it did was make her mad. What could there be about her he found attractive?

"Looking good, girl!" he said in her ear as he reached around from behind and cupped her breasts.

Duane's hands were big, but still not up to the task of holding in the cascading mounds of flesh that made up her DD-cup breasts. He gently squeezed her nipple, and despite her disgust, a jolt of electricity ran through her body.

"Damn, baby, you are sexy!" he said, breathing hard in her ear.

Liar, she thought. There was no way he thought she was sexy, but despite her misgivings, she had to admit his body felt good on hers and she gave in to the sensation, leaning her head back, exposing her neck. Duane took this as a sign to continue his attentions and kissed her neck while he lightly caressed her breasts. She slowly opened her eyes and instantly regretted it because she caught sight of their reflection in her vanity mirror. A fat and disgusting-looking woman stood in her bedroom, while a tall, muscular, handsome man ran his hands over mounds of disgusting fat and flesh. Jessica looked away quickly, all arousal and desire snuffed out like a candle in the wind. Duane, unaware her mood had shifted, continued his attention, but now she tensed each time he touched her.

"Baby, what's the matter?" he asked a moment later.

She picked up her robe from the floor and put it back on, draping it securely around her entire body and tightening the belt.

Jessica's headset buzzed in her ear again, jolting her out of the memory of the previous night. It was Duane calling, and she pressed the ignore button as she thought back to last night when she put her robe back on. The thick terrycloth was like a suit of armor. Putting it back on made her feel better, despite the hurt look on her husband's face.

"What's the matter?" he asked again.

"Nothing. I just don't feel well," she'd lied and retreated to the bathroom and locked the door. A minute later, she heard him leave the bedroom, so she emerged from the bathroom, got dressed, and quickly fell into bed, covering herself up to the neck with blankets. Thankfully, Duane still wasn't there. *I'll talk to him in the morning,* she thought to herself, but had no idea what she would say. Maybe she would lie and say she had her period or claim some other vague feminine issue. She certainly couldn't tell him the truth.

Duane had already left for work by the time she woke up, so she woke Brianne up for school and went about preparing for the day, feeling a little guilty for denying her husband, and for planning on lying to him, but those feelings quickly abated. Lately it had been harder and harder to pretend she had any desire for him. They hadn't slept together in weeks, and now when he reached for her, she couldn't even fake interest, her body language gave her away. On the rare occasion they actually did make love, he would want to be inside her for hours, changing positions God knows how many times until the sheets were wet with perspiration. *Why can't you be like other men your age,* she thought. *Just get your rocks off quickly and leave me the hell alone.* No such luck—the man had the stamina and endurance of a man half his age. It wasn't that he was horny, he loved to tell her, it was that he was horny for *her.*

Whatever.

Duane was a big strong man, but also a sensitive and loving one who showered affection on his family and expected it in return, so the complete absence of love and intimacy in their relationship weighed heavily on him. Duane would tell anyone who would listen he fell for Jessica the first moment he saw her. That might sound romantic and all, but the larger part of her didn't trust that "love" for one minute, and she didn't trust *him*, even after eight years of marriage. How could he be attracted to her when she looked like she did? Maybe he has some skinny little slut on the side, and all this so-called desire for her was his way of trying to camouflage his cheating, but there was no indication of another woman. She knew, because she became a snoop, something she swore she would never do.

She bought software designed to sniff out a cheating spouse and surreptitiously installed it on his devices, determined to find correspondence or pictures, anything that proved he had a lover. As it turned out, her money was wasted. Duane was an open book. All she had to do was open his laptop to see his emails. He almost never shut down his email account. His browser history was never deleted. She found no secret email accounts or dating site memberships, only way too much activity on ESPN. She didn't need special software to open his cell phone, since the lock code was their daughter's birthday. His messages were stunningly boring, texts to her, to friends, family, and work colleagues. There were no salacious images whatsoever, the vast majority of pictures on his phone were of her and their daughter. Undaunted, she checked his social media, convinced that was where he and his whore communicated, but once again, she didn't need to be much of a detective since the passwords to his social media accounts were stored on his devices. There was nothing. All the women he had connections with were relatives, work colleagues, or mutual friends. There were no incriminating direct messages or sexting, just an endless chatter with his buddies about fantasy teams and sports scores. He has another phone, she reasoned, so she performed exhaustive searches of the house and his car and found nothing. Undaunted, she spent more money to buy a device called a ferrous wand which the internet claimed could sniff out a hidden cell phone like a bloodhound, but again, her time (and money) were wasted. She found nothing.

Finally, she was satisfied there was no other woman in his life, which only deepened the mystery. How could he love and respect someone who looked like her? And in the unlikely event his love for her was actually real, how could *she* love and respect someone who loved someone who looked like her?

There must be something wrong with him.

There had to be.

Her phone began to ring with an incoming video call, and she sighed when she heard the ringtone. It was the song "Jolene," her mother's favorite. She loved her mother fiercely but didn't have the strength or the patience to deal with her right now. Yet she knew if she didn't pick up, her mother would only call back again and again until Jessica answered. Her mother was nothing if not persistent.

She took a breath and picked up.

"Hello, Mother."

"What took you so long to answer?" her mother asked, sipping a drink.

"I was dropping Bri off at dance class, Mother. How are you?"

"What color lip gloss is that? It looks terrible for your skin tone. Anyway, bad news—the lawyers decided not to take my case, sons of bitches. Some bullshit excuse about the case not being credible. It's *criminal* what they let that man get away with. But mark my words, I'm filing another one as soon as I find another lawyer if that bastard Harold thinks he can get away with this . . ."

Jessica let her mind wander as her mother ranted. Jessica's parents, Delilah and Harold were divorced for over twenty years, but Delilah never stopped trying to make Harold's life miserable. After the alimony and child support payments were over, Delilah tried a series of frivolous lawsuits designed to pull more money from her ex-husband. So far none of them had worked.

"Did you know that son of a bitch got another job?" Delilah said, draining her glass.

"Did he?" Jessica asked, although she knew full well her father was the new assistant general manager of the New York Knicks.

"Do you know how much he makes now? Millions!"

"Don't exaggerate, Mother."

"Whatever he sure makes a hell of a lot more than he did when we were married, and that skinny bitch whore he cheated on me with is getting all I'm entitled to."

Jessica tuned out again. She knew the diatribe by heart. Her father was a loser. He was coaching high school basketball when they were first married and barely making ends meet. He cheated on her with a younger woman, a white woman no less. Now they lived in a mansion, and she lived in the same house they did when they first got married.

" . . . and just because he can pass the paper bag test, he thinks he's better than me."

"I'm sure that's not true mother."

"Oh, so you're on his side now?"

"I'm not on anyone's side, Mother."

"If you would calm down and listen you'd see."

"Mother, I'm calm. *You* need to listen."

"No! You calm down and listen! Your father . . ."

With great effort, Jessica held her tongue and listened to her mother's rant. The truth was Harold never thought about his ex-wife at all. He got married again and had a great life. After the divorce, his fortunes seemed to change, and he did better and better as the years passed. The better he did, the more angry and bitter Delilah became. Delilah's obsessive behavior had alienated just about everyone in their family, including Jessica's brother and sister, who would have nothing to do with their mother. Jessica was the only one who felt any loyalty towards her, despite Delilah's sharp tongue and constant put-downs.

The caller ID sounded with an incoming call in the middle of Delilah's diatribe.

"Mom, I have to go, I'm getting another call. It's Duane."

Delilah made a face. There was no love lost between her and her son-in-law.

"Taking the time out from some floozy to call you, huh? What a great guy."

"There's no floozy, Mother."

"There's always a floozy. Especially with those damn Caribbean men."

"I have to go, Mother."

"Fine. Bring my grandbaby to see me!"

"I will, Mother. I love—" Jessica began, but Delilah had already hung up, and she reluctantly picked up her husband's call.

"Hello," she said in an exasperated tone, sounding eerily like her mother did just moments ago.

"Hey, baby. What's going on? Just calling to see how your day was."

"It's okay, but I'm still kind of busy. Bri is in ballet class, and I was just talking to Mother. She's going through a crisis."

Duane chuckled. "So what else is new? This is probably her third crisis this week."

"My mother's emotional state is funny, Duane?"

"I think I would care about her emotional state more if she wasn't constantly putting you down. I have no idea why you continue to take her abuse."

"Whatever, Duane. I have to go, I'm gonna call her back."

"Damn, Jessica, can't we talk? Your mother will survive for a few minutes without you."

"Fine. Go ahead and talk then," she said rudely.

"I don't want to talk about your mother," he said calmly. "We need to talk about us. What happened last night?"

"Nothing happened," she lied.

"That's not true. Something definitely happened. If I did anything to hurt or offend you, I'm sorry. For months now, I've felt this distance from you. Please just be truthful with me and tell me what's going on."

Duane's voice was calm and even, but she heard hints of the Jamaican accent that only surfaced when he was angry.

She knew if she were truthful, he would be supportive and do whatever she needed until things got better. Or, he would feel sorry for his fat, disgusting wife and run to some young skinny bitch who would happily supply him with all the perverted sex he wanted.

The thought made her blood boil, and suddenly she was

furious at him.

"There's nothing wrong," she lied again. "Everything is fine."

"Come on, Jessie. Talk to me, please."

Jessie.

There was a time she loved being called that, but now all the nickname did was make her angry.

"Don't call me that, Duane. That's not my name."

"What the hell? Since when?"

"Since now."

"See, that's the kind of thing I mean. You've changed."

"No, I haven't."

"Don't give me that bullshit. Last night things were going great, then suddenly you flinched and stiffened up on me like I had some kind of disease. You acted like my touch disgusted you. I can't tell the last time you said you loved me, Jessica. I feel like an inconvenience to you, like you don't even want me around, and I'm tired of it. I want to know once and for all what the problem is."

Jessica rolled her eyes. They had this conversation every so often, and she was sick of it.

"It's nothing"

"Don' gimme dat!" Duane's Jamaican accent had completely taken over. "Fuck it. I'm just gon' ask. Is there someone else, Jessica? You have another man?"

Jessica almost laughed out loud but just managed to stop herself.

"Oh, this is funny to you?"

She rolled her eyes. "No, Duane, there is no one else. It's just about me . . . I just have some things to work out. I think maybe I need to talk to someone."

"You said this same shit 'bout having things to work out three months ago, and you said it six months ago. I found you a therapist, and you never even made an appointment."

"Duane!" Jessica shouted. "Just . . . stop! I don't want to talk about this."

"Why are you shouting, Jessica? Calm down. And, that 'this' you're talking about is our life together. You don't think that's important enough to try to save?"

Jessica sat with fists clenched, blood boiling. Why did he ask these kinds of questions? Why did he have to care so much? Why couldn't he just leave her alone?

"First of all, don't tell me to be calm, I hate that. And you're the one who's all dramatic. God, you're being such a b—"

Jessica knew the second she started saying the word, she had made a terrible mistake.

Duane went silent. When he spoke again the Jamaican accent disappeared, replaced by a chill in his voice she had never heard before.

"I didn't think you would ever disrespect me like that."

"Duane . . . I didn't mean to."

"It's okay. Save it. You said what you needed to say, and now I know how you truly feel. You don't care about me, that's plain. What's worse is you don't care about our marriage. And way worse, you don't care about our daughter."

"It's not like that, Duane. You're exaggerating."

"Just be honest with me. If you can't, then at least be honest with yourself. You meant what you said. Now I know."

Jessica paled at his words and the sadness in his tone.

"Mark my words," he continued. "I promise you this is the very last time I'll talk to you about our issues." He drew the words out for emphasis: "*The very last time*."

"I'm finished beating my head against the wall. When it's all said and done, I hope you remember I tried hard to fix whatever this fucked up situation is between us, because apparently I was the only one who gave a damn."

"What does that mean 'the very last time'?" she asked, her heart pounding in her chest. With every word, his voice became colder until it sounded like some hateful stranger was on the line.

"What do you think it means? I'm done trying."

"I really don't know what you want from me."

"You don't know what I want? I want my fucking wife. I want to laugh with her every day, I want to show her love and get love back. I want us to have each other's backs, I want to show our daughter what a loving partnership is. I want my wife. I just want my wife. Can you give me that, Jessica? Can you be the wife I need?"

"I'm trying my best, Duane."

He chuckled, and the sound chilled Jessica even more than his cold voice had.

"No, you're not. Not even a little bit."

"I am," she said weakly.

"If you were trying, you wouldn't have called me what you just called me. If you were trying, we would communicate about our problems and we would work at them together. What you're doing is ignoring our problem, hoping I'll be content with the crumbs you decide to throw me once in a while."

Jessica stayed silent. The emotion in her man's voice touched her deeply. She wanted to tell Duane she knew he was a good and decent man and she loved him, too, in her own way. She wanted to say there was a part of her that didn't want to ever live without him. She felt a sob building in her throat. *It's time to be honest, Jessica,* she thought. *Talk to your husband.* She knew there was nothing to fear, if there was anyone in the world who would love and support her without judgment, it was Duane. Tears formed in her eyes, and she reached over to the dash to pull a Kleenex from the small pack she kept there. As she did so, she caught a glimpse of her face in the rearview mirror.

Her fat face.

Her fat face sprinkled with the freckles she hated.

Her fat face sprinkled with the freckles she hated and with wrinkles beginning to form at the corner of her eyes.

Her fat face sprinkled with the freckles she hated and with wrinkles beginning to form at the corner of her eyes and an ugly roll of fat at her neck.

The voices always at the edge of her consciousness

spoke, repeating all the hateful comments she'd overheard over the years.

"How the hell did she land that fine ass man?"

"What the hell was Duane thinking? He must love fat bitches."

"She's lucky she got her a West Indian man. They love them some big girls."

"That's his wife? Get outta here! He must have a chick on the side."

Like the night before, the loving sentiments forming in her heart evaporated under the heat of the voices. She stared at her reflection and asked herself again for the thousandth time: *How could he love me?* The mirror had no answer for her, and so, instead of beginning the process that would salvage her marriage, what she did was . . . nothing.

Duane sighed. "Okay, Jessica. I have my answer."

Duane's voice sounded resigned as if he had come to a difficult decision.

"I tried real hard to be a good husband, Jessica, but like you said, I'm being a bitch. I'm just . . . done. Kiss the baby for me. I'll be home late. I have some things I need to do." He paused. "You know, you're a lot more like your mother than you want to admit."

Those words, more than anything else he'd said, hit her hard, and she choked back tears. "Duane, listen, I'm sorry. Maybe we can . . ." she stopped when she realized she spoke to dead air. He already killed the call.

Duane was done talking.

CHAPTER TWENTY-ONE

"That's it, bitch. I'm gonna beat your ass," Brooke said. She advanced on Jessica, but Bianca blocked her way.

"Brooke, don't do this."

"What? She threw a fucking vase at my head!"

"I think she's having some kind of breakdown," Bianca said. "Look."

Jessica paced the room, wild-eyed and crying. "I'm tired of people telling me to calm down. I won't calm down, I won't."

She stopped pacing as tears streamed down her cheeks.

"We have to have careers and a perfect marriage and perfect children and the perfect house like something out of a magazine, and there better not be one dish in the sink or a blade of grass out of place. Ohhhhhhh no, then you're a terrible wife and everyone judges you. Then a baby comes, and then it's all about losing the weight—but guess what? It won't come off. You just gain more. Then you do Pilates and yoga with a bunch of skinny bitches with their flat asses and chests and fake smiles who don't think you know they laugh at you behind your back."

"Jessica! It's okay, honey, just take it easy," Kristin said.

"It wouldn't be so bad if the stupid exercises actually

worked, but all you get is sweaty and sore. And don't get me started on those diets. I haven't eaten bread in *nine whole months*. No carbs, no pasta, and meal prep every day, and do keto, and all the other useless diets, but not a goddamn thing works. Yet guess what *he* stuffs his face with? Pizza and rice and bread, and *he* still looks great."

"Yo, shouldn't someone do something?" Brooke asked. "She's losing it."

"He's got a few gray hairs, but on *him* it's 'dignified,' but God forbid there's one on your head. Holy God, then it's panic mode because you're not dignified. You're just fucking old, and *he* wants you to jump into bed with him morning, noon, and night. I mean, how can you be naked with him constantly when you can't even stand the sight of yourself in the mirror? I can't figure it out—Why does he want you? How can he, when you're just . . . just . . .FAT? Why can't he just leave me alone?"

Jessica finally stopped pacing and Kristin detached herself from the group and put an arm around her.

"Well, damn," said Brooke.

The sound of Laura's raucous laughter tore their attention away from the distraught Jessica.

"You think that was funny?" Tina asked her.

Laura's response was a loud guffaw. "Hell, yes, that shit was funny."

"She stood up for you, and look how you treat her," Kristin said, her face reddening. "You really are a monster."

"Hey! I didn't ask that fat bitch to stand up for me."

"And you wonder why people hate you," Veronica said.

"Don't think I forgot you. Your time is coming," Laura said.

"If you're going to do it, then just do it," Veronica said, standing up. "I'm sick of hearing you talk."

"Sit the fuck down," Laura ordered.

"No."

"She's fulla shit. She ain't gonna do a damn thing," Brooke said.

"Keep talking. You might be next," Laura said.

"Yeah right, you're all talk. You know what? Fuck this. I'm out of here." Brooke stuck her hand in the bowl where Laura stashed their phones and fished around for hers.

"Bitch, you better sit down," Laura said, raising the pistol.

"What did I tell you about calling me a bitch?" Brooke asked.

"I said *sit down.*"

Brooke ignored her and searched for her phone.

"We've all had enough of you," Veronica said, taking a step closer to her tormentor.

"Get the fuck back and sit down!" Laura screamed as her shaking hand pointed the gun from Brooke to Veronica and back again.

"Got it," Brooke said, pulling an iPhone in a bedazzled case from the bowl.

"Put it down," Laura ordered as Brooke powered up her phone.

"Whatever," Brooke said, still staring at her phone. "Damn, I missed like three calls."

"I said put it back!"

Brooke ignored her and stuck her phone in her back pocket. "Ladies, you all can stay if you want, but I'm gonna bounce. It's been real."

"You're not going anywhere."

"Looks like she is," Veronica said. "What are you gonna do?"

Heart beating fast, Deepa put her hand in her pocket and stepped closer to Laura.

"I'm going to kill—"

"You ain't killin' shit," Brooke said.

"You better get back or—"

Veronica took another step, and Laura suddenly swung at her, but Veronica was ready. She put her hands up instinctively, blocking the blow. The impact was jarring and sent the gun flying. Nine pairs of eyes watched it fly across the room, hit the floor with a heavy "thunk," and slide under a chair.

There was dead silence.

No one moved.

Then, all hell broke loose.

Brooke, realizing Laura was unarmed, quickly covered the distance separating them and punched Laura hard in the face. Laura staggered back, but Brooke grabbed a handful of her hair and punched her again, causing blood to explode from her broken nose. Deepa, tiny scissors in hand, tried to stab Laura, but Laura saw movement from her peripheral vision and put her hand up at the last moment, causing the scissors to sink deeply into her palm. Laura screamed in pain and thrashed about, freeing herself from Brooke's grasp, and stared at the scissors embedded in her hand in disbelief.

"You stabbed—"

Before she could finish the sentence, Veronica hit her with a powerful roundhouse punch that dropped her to the floor.

Jessica ran over and stood between Laura and the mob of women now coming forward, blood in their eyes.

"Okay," she pleaded. "She's had enough."

"Move!" Kristin screamed, pushing Jessica roughly out of the way, causing her to stumble over an ottoman and fall. Laura, still dazed from Veronica's punch, tried to sit up, but Kristin aimed a savage kick at her ribs that connected squarely, driving Laura backward. Laura lay on her back, bleeding and trying to catch her breath, when Bianca ran in and stomped Laura in the stomach.

"Noooooo. Stop. Leave her alone, please," Jessica pleaded.

No one paid Jessica any mind as they surrounded Laura, kicking and stomping her viciously. Time slowed down as each woman used the terror of the past hours to fuel her rage. Gloria felt her ankle turn as she directed a particularly hard kick at Laura's face. Maya and Tina stood beside one another and kicked Laura almost in tandem. Brooke, a smile on her face, swore at Laura under her breath as she stomped her repeatedly in the stomach, and Deepa kicked off her shoes and stomped on Laura's knee in her stockinged feet.

The violence seemed to go on for hours, but in reality only lasted a few seconds. Just as quickly as it began, it was over, and the women beheld their handiwork, the bloodlust slowly leaving their faces.

"What have you done?" Jessica asked as she rushed to where Laura lay, bleeding and motionless. "You animals!" she said. "You killed her. You killed Laura."

#

CHAPTER TWENTY-TWO

"She ain't dead," Brooke said. "She'll be all right."

In the aftermath of the beating, everyone seemed subdued, except for Brooke, who seemed to take the violence in stride.

"What have we done?" Deepa asked.

"We defended ourselves," Brooke said. "I like what you did with those scissors, by the way. That was slick."

Kristin reluctantly glanced over at Laura's body. "Is she . . . ?"

A pained groan from Laura answered her question.

"Like I said, she'll live," Brooke added.

Jessica left Laura's side and sat down heavily on an ottoman. "Thank God she's alive," she said, relieved.

"What is it with you?" Brooke asked. "You got Kingston Syndrome or something?"

"Wait. *What?*" Maya asked.

"Jessica. She got Kingston Syndrome. You know, when hostages get close to a terrorist or whatever. Kingston Syndrome."

Despite the somber mood, Kristin grinned. The grin turned into a smile, which turned into a chuckle, which transformed into a loud belly laugh.

"What's with her?" Brooke asked.

Kristin's laughter was contagious, and in seconds, the others were laughing hard, as well.

"I think you mean Stockholm Syndrome, Brooke," Tina said when the laughter subsided.

"Whatever. Stockholm, Kingston, y'all know what I mean."

"So what do we do now?" Bianca asked, once all their laughter had subsided. "Should we—"

Her question was cut short by the sounds of Laura's harsh, wheezing breaths.

"You bitches think this is funny?" Laura asked. With her split and swollen lips, the words were garbled, but all understood what she said. She finally made it to her feet and leaned against the front door. She slowly touched her left eye, which was swollen shut. Then she spat a mouthful of blood onto the floor and pointed to Veronica, hate burning in her one good eye, and the broken fingers of her hand hanging at unnatural angles.

"I should have killed you, bitch."

"I was just thinking the same thing," Veronica said. She rose from her seat, but Maya held her back.

"She's had enough. It's over," Maya said.

"It's not over," Laura said.

"Are you going to the cops? Play the victim as usual and tell them how we beat your ass?" Veronica asked.

Maya grinned. "No, ladies, she won't say a word. Then we would have to tell how she held us hostage here, and maybe some other choice details might leak out, too, like those parties Veronica told us about."

The hate burning in Laura's good eye turned on Maya.

"Cops?" Laura responded, the S's in her words causing bloody saliva to spray as she spoke. "I don't need no cops. It's me that's gonna get this bitch, when she least expects it. This ain't over." She opened the door and gave them one last, hateful look.

"This ain't over," she said again and shuffled down the driveway.

#

CHAPTER TWENTY-THREE

Laura

Laura lurched down the driveway toward her car. She could see out of only one eye, her broken fingers were in agony, and her chest felt like it was being poked with sharp blades with every breath. She wanted to lay down and die, but she could almost feel them watching her. No, she would keep going; she would never give those bitches the satisfaction of seeing her stumble.

After what seemed like forever, she got to her car and slowly sat down, the act of sitting causing agonizing new levels of pain. She started the engine and took off down the street like a bat out of hell but slowed down and pulled over once she was a block or two away and out of sight. She pulled the visor down and looked at her face in the mirror, gasping when she saw what damage had been done to her.

I need the emergency room, she thought. The hospital was only a couple of miles away, but she thought better of it. There would be all kinds of questions she wasn't prepared to answer. Better to go home. She pushed the button to start her car and cried out at the agony even that simple action cost her. She took a moment to let the pain die down then began driving. Her broken fingers and swollen eye made the journey challenging, it took double the time it normally would have, but she almost cried in relief when she finally parked the car in her driveway thirty minutes later.

The blood dripped down her chin and onto her blouse from her split lips and gums as she used shaking hands to punch in the alarm code, not bothering to reset it once she was in the house. Once inside, Paris and London ran toward her, yapping happily.

"Get the fuck away from me," she said. The dogs ran underfoot, and she lashed out with her foot, managed to score a glancing kick on the unlucky Paris. The little dog whimpered but shook off the blow and continued to scamper around Laura's feet. Annoyed, Laura picked up one of their toys, opened a pantry door and tossed the toys in. The ecstatic dogs ran in to get it and Laura slammed the door, locking them in. Immediately they began whimpering and scratching at the door but she ignored them and headed for the bar where she poured a double of Macallan single malt and gulped it down. She screamed as the alcohol burned the cuts in her lips and mouth but almost instantly felt better once it hit her system. She mixed another double and drank it slowly, not caring that the blood from her lips swirled into the glass, giving the drink a red tint. The alcohol dulled the pain and made her drowsy, so she grabbed the bottle and the glass and limped slowly up the stairs. Halfway up, her leg gave way and she slipped and fell to her knees. She stayed there for a moment, blood from her mouth dripping blood onto the pristine stairs. She rose again, smearing blood on the stairs and banister as she slowly made her way to the bedroom.

Even in her drunken haze, she realized she would need help. There was no way she could take care of herself with her injuries. *I'll call Lily,* she thought, but just as quickly discarded the idea. The first thing her treacherous daughter would do was call the police. No, there was only one person she could rely on. She pulled out her phone and searched until she found the number for her maid, Lupe, and dialed it.

The phone rang twice before Lupe picked up. In the background, people laughed while Mariachi music played softly.

"Ms. Laura?"

"Lupe. Can you hear me? Lupe?" Laura slurred.

There were footsteps and then the sound of a door opening and closing, and the volume of the music lowered.

"Ms. Laura?" Lupe said again.

"I need you, Lupe. Can you come over?"

"Ms. Laura, it's my day off, remember?"

"Lupe, I need you. Just come over, okay? Please."

"You all right, Ms. Laura? Something happen?"

"I need you," Laura said again. "Please."

There was silence for a moment. "Okay Ms. Laura. I come later."

"Thank you, Lupe. Thank you."

Laura felt better, Lupe would take care of her, she would be okay. Exhausted, she slowly began to undress, crying out in pain every time she tried to use her mangled fingers. She intended to fall into bed, but disgusting dried blood covered her chin and chest, so she took the bottle and glass into the bathroom with her and set them on the edge of the huge jacuzzi tub and gingerly lowered herself in. She turned the jets on, crying out in pain as they roughly hammered her bruises. Soon, however, the jets and the hot water did their work and Laura took sips of whiskey and relaxed, allowing her mind to wander and process the events of the day. She'd fully intended to kill that whore Veronica (she refused to think of Veronica as David's wife), but then she saw the picture of the baby.

David's baby.

He looked so much like David. They had the same nose, the same lips, and the same crooked smile. Her resolve faltered, and she just couldn't do it.

But what now? she asked herself. Not only did she have to deal with the embarrassment of being deserted by her husband for a younger woman. Now the whole world would know his son was out there too.

Fuck that, she thought. *I'm gonna kill that bitch.* She took another mouthful of the whiskey and tried to make her mind a blank. She didn't know how long she lay in the hot water, but soon the bottle was empty. She dropped it on the floor and heard it break. Then she passed out.

When she came to, it was much darker in the bathroom, and she sensed someone in the room with her. She tried to open her eyes, but one was still swollen shut, and the other was blurry, courtesy of the whiskey. She vaguely recalled calling Lupe, but whether that was one hour or one day ago, she couldn't say.

She squinted and tried to make out who was in the room with her. Was that . . . David?

"David, is that you?"

She felt him take her hand, and she grabbed onto it with all the strength she could muster.

"David, I saw your son," she said, crying. "He's so beautiful. He looks just like you."

As she squeezed his hand, she felt a sharp pain in her wrist and tried to pull her hand back, but David was too strong.

"David ... what ...," she began but stopped talking as the pain lessened and she began to feel even more drowsy. She opened her good eye and saw the water was turning red. She wanted to panic, she wanted to jump out of the tub and get away from there, but the tired feeling washed over her. With an enormous effort, she turned her head to look at her dead husband. Her eye was still blurred; all she could see was a hazy outline of a person sitting on the edge of the tub. She held out her hand for his, not seeing the blood flowing down her wrist and into the water.

"I love you, David. I love you so much," she said. Then, all energy depleted, she slipped under the blood-red water.

#

CHAPTER TWENTY-FOUR

"Good riddance," Tina said as they watched Laura get in her car and speed away.

They were gathered at a window, and one by one, they all sat down again until only Veronica remained, looking out.

"She won't forget this," Veronica said.

"Do you think she'll go to the police?" Kristin asked.

"And tell them what?" Maya asked.

"No, she won't go to the police," Veronica said. "She'll go home and lick her wounds and get even more angry."

"She's pretty beat up," Gloria said. "Maybe she learned her lesson."

Veronica shook her head. "No. She'll never forget this. Never. I'll be looking over my shoulder as long as she's alive. And now you all will be too."

"So maybe we are the ones who should go to the police. After all, she was the one who threatened us," Deepa said.

"That might have worked if we didn't all beat the stuffing out of her," Maya replied.

"So what then?" Kristin asked. "Just sit around and wait for her to kill one of us?"

"She won't do anything," Brooke said. "You saw what

happened. She's all talk."

"I suggest we all exchange phone numbers," Kristin said. "Just in case anything happens, we can make all communicate."

"Great idea," Gloria said.

One by one, the women entered their phone numbers in each other's phones.

"You can underestimate her if you want, but I won't," Veronica said, after she had given all the women her number. She put her cell phone in her purse and headed for the door.

"So what are you going to do?" Gloria asked.

"What I have to do," Veronica said. She walked out of the house and shut the door behind her.

"What does that mean? What's she going to do?" Jessica asked. No one paid her any mind.

"I'm going too," Maya said.

"Maybe you should wait for a bit. Your head is still a bit iffy," she said as she reached out to her.

"Don't worry about my head," Maya said, shrugging her off.

"Maya, let's go and talk."

Maya ignored her. "Nice to meet you all," she said. "I wish it didn't have to go like this." She gave Tina a dirty look. "But you know what they say—everything happens for a reason."

She walked out the door, leaving the embarrassed Tina behind.

Tina looked at them, face red, and walked out the door after Maya without saying a word of goodbye.

"Drama to the end, huh?" Brooke said. "I'm gonna bounce, too, ladies. This was a hell of a party. Do me a favor and don't invite me to the next one, okay?"

She blew them a kiss, and then she, too, was gone.

"There goes a very troubled young woman," Gloria said when Brooke had left.

"You got some—" Bianca began, but Kristin interrupted her.

"Ladies, I'm going to clean up. I would love some help," she said.

Kristin thrust a platter of untouched appetizers into Bianca's hands. Deepa and Jessica each picked up pitchers and followed Kristin and Bianca into the kitchen.

Alone in the living room, Gloria got onto her knees and peeked under the ottoman the gun had slid under. It was dark, so she stretched out her arm and was rewarded by the feel of cold steel. She stretched and stretched and was eventually able to grab it and pull it closer to her until finally it was in her hands. In the melee, no one had thought to ask where the gun was. She alone had followed its flight and saw where it ended up. Now it was in her hands. She heard voices and quickly thrust the pistol into her purse just before anyone looked in her direction, then pretended to fluff cushions, feeling better and more powerful than she had in a long time.

#

CHAPTER TWENTY-FIVE

Tina

Tina hurried after Maya, catching up with her just as Maya arrived at her car.

"Maya, listen."

Maya raised a hand to stop her. "I think you've said enough."

Tina sighed. "I'm sorry about what I said. It didn't come out right, okay? You know I care about you."

"You're full of shit. How can you care about a . . . diversion? I'm just a hobby, like crocheting or reading trashy novels. I'm tired of being your diversion."

"Maya, I didn't mean it. I'm sorry."

"Please just stop. You were finally honest. Don't start lying again now!" She pressed a button on her key fob and her car roared to life.

"Are you sure you're able to drive?" Tina asked. "Your head . . ."

"Didn't you hear what I said in the house? Don't worry about my head or my anything else. Go get yourself another diversion. We're done."

Maya's talk was tough, but Tina saw the tears in her eyes and heard her voice cracking. "Maya come on. You don't mean that. Please, let's just talk about it."

"I do mean it. You humiliated me. I feel cheap and used, and I've never felt that way in my life. So, fuck you. There's nothing to talk about. I'm done," she said. She slammed her car door and sped off.

Tina watched Maya leave, conflicted. Despite what she'd said at the party, Maya was more than just a diversion to her. But she lived in this life, her *real* life, which had only so much room for Maya in it.

No, it was better this way.

She got into her car, resigned to start over and close the Maya chapter once and for all, but as she started the engine, she realized this moment, this very second, was the beginning of her new life. A life without Maya. The loss and pain sat on her like a weight because it was now, when Maya was well and truly gone, that Tina realized she didn't want to be without her.

A couple walking their dog headed in her direction, so Tina dried her tears, pulled out of the parking space, and headed home. She knew now her feelings for Maya were much, much deeper than she had let herself admit. Her heart grieved the loss of her lover, but her head knew the right thing had happened.

She needed to try to salvage what she could of her marriage. She still loved Ted, and she knew he loved her too. They needed to communicate with each other openly and honestly to give their marriage the shot in the arm it so desperately needed. She didn't know if he would give up his young girlfriend—God knows she knew how intoxicating being with a younger woman could be—but they had raised a family and overcome decades of challenges together. Surely that trumped young pussy?

She would see.

A few minutes later, she arrived home, pleased to see Ted's car in the driveway. In the minutes since leaving Maya, her mood began to shift, and now she looked forward to the challenge of trying to save her marriage. She opened their front door and saw Ted in the kitchen, whispering on the phone, a huge smile on his face. She rolled her eyes. Ted thought it was a secret he was screwing his personal trainer, a dizzy young blond hussy with daddy issues who seemed determined to sleep with every male client old enough to be her father, which Ted certainly was. She had to admit, though, there was no better motivation to get in shape than a young lover. Ted looked great. He'd taken up CrossFit and completely transformed his body over the past year or so.

Ted saw her arrive and ended the call before she came into earshot.

"Hey," he said, kissing her on the cheek. "How was the party?"

The oven dinged and he turned it off then removed a platter of chicken wings, put them in a bowl, and poured a batch of his secret sauce over them, a recipe he only made for special occasions.

"It was fun," she lied, knowing he was only making conversation. She could actually tell him the truth—*oh, well, a crazy woman was there, and she held us hostage the whole time*—and it wouldn't get any reaction but a distracted "wow" or a half-hearted "that's great."

"Wow," he said. "That's great."

"Who's that for?" she asked, pointing at the wings, which by now were all thoroughly bathed in his sauce. "We having company? I was kind of hoping it would be just the two of us tonight."

He put a dollop of sauce in his palm, tasted it, and frowned. "Taste this," he said, thrusting the spoon at her. "Do you think it needs more sweet chili?"

She tasted it and nodded. "Maybe just a little bit more. Did you hear what I said? I was hoping it would be just the two of us."

He made a face as if he had misheard her. "Don't you remember? TJ, Fran, and the baby are coming over. We're going to watch UFC tonight. Mary heard the baby was going to be here, so she's actually going to sacrifice a Saturday night out with her weird hipster friends and spend time with her family."

"I completely forgot," Tina said. In all the excitement of the day, she had forgotten their son, Ted Jr., his wife, and baby son were coming over. They didn't live very far, but with schedules being so busy, it was rare they were all together. Their daughter, Mary, was home from college on a break, so the entire family would be present tonight.

"Hey, can we talk before the kids get here?" she asked.

"Huh? What did you say, babe?" he asked, stirring his sauce then tasting it again.

"Ted! The sauce is fine. Can we talk, please?"

He gave the wings one last stir, then put a cover on the bowl.

"No can do, babe. They're going to be here soon, and the prelims are going to begin. We can't miss them."

"The what?"

"Prelims. You know, the preliminary fights. I'm gonna shower before the kids get here. Can we talk tomorrow? Great! Thanks, babe."

Ted ran up the stairs, peeling off his shirt as he went. "I bet you'd stop and talk to your young girlfriend," Tina muttered to herself as she watched him go.

She banged her fist on the counter, rattling the bowl of wings and spilling the sauce. She was furious at Ted for leaving when she needed so badly to talk, but she was madder at herself for actually *needing* to communicate with him. It had been a long time since she needed him for anything, and now the one time she did, he ran away. A tear squeezed from her eye, and she wiped it away quickly, completely at a loss for what to do. She picked up her phone, tempted to call Maya, then put it down again.

"No," she said to herself. Calling Maya would cause more problems than it would solve, and anyway, she doubted

Maya would pick up the phone. Knowing her, she had already blocked Tina's number.

On the way home, she mentally began the process of getting over Maya by thinking about Ted and the work they might do to fix their marriage. In a weird way, she figured it would help heal her broken heart, but now Ted had completely ignored her, and she felt more alone than she felt in a long time. The tears began again, and she wiped them away angrily. *I'll be damned if either Maya or Ted make me cry any more*, she thought. She'd given way too much emotional energy to them both, and it was time she thought about herself. It still hurt, but she would enjoy the time with her kids and grandson this evening, get a good night's sleep, and tomorrow contemplate her next move.

Mind made up, she went up to their bedroom to shower and change before the kids arrived. Ted had already undressed, and seeing him made her do a double take. This was the first time in a long time she'd seen him naked. For a man who would be sixty years old in a couple of years, he looked good. Damn good. His body wasn't smooth and sculpted but had a more rugged, athletic look she had always found sexy. Tina had to admit his young girlfriend was a great trainer. Ted looked amazing.

"Tina, have you seen my black UFC shirt? With the white logo?" he asked from the shower. "I think it's in my top dresser drawer. Could you find it for me please? Thanks, babe."

She said nothing. Seeing her husband's body ignited something in her, and she undressed quickly, slid the shower door open, and stepped in behind him.

"Tina, what the?"

"Shut up, Ted," she said, placing her hand between his legs.

He turned to face her. "C'mon, babe, the kids are almost . . ." He stopped when he saw her body. Ted wasn't the only one who had been working out. Early morning yoga and strength training several times a week made her more defined, while at the same time making her curves stand out. She hadn't been doing it to impress Ted, but the look on his face at the sight of her made every impossible pose, every weight she'd lifted, every ache and pain worth it.

"You look great," he said.

"So do you."

She drew him closer as the warm shower spray rained on them and kissed him hard, then turned the water off and led him from the bathroom to their bed. They made out like teenagers, and it felt strange to Tina, familiar and unfamiliar all at once. They had been together for thirty years—she should know every nook, cranny, and crevice of his body almost as well as she knew her own, but Ted felt new to her. Not only because of the changes in his physique but also because she'd become used to making love to a woman. As she kissed Ted, she felt his energy shift. Whatever hesitation he felt was gone, and he grabbed her behind the neck as he kissed her. She couldn't help but smile. His lovemaking was predictable, she knew his every move before he made it, starting with the neck grab. Instead of being annoyed by his lack of inventiveness as she might have been in times past, she felt comforted by it. It was like being away from home for a time, then returning and having a restful night's sleep in your own familiar bed.

"Wow," he said when it was over and they lay next to one another, covered in perspiration and trying to catch their breath. "That was amazing."

She nodded in agreement, still breathing hard. Sex with a man could never compare to the pure pleasure and intimacy of being with a woman, but in a way, sex with Ted was just as good because it was familiar and safe.

"Babe, you look great," he said when he finally caught his breath. "I should have told you a long time ago."

The compliment made her blush and smile shyly.

"I'm curious. What possessed you to do this?" he asked. "I mean, I'm not complaining or anything. It was great, but . . . what's up?

"Oh, I don't know," she said. "You looked so good, I just had to."

"Well, you're not the only one who can rock a hard body in this house," he said, smiling. He raised up on one elbow and looked at her. "We have to do this again. A lot!"

She nodded in agreement.

"C'mon, babe, the kids are almost here. Let's get dressed."

"I'm sorry, Ted," she said.

"For what?" he asked, puzzled. "For the shower?"

"No. Not that."

"Then what?"

Unexpected tears fell, and she turned away, suddenly not being able to meet his gaze.

"I haven't been a good wife."

"Why would you say that?"

"I just haven't."

"That's not true, Tina."

"It is, Ted. I haven't. I've been—"

"Babe. Stop. You don't have to say it."

"I have to, Ted. I want you to know."

"That you're not the only one with someone on the side?"

Tina sat upright, shocked.

"You . . . you knew?"

"I've suspected for a while."

"Why didn't you say something? Didn't it upset you? Didn't you want to fight for me? For us?"

"My God, how could I confront you, Tina? I'm guilty of the same damn thing? I'm a lot of things, but I'm not a hypocrite."

They sat in silence, each absorbing what the other had said.

"I bet you knew the moment I started messing with Aurora," he said.

She chuckled. "Good grief Ted. Aurora? Is that really her name. You could've found a Candi with an I or Brandi who dots I's with a heart. I'd even take a Sinnamon with an S. But Aurora?"

He laughed and swatted her with a pillow.

"So, now that we're finally being honest," he said, "let me ask you something. Your side guy. Do you love him?"

His voice broke, and Tina was shocked to see the emotion plain on his face.

"No, I don't," she said, not bothering to correct him about the gender of her affair. "I was afraid maybe I did, but now I know I don't."

Ted nodded, relieved.

"Why did you ask? Do you love Aurora?"

"Not at all. I mean, we have a good time, and she's a good person, but that's about it. Tina, I know it sounds crazy after all I've done, but I really don't want to lose you."

"I don't know, Ted. It seems we lost one another a long time ago."

"And yet here we sit. We just made love, and now we're telling each other our truth. Maybe we lost our way a little bit, but I don't think we ever truly lost one another."

Tina shook her head. "I wish that were true. I abandoned you, and I abandoned our family. I left you alone all these years, chasing my career, and you found someone else to be with."

"Are you kidding? Tina, you cannot possibly take the blame for my behavior. Was I lonely sometimes? Sure. But don't act like you were the only ambitious one in this house. I went after my job just as hard you did yours. I knew you were a hard charger when I married you. I never once asked you to change, did I?"

"No, you never did. But, Ted, you and the kids needed me sometimes, and I wasn't there."

"I did the same thing. Many times. But I knew if I really needed you, you would be there. And you always were."

"I want to believe that, but . . ."

"But?"

"But I just don't think I was. I was so selfish."

"Bullshit, Tina. Hey, remember when I got shot on the job?"

Tina nodded. Ted was shot while trying to foil a robbery about fifteen years ago while still a detective. He was off duty at the time and had left the house because she asked him to go get ice cream. She still felt guilty whenever she thought of it.

"Of course I do," she said. "It was horrible."

"I woke up in the hospital, and who was there? You were. I stayed in hospital for a month, and you were there every single day."

"Yes, with a laptop and phone, working. I turned your room into my office."

"I didn't give a damn you were working. You were there, and that's what mattered. I was in a lot of pain. There were times I wasn't sure I was going to make it, but every time I woke up, there you were. You gave me the strength to fight."

"I did?"

"Yes, you did. Honey, we haven't been exactly good, but I think we've been good for one another. We let each other have the freedom to be who we are and to do what we had to do for our careers. Maybe we weren't the perfect family, we didn't sit at the table and have dinner every night, but one of us was always here for the kids."

"We made it work," she agreed.

"We did. Maybe this kind of life, maybe it just works for us."

"Maybe it does," she agreed.

Downstairs, the front door opened, and they heard their son's voice.

"The kids are here," she said. "Go watch your intros."

Ted chuckled. "The prelims, they're called prelims."

"Whatever. Go watch them."

"You watching with us?"

"Sure. I'll shower and come down in a few."

She started to get out of bed, but Ted stopped her. "You

said a minute ago that I found someone else to be with. I didn't. I found someone else to fuck. I know that sounds bad, and maybe it is, but there's a big difference between the two."

"I understand what you mean," she said, and she did.

He looked into her eyes, then kissed her passionately. "God, I love you so much," he said. "I'm glad we talked."

"Me too," she said.

Ted dressed quickly and ran downstairs. She stayed in bed for a minute longer, luxuriating in the feeling that had come over her.

It was relief.

She knew about Ted's extracurricular activities, and he knew about hers, and the Earth didn't open up and swallow them both. Each had had a lover, but they were still committed to one another. There was no precedent in her life for such an arrangement working. If someone had suggested it to her, she would have laughed. But here she was. Here *they* were.

She showered and dressed quickly and ran downstairs. Ted and Ted Jr. were already sitting in front of the television with their plates, watching a man in an outrageously colored blazer standing in a cage introducing the fighters. In the kitchen, her daughter and daughter-in-law chatted while piling pizza and wings on plates.

"Hiiiii Grandma," her grandson screamed as he ran to her. She lifted him up and kissed him then hugged her daughter and daughter-in-law. She poured herself a large cup of diet soda and put a slice of pizza and some wings on her plate, reveling in the noise and happy chaos around her. As she sat between her husband and son with her grandson squirming on her lap, she wished she could apologize to Gloria for what she'd said to her in the party because now she knew what she meant. Everyone Tina loved most in the world was in this house at this very moment, and there was nowhere she would rather be. This was what was important.

Her phone buzzed with an incoming text, and she turned it off without looking at the message. It might be Maya, it might not, she didn't care. Tomorrow she might call Maya and patch things up, or she might not. She didn't know, but there was one thing she knew for certain: Maya had no place in *this* world. She could never be anything more than a diversion.

#

CHAPTER TWENTY-SIX

Maya

"Fuck you, Tina," Maya said as she sped off. "Fuck you! Fuck you! Fuck you!"

Distraught, she drove her Mustang much faster than she should have down the quiet residential streets and flew through three stop signs until she got to the highway on-ramp. She'd bought herself the car when she made detective. It was a popular car in the department, and she hoped owning it would help her fit in, but she quickly grew to love everything about it. She loved its imposing deep ebony color, the bass roar of its huge engine, the way the leather seats enveloped her, making her feel like she and the machine were one. Most of all, though, she loved the speed. The Mustang went from zero to sixty in what felt like nanoseconds, and for her, there was no bigger thrill. Now that she was on the highway, she pushed the powerful muscle car even harder, blowing past the speed limit in seconds.

"Fuck you, Tina!" she screamed to a motorist who gave her the finger as she weaved in and out of the weekend traffic.

The tears flowed fast, and she angrily wiped them away as she thought about just how she was going to live without Tina in her life. She'd put up with a lot from her over their affair, but being called "just a diversion," and in front of a room full of strangers no less, had hurt her even more than Laura cracking her in the head with the pistol. Still, she already regretted her angry talk of a few minutes ago and wished she could take it all back. She was strong. Yet, Tina made her weak. She put up with things from her she would never stand for from anyone else, and if she were honest with herself, despite what she had said about being done with her, if Tina came back to her, she would put up with this too.

She pushed down harder on the gas pedal and the Mustang's engine responded almost instantly, pushing the speedometer over one hundred miles per hour. She could almost hear Tina's voice in her head urging her to slow down, so she slammed harder on the gas pedal, watching in satisfaction as the needle moved closer to one hundred and ten. A few minutes later, she arrived at her apartment, threw her keys on her coffee table, and dropped heavily onto her couch. She began to cry, but angrily wiped the tears.

"No!" she told herself. She wouldn't cry about Tina. Not anymore. It was stupid to hurt so much over someone who obviously didn't value her.

Their affair had lasted only about a year, but in that time, Maya had filled her home with mementos of life with Tina. Tina was always reluctant for them to take pictures together, but the few Maya had convinced her to take were in frames in every room of the apartment. There were other things, too, a juicer Tina bought her for her birthday, a crystal vase Tina got her on one of their rare trips together to the mall, a throw rug she brought back from a business trip to Greece. The apartment reeked of memories of Tina. Suddenly, a fit of rage overcame Maya, and she found a garbage bag and began to throw every item that reminded her of Tina into it. Every picture, every gift; even the coffee cup that Tina liked to use when she was here went into the trash bag. Before she met Tina, the apartment was just a place to store her stuff and to lay her head between shifts, nothing more. Sure, it was comfortable, but it was just a place. Then she met Tina, and it became more of a home of sorts. Now, it was just an empty place again.

The clock on her mantle struck the hour, reminding Maya that she would have to go to work soon. As the newest detective, she got stuck with some of the crappy shifts, and the graveyard shift was the worst of them. She had a little time and was tempted to have a glass or three of wine, but thought better of it. The very last thing she needed was to get tongues wagging by showing up for work reeking of alcohol. She gave the wine bottles a covetous glance then decided the time before work would be spent relaxing, and what better way than to have a good soak in the tub? Her apartment was unremarkable in just about every way, but for some reason it featured an enormous tub that she took full advantage of. While the water ran, she removed the bandage from her head, wincing as she saw the multicolored bruise. The actual wound was a lot smaller than she thought it was, and the swelling had already gone done a fair amount, but she knew it would be a while before it was gone completely. Until then, the phony racquetball accident excuse would have to suffice.

She drew the bath, undressed slowly, and stepped into the tub. She tried to make her mind a blank and just relax and enjoy the warm water, but the tub held vivid memories of her and Tina. Many times, they had sat in the water, talking until the water ran cold, then dried each other off and made passionate love. Maya could almost see Tina sitting across from her in the tub, eyes closed, with that contented half-smile she always had on her face when she was in relaxation mode.

Maya treasured these times the most; she loved to gaze at and admire Tina's body. Tina had ceaseless complaints about her body, the sag in her breasts, the stretch marks that never went away after she had her daughter, the ass that would never be tight enough for her liking, no matter how many hours she ran or worked out. Maya would listen to none of it, she loved it all. But Tina was more than that. She was a mentor, someone Maya could talk to about the jealousy of her fellow officers, the rampant sexism she experienced, the endless, soul-numbing paperwork, not to mention trying to work within a system that sometimes seemed constructed for the benefit of the very criminals she tried to bring to justice. Being a detective was nothing at all like she thought it would be, and very soon she became disillusioned and unhappy.

Then she met Tina and everything changed. They only saw each other a couple of times a week at most, and then only for two or three hours at a time, but those times filled Maya's soul and gave her the drive to continue for another day. The job became bearable, at times even enjoyable. The apartment went from just somewhere she lay her head to a love nest where she and her lover could be safe and alone. Life finally had meaning with Tina in it. She heard what Tina repeated again and again —that her family was most important and she would never leave them, but Maya knew despite what Tina said, one day she would come to her senses and see she could only be truly happy if they were together. And so, she lived in hope, existing from one brief encounter with Tina to the other until the day when they could be together.

Now, that hope was gone.

The dream was dead, and she had nothing to live for. Life had become what it had been before Tina. No, even worse, because now she knew there was another side to life, a side she briefly experienced before it was cruelly snatched away from her. She realized that Tina was well and truly gone from her life, and she now had nothing besides a soul-crushing career and a soulless apartment, and she cried.

She didn't know how long she lay in the tub weeping, but the water had become cold, and goose pimples covered her arms. She was tempted to draw another bath, but it was almost time for her to get ready for her shift, plus her crying spell had made her throbbing head feel worse, and she needed to take something for the pain. She opened the medicine cabinet and rifled through it, looking for anything that would bring her some relief. As she did so, a small bottle of pills fell from the cabinet, and she caught it before it could hit the floor. The bottle had Tina's name on it. A few months ago, Maya had been plagued with insomnia, and Tina gave her the rest of a prescription of the sleeping aidAmbien.

"You know this is illegal, right? I can't accept your drugs," Maya had said jokingly.

"Fine, give it back to me then," Tina replied, trying to grab the bottle back. "If you're looking for me, I'll be the one getting a good night's sleep."

Maya laughed and held the bottle close. "Okay, okay I'll try them," she said.

And she did. The pills worked like a charm, and after a few nights, she hadn't needed them anymore. She'd put them in the medicine cabinet and hadn't given them a second thought since. She opened the bottle and emptied the pills into her hand, wondering how many of them she would have to take to sleep and never wake up. She was seriously contemplating drawing another bath and washing down a handful of pills with a few glasses of wine, when her phone rang. She snatched it up, hoping it was Tina, but the number showing was of the precinct, and before she could stop herself, out of sheer habit, she answered the call.

"Hello."

"Maya, it's Frank. I got a body for you. Take down this address."

"Sarge, I don't start for another hour."

Maya heard the veteran sergeant sigh. "Maya, don't give me a hard time, okay? I need you on this. I got no one else."

Maya owed the desk sergeant a lot. He was one of the few who didn't oppose her promotion, and he often spoke up for her when the other officers gave her a hard time.

"Okay, Sarge, no problem," she said.

She took down the address, then hung up the phone.

"Soon," she said to the pills before she put them back in the medicine cabinet and prepared to go to work.

#

CHAPTER TWENTY-SEVEN

Deepa

"Are you sure you don't need anything else done?" Deepa asked.

"No, Dee, I think we're okay," Kristin said.

"All right," she said. "Goodbye."

"Are you okay?" Bianca asked.

"I am," she lied.

"Well, I'm not," Bianca said, rubbing her temple. "If you need to talk, just call me or Kristin, okay?"

She nodded and turned to leave, but Bianca hugged her tightly. Kristin joined them. Then Gloria and the four women stood embracing one another.

"Are you sure you're okay, sweetheart?" Gloria asked when Deepa turned to leave. "You look a little pale."

"I am okay," Deepa lied again. "Please don't worry about me."

The last thing she wanted to do was leave. Now that the ordeal was over, it was fast beginning to feel like a bad dream and not something that had actually happened to her. The terror she'd felt had largely subsided, but still she didn't want to leave the safety of the company of these women to venture out into the world. Still,, she smiled bravely and walked out the door.

Outside, things seemed normal, but the past few hours had been so completely divorced from anything in her experience that she would not have been surprised if an alien spaceship hovered menacingly above the town, or the cat that sat on the sidewalk suddenly opened its mouth and began singing an aria. None of that happened; the world was completely ordinary, free of crazy, raging women bent on murder. The night was warm, and neighborhood children played a loud game of basketball down the street. Fireflies were beginning to sparkle, and the smell of barbecue was in the air. Deepa mentally embraced the complete normality of the suburban summer evening, wrapping it like a cloak around her mind, hoping it would help to keep the small nugget of terror she still felt from growing any larger. Her car was still blue, it started like always, the radio came on, still tuned to the 90's R&B station she enjoyed. The car moved when she put her foot on the accelerator, and the kids down the street parted when she approached and began their game anew as soon as she passed.

The tears began when she was about halfway home. They didn't start slowly and build, but came all at once in a sudden salty deluge that caught her by surprise. Vision obscured, she carefully pulled her car over, laid her head on the steering wheel, and wept bitterly.

She hadn't thought herself capable of violence until today, but she had unthinkingly assaulted Laura, the same as the other women. Her stomach heaved as she remembered stomping on her in a frenzied blood lust she had never felt before. All her life, she thought herself to be a civilized person, immune to the call of violence. Decades of education and refinement had gone out the window in a few seconds, and now she had no idea who she was.

She dried her tears and started the car up again, and in a few minutes, she pulled into her driveway. She checked her face to make sure that no one would be able to tell she had been crying, then plastered a fake smile on and went inside.

"Hello, everyone," Deepa said. As usual, Hanif and his father were engrossed in a cricket match and neither turned to greet or even look at her. The tray tables were out and laden with boxes from a nearby Indian restaurant.

"Hi, Mommy," Anima said, running to her.

"Hello, my love," Deepa said. She knelt and hugged her daughter tightly. "How are you?"

"I'm good, Mommy. I watched cricket with Daddy and Grandpa."

"That's great. Are you ready for bed?"

"Yes, can you tuck me in, please?"

"Okay. Go kiss your dad and grandfather goodnight."

Anima did as she was told, then ran to her room, Deepa in tow. Deepa tucked her tired daughter in, then turned on her night-light. She wished Anima were still at the bedtime-story stage. But since learning to read, she much preferred to read on her own, so Deepa didn't have an excuse to delay the inevitable storm from her husband and father-in-law. She took a deep breath and mentally prepared herself as she walked back into the family room, where the men were still watching the match.

"Where have you been, Deepa?" Hanif asked. He muted the television and turned around to face her.

"I . . . I . . ."

"We had to order takeout food from a restaurant," Anuj said, spitting out the word *restaurant* as if it were dirty. Anuj believed that the only good food was food made in the home by a woman's hands. He only consented to go to a restaurant on the most special of occasions, and even then, he incessantly complained about everything, from the seasonings to the silverware.

"We expected you home hours ago. We didn't have a choice but to eat from that place. It was very inconvenient," Hanif said. He gave her a nasty look then turned the sound back up on the television. "Clean up these containers."

Complaints aired and nasty looks given, the men turned their attention back to their cricket match. Deepa shook with rage as she walked into the kitchen, got a trash bag, then returned to the family room, where the men cheered as their team scored. Miraculously, they had managed to make iced tea to enjoy along with their dinner, and the mostly-empty pitcher stood among the takeout containers. It was a heavy, brass thing that was part of a set they had received as a wedding present. She picked it up, liking the stout weight of it in her hand, and imagined herself lifting it high then bringing it down hard to connect with the back of her husband's head then on her father-in-law's gray head.

Just minutes ago, the memory of violence she had committed literally made her sick to her stomach. But now the thought of committing violence again, and against her husband and father-in-law, no less, gave her a strange peace. That sense of peace gave her courage, and before she realized what she was doing, she snatched up the remote control and turned the television off.

Instantly, the men pivoted in their seats, eyes flashing, faces dark with anger.

"Deepa, what are you doing? Turn the television on right now!" Hanif demanded.

"Not until you hear what I have to say," she said.

"I said, turn it back on. Right now!" Hanif said. He rose and took a step toward her, and she flung the remote control hard against the nearest wall, where it broke into several pieces.

"What did you do?" Hanif said. He looked like a little boy witnessing the destruction of his favorite toy.

Deepa approached her husband and poked a finger into his bony chest. Hanif took a step back, shocked.

"You didn't ask me where I was, or if I was okay," Deepa said. "I could have been dead by the side of the road for all you knew, but all you cared about was that I wasn't here to cook your damn dinner."

Hanif looked aghast. He looked to his father as if searching for an answer from him.

"Why are you looking at your father? You're a grown man. Speak for yourself!" Deepa demanded.

Embarrassed, Hanif puffed himself up. "That's right. I am your husband. Now stop this foolishness."

"This is not foolishness, and I will not stop!" Deepa pounded a fist on a tray table, sending glasses and takeout containers flying. "I work just as hard as you do, but you expect me to come home and do everything in this house. I am your wife, not your damn slave."

The anger rose up inside her, and Deepa poked her finger in her husband's chest again for emphasis. Hanif took another step back, almost tripping over the ottoman his father still rested his feet on.

"It wouldn't be so bad if you would show some appreciation once in a while," she said. "But neither of you even dream of saying please or thank you. Do you think I am a robot, Hanif? Do you think I don't have feelings? You just declared that you are my husband, so then treat me like a husband should treat a wife. With love and respect!"

Hanif glared at her, his mouth open in shock.

"And if you don't love me," she said as she began to cry, "then at least show me respect so our daughter can see the right way that a man should treat his wife."

Hanif recoiled as if he had been slapped.

"Anima? What about her? What do you mean?"

"Yes, what do you mean?" Anuj piped up for the first time, indignant. "We love her. We certainly don't mistreat her."

Deepa laughed. "You love her? Do you really?" Deepa asked. "Do you want her to be treated the way you both treat me? How would you like her husband to treat her like a slave, and show her no love or appreciation for her hard work? Do you want her husband to not even give her the courtesy of saying good morning or good night to her?"

Suddenly all the anger drained out of Deepa and she began to cry harder. "Do you want her to feel unloved and unwanted and unappreciated by the men in her life every single day?"

Hanif's face went pale and he sat down. His mouth opened, but no words came out. And for long moments, they all sat in silence, letting Deepa's words sink in. Finally, Deepa picked up her car keys and walked out of the house. She had no idea where she was going, and she didn't know if what she had done was right or wrong, but she knew she needed to get away from this house for a while.

She peeled out of the driveway, narrowly missing Hanif's car, and sped off down the block. For years she had fantasized about telling her husband off, but even thinking about putting Hanif in his place brought on a fear and anxiety that took long minutes to shake. Now, as she sped through town having done the thing she'd dreamed of, she found there was no fear or anxiety. Her heart beat wildly, not out of fear, but exhilaration. She turned the radio on to Mary J. Blige singing about how she was just fine. Deepa laughed out loud when she heard the song, it was one of her favorites, and fit her mood perfectly. She turned up the radio full blast and sang along. She got more of the words wrong than than she did right, but she didn't care, she was just fine.

As she sang she drove past a new coffee shop, Sacred Grounds, that had opened up a few months before. It seemed to be one of those new hip places that only actors and artists would feel comfortable in, so she had never tried it. But on whim, she made a U-turn and headed back toward it.

Inside, the coffee shop was not much different from what she'd envisioned, and she loved it immediately. Colorful, handwritten menus on chalkboards competed for attention with loud posters decorating the walls. The space was much bigger than it looked from the outside, and everywhere people lounged on comfortable-looking overstuffed couches and armchairs or at small tables, drinking from enormous mugs.

She joined the line to place her order, slightly nervous about what to select, since the strongest thing she ever drank was tea. Finally she picked out a delicious-sounding drink, called a mocha, and at the last minute bought an enormous slice of cake to go with it. She was certain the combination of the caffeine and the sugar would keep up her for days, but she didn't care. She was just fine!

The coffee shop was getting more crowded by the minute, but she managed to find a small table in a corner and sat down with her coffee and cake. There were magazines strewn about, and she picked one up to browse as she ate, but barely read a word, completely absorbed in people watching. She took a forkful of her cake, then another, and very soon the slice that looked so enormous a few minutes ago was almost gone. She was about to eat the last bit of cake when a tall man approached her table.

"Hi, Dr. Dee," the man said.

Surprised, and at a loss for words, Deepa swallowed her cake quickly. She looked to see a tall African American man smiling down at her.

"It's me, Winston," the man said. "You take your car to my shop. Blue Beemer, right?"

She had no idea why, but she was suddenly nervous and was sure that her blushing cheeks stood out like beacons. "Oh, hello," she said.

"Is anyone sitting here?" he asked, pointing to the empty seat at her table.

She felt her cheeks redden even more. "No," she said nervously. "No one is sitting here."

"Do you mind?"

"Uh . . . no. Please sit."

Winston smiled again and sat down. She looked around and saw that while she was absorbed in her cake and coffee, the shop had filled up; all the tables and seats were taken. There was now a small makeshift stage in one corner of the shop, and a young man with the longest hair she had ever seen on a male was busy installing a microphone stand and speakers.

"It's good to see you, Dr. Dee," Winston said. "You haven't been in the shop for a while. Car running okay?"

"Oh, yes, it's running very well, thank you."

Winston sipped his coffee. "I don't know if you knew, but my sister was a patient of yours. She always raved about you."

"She was? What was her name?" Deepa asked, glad to have a subject that would distract her from Winston's dazzling smile.

"Miriam. Miriam Buckley."

Deepa smiled. Miriam had been one of her favorite patients. Married in her late thirties, Miriam and her husband tried in vain for a few years to conceive before she came to see Deepa. After a few failed attempts using various methods, Miriam had finally gotten pregnant. Deepa had cried right along with Miriam the day she gave her the happy news. Not long afterward, Miriam's husband received a job offer in California and they'd moved across the country, but she still sent Deepa pictures of the baby from time to time.

"I remember Miriam! Her baby is so beautiful. How is she doing?"

"She's walking already. Can you believe it? I was just in California visiting them. Want to see pictures?"

"Oh yes, please."

Winston pulled out his phone and scooted his chair closer to Deepa, and for the next few minutes, she oohed and ahhed over images of the baby, trying hard not to get distracted by Winston's scent and his beautiful smile, which he flashed often.

He was about at the end of the photo album of his trip when one of the coffee shop employees tapped him on the shoulder.

"Winston, you're up first, okay?"

"Sure, Jerry. Thanks a lot."

"It's poetry night," he said when he saw Deepa's puzzled look. "That's why it's so packed in here. Poets from all over the state come here to read their stuff."

"You're a poet?"

Winston smiled. "I don't know if I can be called a poet yet, but I'm trying."

Just then the man with the very long hair tapped the microphone to get everyone's attention.

"Hey, everybody," he said. "Welcome and thank you for coming out. We have a lot of talent in the room tonight. We're gonna start with Willows's own, a crowd favorite here at Sacred Grounds, and a hell of a nice guy. Give it up for my man, Winston."

Winston rose and made his way to the stage, a well-worn notebook in his hand. He adjusted the microphone, looked out over the audience, and smiled. Deepa blushed again at seeing his smile, but as she looked around the room, she noticed that almost every woman had a similar reaction.

"What's up, y'all?" Winston said. "I'm gonna read this poem for you. It doesn't have a title."

The room went quiet as Winston began to read. Deepa didn't know much about poetry, the little she'd read was what they taught in school, but as Winston began to read, she resolved to read more. His poem was about love and family and loneliness. He talked about life and work and coming home to an empty house, but still being happy and content with his lot. The poem was long. It took a few minutes for him to read it, but for that time, the audience was mesmerized. When he was done, he looked up and smiled, and the audience broke out into applause.

He left the stage, stopping here and there to shake hands and receive compliments, then returned to his seat. He seemed exhilarated, as if he had just run a long and grueling race.

"So? What do you think?" he asked.

"Wow," she said. "It was . . .wow."

"I guess that's good," he said with a smile.

"It was amazing. I would never have thought that you . . ."

"You would never have thought the big Black man that fixes cars for a living had a soul?"

"No, no . . . I'm sorry, that's not what I meant," Deepa said quickly, wanting to kick herself.

"No, it's okay, Dr. Dee," he said. "I get it all the time. We put these labels on one another without knowing anything about the person. We're all guilty of that, don't you think?"

Deepa nodded, still embarrassed.

"Speaking of getting to know someone, your name is Deepa, right?" he asked. "I feel silly calling you Dr. Dee all night."

"How did you know?"

"From my files at the garage."

"Ohhhhh. Yes It's Deepa," she said. "But you can call me Dee, it's okay."

"No. Your mom didn't name you Dee, did she? It's Deepa, and that's what I'll call you. That's a beautiful name. What does it mean?"

"It means light," Deepa said, astounded. In her entire life, no one had ever asked her that question.

"Deepa," he repeated, rolling the word around in his mouth like he was tasting a new wine. She wanted to smile at his pronunciation, his emphasis was in all the wrong places, but she loved the way it sounded in his deep voice.

"So, I've never seen you in here before. You're not just here for the excellent carrot cake, are you?"

"No. I'm not," she confessed.

Later on, if you had asked her if she had meant to tell this stranger the details of her run in with Hanif and Anuj, she would have said certainly not, but that is just what she did. The man with the long hair introduced another poet, and they spent the next hours talking and listening to poetry. After the last poet performed, the MC brought all the poets back onto the stage for a round of applause, then the audience began to file out.

"Walk you to your car?" Winston asked.

"Sure," she said.

"So, did you have fun?"

"Oh yes! I did."

"Well, we're here every Saturday night. You should come some other time."

"I will," Deepa said.

"Ahh, there she is. Nice to see you, honey," Winston said when they arrived at her car. "She looks good. You're taking good care of her."

Deepa smiled. "She's doing well. She has a good doctor."

They stood together awkwardly for a moment and Deepa's heart beat wildly. Would he try to kiss her? What would she do if he did? It was obvious she was married—she had a ring on, after all.

"Deepa, I'm going to give you my number. Please text me when you get home, okay? I want to make sure you made it back safely."

He read the number to her, and she added it to her contacts, wishing that he had kissed her instead.

"I had fun," he said. "Thank you."

"I had a great time too," she put out her hand awkwardly to shake his, but instead he hugged her. She was surprised, but she hugged him back, instantly aroused by the feel of his body against hers and the woodsy, masculine scent of him. The arousal quickly morphed into a warm glow that spread through her entire body. Entranced by the feeling, she held him close for several beats longer than she should have, but she didn't care. She knew she should feel weird or embarrassed or awkward, anything but the safe, contented feeling she had being held in Winston's arms. She didn't know if she would ever see him again, or feel another man's body against hers except her husband, so she tried to memorize the scent of him, the feel of her head on his chest, the press of her arms against the hard muscles of his back. Winston seemed surprised. His body tensed for a moment but quickly relaxed. He seemed to sense that she needed this closeness, and he melded his body closer into hers. Behind them, the coffee shop's lights went off, and the last of the staff headed to their cars, oblivious to the two people holding onto one another in the parking lot.

After what seemed an eternity, she let Winston go. She felt strangely emotional and dared not say anything, not trusting herself to speak in such a state.

"That was nice," Winston said.

She nodded and smiled.

"I have to go," she said a moment later, when she finally found her voice again.

"Me too," he said, but neither but made a move.

"Hey," he said, "I read a new poem here just about every Saturday night. I'll be here next week. Will I see you?"

"I don't know," she answered. "I will try."

Smiling like an awkward teenager, Winston opened her car door and she got in.

"Don't forget to text me when you get home, okay?"

"I will," she promised.

Minutes later, Deepa pulled into her driveway and looked up at the bedroom window, breathing a sigh of relief when she saw there were no lights on. Hanif was sure to be furious with her for telling him off earlier, not to mention for being out so late. She was sure to hear an earful from him tomorrow, but right now, the last thing she needed to do was argue. It had been an eventful day, to say the least, and she needed to rest and try to get her mind around all that had happened. She'd spent the drive home trying to relive the feeling of Winston holding her. She'd had sex with her husband many times, but the moments she had spent in Winston's arms was the most intimacy she had ever experienced. They hadn't even kissed, but if he had kissed her, she knew for certain she would have kissed him back. And if he had suggested she come home with him, she would have gone and even now be in his bed. When she fantasized about being with another man, a part of her had always felt guilty about betraying Hanif, even if it was only in her mind. Now that she had done it—sort of—there was no guilt, only a quiet elation and a hope that it would happen again.

She picked up her phone and sent a text to Winston to let him know she was home, smiling the entire time. This stranger, this man she had just met, had cared enough to ask her to tell him that she had gotten home safely, something her husband had never cared enough to do, not even once in all their years together.

Moments after she sent the text, her phone rang. She smiled and her heart beat faster, convinced that the call was from Winston, but when she looked at the iPhone display, it was an unfamiliar number that lit up the screen. Disappointed it wasn't Winston calling, but concerned that one of her patients might have gone into labor, she quickly answered the call.

"Hello?"

"Hi, Dr. Dee. It's Maya . . . from the party earlier. I'm sorry to call so late. Listen, I have some news."

"Oh. Hello. News? What news?"

"It's about Laura."

Deepa's heart skipped a beat. She was scared that after the beating she had taken, Laura would go to the police, but Maya had assured her that even if Laura did—and she was sure that she wouldn't—she would make sure the police knew what they did to her was in self-defense. Now Maya was calling her, which could only mean that the worst had happened, and the police were on their way to arrest her.

"Dr. Dee, are you there? Did I lose you?"

"I am here."

"Good. I'm at Laura's house."

A minute later, Dee hung up the phone, stunned. She walked toward the house slowly, still trying to process what Maya had told her.

Laura had committed suicide. Out of all the possible outcomes, Deepa had to admit she had not seen that one coming.

She opened the front door, still deep in thought, not noticing that her father-in-law sat on the couch. He rose, startling her badly.

"I'm sorry, Daughter," he began, which puzzled her, since as long as she could remember, he had never called her that.

She had been concerned about having to deal with Hanif. She had never imagined Anuj would be up and waiting for her. She'd never seen him be up past nine o'clock for as long as she had known him. She took a deep breath, steeling herself for a tongue lashing.

Anuj fingered the hem of his shirt nervously. "Daughter, I am ashamed of myself," he said. "If my Reeva were alive, she would have gotten up and cheered for you this evening."

"What do you mean?" Deepa asked, shocked.

Anuj chuckled. "What you did earlier today reminded me of the many, many times my wife told me off. As you know, she was a very kind and loving woman, but she also was not a woman to ever hold her tongue. She told me off many times, and there was not one time I can remember when I did not deserve it. Like I deserved it today."

Anuj took her hand.

"I think Reeva's spirit was here, cheering you on. She loved you very much. She always said you were much too good for our son."

Deepa nodded, crying and smiling at the same time. Her late mother-in-law had been that very, very rare Indian mother who did not think the sun rose and set in her son's eyes. She loved Hanif and her husband and had been devoted to them, but she didn't turn a blind eye to their shortcomings and never hesitated to put either of them in their place when needed.

"I tried to sleep tonight," Anuj said, "but I could not. I heard Reeva's voice in my head, and she was quite angry with me. If she were here, she would never tolerate our treatment of you. You were quite right. We treat you very badly. I am ashamed of myself, and I apologize. I cannot speak for my son, but I promise you I will try to do better. You took me into your home, and you treat me with the same love and respect you would give to your own father, and for that I am grateful.

Thank you, Daughter."

Deepa profoundly touched and surprised by the old man's words, searched for the right response, but words escaped her. "Thank you, Baba," was all she said.

"Now, I will go to bed," Anuj said, smiling. "Hopefully my wife will let me sleep this time."

"I'm sure she will, Baba. Good night."

"Good night, Daughter," he said, shuffling off to his bedroom.

Deepa watched him go. This day had been one revelation after another. If you had asked her just five minutes ago if this day could hold any more surprises, she would have said certainly not, but how wrong she would have been.

While she was talking to Anuj she had received a text, and she opened it, beaming when she saw that it came from Winston.

You made my night, Deepa. I hope I'll see you next week.

Upstairs, Hanif slept soundly, and she slipped into the bathroom and undressed quickly, then read Winston's message again. She began to use her phone to navigate to one of her favorite porn videos, but stopped because she didn't need to. Reading Winston's text and thinking of the feel of her body on his aroused her much more than any simple video ever could. She picked up her blouse and inhaled. His scent was still there. Faint, but enough to get her heart racing. She put her hand between her legs and imagined what his big hand would feel like down there. The thought excited her and she moaned, not trying to silence herself as she usually did. She touched herself in the spots she wanted him to touch, and in seconds, the most enormous orgasm she had ever had shook her body, leaving her sweaty and weak. Exhausted, she ran a bath and sank into the warm water.

When she had her strength back, she grabbed her phone and responded to Winston's text.

Yes, she typed. *I will be there. See you then.*

#

CHAPTER TWENTY-EIGHT

Jessica

"What have we done?" Jessica asked.

Most of the women had already gone; only Bianca, Gloria, and Jessica remained. Jessica stayed to help clean up, but unlike the others, who seemed to get over their shock fairly quickly and were busy helping to straighten the room, Jessica sat in an easy chair, wringing her hands, still in disbelief.

"It's okay, Jessica," Kristin said, her tone betraying her annoyance with the question. For the past thirty minutes, Jessica asked the same question over and over again in the same shell-shocked tone of voice. They had been concerned at first, but it quickly became tiresome.

Jessica seemed not to notice the tone in Kristin's voice.

"Girls, what have we . . ."

"Jessica!" Bianca shouted. "Enough!"

"Have some patience with her, dear," Gloria said. "It's been a challenging day for all of us."

Bianca ignored her mother-in-law and squatted in front of Jessica.

"Jessica, that's enough. If you're not going to help clean up, then maybe you should go home."

"You kicked her," Jessica said in an accusing tone. "You kicked Laura."

"No, I didn't."

"Liar! You kicked her. I saw you."

"I didn't kick her. I stomped that bitch. I stomped the fuck out of her." She pointed to Kristin and Gloria. "And so did they."

Tears began to flow down Jessica's face. "You hurt her. Why did you do that?"

"If we didn't do what we did, that woman would have killed us. Don't you see that?"

Jessica shook her head like a petulant child.

"No, she wouldn't have hurt us. If we just had patience and talked to her, she would have worked it out. Once she knew we cared, she would have—"

Bianca rolled her eyes. "Oh, so you think all she needed was a therapy session, huh? A good cry with the girls, then we would have all laughed about it while we drank sangria? No, Jessica, that would never have happened. That bitch was crazy."

"Don't call her that! That's so insulting. You don't know what she's been through. She lost her family. Her husband left her for that whore, Veronica. How would you—"

"Hey!" Kristin said suddenly. She was placing glasses on a tray, but she dropped the tray and glared at Jessica. "Don't call her a whore!"

"That's what she is, isn't she?"

"Why?" Kristin asked. Her face went red and she put her hands on her hips. "Just because she dated a married man? That does not make her a whore."

Bianca and Gloria exchanged puzzled looks at Kristin's reaction.

"Okay, ladies, just calm down. There's been enough fighting for one day," Gloria said.

Kristin shot Jessica a dirty look, then picked up the tray and walked into the kitchen.

"Listen, Jessica, let's just try and forget this all ever happened, okay?" Bianca said.

"I can't. I just can't. What we did to Laura was awful. She was just sad. It was all just talk. Don't you see that? She was so sad."

Bianca chuckled. "If you think that, then you're as crazy as she was."

"Stop calling her that!" Jessica said. "Everything she had was taken away from her. How would you feel if that happened to you?"

"Maybe you're right. Maybe she was sad," Gloria said. "But she was angry, as well. She was so very angry."

"She just wanted someone to listen to her, to understand what she was feeling," Jessica said. "If we tried to help her, things would have turned out differently."

Bianca laughed again. "I guess you don't remember that Maya was trying to talk to her when she got knocked out. Or did you forget?"

Jessica shook her head again. "I tried to stop you," she said as more tears flowed. "I tried to stop you, but no one listened to me. You were like . . . animals."

"This is a waste of time," Bianca said. "I have no patience for this shit. I'm done trying to make this chick see reason." She picked up a tray of food and walked to the kitchen, leaving Gloria alone with Jessica.

"Look at me, dear," Gloria said in a stern voice, handing Jessica tissues. "We were all scared. Very scared. We thought she was going to kill us."

Jessica shook her head, but Gloria held firm.

"Yes, Jessica. She would have. She would have murdered Veronica, then you were next. You heard how she insulted you all night. We did what we had to do. I know you don't like it, but at least you can take comfort in the fact you tried to stop us."

Jessica dabbed her face with the tissue and said nothing.

"I understand you're upset, sweetheart. This has been a difficult day for all of us. Maybe you should just go home. Some time with your family might be just what you need to feel better."

At the mention of her family, Jessica's weeping began afresh as she thought of all she had revealed about herself and her marriage to this group of strangers.

"Don't worry about the things you shared here today," Gloria said as if reading her mind. "We all said things maybe we shouldn't have. The good thing is this can be a clean slate for you. Just go home to your man and be the wife he needs."

Jessica wiped her tears. "How do I do that?

"Is your husband a good man?" Gloria asked.

"Yes. He is."

"Do you love him?"

"Um," she said, looking down at her hands, "I don't know. I should love him, but sometimes the feelings get all mixed up. I mean, how can he love someone like me? There must be something wrong with him and I, well, I don't know if I can trust someone like that with my heart."

"Okay then. Do you love the home and the life you have together?"

Jessica smiled through her tears. "I do. I really do."

"Then here's how you do it," Gloria said. "You go back to the home you and your husband made and look at it. I mean, *really* look at it. See what there is to lose. I don't mean just the things in your house, the 'stuff.' Your home isn't the appliances or the televisions or the furniture. It's all the memories you made there. Think about the time you first saw the house, the first night you spent in it, the time you brought your baby home, all the holidays, all the birthdays. It's everything. Do you want to lose that?"

Jessica shook her head.

"Then go home and fight for it. Go be the woman he wants. If he wants to make love ten times a day, do it. If he likes cakes, cookies, and pies, learn how to bake. If he wants to sit undisturbed all day Sunday and watch football games, make him something to eat, chill his beer, and leave him alone."

"But what does he have to do for me? What do I get?"

Gloria threw up her hands in exasperation. "I'm going to ask you again, Jessica. Is your husband a good man? Does he work hard every day? Does he provide for you and your daughter?"

"Yes, he does."

"Then that's what you get."

"What? I deserve more than that."

"Does he run around town with floozies? Any kids on the side?"

"No," Jessica said. "Nothing like that. Believe me, I checked."

"Then you have so much more than many of us have. Myself included. I don't understand what more you could ask for? You have a hardworking man who provides for his family. You just confessed you didn't love this man, but you say he loves you. And even though he *knows* how you feel, he doesn't cheat on you. I ask you again: What more do you want?"

Jessica hung her head. "I don't know. But I feel like there should be more. I deserve more. Don't I?"

Gloria sat up. Her face lost its compassionate look and became hard and stern. "I was hoping you would understand me, Jessica. But I see it's time to stop sugarcoating things."

"What are you talking about?"

"You don't *deserve* anything, you stupid woman."

"You can't talk to me like that!" Jessica said, her face reddening.

"It's about time somebody did," Gloria said. "I've known so many women like you over the years, and for the life of me, I can't understand what makes you tick. You expect so much, yet give nothing and have the nerve to talk about what *you* deserve. Oh please! Let me tell you something your mother should have taught you—you don't deserve a damn thing! No one does. Everything we get in this world, we have to earn. And guess what? You have to give something to get something. You're a sponge, Jessica, a parasite that expects to get, get, get but never gives because you have nothing *to* give. Therefore, you get nothing."

Jessica recoiled as if she had been slapped. "Why are you saying these things to me?"

"You need to hear them, so you'll wake up. Here's some more truth. The feeling you're missing is the love you should have for yourself. That's why you can't accept or trust your husband's love."

"That's not true. You're wrong," Jessica said, shaking her head. "You're wrong."

"No, dear. I'm right. Go home now. Go home and try to figure out how to love yourself. Go home and fix your relationship. If not for your husband, then do it for your daughter."

Gloria leaned over into Jessica's face until they were almost nose to nose.

"And if you can't do that," she said, "then get out of their lives and make room for someone who can actually love them."

Jessica's jaw dropped. "I . . .I . . ."

Gloria got to her feet. "Go home," she said again. Then she picked up an empty pitcher and walked out of the room, leaving Jessica alone with her tears.

Shocked, Jessica wanted to scream at Gloria that she was wrong, that she loved herself plenty, thank you very much.

Instead, she said nothing.

Then she walked toward the door on unsteady legs, opened it, and turned and looked back at the room where so much had happened. It was mostly cleaned up. There was almost no sign of the carnage, both mental and physical, that had occurred inside it.

"You're wrong," Jessica said to the empty room. "I deserve more." She slammed the door and walked out to her car.

Jessica thought about all Gloria said as she drove home, mentally kicking herself as all the retorts and rebuttals she might have said came to her much too late.

"Who the hell does that bitch think she is?" she asked,

slamming her palm on the steering wheel, inadvertently sounding the horn and startling the elderly man and his equally elderly dog slowly crossing the street.

Gloria was full of it, but she did get one thing right. She had to fix her marriage. Duane was a good man. She needed to treat him better. He didn't run around town with a young girlfriend like Tina's husband, or have a history of screwing around like Gloria's husband or neglected her like Deepa's husband. And she definitely didn't want to end up like Laura, whose husband, David, was faithful for most of their marriage until the day came when he'd had enough.

She called Duane and got his voice mail. Duane and Brianne were spending the day at an amusement park, but they should have been on the way home by now, and he was fanatical about not using his phone while driving with their daughter in the car.

She glanced at the clock on the dashboard. She would have liked Duane to have a home-cooked meal, but there wasn't enough time before they arrived home, so she stopped at their favorite pizzeria, got them all their favorites, then rushed back with the food. Once home, she set the table, put the food in the oven to keep warm, then ran to take a shower. In their bedroom, she searched her dresser for a lingerie set she bought long ago but never wore. She held it against her body, liking the look of the color against her skin but hating just about everything else about it. The plunging neckline would expose her huge breasts, the short length would expose her fat thighs, and the sheer material would expose everything else. She envisioned how she would look wearing it, and, disgusted, she opened the drawer and threw it back in, but heard Gloria's voice in her head.

" . . . you're a sponge, Jessica, a parasite that expects to get, get, get but never gives."

"Fuck you, you old bitch," Jessica said, retrieving the lingerie from the drawer. She didn't feel any better about it than she did a few seconds ago, but she knew Duane would appreciate it, and this evening would be for him. She brought dinner for her man, but she would be the dessert.

She left the lingerie laid out on the bed, got dressed, and hurried downstairs just in time to see Duane walk in the door holding the sleeping Brianne in one arm and an enormous stuffed animal in another.

"Here, honey, let me help you," Jessica said, taking the stuffed toy.

"Thanks," Duane said. "I'll bring Brianne upstairs."

Something in Duane's stiff and formal tone set off an alarm bell in Jessica's mind, but she silenced it, attributing it to the argument they'd had. *Once he sees the food and then me in the lingerie, he'll feel better*, she thought.

She put Brianne's stuffed animal in the living room, then took the food out of the oven and plated it. She grabbed a bottle of Duane's favorite beer from the fridge and poured it into a glass.

"How was the park?" she asked Duane when he returned downstairs.

"We had a great time," he said.

"How was the party?" he asked.

"It was . . . eventful," she said. "I don't want to talk about that right now. Sit down. I got you dinner."

Duane seemed reluctant, but he sat down and Jessica put the food in front of him. She made a plate for herself then sat across from him.

"You're not eating. Are you okay?" she asked.

"I'm fine. Listen . . . we have to talk."

"I know, Duane. Listen, I'm—"

Before she could finish, he pulled a large envelope from his back pocket and handed it to her.

Jessica's blood ran cold, and she stared at it as if it were poisonous.

"What's that?"

"What you've wanted."

"What I wanted?"

Jessica reluctantly took the envelope and pulled out a thick sheaf of papers all on law firm letterhead.

"Enclosed please find an original and two copies of a complaint for divorce . . ."

Her heart beat faster and she looked at her husband in shock. "Divorce? I never said I wanted this."

"You didn't have the courage to say it, but you certainly showed it. Actions speak louder than words, Jessica."

"But I don't want this. I don't want this at all."

She read the papers again, as if willing the words to change in the scant few seconds since she read them.

"Duane, please can't we talk?"

"Talk about what, Jessica? I've been trying to talk to you for a very long time, and all you've done is ignore me or blow me off. I said on the phone the other day I was done, and I meant it."

Jessica said nothing as the tears flowed down her face and onto the papers.

"We can do this the easy way or the hard way," he said. "If you read the papers, you'll see my lawyer has divided everything. I think it's pretty fair. I'll leave, and you can stay here in the house with the baby."

"Leave the house? Where are you going to live?"

"Don't worry about me. What you need to do is get an attorney to look over those papers. Let's not draw this out any more than we have to, okay?"

"Draw this out? This is our life you're talking about, Duane, not some game. Isn't it important enough to try to save?"

Duane laughed out loud. "Wow! Talk about irony. Aren't those almost the exact same words I said to you before you called me a bitch?"

"I'm sorry, Duane, okay? I'm sorry! I didn't mean that. I wasn't in a good place."

"I meant what I said. I'm done. There's nothing else to talk about. I packed a bag already and booked a hotel room for a few days until my new place is ready. I told Brianne I was going away for a few days for work, but soon you and I are going to have to have a conversation with her."

Duane continued speaking, but Jessica heard nothing. She stared at the papers in her hand and thought about Laura and what she'd been driven to do. She understood her now more than ever. The anger built in her, and her breath came harder and faster.

"Jessica! Are you listening to me?"

Jessica snapped her out of her rage-induced stupor and flung the divorce papers to the floor.

Duane sighed. "Okay," he said, picking up his phone and keys. "I see you're not ready to have this conversation, so I'm gonna go."

"Get out! Get the hell out," she shouted. "I bet you're leaving your family so you can be with some skinny whore."

Duane's face darkened, and he looked so angry Jessica took a step back, fearing she had gone too far.

"You have some goddamn nerve!" he said through gritted teeth. "There is no side chick, much less a skinny one. I've never been with a skinny chick in my whole damn life, and you know that! You think I don't know you went snooping through my phone and my computer? What did you find? Not a damn thing, because there is nothing *to* find. I probably should have found me a side piece a long time ago, but my problem is I love my wife and I wanted our marriage to work."

"Yeah right, you have some whore out there and you're just—"

Duane banged his fist on the kitchen counter so hard it caused the dishes to jump.

"No, Jessica! There is no one else! I love *you*, Jessica, but I am sick and damn tired of loving a woman who doesn't love me back. So don't blame this on some nonexistent girlfriend." He pointed his finger at her. "It's *your* fault," he shouted. *You* did this. *You* killed our marriage. No one else."

Jessica wept because she knew he was right. Everything

Gloria said earlier was correct, but it didn't matter now. It was much too late to save her marriage and keep her family intact. Suddenly, she heard Gloria's voice in her head.

"You don't deserve anything, you stupid woman."

She put her hands on her ears to block it out, but the voice wouldn't be silenced.

"You don't deserve a damn thing."

"Yes, I do," she said. "I deserve more!"

"What the hell are you talking about, Jessica?" Duane asked.

"You have nothing to give. Therefore, you get nothing."

"I deserve more," she said. "I do, I do, I do."

The feeling you're missing is the love you should have for yourself. That's why you can't accept or trust your husband's love."

Suddenly, she swept the food-laden dishes off the table. They crashed to the floor sending slices of pizza, chicken wings and salad everywhere.

"Jessica, what the—"

Before Duane could finish his sentence, Jessica picked the toaster up from the counter and hurled it across the room. It smashed into the cabinets with a huge bang and pieces of toaster and shards of glass rained down onto the kitchen floor.

"And if you can't do that, then get out of their lives and make room for someone who can actually love them."

"No! Never! I deserve more!" Jessica's breath came in frantic gasps and the rage gave her tunnel vision. She picked the appliances up from the counter one by one and hurled them as hard as possible across the room. When there were no more appliances to destroy, she snatched a frying pan from its hook on the wall and began to shatter the glass of the cabinets. In a frenzy, she threw the pan across the room and heard something break, then picked up another pot and threw that one too. The destruction she had wrought so far did nothing to satisfy her rage, she had an undeniable urge to destroy everything, so she grabbed a third pot, a heavy cast-iron frying pan, and used it to bludgeon everything in sight.

"Mommy, what's going on?"

There was a lone glass left on the kitchen counter, and before she could stop herself, Jessica used the pan to hit it like a tennis ball, watching in horror as it catapulted through the air almost in slow motion and shattered against Brianne's forehead.

Brianne screamed and fell to the floor, blood pouring from the gash in her head.

Instantly, the rage evaporated from Jessica, leaving her weak and unable to move.

"Bri, I'm sorry, honey," she consoled.

"Don't touch her!" Duane hollered. He stuffed his phone in his pocket, and she realized with a start he had recorded her entire rage-induced tantrum. He grabbed a dishcloth and put it to Brianne's head. "It's okay, honey," he said to the hysterically crying little girl, dabbing her forehead with the cloth.

"Baby, I'm sorry," Jessica said, reaching out to her daughter. "It was an accident."

"I said don't touch her!" Duane called even louder as he dialed 911.

Her mind in turmoil, Jessica ran up the stairs to their bedroom. She saw the lingerie she so carefully laid out earlier and picked it up, looking at it as if it were responsible for her earlier actions, then ripped it to shreds.

Shortly after, she heard the doorbell then voices as the police and the EMTs arrived. She watched from the top of the stairs as the medics tended to Brianne's head and Duane spoke to the police. He pointed to the crumpled divorce papers on the floor before showing them the video. The police, a male and a female officer, watched the video, their faces growing more serious by the second.

The female officer said something to Duane and he pointed up the stairs. The officer approached the steps.

"Ma'am, can you come downstairs, please?" she requested.

Jessica walked slowly down to the grim-faced policewoman.

"Is my daughter okay?" Jessica asked.

"I think so, ma'am. The EMTs are checking her out now."

"Can I go see her? I want to apologize."

"You can see her in a minute, ma'am. Can we talk first?"

They walked past the kitchen on the way to the living room, and Jessica stopped and stared in shock. The oven door was shattered, as was the glass front of their microwave. Every shiny appliance that used to sit on the counter was in pieces, and the floor was a minefield of broken glass and metal. The kitchen cabinets she painstakingly picked out and took so much pride in were smashed, and a couple of them hung from hinges.

"Let's go, ma'am," the cop said, guiding her to the living room.

Jessica walked like a zombie, unable to believe the carnage she'd committed in the home she loved.

". . . the feeling you're missing is the love you should have for yourself." Gloria's words echoed in her head again.

"Ma'am, ma'am, did you hear what I said?" the officer asked in an exasperated tone. She had a notepad out and a pen in hand poised to write.

"I'm sorry. What did you say?"

"What happened here, ma'am?"

Jessica began crying. "Uh, my husband gave me papers."

"What kind of papers? Divorce?"

"Yes. I tried to talk to him and—"

"Did he threaten you? Did he physically or verbally abuse you, ma'am? Was there a physical altercation?"

Jessica shook her head. "No, no, nothing like that."

The officer made a note in her pad as she spoke. "Can you tell me what happened in the kitchen, ma'am?"

"Call me Jessica. Uh, he gave me the papers and I, uh, lost it. I can't lose my family. He can't do this."

"So he didn't hurt you in any way, ma'am? Is that what you're saying?"

"I already said he didn't. Is my daughter okay? I need to see her."

Jessica began to get up.

"Ma'am, sit down, please," she said in a no-nonsense voice. You can check on her in a minute." She made another note, then continued. "We saw the video, ma'am, and I don't think you meant to hit your daughter."

"I didn't," Jessica said, sobbing. "I didn't even see her there."

"Be that as it may, she's got a pretty good cut on her head, and your husband told us he's going to file a restraining order first thing in the morning. Based on your daughter's injury and the damage you did to your home, not to mention the video, I think there's a pretty good bet the judge will grant it."

"A what? But that's crazy. I didn't mean to hurt her!"

"Ma'am . . ."

"Duane!" Jessica shouted. "Duane, don't do this."

"Ma'am, calm down."

"Duane, please don't do this!"

"Ma'am!" the officer said louder to get her attention. "You are not helping. Calm down. You need to realize this is happening. What you're doing right now is making things worse."

"Am I under arrest?" Jessica asked.

"We're not going to arrest you, ma'am, but you should pack a bag and leave this house."

"What? You're making me leave?"

"No, ma'am, we can't make you leave. But my advice to you is to go, at least for the night. Maybe tomorrow you and your husband can speak and try to work things out, but for tonight, you should go."

"But I didn't do anything. I mean, I didn't mean to."

"Ma'am, your daughter's head has a huge cut on it, and your kitchen looks like a war zone. Your husband didn't touch you. There was no fight. You destroyed your kitchen because you lost control of yourself."

Jessica sobbed. “I didn’t mean to.”

“Things are pretty heated right now, ma’am, but like I said, maybe tomorrow you and your husband can work things out. For now, you need to leave.”

“Fine,” Jessica said. “Can I go upstairs and pack some things?”

“Go ahead, but don’t take too long.”

Jessica walked through the living room and trudged up the stairs, trying to figure out how this evening had gone so horribly, incredibly wrong. She sat on her bed among the tatters of the lingerie and put her face in her hands, wondering if this was how Laura had felt before her life had spiraled out of control.

“... get out of their lives and make room for someone who can actually love them.”

“Ma’am, we’re waiting,” the officer called from the bottom of the stairs.

“I’m coming,” she said in a small voice. She pulled a weekend bag from the closet, filled it with clothes, then took one last look at the bedroom and the life that used to be hers and walked downstairs to the waiting police officer.

#

CHAPTER TWENTY-NINE

Kristin

Kristin restlessly drifted from the kitchen to the living room and back again, looking for something to clean or put back in order, anything to occupy her restless mind. Now that everyone was gone and the events of the day had sunk in, her earlier calm was replaced by a nervous energy she couldn't shake. There was nothing to clean.

Everything had been put back in order with the help of Bianca and Gloria. She used to be so proud of this room. Every stick of furniture, every photo, and piece of artwork had special meaning, and each one had been carefully placed. Now all she saw was a space where a group of civilized women acted like animals. Her training as a mental health professional told her she needed to take the time to process what had happened, but that she was unwilling to do because it meant she would have to force herself to think about what they had done.

Desperate, she turned the television on, hoping for something to distract her mind. She flipped the channel, and suddenly an intense fight scene erupted on the huge screen. She watched in horror as one of the characters, a handsome man in a black suit, hit a large, evil-looking man with an enormous handgun, then brutally kicked him in the face, causing droplets of blood to rain across the screen in ultra-vivid high definition. Kristin had never been a big fan of action movies; the violence on the screen seemed too real and too disturbing to watch. But now that she had experienced violence firsthand, she found movies weren't even close to the real thing. Hands shaking, she pointed the remote control at the television and punched the power button repeatedly until it powered off, but the damage was done.

The violent scene somehow broke down the fragile walls she'd built around the memories, and she heard the dull thuds of her vicious kicks impacting Laura's body, then the sharp crack of a breaking rib combined with Laura's anguished cries of pain. She saw the wild looks of the other women and heard their grunts and labored breathing as they, too, rained kicks on Laura until, finally, she was still. Even then, Kristin remembered, she'd felt nothing as she gazed upon Laura's battered and bleeding body.

No, that's not true, she corrected herself.

She felt exhilarated.

In those moments of savage, merciless violence, she felt on top of the world. She hadn't cared that maybe Gloria knew about her affair with Ed. She hadn't cared that a police detective was assaulted in her home. She didn't care that they had hurt Laura badly. Nothing mattered. She saw the euphoric looks on the other women's faces and knew the very same look was mirrored on hers. In that one breathless, intoxicating moment, she reveled in the violence she had committed. She stood over the body of her vanquished enemy and let the electricity wash over her, feeling like a new person, like a brave, fearless trespasser in her own body. She had behaved like a barbarian, and God help her, she had enjoyed it. In that moment, she could run a marathon, she could lift a car, she could fly.

At the realization, her hands shook uncontrollably, and she began to cry. Her phone rang just then, the screen lighting up with a picture of her son's face.

"Hey, buddy," she said as she wiped her eyes, trying to keep her voice even and calm, thankful her son was with his father for the weekend.

"Hi, Mom. How was your party?"

"It was great, honey. We had a lot of fun." She cleared her throat.

"Why do you sound weird?" he asked.

"Weird? No, honey, I'm okay. It was a long day. I'm just a little tired." She smiled even as she told the lie. She loved how very perceptive Lucas was of her moods. He always seemed to know when she was upset, no matter what effort she made to hide her emotions.

"Did you do anything fun with Dad?" she asked.

"Yeah, we went to the new arcade in the mall. Did you know they have a . . ."

Kristin listened with half an ear as Lucas told her about the day with his father. A few minutes later, they said goodbye and she hung up and exhaled. The call with her son had calmed her down a bit, but her mind was still unsettled. What she needed was some company, even for a little while. She was about to pick up the phone and send a text when it vibrated with an incoming message.

How was the party?

She smiled. She loved that about Ed. Even though he'd worked late and was probably exhausted, he cared enough to ask how things went, something Stan would never have done.

It was good. Are you still in New York?

No, I just got off the train.

Kristin smiled again. The train station was only a few blocks from her house. Ed often left his car there and walked over so his car wouldn't be seen at her house.

Coming over?

I was about to ask you if I could come over. We need to talk.

The dreaded "we need to talk." Kristin sighed and sent him a text back hoping against hope that their talk wouldn't be about what she thought.

Okay. I'll open the back door. See you in a few minutes.

She unlocked the door for him then ran upstairs, undressed quickly, and was about to step into the shower when she stopped and looked at her body in the full-length mirror.

I'm . . . okay. Nothing to write home about, she thought. *A few extra pounds maybe. Okay, more than a few.*

But Ed seemed to thoroughly enjoy them, much more than any man in her life ever had. It didn't hurt that the sex that had started out being just good was now much better as they became more comfortable with each other. The last time they made love—no, that wasn't lovemaking, it was fucking. Raw, animal fucking that made her lose control and scream and holler so loudly they were afraid the cops would come knocking. When they were done, she lay limp as a rag in his arms and cried. Ed made her feel like a complete woman for the first time in her life, and her tears were partly because she loved the feeling, partly because she was falling in love, but mostly because she knew what they had couldn't last forever.

As she showered, she wondered if this was the last time she would be alone with him. She knew this day was bound to come, what they were doing couldn't last forever. It was inevitable, and she had prepared herself for it, or so she thought. Now it was here, but God help her, she just didn't want to give him up.

How much trauma can a person take in one day? she thought. First, she was held hostage in her own home, then she helped to beat someone almost to death, and now her man—yes she thought of Ed as her man—was probably breaking up with her.

As she emerged from the shower, she heard the door open downstairs and smiled, despite the pity party in full swing in her head.

"Kris, I'm here, baby," Ed called up to her.

Baby. He called me baby, she thought. The hope flared in her heart that just maybe she was wrong about his intentions.

"I'll be right there," she called back. "There's food in the kitchen. Help yourself."

Her hair and skin were still damp, but she threw on a

white T-shirt and was about to put on a pair of panties but stopped. If this really were to be the last time they were together, then she was going to give him a hell of a memory, and panties weren't going to be a part of it.

She ran downstairs to see him waiting at the foot of the stairs, suit jacket on and briefcase still in hand. Usually by now he would have abandoned both, but he looked like a man who intended to say his piece quickly and leave. The hope that began only moments ago died and her heart sank.

She gestured to the briefcase. "Not staying?"

His eyes lit up as he took in her wet hair and the white T-shirt clinging to the curves of her damp body, but he looked away quickly.

"We have to talk," he said.

"So talk."

"I've been thinking about this, Kris. We have to stop. We can't do this anymore."

"Did I do something to make you want to end it?" she asked.

"No! Of course not. You didn't do a thing. It's, well, it's just wrong. I sneak in the back door, then sneak out again, after ... after ..."

"You fuck your side chick?"

"See, that's what I mean. It's so . . . dirty."

The pained look on his face said much more than his words, and she sensed there was something else behind his decision.

"Is that the truth, Ed? Is that why you want to leave me?"

He hung his head. "I'm not leaving you. We just can't keep doing it this way."

"The truth," she said. "Please."

Ed said nothing.

"Please, Ed. I deserve that much."

"Kris, I'm falling in love with you," he said, his eyes wet with tears. "No. I *am* in love with you. And that just can't happen."

"Sounds like it already did. For both of us. Ed, I'm in love with you too."

Despite Ed's somber look and the gravity of the moment, Kristin's heart sang at finally being able to admit how she felt.

"Kris, that can't happen," he said again.

As he spoke, all the events of the day and all the things the women who stood in this very room said ran through her mind in a heartbeat. Not just the things they said, but the way they had said them. And suddenly she realized the one thing that ruled them all, the thing that underlined everything all of them had said and done today, was fear.

Fear of facing who they really were.

Fear of facing the past.

Fear of what others would think.

Fear of jumping outside the tight, constricting boxes they lived in.

As she looked at Ed, she saw the same fear etched in his face, the very same fear she saw reflected in her bathroom mirror just a few minutes ago.

Ironically, the only time she had felt truly alive was while she helped to beat Laura. Not because of the violence, but because in that moment they had had enough and finally took their power back. That was why she felt exhilarated, she realized, because when you take your power back, you can feel no fear. And when fear is gone, you are truly living.

And just like that, her fear evaporated and she saw things clearly.

She saw her ex-husband, Stan, for what he was. A nervous, neurotic, scared little man who used meanness and false bravado to hide his fear.

She saw her best friend, Bianca, whom she loved, but now realized was a quivering ball of fear just barely holding it together, totally incapable of loving herself, much less a good man.

She saw herself at almost forty years old, an educated and accomplished woman, raising an incredible child. She was curvy and sexy, and there were *plenty* of men who would love to be with her. She had done a lot to be proud of, but a man had taken that feeling of pride and accomplishment away from her. No, she had *allowed* it to be taken away. Never again!

She saw Ed. A good man who deserved more, but had the poor fortune to be raised by a mother whose only concern was for appearances and by a father who cared only for his perverted appetites. He grew up and became chained to a woman who loved herself so little she would rather be abused than show a good man the love he deserved.

There was a time only a few short minutes ago when she would have understood Ed's reluctance—hell, she had felt it herself—but this new and reborn Kristin had no patience for it.

"Ed," she said as she walked down the last two stairs toward him, "it was a hell of a day. A *hell* of a day. I learned life is short, and we have to make the most of it."

"I know, Kris, but—"

"Picture yourself fifty years from now, Ed," she interrupted. "You're almost ninety years old. Your body is shot, your mind isn't as sharp as it once was, and all you have are two things. Memories and regrets."

"What are you talking about, Kris?"

"Listen to me, Ed. You're ninety years old, and memories and regrets are all you have. You're sitting in a rocking chair with your grandchildren all around you, and you're thinking back on the day you decided to never see me again. Tell me, will this be a memory, or will this be a regret?"

"I ... I don't know, Kris."

"Well, I do, Ed! Goddamn it, I do. If you decide to walk out now, you will always regret it. Always!"

He tried to respond, but she put a finger to his lips.

"Before you make your decision, think about what you're leaving, and then think about what you're going home to."

She could almost see the battle going on in his head. His eyes had the haunted look of a deeply conflicted man, and he gripped the handle of his briefcase so tightly his knuckles turned white. “Kris, I guess I—”

“No, Ed! No guessing. Be sure. Do this because your eyes are open. Do this because you want to be happy, even if only for a little while. Do this because you love me. Don’t guess, Ed. Know!”

Then she went up on her tiptoes and kissed him, putting all her passion, all her newfound confidence, and every ounce of the love she felt for him into the kiss. When she let him go, he looked at her with wide eyes.

“I love you, Ed. And I’m yours. All yours. If you want me.”

“I love you, too, Kris. And I do want you. You know I do.”

“Fine. Then show me.”

She peeled off the damp T-shirt and dropped it on the floor.

“I’m going back upstairs. I guess in a minute I’ll find out if we just kissed hello or kissed goodbye.”

As she reached the top of the stairs, she heard a thud as his briefcase hit the floor. She walked into the bedroom without looking back and smiled when she heard his footsteps on the stairs.

The sound of her vibrating phone woke Kristin up from a light sleep. Ed’s arm was draped around her, and she gently lifted it off to check the screen. The call was from a number she didn’t know, and her first thought was one every mother had when their kids weren’t safe under their roof, that it was the police or some stranger calling to give her bad news. She quickly answered the call, prepared to hear the worst.

“Hello,” she whispered so as not to wake Ed.

“Um, hi, Kristin. It’s Maya. From earlier. The party.”

“Yeah. Yeah. Hey, Maya, what’s up?”

Before the women left her house, they had all exchanged numbers. Maya had promised to keep in touch with all of them if she heard anything about Laura, but in all honesty, Kristin had hoped never to hear from her again.

"Yeah, I'm at Laura's. Hang on a sec."

Kristin heard Maya speaking with someone in the background then footsteps as she moved to a quieter location. She was relieved that the call had nothing to do with her son, but her heart beat double time in anticipation of whatever terrible news prompted Maya's call. In her mind's eye, she envisioned a dark truck pulling up outside her house with police in SWAT gear silently swarming out of it like ants from an anthill before they kicked down her door and dragged her from her bed.

"Hey. Sorry. You there?"

"I'm here," Kristin said, heart pounding.

"I'm at a crime scene. It's at Laura's house. She killed herself. Slit her wrists in a tub. She looks pretty beat up, like maybe she was drunk and fell down some stairs before she offed herself."

Kristin's heart beat so loudly she was afraid Ed could hear it.

"Kristin? You there?"

"Yes. Yes, I'm here. Wait, you say she fell?"

"Looks that way. There's blood on her stairs. Seems like she might have been drunk and fell before she killed herself."

Kristin took a moment to read between the lines of what Maya said.

"My God. Okay, I understand. Thanks for telling me."

"I'm going to call everyone else now and let them know. You take care of yourself, okay? You probably won't hear from me again."

"Oh, okay. Thanks, Maya. Yes, you too."

Kristin ended the call and tried to process what she'd heard. She got the message that Maya was trying to tell her, that Laura's many injuries would never be suspect because she had "fallen" before she killed herself. She knew a part of her should feel some pity for poor dead Laura, but fuck her. She almost screamed in happiness, but instead snuggled closer to Ed. The day had been absolutely insane, but the night was turning out great. Ed—they hadn't spoken any more about breaking off their affair, but Kristin knew the discussion was over by the way he made love to her. Their lovemaking tonight had been mind-blowing, as if Ed had taken her words to heart. She had no idea where the sentiments she'd expressed to him earlier came from; they sounded like some well-rehearsed speech. But they were from her heart, and she meant every word.

Kristin was no fool. She knew Ed wasn't all hers and probably would never be, but that was okay with her. She was content with what they had. If their love had to be a secret, that was a price she was willing to pay. He was hers in all the ways that mattered. She remembered what Veronica said earlier about not feeling guilty about her affair with David. Only a few short hours ago, she couldn't conceive of such a thing, but now she understood. She heard the buzzing of a phone again. It was Ed's this time, and she reached over and grabbed it, intending to wake him up and give it to him, but as she started to shake him awake, she saw the alert was a text message from Bianca.

"Hell, no!" Kristin whispered to herself. She deleted the text before she returned the phone to the nightstand and snuggled closer to her man.

#

CHAPTER THIRTY

Bianca

"Are you okay, dear?"

Bitch, I'm fine, Bianca wanted to say. Gloria had asked her the same question multiple times on the ride home, but she bit her tongue, plastered a fake smile on her face, and nodded.

"I'm good, Gloria, really."

The lie flowed from her lips easily. She was anything but okay, but she was happy she was about be home. She needed a nice, hot bath with a huge glass of wine, but most of all, she needed to be away from her mother-in-law.

"I don't know, sweetheart. If you grip the steering wheel any harder, you might just rip it right off."

Bianca loosened her grip on the wheel and exhaled.

"I'm just tired."

"Yes, me too, dear. It was an exhausting day, to say the least. Being around that terrible, deranged woman brought out the worst in all of us."

They arrived at the house, and Bianca used the remote control to open the garage door, glad to be home at last. She was a little sad to see the other side of the two-car garage sat empty; Ed was still working late in New York. She had been actually looking forward to seeing her husband. The calming presence that had usually annoyed her would be a godsend right now.

"Ed's not home yet? That man works so hard," Gloria said in the grating, over-sympathetic tone only a mother-in-law can muster.

"Yes, the firm is litigating a huge case, and he's been working late a lot lately. He texted me earlier to say he and his friends from the firm were going to get a drink after work."

"I remember those days," Gloria said with a smile. "Many a night Will had to work incredibly long hours on some huge case or another. There were times we barely saw him for weeks on end."

Yeah right, Bianca thought. She wanted to say the huge cases Will worked on probably involved him screwing some side chick, but only nodded, astounded at the depth of Gloria's self-delusion.

"Ed's a genius at the law, just like his father. It must be in the genes," she said proudly. "Maybe one day your boys will be attorneys, too. You never know."

Yes, Ed was good at the law, but he absolutely hated being a lawyer, and his mother knew it. She was the one who pushed him into a law career when she knew his passion was for photography. He was partner at the same firm that his father worked at for years and would like nothing better than to tell them all to go stuff it and take photographs full-time, but he never would because it would upset his mother.

"We won't push them into anything," Bianca said through gritted teeth. "We want them to find their own way."

She got out of the car, thankful they were home and she could retreat to the safety of her bedroom and not have to listen to her mother-in-law any more.

"Of course, dear. It's so important for men to be able to find their own way in life, but sometimes it's up to us to, well, guide them along, don't you agree?"

Gloria stopped talking abruptly as her leg seemed to give way and she stumbled and fell. She screamed as she tried to hold onto the car, but her hands slipped, and she fell to the concrete with a heavy thud.

"Oh my God, Gloria, are you okay?"

"I think I'm okay, dear," she said. She tried to pick herself up off the floor but fell back down.

"Here, let me help you." Bianca helped to lift Gloria up off the floor and lean her on the car.

"What happened? Did you trip?"

"I don't think so, dear. It was my ankle." She leaned against Bianca and lifted a hugely swollen ankle.

"It happened at the party," she said.

She didn't have to elaborate. Bianca knew exactly what she meant. The women at the party, level-headed Gloria included, had formed an out-of-control mob bent on hurting Laura as much as they could. At one point, Gloria had stomped Laura in her face, twisting her ankle as she did.

"I guess when *it* happened, we were so worked up I didn't even notice it," Gloria said.

"Here, lean on me. I'll help you into the house."

Gloria leaned on Bianca, and together they slowly made their way inside, where Bianca helped her mother-in-law settle onto the couch. Then she dragged an ottoman over and elevated Gloria's leg.

"I'm afraid you're going to have to help me take my shoe off," Gloria said.

"It's going to hurt."

"I know."

Bianca gave the shoe a gentle tug, hoping that it would just slide off, but Gloria's ankle and foot were so swollen the shoe didn't budge.

"Just pull it off, sweetheart. It's okay."

Bianca gave the shoe a harder tug, and it moved a little but not nearly enough. She pulled it again, twisting it slightly. Gloria's breathing quickened and her face paled, and Bianca pulled the shoe again, harder this time, and it slowly slid off.

"That's going to need some ice," Bianca said. Gloria's foot was grotesquely swollen. Her ankle blue-black and bruised.

Gloria only nodded, her fast breathing and pale face the only indications of the pain she was in.

"Can I get you anything?" Bianca asked.

Gloria took a moment to catch her breath. "Thank you, dear. I think a cup of tea would hit the spot right now."

Bianca put the kettle on, then dialed her husband as she made an ice pack for Gloria. She got his voice mail and left a message explaining what had happened.

"Are the boys home?" Gloria asked as Bianca returned with her tea and the ice pack.

"No, they're at a sleepover."

"Good, I'm glad they're out. It wouldn't do for them to see me like this."

"Why not? You're human; things happen."

"Like you say, things happen, and sometimes it can't be helped. But, generally, men don't need to see us in a weakened state if we can help it."

"Weakened state?"

"Yes, like this. She pointed to her swollen foot. Hurt or incapacitated or sick. You have to understand, Bianca, there is nothing stronger in this world than a woman. But we don't start that way. We're born weak."

"I don't understand? What are you saying?"

"We're born weak, dear. To get strong, we have to work at it. And I don't mean just physically. No, that's the easy part. It's up here." She tapped her head. "We women pretend we're strong. We say it a lot to convince ourselves. I hate to tell you, but constantly boasting about how strong you are . . . is weakness. Constantly browbeating your man is weakness. Not letting your man be a man is weakness."

"Gloria, you sound like a dinosaur. That's outdated thinking."

"Maybe. Doesn't mean it's wrong. Sometimes the old ways of thinking are the best."

"How can we live like that? Always having to be 'on'? Isn't that exhausting?"

Gloria sipped her tea. "I admit, sometimes it can get . . . tiring."

"Then why be that way?"

"Because the alternative is far worse. "Letting them see us weakened makes them think they are better than us, and when they think they are better than us, that's when they try to dominate us. Either that or they just up and leave. The moment either thing happens, it's chaos."

Bianca rolled her eyes. "Come on, Gloria. Chaos? Really?"

"Yes, chaos. Really!"

"Aren't you exaggerating just a little?"

Gloria put down her teacup. "No, not at all. I know because I lived it. My grandmother had eleven children, and while she struggled to provide for them, her husband, my grandfather, ran off to live with a floozy across town. To add insult to injury, my mother and her brothers and sisters went around in rags and barely had enough to eat, but the kids of the woman Grandfather took up with were always well fed and dressed. Mother and her siblings went to school with those children every day. Think about what that would do to a young mind. Chaos. But mother was determined not to let it continue to the next generation. My mother saw her dad leave, so she vowed, no matter what, her family would always stay intact." Gloria sighed. "No matter what Daddy did, Mother put aside her ego for the good of the family. She taught me how to put my family before anything."

"I still think *chaos* is a bit strong."

"It's not strong enough." Gloria's eyes lit up, and the anger she held in check began to show itself.

"Chaos is like a virus. It spreads so easily and infects everyone until you have generations and generations of chaos. And only we women can cure it, Bianca. Only us."

"How?"

"We accept that men are weak and, well, men are going to be men, no matter what we do or what we say, and there's nothing you or I can do to change that. We shouldn't make demands they can't possibly live up to. And we should make a soft place for them to land."

Her eyes got a sad, faraway look. "Sometimes they can't or won't control their desires. And let me tell you this, if you think denying a man something he desires will make the desire go away, you're a fool. Desire grows stronger until one day it consumes him and you and the entire family. Mark my words."

"So what do we do?" Bianca asked. She knew all too well the power of desire.

"Simple. I say then let them indulge themselves. Let them go get their fill of whatever . . . then leave it where they found it and come home. Always come home."

"And what do we do about *our* desires? What do we do about our hurt and our pride and our pain? Are we just supposed to act like they don't exist?"

"Yes, that is precisely what you need to do, because we know a secret they don't. Those desires don't exist. They're your ego's way of getting you to indulge in the things you know you shouldn't have. That hurt and pride and pain you mentioned are also not real. It's ego. Accept that your man is fallible, and love and accept him even in his weakness, and your ego will no longer have any control over you, and all those desires will disappear. But that takes work. Work men can't do. Work that we *must* do."

"Do you really believe that?" Bianca asked in shock.

"Oh, absolutely, dear! I believe it with all my soul, and I live it every day of my life! When you have a family, the only thing that matters, the one and *only* thing, is keeping that family together and protecting its good name. Nothing else, not your fragile ego, not your hurt, not your pride, not a thing else matters except for the family!"

"So we're just supposed to let men get away with their bad behavior?"

"What you call letting them get away with it, I call preserving the family."

Bianca rolled her eyes. "So men get a pass to do whatever they want any time? Great."

"Don't be naive dear," she said, looking Bianca in the eye. "Let's not pretend like we're any better than them. We're just as fallible as they are. There is plenty we do we should be ashamed of. Plenty! Let she who is without sin cast the first stone and all that. But the difference is as women, we have a duty to be better than them. We are the heart and soul of our families, and we need to rise above."

"I don't know if I can do that."

"If you love your boys, then you will," Gloria said, then she glanced at her watch. "Lord, look at the time. I need to turn in. Can you help me, dear?"

"Sure, sure, no problem."

Bianca took her mother-in-law's arm, and slowly they made their way to the guest room. "Today was a strange day, to say the least," Gloria said as she sat on the bed. "But I'm glad we spent this time together. It was long overdue. Good night, dear."

"Good night," Bianca said. She started to leave, but turned back.

"Gloria, one more thing about what you said." Bianca shuffled her feet. "How can you forgive? When someone does something to you or they betray you, how can you forgive them?"

"Who said anything about forgiveness?" Gloria replied as she removed her watch and put it on the side table. "If I knew how to do that, I would be a saint. I'm certainly no saint, no matter what that awful Tina woman said. No, dear, I don't even try to forgive. I used to try, but I just couldn't. So now I forget. I only remember the good things about those who wronged me. I make myself forget for the good of the family."

"You forget? How can you force yourself to forget everything. Don't some things just stick with you?"

Gloria's eyes took on a hard look.

"Yes, sometimes they do. They most certainly do."

"Then how?"

Gloria paused as she removed an earring and laid it carefully beside the watch.

"No, dear, they don't. I let them go."

"Don't you ever want to face those people?" Bianca asked. "Don't you ever want to punish them for what they did to you?"

"Yes," she said. "Yes, I most certainly do." She stared at Bianca for an uncomfortable moment, then she took another earring off and set it next to its twin. "But if I did that, I would be no better than them. I take comfort in the fact that those who have wronged me know what they did, and living with their guilt is punishment enough, isn't it? Good night, dear."

"Good night," Bianca said. She went to her bedroom and thought to call Kristin to tell her about the conversation between her and Gloria, but hesitated. Something between her and her best friend had shifted. She couldn't tell what that was, but something had changed between them. Maybe she had confided in Kristin too much lately. Maybe it was time to keep her secrets to herself and work them out on her own. She wished she could confide in Ed, but there was no way to do that without telling him everything. No, this one she was going to have to deal with on her own.

Gloria is rubbing off on me already, she thought. She lay in the dark, thinking about all her mother-in-law said. She knew now that her suspicions were correct. Gloria knew she'd had an affair. She also knew that Gloria would take that secret to her grave, rather than do anything to upset the artificial happiness of their family, despite the anger she held in check. Underneath Gloria's calm veneer was a seething cauldron of rage. She'd seen it today in the way she had confronted Tina, and even more so when Gloria had cheerfully helped to beat Laura half to death. She realized now Ed was exactly like his mother, which was why he had been so calm on the night she told him of her supposed affair. He didn't go out and have a drink or two to think it over like Kristin had suggested. No, he'd run straight to his mother. She'd probably laid her whole "don't say anything for the good of the family" rap on him, and he bought it hook, line, and sinker. The thought of Ed confiding their business to his mother filled her with rage, and she wished he were here so she could give him a piece of her mind.

Where is that sneaky little mama's boy? she wondered. She checked her phone to see if he had called or texted, but all she had was his earlier message saying he would be late. She texted him to see where he was, then threw the phone on the bed in frustration.

She had to admit that Gloria had been right about some things. One selfish act could have unforeseen consequences, not just for the doer but for the family caught up in the vortex of lies and hate. Look what effect David's affair had on Laura, and in turn what Laura's actions had done to a group of strangers. Maybe the key to taming the beast of desire that Will awakened was to bury it deep inside, as Gloria suggested. If she ignored it, surely it would grow weaker and eventually die. Bianca tried to envision what life would be like if she did that. There would be no chance of sleeping with Will again. She wouldn't even think about him in that way. And if she did, she would abort those thoughts before they were born. She would settle for—no, she would appreciate—the sex with her husband and force herself to want no one but him and want only what he had to offer. She would be more like Gloria. She would put anything that didn't conform to her new way of thinking out of her mind, and she would be happy.

Finally.

Even as she thought it, she knew it wasn't true. What was it Gloria said about desires? Deny them and they grow stronger. Right on cue, thoughts of her and Will in this very bed came to her, as if her mind were testing her resolve. She'd revisited the memories of those weeks many, many times and remembered every moment as if they had happened that very day, but tonight the memories were especially vivid. Her hand slowly found its way between her legs as she quit the futile effort of trying to deny the memory and instead let it play freely. She felt her father-in-law deep inside her, she smelled his aftershave, she felt his strong hands on her neck, threatening to cut off her air, and she smiled as her orgasm washed over her in waves.

She lay in her bed, a light sheen of perspiration on her face and her heart beating wildly.

"No," she said to herself.

No. She would not bury the memories.

No. She would not try to pretend they had never happened.

No. She would not live each day denying her desires.

She still felt the same familiar emptiness she always felt after Will used her and walked away, but she didn't care. The memories were hers. Yes, it was a terrible mistake she'd made over and over and over again, but it was hers, and she could no more deny it than she could cut off her own head. If she denied what she wanted, she would be dead long before the flame of desire went out. There was no way she could be like Gloria and Ed, no way she could just take what she felt and file it away, suppressing her needs and desires to ensure that she could live a lie, pretending day after sad, soulless day everything was all right while becoming a bottomless pit of rage like her mother-in-law.

Bianca sat up in bed. She knew her desires were not "normal." What woman wants to be used and abused day in and day out? No, it wasn't normal, but neither was living a lie and presenting a false face to the world. She could never live that way. She would kill herself first.

Say what you want about Will, but at least he was true to his nature, and she needed to be the same. There was no way she was the only person in the world with her kinds of needs. There had to be a way she could get what she required. She picked up her phone, not noticing or caring that Ed had not responded to her text, and began to search.

A few minutes later, the phone vibrated in her hand and

she was surprised to see it was Maya calling. They had all exchanged phone numbers earlier but the truth was she had expected to never hear from any of them again.

"Hello ... Maya."

"Hi, Bianca."

"What's going on? Everything okay?"

"Sorry to call so late, but I wanted you to know . . ."

A minute later, Bianca ended the call and sat up in bed, stunned. Down the hall she heard Gloria's phone ring and knew Maya was giving her the same news she just received.

She waited a minute, then walked down the hall to the guest room and knocked softly on the door.

"Come in, dear."

Bianca opened the door to find a stricken-looking Gloria sitting up in bed, her face pale.

"I guess you heard," Bianca said.

Gloria nodded. "Come sit with me," she said, patting the space on the bed next to her.

Gloria turned off the light, and the two women sat together in the dark.

"That poor woman. Can you imagine her pain? And all we did was beat her half to death."

"Gloria, she might have killed us. We didn't have a choice."

"You're right, of course. We did what we had to do, but I still feel somehow responsible. Like I could have done something. She was so angry, and all the anger did was consume her."

Gloria began to weep softly, and Bianca put her arm around her mother-in-law and held her close as she cried.

#

CHAPTER THIRTY-ONE

Gloria

Gloria leaned on the banister and slowly made her way down the stairs. Her foot was less swollen than the night before, but she still winced when it touched the ground. It was a Sunday morning, and the house was quiet, but to her surprise, there was already a fresh pot of coffee on. As she poured herself a cup, she glanced outside and saw Bianca sitting by the pool.

Gloria took her coffee and slowly limped outside. "Hey there, good morning."

"Morning."

"Are you all right?"

Bianca shook her head. "No, not really. I didn't sleep much."

"To tell you the truth, neither did I. I'm not much for sleeping in, but this is one time I wouldn't have minded getting a little extra rest."

For a minute, the two women sipped coffee and stared at the still water.

"Will is on his way to pick me up, but I wanted to talk to you before he got here."

Gloria put down her coffee cup and rested her hand on Bianca's. "First thing is I wanted to tell you thank you for staying with me last night. I didn't want to be alone, and you were a tremendous comfort, and I'm so grateful."

Surprised, Bianca said, "You're welcome."

"And the other things is, I was wrong about what I said last night."

"About?"

"Forgiveness. I was wrong."

"You were?"

"I was. I always thought I had only one choice when someone did me wrong. I figured the only way to deal was to bury the resentment and anger inside. It's been a while since I thought about a second option. Forgiveness. I've been thinking about the last twenty-four hours, and I can't help but think if Laura learned to forgive, maybe we could have avoided all that unpleasantness yesterday and she would still be alive."

"Forgive? Forgive her husband? Forgive Veronica?"

"Them, too, but mostly herself."

"What do you mean?"

Gloria hesitated before she answered. "I've done . . ." she began, but hesitated again. How could she tell her daughter-in-law about the things she'd done? The abortions she paid for, the woman who had killed herself over Will because of her. How could she explain that the things she'd done still haunted her, but she had done them for her family.

She couldn't.

"I've done a lot of things I'm not proud of. Just like Laura, I haven't been the perfect wife. My sins were different from hers, but they're sins all the same."

"Have you forgiven yourself?"

"No," she admitted. "My mistakes haunt me."

"Mine too," Bianca said.

"Nobody is perfect, Bianca. Laura did some things she shouldn't have done, so have I, and so have you. When we women make a mistake, we tend to hold it close like we gave birth to it. We feed it and nurture it until it's a parasite sucking all the joy out of us. Eventually, it begins to seep into our relationships with our family, our children, our friends. I doubt that men dwell on their bad behavior like we do. They do something terrible then release it right away. Poof—like it never happened. Lord, I envy them that," she said, sipping the last of her coffee.

"So how do we live with the things we did?" Bianca asked.

Gloria sighed.

"I lied to you last night when I said I just let things go. I don't let them go . . . not exactly. What I do is take those feelings and force them down deep where they can't hurt anybody. If I didn't, I'm afraid I would be out of control like Laura was yesterday. That is something I will never be, because I know I would very easily do what Laura couldn't. I would leave bodies behind. If you can't forgive and let go, then bury your hurt. Bury it deep. I know people will say, 'Oh no, get them out in the open.' Seems like nowadays everyone parades their deepest darkest secrets out in the light of day for the world to comment on, but that's bullshit."

Bianca looked up from her coffee cup, surprised to hear her mother-in-law curse.

"Bury those secrets, dear," Gloria said. And if they claw their way up and start haunting you again, and you get tempted to drag them into the light, think of your boys. Think of your husband. Think of your family. What good would it do to have those secrets out in the light of day?"

"Maybe some secrets shouldn't be secrets," Bianca said. "Maybe they need to be dragged out into the light. Maybe that's the only way for them to stop haunting you."

"That's ego talking. Ego, and too many years of listening to Oprah. God knows I love Oprah dearly, but she's wrong about this."

Bianca hung her head. "But what if you can't live with your secret? What if it burns you up inside and makes you do things you don't want to do?"

Gloria shook her head. "Ego again. You're only thinking

of yourself. You'll let the secret out to burn your husband? Your boys? Do they deserve to suffer for your mistake?"

Bianca said nothing.

"No, they don't. They certainly don't," Gloria said. "It burns now, but trust me, one day you'll have buried it so deep that it can't hurt you or anyone else ever again."

The patio door opened, and they watched Will walk toward them, a cup of coffee in his hand. He seemed not to notice Bianca's red, teary eyes as he hugged her then hugged and kissed his wife.

"How are my best girls?" he asked.

"We're fine, darling," Gloria said. "Just saying goodbye."

"That's great, baby. You girls finish up, and I'll meet you in the house."

He held up his coffee cup and gestured toward Bianca. "Glo, did I tell you how much I love Bianca's coffee? I missed your coffee," he said, staring at Bianca with a gleam in his eye. "Mmm, mmm, mmm, I missed your coffee a whole lot." He grinned. "I had her coffee then swam laps in the pool. It kept me going all damn day. I felt like a new man after that, didn't I, Bianca?"

He took a long sip of coffee and smiled as he stared hungrily at his daughter-in-law.

"Damn, that's good. Anyway, girls, continue your gabbing, I'll be in the house."

He walked into the house as his wife and daughter-in-law sat, speechless, watching him go.

"Gloria, are you okay?" Bianca asked.

Gloria's skin paled, her body tensed, and her breathing became fast and shallow. The transformation from placid grandmother to an enraged creature scared Bianca, but just as quickly as it started, it ended, and Gloria became herself again. She rose from her seat and smoothed out her skirt, her hands shaking slightly.

"Yes, dear, I'm fine, I'm fine. Come on, give me a hug."

Bianca hugged her mother-in-law, a fierce hug that

caught the older woman by surprise.

"You remember what I said, you hear?" Gloria said.

"I will."

They walked inside together, Bianca supporting Gloria, who still walked with a slight limp. Outside, Will leaned on his car, smoking a huge cigar.

"Bianca, where's that son of mine?" Will asked.

"Still sleeping. He got in late. They're working on the senator's case, and he went out with some guys in the firm after work for dinner."

"Ah, good, good, he needs to blow off some steam," Will said as he exhaled thick, fragrant smoke. "God, I miss those days."

He noticed Gloria's limp and gestured toward her foot with the cigar.

"What happened, Glo?"

"It's nothing, sweetheart. Ready to go?"

"Sure, baby. See you soon, Bianca."

"Take care, Will."

"So, how was the party. Did you buy anything?" Will asked with a grin as they drove away from the house.

"It was *fun*. And, no, I didn't buy anything."

"That's a shame, you should have."

"So, what did you get up to while I was away," Gloria asked, eager to change the subject.

Will paused before he answered, his dead giveaway that what he was about to say was a lie.

"Nothing much. My plan was to stay in and grill a steak, grab a couple of beers, and watch the Knicks, but the boys called, so I ended up hanging out for a bit. We had a few beers and played some pool."

Gloria nodded, not believing a word. She could only imagine what they had gotten up to. The "boys" were a group of retirees who lived in their exclusive Chappaqua neighborhood. They were all former politicians, CEOs, and entrepreneurs, most of whom were forced to "retire" due to some scandal or another. They were all degenerates, in her opinion, sharing Will's appetite for women and debauchery. All a man needed to get into trouble was time. If they had that, then an opportunity would present itself, and being retired, the "boys" had plenty of time. They were all wealthy, too, which only exacerbated the amount of damage they could do.

"The Knicks screwed the pooch again," Will said. "What a shocker. They were up in the third quarter, but I knew they were going to blow it, and blow it they did. I told Joaquin those fools don't know how to win anymore, but he insisted on betting anyway, and now that moron owes me a grand. I mean, how can he possibly still support the Knicks? They haven't been a good team for at least a damn decade. Now if you want to talk the Nets, that's another story."

Will's ringing phone interrupted his diatribe, and he smiled when he saw the caller ID. "Speak of the devil, and in he walks," he said with a sly grin. "You don't mind if I take this, do you, Glo? It's Joaquin, probably telling when he'll be coming over to pay me my grand."

Will found his Bluetooth earpiece and secured it in his ear without waiting for her to respond, then picked up the call.

"Hey, fool. I just mentioned your name . . . yeah, yeah, I'm driving home from Jersey, I got Glo in the car with me."

Gloria rolled her eyes. That was probably a not-so-subtle code to let his degenerate friend know not to talk about anything too scandalous since the ol' ball and chain was present, but she didn't care. The interruption was welcome. She was still fuming at Will's behavior at Ed and Bianca's home. To openly taunt Bianca . . . no, to openly taunt the both of them the way he did, showed an astounding disrespect. Gloria shot Will a nasty look, but he was absorbed in the inane conversation with his friend and was oblivious, which only made her angrier. He must think she was a complete fool with no clue what he did behind her back.

But why shouldn't he think that? she asked herself, thinking back to what Kristin said the day before about enabling her ex-husband's behavior. Why shouldn't he sit here smoking his cigar with not a care in the world, having a stupid conversation with his degenerate friend? He's gotten away with it so many times over the decades he thinks he's invincible. And that, Gloria realized, was her fault. It was her fault Will felt he could violate his own daughter-in-law and get away with it. It was her fault he had continued his behavior because not once, not one single time in decades of marriage, did she ever call him out for the lives he ruined.

No, the lives *they* ruined.

She was complicit in everything he did, and all for the sake of keeping up appearances to the outside world. The right education, the right spouse, the right job, the right car, the right home in the right neighborhood. Then she had made sure her son did the same—right education, right spouse, right neighborhood, on and on and on.

How many families look just like ours? she thought. Picture-perfect from the outside, but inside a festering cycle of misery and unhappiness that grew more rotten with each passing generation?

The advice she gave Bianca was not for Bianca's sake but for her own. She had only told her that to stop her from blowing up their tidy little lives. If Ed knew what his father had done, their family would be torn apart. That much was true. But telling Bianca to bury her feelings and forget about what happened would keep the family intact for now, but what would happen months or years from now, when the pressure on Bianca became too much to bear? What would happen when the suppressed emotions built up over years suddenly overflowed and exploded? Would her daughter-in-law become another Laura? For that matter, how long would it be before *she* snapped just like Laura did? After all, they were very much alike. They were both almost the same age. They both had very successful husbands who cheated on them, and they both had massive reservoirs of anger inside them. The only difference was Laura vented her anger daily, while Gloria kept hers tightly contained. Maybe she had judged Laura too harshly, she now realized. Who was really the better person? Laura, the one who never covered up who she was or how she felt? Or was it she, who lived a lie for decades? On the outside, her life looked pristine, a shining example of right-living, but on the inside, things were rotten. Things were rotten and corrupted.

She was such a hypocrite. She had spoken with Bianca about the chaos men caused, but what about the chaos she caused? Her chaos was much more subtle, but no less damaging. Maybe even more so. The difference would be it likely wouldn't be a room full of strangers who would suffer—it would be her family who would bear the brunt. The thought suddenly made her sad and a sob caught in her throat. She looked out the window as they sped up the turnpike, not wanting Will to see her tears. Despite all her good intentions, all her lofty talk of keeping the family together, all she'd done was begin the process that would cause generations of misery by enabling an evil man.

Yes, Will was evil.

She saw that now.

And she had to do something about it.

As Will was still engrossed in his conversation, she opened the snap on her purse, put her hand inside, and caressed Laura's revolver. In the melee yesterday, no one but Gloria had remembered the gun had flown from Laura's hand and slid under an ottoman. Gloria picked it up and put it in her purse during the cleanup, grateful no one had thought to ask what became of it. She'd never held a gun in her life, but she didn't have to be an expert to point it, put it to Will's evil head, and pull the trigger. She would probably end up killing them both, but that was just as well because she was as guilty as he was. They would both be dead, and the chaos would end with them.

"You okay, Glo?" Will asked while she caressed the shiny metal of the revolver. "You look deep in thought."

Gloria had been in such contemplation of the weapon in

her purse she hadn't realized Will's call had ended.

"Yes, dear, I am."

"What's on your mind?"

She said nothing. She closed her hand around the grip of the gun, closed her eyes, and began to pull it out.

Will's phone buzzed again, and he glanced at the text message.

"Glo, I just got a text from Steve. He wants to know if we want to have dinner tonight with him and his fiancée."

The text message was from Steven Booker, a charismatic and intelligent young intern whom Will took under his wing during his time as a partner at the law firm. Will had seen something in the young man from the wrong side of the tracks and staunchly advocated for him when no one else believed in him. With Will's support, Steven had gone from lawyer to councilman to mayor and had recently completed a successful senatorial bid. He was almost never in town, but when he was, he never failed to get together with his mentor.

"Um, sure," she said. Her hand was still wrapped around the grip of the revolver.

"I'll call him," Will said. "Maybe we can eat at that Italian place, you know, the place where Hilary had her fundraiser during her campaign? Can you give them a call and make the reservations?"

Gloria's hand tightened on the handle of the gun, and she closed her eyes and tried not to cry. Just the thought of dinner reservations with a politician in an expensive and very exclusive buttoned-down restaurant made her want to scream. Everything about that scene was fake. Lots of insincere handshakes and fake smiles hiding the dirty, disgusting truth behind their seemingly upstanding lives.

It had to end.

She pulled her hand slowly out of her purse, but when it emerged, it wasn't the gun she held but her phone.

It had to end.

But not now.

She stomped her anger down, down, down, until it was securely locked away, then opened her eyes and looked lovingly at her husband, smiling broadly.

"So," she said, "reservations for four?"

CHAPTER THIRTY-TWO

Brooke

Brooke heard the bedroom door opening, followed by the click of the light switch, and immediately burrowed deeper into the blankets.

"Mom, wake up."

"Huh? What?"

"Mom, wake up, we're going. I saw your note on the fridge that said you wanted us to wake you up when we were leaving for school."

Brooke opened her eyes and immediately shut them again against the bright light.

"Oh, right. Yeah, okay, I'm up, I'm up."

Brooke reluctantly opened her eyes again to see her daughter, Amy, standing over her, hands on her hips.

"Are you up, Mom?"

"I'm up, honey. I'm awake. I'll be down in a minute."

"Don't go back to sleep, Mom. We're not gonna wait for you. We have to go," Amy said. She gave her mother one last exasperated look and left the room.

Brooke stretched and immediately regretted the movement since it made her pounding headache worse. She swung her legs over the side of the bed, wincing as warm toes met cold floor, and used her feet to feel around for her slippers. What she felt instead was the cold glass of an empty tequila bottle. Brooke groaned. The events at the party had rattled her much more than she'd let on, and the moment she arrived home, she found a bottle and began the process of trying to forget. The alcohol worked too well. She didn't remember much, but she had a vague memory of receiving a phone call. Something about Laura?

Her phone was on the floor, and she picked it up and checked her calls. Sure enough, there was a call from an unknown number that lasted for over a minute. Her head pounded as she tried to remember what the call was about, but the alcohol still fogged her brain, and nothing came to mind. She felt around again for her slippers, found one, but its twin was missing, so she gave up the search, quickly slipped on one of Nick's oversized hoodies, and trudged wearily down the stairs.

It was only seven thirty in the morning, but her husband, Nick, had long departed for work, and the ever-present Portia was already in the kitchen, helping to see the twins off to school, fussing over them like a mother hen as always. Just hearing Portia's voice made her headache worse, and for the millionth time, Brooke wished she could erase the old Jamaican maid from their lives. Despite her annoyance, the horrible headache, and her exhaustion, Brooke plastered on a huge fake smile and bounced into the kitchen as if she saw her kids off to school every day.

"Morning, guys," she said in her most cheerful-sounding voice.

"Hey, Mom," Alex replied. Smiling, he put his backpack down and hugged her tightly. Of the twins, Alex was closest to her.

"Alex, we gotta go. We're gonna be late," Amy said, annoyed.

"Relax, Amy," Alex said in a no-nonsense tone.

Amy crossed her arms and scowled as Brooke silently

cheered her son. Amy had always been the more assertive of the twins, but she could only push her brother so far before he pushed back.

Alex hugged her again. "Mom, you okay?" he whispered in her ear.

"Yeah, baby, I'm good. Don't worry about me."

"I always worry about you."

"Don't, baby. I'm okay, I promise."

"Okay, Mom. See you later. I love you."

"I love you too."

He kissed her on the cheek, grabbed his backpack, and headed for the door. "Ready?" he asked his sister.

Amy made a face as she picked up her own backpack.

"Love you, hon," Brooke said to Amy, but her daughter was already gone.

Brooke exhaled. She could tell the twins were confused. She hadn't seen them off to school in a long time. She hadn't made much of an effort to be a mother to them for years, but she was determined things would change. It would be damn hard, but she would show them she could be the mother they needed. Kids gone, she abandoned the bright and bubbly facade and sat down wearily at the kitchen table.

"It's good to see you up so early, Ms. Brooke. Everything all right?"

"Don't worry about it, Portia. Just give me my damn . . ."

Before she could finish the sentence, Portia put a plate with her scrambled egg whites and toast on the table.

Brooke shot the maid a nasty look, but said nothing. The thought of getting into it right now with the older woman made her head hurt more, so she took a bite of her toast and ignored Portia.

"You did a good thing this morning," Portia said as she washed the twins' breakfast dishes.

"What?"

"Seeing the children off. It was good."

"Amy didn't seem too damn pleased about it."

Portia smiled. "One one coco full basket."

"Portia, I'm from South Jersey, not South Kingston. I have no idea what you just said."

"It's a Jamaican saying that means you have to take things one step at a time."

"Yeah, well, you see how well it worked out just now. Amy hates me."

Portia put away the last dish, wiped her hands dry on a dishtowel, then sat down at the table and stared at Brooke. Her usually hard and unyielding brown eyes had a softer look in them. "How could you think that, Ms. Brooke?" she asked.

"Come on, Portia. You see it. She can't stand to be around me. She barely talks to me. It's pretty obvious, don't you think?"

"Ms. Brooke, I know these children from when they were born until now, and I can tell you they love you. Amy especially."

"I don't think so."

"That girl is just like you. Sometimes when I look at her, I think I'm seeing you. That girl loves you. She just has a hard time expressing it."

"Just like me," Brooke said.

"Just like you," Portia agreed.

"I screwed up bad, Portia. I wasn't a mother to those kids," she said, inspecting her breakfast. "And I just don't know how to fix that."

"One one coco—"

"Portia! Enough with the Jamaican sayings."

Portia grinned. "Ms. Brooke, you made mistakes, but that's in the past. There's not a thing you can do to change it. But what you can do is be better going forward."

"How, Portia? How?"

"Just be there for them. Even when they act like they don't want you around. Just be there. Make them know they can depend on you. Make them feel safe. That's what they need."

"I'll try Portia," she said.

"You'll figure it out, Ms. Brooke. You wait and see."

The maid patted Brooke on the shoulder and left the room smiling, but Brooke wasn't reassured in the least. Appetite killed, Brooke threw the rest of her breakfast in the trash, then went upstairs to her bedroom, where she fell onto the bed and lay in a fetal position, shrinking into Nick's large sweatshirt like a turtle in a shell and thinking about the advice Portia gave her. Make them feel safe. "How can I make them feel safe, Portia," she said to herself, "when I haven't felt safe in all my damn life?"

No, that wasn't entirely true. Nick made her feel safe. At least he used to. Nick was damn near perfect. A great husband and father, a successful businessman and ex-Marine with a slew of medals from Desert Storm. Everyone loved her husband, like they loved Laura's husband, and like Laura, she was a bitch to her man. She completely ignored him, and he still cared enough to tell her he loved her every day, and she was too fucked up and broken to accept his love and appreciate the family she had.

Exactly like Laura was.

And it was at that moment that her alcohol-soaked brain chose to make her remember the phone call last night. It was Maya. She was calling to give her some news about Laura.

Laura was dead. She had killed herself.

And with that memory, everything that Laura did came into high-definition focus.

From the day she'd met Nick, his love and support had been a constant in her life. Even at her worst, and her worst was pretty damn bad, Nick had been there. She now realized that his love and devotion were the things that ensured she didn't completely run off the rails. Now she understood, really, really understood, why Laura had done what she'd done. Laura had known she was broken and completely unlovable, but there was one person in the world who had loved her without hesitation, her husband. He had been her lifeline, and when she'd lost him, she lost the one thing holding her back from truly becoming the monster she imagined herself to be.

"Do they look at me like that?" Brooke asked herself. "Do Alex and Amy see me the way Laura's kids saw her?"

Her hands shook and her heart began beating fast with the onset of an anxiety attack. Getting high was the only cure. Getting high would slow down the anxiousness and take her away from the reality she wasn't equipped to face. She frantically rummaged around her hiding places and brought out all the pills and alcohol she had hidden, determined to get so drunk and so high the events of the last day would be completely erased from her mind. Just sitting on the bed and looking at her stash comforted her. The liquor and pills were like old friends, ready to give her comfort without demanding a thing in return. She cracked open a bottle and took a deep swig. The liquor fell like a rock into her stomach, and she waited for the calming effect, but there was none. Her hands still shook, and her heart still beat fast. She took another huge mouthful, then another, but nothing happened. No usual sense of calm, no peace that fell gently on her like a mist, nothing. Only the alcohol burning in her stomach and the burning in her spirit from the realization of what she must look like to her family.

She knew what she had to do. She had to turn things around. She sprang from the bed, gathered up all the liquor and pills, and took them with her to the bathroom. She opened all the bottles quickly before she had a chance to talk herself out of it, and poured them down the drain. Then she took all the pills, dropped them into the toilet and quickly flushed it. She watched the pills swirl around, fighting the urge to scoop them up and swallow each and every one. She took the empty bottles and ziplock bags outside and thrust them deep into the recycling bin, then went back and collapsed onto her bed and cried herself to sleep.

Brooke woke up a couple of hours later as her body gave her the first, faint warnings that her addictions were about to come calling. For a moment she forgot what she'd done, but with a stab of terror, she quickly remembered throwing away her drugs and alcohol. As the hunger inside of her slowly built, she cursed herself for a fool because she knew a very bad time was about to begin.

Brooke's phone rang, startling her, and she dug it out of the hoodie's roomy pocket and looked at the screen. The caller ID said UNKNOWN NUMBER, but she was pretty sure it was D-Mo calling. D changed his number often, one of the many precautions he had to take as a drug dealer.

"Hey D."

"Hey, girl, haven't heard from you in a couple of days. Everything okay?"

She thought about telling D the story of what happened. If there was anyone who could keep his mouth shut, it was him, but she didn't have the energy. "Long story," she said. "I'll tell you another time."

D-Mo said nothing, and Brooke could tell by his silence he wanted to push the issue but knew this wasn't the time.

"Okay, girl," he said after a moment. "You sure you okay? You need anything?"

The "anything" was the drugs that would curb the anxious feeling that even now was creeping up on her.

"No," she said. "I think I'm good."

"Cool."

"Hey, D?"

"What's up, baby?"

"I love you. Thank you for looking out for me."

I love you too, girl. You hang in there, aight?"

"I will."

Brooke ended the call and smiled. It was good hearing D's voice. Just knowing he cared gave her the strength to do what she had to do next. She didn't know if she still loved Nick. The drugs, alcohol, and general depravity of her life had dulled all feeling for anything but the drugs and alcohol and depravity, but she had to try to cut them out of her life then figure out her next move. It all had to begin with a hard conversation with her husband, so she picked her phone up, but as she did so, it began to ring and she picked it up without looking at the caller ID.

"What's up, D? You got freaked out because I said I love you?"

"Um . . . what?" A female voice on the other end asked?

"Sorry. Thought it was somebody else calling. Who is this?"

"Hi, Brooke. It's Bianca. From the party, remember? We all exchanged numbers after."

"I remember you," Brooke said.

"Yeah. I'm sorry to call out of the blue like this, but I was wondering if we could talk."

"Okay. Talk."

"I meant in person."

Goddamn it, Brooke thought. This was the last thing she needed.

"Listen," Bianca said, as if sensing Brooke's reticence, "I'm sorry to bother you like this, but I just need to ask you some things. I'll only take a few minutes."

"Okay," Brooke said. "I'm free now."

"Thanks. I won't take long, I promise."

Brooke gave her the address then went outside to the patio, wondering why in the hell she agreed to meet, but there was something in Bianca's voice that nagged at her and told her this was probably not going to be just another girl talk session.

A few minutes later, Portia appeared on the patio with Bianca in tow.

"Ms. Brooke, you have a guest."

"Thanks, Portia."

Now that Brooke saw Bianca, she was glad she agreed to talk to her. Something about her struck a chord with Brooke she couldn't quite put her finger on.

"Thanks for seeing me," Bianca said as they exchanged an uncomfortable hello hug.

Brooke could tell at a glance Bianca was in distress. Her fingernails were bitten down and even her expertly applied makeup couldn't hide the bags under her eyes.

"You look like shit," Brooke said.

"I feel like it. Hey, did Maya call you?"

"She did. Can't say I'm surprised. That bitch Laura was a basket case. Anyway, what's going on? Is it the party? Is all that craziness still on your mind?"

"Kind of. There was something you said, something about being mistreated, and it was the only way you could feel love. Do you remember that?"

Brooke nodded. She wished she hadn't said it, but it was the truth.

"Why did you say that?" Bianca asked.

"Listen, Bianca, I like you, okay? But I'm not going to get into that. It's too complicated. Why do you want to know anyway? You a shrink or something?"

"No," she said. "Nothing like that." Bianca's eyes watered, and in a moment, huge tears began to stream down her cheeks.

"What the? Are you crying?"

As Bianca wiped her tears, it finally hit Brooke what it was about Bianca that nagged at her. Everything about her, the tone of her voice, her demeanor, the slump of her shoulders, the defeated look, reminded Brooke . . . of Brooke. And suddenly, she knew why Bianca was there.

"There's something I want. No, there's something I need," Bianca said. "And I don't know how to get it."

"What do you need?" Brooke asked. She knew the answer, but she wanted to hear Bianca say it.

"Someone did something to me, Brooke. Something I didn't think I wanted. Turns out I did want it. Now I don't have it, and I'm going crazy."

"English, please."

Bianca wiped the tears from her eyes. "God, I can't believe I'm telling you this. Last year, my father-in-law came to help us with some repairs to the house. One day we . . ."

Fifteen minutes later, Bianca finished her story as Brooke sat speechless. She had expected to hear some suburban housewife sob story about Bianca hooking up with some random guy who rocked her world in a way her husband couldn't, which, now she thought about it, wasn't far from the truth.

"That is fucked up!" Brooke said.

"Yes."

"And just about the hottest thing I have ever heard in my life."

"Oh yes," Bianca agreed. "Now do you see my problem?"

Brooke nodded. "I do. But what do you think I can do about it?"

"I guess I thought you might know about that kind of . . . life."

Brooke's first reaction was to lie to Bianca, to tell her she was mistaken, thank you very much, and get the hell out of her yard and her life. She needed this like she needed a hole in the head. She had resolved to make changes in life, but this . . . this put a whole new wrinkle on things. A very hot new wrinkle that caused her to shiver with excitement. She took a good look at Bianca. Minus the runny mascara and defeated look, Bianca was hot. She had big tits, a beautiful ass, and a pretty face. She would be a big hit. Plus it would be nice to have someone to take under her wing and teach the ropes to. If she told her no, Bianca would only go out and try to do it herself and end up getting hurt or worse. If she told her yes, she would have to convince D-Mo. He might resist initially, but she had a way of convincing him. That wouldn't be a problem. She thought about her resolve of the night before to leave the life and never look back. Now, she wasn't just returning to the life, she was about to jump back in and take someone else along for the ride.

"Do you know what you're getting into?" Brooke asked her.

"Truthfully? No."

Brooke looked her in the eye. "I need you to understand

that you're turning your back on everything decent. You'll be around people who don't care about you. You'll be a toy to them. Less than a toy, you will be something to use and then throw away. You okay with that?"

"God, yes!"

"Okay," Brooke said. "I'll help you."

Bianca smiled broadly. "Thank you, thank you," she said. "What do I have to do?"

"Right now, nothing. Just sit tight. I have to make a call. I know a guy."

"And then what?"

"And then . . . then you'll find out what it's like to become an object."

CHAPTER THIRTY-THREE

Veronica

Veronica arrived at a gated home and entered a code on a keypad. The large gate swung open silently and closed again after she drove past. The garage door was already open as she pulled up to the house and she drove in, put the car in park and sat in the car for a moment, the same as she did every single time she arrived home. David's sports equipment sat neatly in their places on the walls, sets of skis here, mountain bikes there, a punching bag in the corner. All gathering dust. She walked through the garage, touching things as she passed them. She should probably get rid of it all, but knew she never would. It was nice to come home and see David's things and think, if only for a second, that one day he would use them all again.

Inside, her son was asleep on the couch next to the babysitter, Erin, a teenager from the neighborhood who was half-asleep herself.

"Hi, Mrs. Green," Erin said. "Isaac's been asleep for a while. He had a bottle and passed out." She stretched and yawned then did a double take. "Hey, what happened to your head?"

Veronica touched the knot on her head; she'd forgotten all about her injury.

"Oh, it's nothing. Just me being a klutz. Hey, Erin, thanks for staying a little longer," she said, changing the subject. "I had a quick errand to run before I came home. Hey, I can still pay you through the app, right?"

"Sure."

Veronica used her phone to pay the teen, giving her a healthy tip.

"Wow, thanks Mrs. Green," Erin said, looking at her phone.

"My pleasure, Erin," Veronica said as she walked the teen to the front door. She watched as Erin walked to her car, then inside and hurried to a door in the back of the house secured with a keypad. She punched in the code and entered a room that looked as if it belonged in a high-security facility, not in a suburban home. Several high-definition monitors covered one wall, and she powered them on and watched as Erin drove through the gate. Satisfied she was alone on the property, she activated the various cameras, alarms, and motion sensors that dotted the grounds, then sat back and exhaled.

Veronica hated living like this. It sometimes felt like the house had more security than most prisons, but she had to remind herself that it was a small price to pay for peace of mind. Since escaping from her family in Los Angeles, Veronica lived in a constant state of vigilance and became more adept at covering her tracks, so it was unlikely her father would find her. But even so, David had insisted on the increased security and she readily agreed.

Alarms set, she checked on her sleeping son before she made her way to the bathroom and peeled off her jacket, revealing the blood splatter covering her blouse. She removed the rest of her clothes, turned the shower as hot as she could stand, and stood under it. After she killed her Uncle Tito, the shower had been like a ritual cleansing that washed away her guilt. This time, there was no cleansing, all she got was wet.

She changed clothes and put the bloody outfit, underwear and all, in a drawstring bag, meaning to dispose of it right away, but the baby was awake again and crying for another bottle. She poured herself a glass of wine and made him a bottle of milk, and, as was her habit, took the baby to sit in David's study while he drank. David had only been able to use it for a month before his death, but she thought of it as his room and hadn't moved one item. She felt his presence in every corner of the house, but it was in this room she felt it strongest. As always, she looked around at David's collection of things, his humidor still filled with the cigars he enjoyed so much, his beloved books, the art on the walls, and the many pictures of his children and grandchildren, and her heart felt a stirring of grief that she knew would never, ever leave.

Minutes later the baby loudly sucked the last of his milk from the bottle then smiled at his mother sleepily before closing his eyes and falling asleep once again. Veronica gently smoothed his hair from his face, then picked up the wine glass, but her phone rang before she could have a sip.

She looked at the name on the caller ID, not entirely surprised to see who was calling.

"Hello, Maya."

"Hi, Veronica. Sorry to bother you."

"It's no bother. What's going on?"

"Hey, I, uh, have some news. I'm at Laura's house. Something's happened."

Veronica's heart beat faster and she gripped the wine glass tightly.

"Laura's house?"

"Yes. She's dead, Veronica."

"Oh . . . what . . . what happened?"

"Looks like she killed herself. Her maid came by to check on her and found her. Slit her wrist in the tub. I can't say I'm surprised."

"I ... I ..." Veronica's face flushed and her legs went weak.

"I know, it's a shock. Well the good news is you won't have to worry about her anymore."

"That's true," Veronica managed to mumble, still at a

loss for words.

"Anyway, I just figured you would want to know. Listen, I got some more calls to make. I gotta go. Take care of yourself, okay?"

"Yes ... Uh ... Thanks, Maya. Bye."

Veronica hung up the phone and put the wine glass down, all appetite for it gone. On the bookshelf in front of her was a picture of her and David, taken shortly before he died. It was one of her favorite pictures of him. Seeing it always made her smile, but now she felt as if his eyes followed her as she moved about the room. She ignored the feeling and put her son to bed, then retrieved the drawstring bag with the bloody clothes, disabled the alarm, and walked outside.

It was dark, but the full moon gave her more than enough light to see by as she walked down to the lake a few hundred yards away. When she reached the sand, she kicked her shoes off and waded barefoot into the lake, savoring the solitude and the feeling of the warm water caressing her skin. She was completely alone. Her closest neighbor lived on the other side of the lake, but their home was completely dark. She stood in the lake for a moment more, enjoying the soothing sound of the water gently caressing the sand, then returned to the shore and quickly found several large rocks, which she dropped into the bag with the clothes before knotting it securely.

A wooden pier stretched out into the lake, and she walked to the end of it, bag in hand, the creaking of the weathered wood sounding loud in the still night. She loved this place. It was where she went to most often after David's death, reliving the many evenings with him spent sitting on the pier and talking. From one of those conversations, she knew that there were parts of the lake that were over a hundred feet deep. Her intention was to drop the bag into the lake's depths and never think about it or this day ever again, but instead her mind brought her back to the massive panic attack she experienced earlier.

She left Kristin's home feeling okay, all things considered. She started her car, but suddenly her hands began to shake and the tears fell like a sudden summer deluge. It took ten minutes of deep breathing to stop her crying and slow down her wildly beating heart.

I'll never have any peace, she thought. If today had taught her anything, it was that Laura would never relent, never give up the campaign to get her revenge, and she was capable of anything to achieve that goal.

Veronica started her car again and drove toward Laura's house with no idea of what she would do when she got there. At least that was what she thought at the time but part of her knew she knew she was just fooling herself because she knew good and damn well what she had to do, the same as she did when she dealt with her Uncle Tito. Now, just as then, if she didn't take action she would have to live every day looking over her shoulder.

That she would not do.

Never again.

She arrived at Laura's house and drove around to the back, the same as she'd done many times when, as David's assistant, she'd gone there to drop off paperwork or on some other errand. The spare key was still in its customary hiding place inside a fake rock, and she used it to open the door, listening for Laura's little dogs and also the series of beeps that would tell her the alarm and security cameras were active, but there was no sound—Laura was notorious for not activating the alarms, and surprisingly the dogs were nowhere to be seen. She made her way to the kitchen where she heard a muted barking and frantic scratching nearby and realized that Paris and London had somehow gotten locked in the pantry. *Good*, she thought. She didn't need them underfoot. She grabbed a knife from a magnetized wall rack and silently walked up the stairs and peeked into the darkened bedroom. Laura was nowhere to be seen, but she heard water running in the bathroom, so she moved without a sound, glanced in, and saw that she needn't have been so stealthy since Laura was passed out drunk, just as she expected. She crept into the bathroom, almost stepping on the broken liquor bottle and realized she wouldn't need the knife after all. She put it down and picked up a razor-sharp shard of the broken glass and held Laura's bony wrist, but her resolve almost faltered when unexpectedly, Laura spoke.

"David, is that you?"

Laura's words startled her badly, and she thought about leaving, but she realized that Laura was much too drunk, high, or both to realize who she was. She sat on the edge of the tub and put the glass to the vein in Laura's wrist.

"David, I saw your son. I saw Isaac ... he's ... he's so beautiful. He looks just like you."

Once again, her courage threatened to abandon her, but she steeled her resolve and ran the shard of glass over Laura's clammy wrist, easily slicing through skin and veins, causing a fine blood mist to spray over her clothes.

"David . . . what ..."

This time Veronica paid no mind to Laura's words. She reached out for Laura's other hand, intending to do the deed on that wrist, as well, but there was no need. The severed vein was already pumping out blood in great crimson gushes. In less than a minute the water in the tub was almost completely red. Already too weak to sit up, Laura began to sink under the water, but before she was completely submerged, she opened her eyes and spoke.

"I love you, David. I love you so much."

Veronica dropped the broken glass into the tub, picked up the knife and quickly left the room as the life left Laura's eyes and she sank under the bloody water. She rushed downstairs into the kitchen, washed the knife thoroughly then holding it with a dish towel put it back in its place on the wall rack and was about to leave the house when she heard the dogs still whining and scratching at the pantry door. She opened the door and the grateful dogs shot out of the pantry, tails wagging in happiness. She ignored them and quickly left the house.

On the drive home, Veronica concentrated on the road, pundits arguing on the radio, people walking their dogs, all the better to avoid thinking about what she had just done and Laura's haunting last words. But now, standing alone on the pier under the full moon in the silent night, there was nothing to distract her mind from replaying Laura's dying words over and over in her mind.

"I love you, David. I love you so much."

Stupid woman, Veronica thought as she looked out onto the horizon, barely visible in the dark summer sky. She would never understand why Laura treated David so horribly for decades, yet with her last words professed her love for him. *Stupid woman*, she thought once again, and with one motion tossed the bag as far as she could out into the lake. It hit the water with a soft splash and sat unmoving for a long moment as if taking one last look at the world, then succumbed to the inevitable gravity of the rocks and began to sink. At the same moment, a cloud drifted over the moon and Veronica stood in the dark, imagining the bag as it sank, down, down, down into the depths to land on the lake floor, kicking up a small cloud of sand and silt before it settled in to join sand and rocks and fish as part of the lake.

The job done, she walked off the pier and back to the house. At the door, she turned and looked back out at the water. The offending cloud had moved on, and the moon cast its reflection unimpeded onto the still water once again. But now the sight gave her no comfort. It wasn't the same. It now seemed . . . dirty. She had recruited the lake as an accomplice to hide the evidence of her crime and in doing so had polluted it. David would be ashamed of her, she knew, but David was dead and gone. She was alive, and she did what she had to do for her and for her son's survival, same as she'd done to her Uncle Tito after he violated her.

No, David wouldn't be happy but I can live with what I did, she thought as she turned her back on the lake and entered the house. Laura was dead and burning in hell.

For the first time all day she felt as if she could finally exhale. She smiled broadly as she locked the door and set her alarm.

Laura was dead.

And burning in hell.

Maybe she would have that glass of wine after all.

The End...

Or is it.

The story isn't over for the women of ***Pleasure Party.***

Not even close.

Turn the page to read a short story featuring one of the ladies of ***Pleasure Party*** and be sure to look out for the second book in the ***Pleasure Party*** series coming in 2023.

FLING OR FOREVER

A *Pleasure Party* short story

Kristin pulled the lingerie out of the bag and lay it flat on her bed. It still had the tags attached, and she considered removing them but left them on since chances were she would only be returning it. She should have tried it on in the store but the thought of taking off her clothes in a tiny mall dressing room only to try on lingerie that would probably look awful on her made her shudder.

She gave the lingerie one last skeptical look, got undressed, then worked her way into it, eyes shut tight as she shimmied and squeezed to get it to fit. She took a deep breath, opened her eyes slowly and looked at herself in the mirror, fully prepared to hate what she saw but surprisingly the sight didn't automatically make her want to rip it off her body and tear it to shreds. She turned this way and that, examining herself from all angles.

"Not bad," she said, smiling. "You're definitely going with me to Miami."

She took the lingerie off, removed the tags, and threw it on the "going with me this weekend" pile, which on second glance was growing much too large for only four days away.

Screw it, she thought. If I overpack, then I overpack. It's not every day she got to go away to Miami with her guy. Ed, her boyfriend, was a lawyer who had been flying back and forth from home in New Jersey to Miami for the past few months preparing for a big case. Just a day into the trial his client dropped dead of a heart attack, so realizing he had a few free days in Miami, Ed called her to propose this weekend getaway and Kristin jumped at the chance. That was two days ago, and she'd spent most of that time in a happy, giddy haze of anticipation. She couldn't wait to see Ed and do the things normal couples take for granted, like walk on a beach holding hands or eat at a cute outdoor restaurant, things they could never do at home since Ed was married, and to her best friend Bianca no less.

Satisfied with her selection of outfits, she began to pack but her phone interrupted. Her friend Veronica's name showed up on the caller ID and she smiled and picked up the phone.

"Hey Veronica," she said. She could hear Veronica's baby son, Isaac, babbling in the background.

"Hi, Kris. Ready for the big weekend away?"

"I just finished trying on lingerie, can you imagine? Me in lingerie?"

Veronica chuckled. "Going all out I see."

"I sure am. This will be a weekend to remember."

"I'm happy for you," Veronica said. She was silent for a moment, then her voice took on a somber tone. "Um... you think I could come over for a little bit. I need to talk."

"Of course!" Kristin said. "Lucas is with his dad until I get back, so we'll have the house to ourselves. Are you okay? The baby..."

"He's fine, I'm okay too... it's just..."

"It's okay honey, just come on over. We'll talk when you get here."

"Okay, Kris. Thank you, see you soon."

#

She was almost done packing a few minutes later when she heard Veronica's car pull into her driveway.

"Good timing," she said as Veronica walked up to her door pushing Isaac in his stroller. "Come on in."

The baby was fast asleep, and Kristin gave him a gentle

kiss on the cheek, then hugged her friend.

"All packed and ready to go?" Veronica asked.

"SO ready," Kristen said. I'm so excited, I'm really doing this. I can't wait!"

"You're gonna have a great time, I'm happy for you."

"You didn't come here to talk about my weekend, what's going on? You okay?"

"Yes... no... kinda. You remember what tomorrow is, right?"

"No, what is it?" Kristin asked.

Veronica made a face.

"Okay, okay, I do," Kristin admitted. "But I've tried for a year to forget."

"Me too," Veronica said. "But how do you forget something like that?"

It was almost a year ago that Kristin and her former best friend Bianca threw the party that was to change all their lives. It began normally enough but soon devolved when one of the guests, Laura Green recognized Veronica as the woman who had an affair with her husband. Laura made a scene and left the party only to return minutes later with a gun, holding them hostage for a few hours. During their ordeal, the terrified women argued with one another, spoke their truths, and revealed secrets. Eventually, they managed to disarm Laura and ended up beating her to within an inch of her life. Laura left the house battered and bruised and hours later took her own life.

In the year since the pleasure party, Kristin and Veronica had become close friends. So close that Kristin had confessed to Veronica about her affair and her feelings for Ed.

"I guess you don't ever forget about something like that," Kristin said. You do the work and learn to live with it."

"I killed her," Veronica blurted out suddenly. "I killed Laura. How do I live with that?

"What? You didn't kill her, Veronica. Laura killed herself. That's not on you."

"Yes but..."

"But nothing, Veronica. Laura had issues, most of which had nothing to do with you. Her demons finally caught up to her and she slit her wrists in her tub. Her death isn't on you. It isn't on any of us."

"No, you don't understand. I..."

"You what?"

"I... I..."

Kristin held her friend's hand. "You did what you had to do, Veronica. We all did. Remember, if we hadn't overpowered her you would have been the first one she killed. And don't forget how vengeful Laura was, if she hadn't taken her own life, you would have been looking over your shoulder every time you left the house."

Veronica only nodded, remembering she had thought the very same thing on the night one year ago when she left the party and sneaked into Laura's home. She found her in a drunken stupor in her tub and slit her wrists to make it look like a suicide.

"Have you spoken with Bianca lately?" Veronica asked, quickly changing the subject.

Kristin sighed. "We've talked, you know, to say hi and how are the kids, stuff like that, but we haven't really talked if you know what I mean. We tried a few days after the party but it just felt... forced and kind of weird."

"Why? Do you think she knows about you and Ed?"

"No!" Kristin said. "No, she doesn't. It's not that. I don't know how to be Bianca's friend and be in love with her husband at the same time. Maybe I could, but she's changed too. She's been hanging out with Brooke for a while now and..."

"Say no more," Veronica said. "That Brooke is a piece of work."

"She sure is," Kristin agreed. "I mean, I like Brooke and all, but you can tell there's a lot of trauma in her past. She's into some freaky, scary stuff."

Veronica nodded, remembering some of the things

Brooke revealed during the party. "Do you think Bianca is into the same kind of things?"

"Yes," she said. "I know she is. That's exactly why she's hanging out with Brooke." Her voice got louder, and she became red in the face. "She says Ed is too boring for her... she doesn't deserve him. He's a good man, he's... he's..."

"Kris, it's okay. Calm down," Veronica said, holding Kristin's hand.

Kristin took a breath. "I'm sorry, I'm sorry, it's just that..."

"The man you love is shackled to a woman who doesn't deserve him."

"Yes," Kristin said through tears. "That's it exactly."

"Been there, done that."

"Any advice for me?" Kristin asked, dabbing at her tears with a tissue.

Veronica exhaled. "Let me ask you a question before I answer that. Do you think Ed really wants to be with you, or are you guys ..."

"Having a fling? No, he wants to be with me! He's said it a thousand times."

"And you believe him?"

"I really do, Veronica. He's not the type of man to have a fling for the hell of it. He wants a divorce, but his boys... he's worried about what it would do to them, and I can't blame him. I know how he feels."

"So you wait?"

Kristen nodded. "I won't have long to wait. The way Bianca's going it's a matter of time before he sees who she really is and then..."

"And then?"

"And then he'll have to end it. It's inevitable. He won't have a choice."

"And if that plan doesn't work, then what?"

"I don't know... I guess... I wait. As long as it takes."

Veronica sighed. "During my affair with David, I was on

top of the world. But there came a time when I wondered if he was playing me for a fool. I started thinking crazy thoughts and pretty soon I convinced myself he was only with me to get back at Laura, just having a good time with the gullible idiot who believed his lies. I kept on asking myself if he was just having a fling or was this forever?"

She took a breath and continued.

"David soon showed me he wasn't like that. I was lucky. Most women in that position aren't."

Kristin searched for the right response but just then the baby woke up, looked around, and started to fuss.

"I think the conversation is too heavy for Isaac," Kristin said, grinning.

"Nah, he's just ready to eat. I swear, this kid eats like a grown man." She dug in one of her diaper bag's many pockets and emerged with a sippy cup which she gave to Isaac. The baby took the cup and began drinking greedily.

"That'll hold him for a little bit, but I better get him home and fed," Veronica said. "Thanks for talking, Kris, I appreciate it. I hope you have a great time in Miami."

"I'll come over and tell you all about it when I get back."

"It's a date," Veronica said, as she hugged Kristin goodbye.

Kristen watched as Veronica put the baby in his car seat, then waved to her and drove off. She shut her door and leaned against it. The conversation with Veronica hit her harder than she cared to admit.

Was Ed just using her for...

"No! Stop!" Kristen scolded herself for her negative thoughts, put them out of her mind and went upstairs to finish packing.

#

Kristin's phone alarm began blaring at 4:00 a.m. jolting her out of a restless sleep that featured a terrible nightmare, something about arriving in Miami only to have Ed disappear on her. She put the terrible dream out of her mind, showered and dressed and in a few minutes she was in the car and on the way to the airport.

Driving down the New Jersey Turnpike at this time of day made her feel like she was the only person in the state. The highway was deserted save for the occasional trucker that blew by her on the way to God knows where. The ride to Newark Airport was normally around forty-five minutes from her home, but according to her GPS she would be there in thirty. She tuned the radio to her favorite 90's R&B station but soon turned it off again, preferring to enjoy the time savoring the sweet anticipation of seeing and spending time with her man. At least that's what she intended but her conversation with Veronica invaded her thoughts. Ever since they spoke the questions Veronica asked her had been playing in a loop in the back of her mind.

Did Ed really want to be with her?

Would he ever divorce Bianca?

What if Ed were just using her as a "distraction?"

Was this a fling or was what they had forever?

She knew that Veronica did what any good friend would do, making sure she saw all sides of the situation. But where she previously had 100% faith in Ed, now the tiniest spark of doubt glowed in her mind.

Kristin arrived at Newark Airport, parked her car in the long-term lot and hopped on the shuttle that would take her to the terminal. The shuttle was only about half-full, but the bulk of the passengers seemed to be happy couples. She felt like the odd woman out, growing increasingly uncomfortable as she watched them hold hands and whisper to each other.

Kristin was the first one off the shuttle as it pulled up to the terminal. She quickly retrieved her bags and walked to a kiosk where she scanned her ticket and got her boarding pass. The doubt that was just a spark minutes before had burst into flame. It was still fairly small but growing steadily throughout her psyche.

She followed the signs to security and stood in line behind a couple who held hands and took every opportunity to look into each other's eyes. The woman had her arm around her man and as she watched, he leaned over and kissed her on the top of her head, looking at her with intense love in his eyes. The woman saw her man's look and held him closer.

The looks the couple exchanged nearly almost broke her. Moments like that were all she wanted. For her man to look at her like that. As long as she was in an affair with another woman's husband, she could never be out with him in public, much less put her arms around him or give him loving looks. She was fooling herself if she thought a couple of hours a week of stolen time in her bed would ever be enough. As she neared security she turned away, unable to stand the sight of the couple. By time she had finished her security screening she was close to tears. She put her shoes back on quickly, ran past the couple, found the nearest ladies' room and ran inside. Luckily, there was no one else in the bathroom and she locked herself in the closest stall and let the tears flow.

"Stupid, stupid, stupid, stupid," she said to herself. When her then-husband Stan cheated on her she vowed to herself never to let another man break her heart, and yet here she was, in an airport bathroom crying her eyes out over another cheating man.

How could he love you. She thought. You're just... pussy. Just a diversion, like Maya was for Tina. He's just using you. God, you're so dumb!

Suddenly she felt as if a great weight had settled on her chest and her breaths came in wheezes and gasps. She could feel and hear her impossibly fast heartbeat and her knees went weak but she held onto the stall door for dear life, refusing the indignity of falling to the disgusting bathroom floor. It seemed like hours, but a few minutes later the weight on her chest subsided and her breathing slowly returned to normal although her heart still beat rapidly in her chest.

When she felt like she could trust her legs to support her, she emerged from the stall, dragging her luggage behind her like an anchor. She splashed water on her face and slowly walked out into the terminal. Her gate was only a few yards away, but she turned her back on it and began walking toward the exit. She wished with all her being she could be on the flight to Miami, but this was for the best. She would rip the boarding pass to shreds, go get her car and go the hell back home. And when he called her to find out what happened, she would tell him it was over and never speak to him again. She would be crying for weeks, she knew, but this heartbreak now would be nothing compared to the heartbreak she'd feel months or years down the line when he decided he was done with her. She gave the gate one last, longing look and started walking toward the exit when her phone rang. It was Ed. She considered not responding but maybe it was best to tell him now.

She sat down on a bench, put her ear buds in and folded her arms.

"Hello," she said in a cold voice.

"Hey... Kris, are you okay honey? Did you get to the airport?"

"Yes. I'm almost at the gate."

"Okay, great you had me worried for a moment there."

"Ed... I don't think..."

"Baby I didn't sleep all night. I'm so damn excited about seeing you. I've missed you so much."

She made a face and rolled her eyes. Yeah, I know what you missed, she thought.

"I know I said it before, but I cannot wait to see you. I can't wait to just... you know... hang out with you and hold your hand. I'm so sick of hiding Kris. I want the world to know how I feel about you."

"You do?"

"Hell yes I do. You know I do. I love what we do, don't get me wrong but there's so much more I want to experience with you. I want to be out with you and take walks and eat fattening food in overpriced restaurants and just hang out together. I want to make memories with you."

Kristin began to cry and a sob escaped her lips.

"Wait, honey, are you crying?"

"I am," she said as she wiped her tears. "They're happy tears. I'm crying in the middle of Newark Airport at six o'clock in the morning and I don't care. Ed, that is the sweetest, most romantic thing anyone ever said to me, and baby believe me when I tell you, I really needed to hear it."

"I'm glad honey. Now hurry up and get here. I love you."

Kristin stood up with renewed vigor and walked toward her gate. "I'm hurrying baby, see you soon. I love you too." She hurried to the gate, wondering how just a minute ago she was about to make the biggest mistake of her life. Veronica, although well-intentioned, triggered her insecurity and almost led her to do something stupid, completely convinced that the man she knew for a fact loved her was only using her. Moral of the story, get better control over your emotions and never, ever tell anyone about your love life. Not even your friends.

The flight began to board, and she showed her boarding pass and stood in line on the jet way with the other passengers. One of the couples from security stood in front of her, still in each other's arms, oblivious to the rest of the world. This time they didn't faze her. Ed loved her and she loved him, and she would wait to have him, no matter how long it took.

She arrived at her seat, put her carry-on away and lay back and smiled.

She was on the way to see her man.

Life was good.

* * *

Want to know what happens with your favorite ***Pleasure Party*** character and don't want to wait until the next book comes out?

Click **HERE** to be put on Hugh's mailing list and get a **FREE** short story featuring one of the ***Pleasure Party*** characters every few weeks.

There's a LOT going on in **Willows,** the town that ***Pleasure Party*** is set in. This town has more than its fair share of secrets. Turn the page to read a sample of ***Candyland*** - another story set in this drama-filled town.

CANDYLAND

Hugh O. Smith

In the wealthy town of Willows, New Jersey things look perfect. From the beautiful homes, to the immaculately kept streets to boasting some of the best schools in the state, Willows seems like the perfect town.

Enter Shaun Harmon. Shaun is a bestselling author who arrives in Willows with his young daughter Tanya to start a new life. After years of trying his books are finally bestsellers and one of them has become a Hollywood blockbuster. Life is good, Shaun just bought his dream home in Willows and he's starting a brand-new relationship. He should be happy, he has all the money and success he worked hard for but he's still mourning the loss of his beloved wife, and for some reason the words that used to come so easily to him no longer flow. And now, Shaun is finding out that Willows, the perfect-seeming town harbors dark secrets. Secrets that it would do anything to hide. Even kill!

You see, Shaun is about to find out that the wealthy have the most to hide.
And the most to lose.

CHAPTER 1

Shaun sprinted through the back door, past the pool and onto the broad expanse of lawn. Adrenaline heightened his senses and gave him a strange clarity, every single blade of grass stood out in high definition and the fireflies' flickering lights blazed brightly in stark relief against the dark backdrop of Willows Lake. He felt his daughter's dead weight in his arms and her terrified breaths, hot against his neck.

The adrenaline also gave him the gift of calm. He should be panicked, but he wasn't. Strangely, all he could think about was how to use this experience in his next novel. After all, Shaun Harmon novels were known for moments like this, a hurt and bleeding hero running in the dark, using only his wits to escape harm and defeat the bad guys. If he were writing this scene, the hero would be injured but unflappable, working out the ways to use the everyday items around him as weapons even as he weakened from blood loss.

He ran across the grass, his mind working to find a way to describe what was happening.

Early evening had given way to full on night. Fireflies were the only light, but terror heightened his senses and his eyes adjusted quickly to the gloom. The grass was damp from the evening's rain, soaking his bare feet and the cuffs of his jeans as he ran.

That was okay, he thought, but not dramatic enough.

He looked right, then left.

Nowhere to run except straight ahead into the dark waters of Willows Lake.

Too dramatic, he thought, and not strictly true. He had choices. He could...

Tanya's frightened breathing in his ear brought him back to reality. Usually he couldn't shut her up, but now her wide and terrified eyes were doing all the talking.

"It's gonna be okay baby, don't worry, everything's gonna be okay," he whispered to her as they ran.

He hoped.

Shaun ran around to the side of the house, sticking close to the building, cursing the floodlights that activated at his movement. He stopped to peer around the corner. His Range Rover was in the driveway and his hopes flared, only to be dashed a moment later when he realized it sat on slashed tires.

"Fuck," he hissed under his breath.

Tanya was usually quick to admonish her father when he let loose the occasional swear word in her presence, but terror had rendered her mute. He peered around the corner once again, looking and listening for their assailant. Seeing and hearing nothing, he scurried across the driveway and took refuge behind his SUV. There was no sign of their attacker, so he took a moment to smooth Tanya's hair out of her eyes.

"It's gonna be okay, Princess," he said again, trying hard to sound convincing. Tanya's eyes were wide open and staring down at his side.

Shaun didn't look. He didn't have to; he could feel his t-shirt sticking to his skin, soaked with blood. There was no pain yet, adrenaline was probably delaying its onset, but Shaun had no doubt it would come soon. In his second book, *Van Cortland*, his hero was injured by a serial killer operating in the Bronx. He'd had his hero chew periwinkle leaves and apply them to the wound to staunch the blood flow. Or was it dandelion? He couldn't remember. His friend Nelson's *Abuela* had told him about that when he was writing the novel. The old woman had insisted on taking him out and actually showing him how to chew the bitter leaves and apply to the wound. He put his hand to his side and they came away red and wet.

He put his hand to his side and it came away wet and red with blood. The knife had been sharp. So sharp, the cut was almost painless. He'd only realized he was hurt when...

Oh, now you want to write, he admonished himself silently. He should be running for his life, their lives, but his mind kept on trying to find the words. Writer's block had plagued him for months and now, in the most unlikely of moments, was when the words chose to come to him again.

He knew they had to keep moving but he hesitated a second longer, trying to stay calm long enough to weigh his options. His first thought was to return to the back of the house but there was nothing for them there except the dark waters of Willows Lake (maybe that line would work after all) and the dilapidated boathouse that he'd been meaning to demolish since he bought the home six months ago. He glanced out at the lights twinkling in the homes on the far shore of the lake. There were far more homes there than on this side; if he were alone he would chance the long swim but making an attempt with Tanya was out of the question.

He thought to creep along the trees that lined his driveway until he reached the main road, but with Tanya in his arms, his wound, and no shoes on his feet, he doubted he would get very far.

To his west was the Murphy estate but it was over three quarters of a mile away; they'd never make it. His neighbors to the east, the Kings, were much closer, but their house was empty. An elderly couple, the Kings spent much of the year in their Florida home. There was no one there and no help for him. Then he remembered the old Duracraft fishing boat that Gerry King kept. The King's had invited Shaun and Tanya over shortly after they'd moved in and Gerry had proudly showed off the lovingly maintained boat he'd rescued from a junkyard and restored. Shaun didn't know the first thing about boats, sailing hadn't been a part of his Bronx upbringing, but he figured that if they made it to the boat, he could at least start it. They didn't have to go far, only to the other side of the lake - then they would be safe. Course of action decided, he glanced toward the house again then ducked into the trees.

Five minutes later Shaun and Tanya emerged onto the edges of the King's property. There was no sign of anyone about, but Shaun paused at the tree line and sat down in the dirt. Tanya was a very petite child, one of the smallest in her Kindergarten class but terror made her a dead weight in his arms that was becoming heavier by the minute.

"Let's rest here honey," he said, trying to put her down.

The scared little girl shook her head and held onto him for dear life.

"We're only gonna rest for a minute, Princess. I'm not going anywhere, I promise."

Gradually, Tanya loosened her grip and he placed her on the warm dirt. Her eyes were wide in the dark and he kissed her forehead gently.

"We're going to be all right honey, don't you worry," he said.

He knelt in the dirt next to his daughter, looking and listening. The King's property was dark except for a dim spotlight that illuminated the front of the massive home. Except for the cicadas there was no sound.

Shaun mapped out the route in his mind, then turned to his daughter.

"We're going to run into the King's backyard, go get Mr. King's boat and ride across the lake. Sound good?"

Tanya's response was to hold up her arms and Shaun lifted her up and held her close. She snuggled her face into the space between his neck and shoulder and wrapped her tiny arms tightly around his neck.

Shaun took one more look around, then keeping low, ran along the side of the King's property hugging the tree line. A minute later they were at the back of the King's property, and he paused again, looking hard into the darkness for any sign of movement. Seeing none, he ran down the slope of King's back lawn and down the steps to the dock and the boathouse.

Now that they were here, he began to question his idea. What if the boathouse was locked? What if the boat was in dry-dock already? What if he couldn't get it started? He shook off the doubts and turned the boathouse doorknob. The door pushed open with a tiny squeak that sounded as loud as a gunshot in the darkness. Shaun put Tanya down and stood for a moment to get his eyes used to the murk.

The boathouse was large and immaculately kept. There were two spaces for boats, one occupied with the Duracraft, the other empty. On each wall were shelves and hooks that held the various canoes and kayaks that the King's grandchildren were constantly paddling on the lake.

Shaun recalled Gerry King explaining that the boat was relatively small, only seventeen feet, but in the darkness it loomed huge in front of them. Shaun lifted Tanya onto the deck and opened the hatch he remembered led to a storage compartment below.

"Get down there honey," he whispered. "We'll be safe soon."

Tanya quickly did as she was told and Shaun sat in the pilot's seat, trying to remember Gerry's lessons. The throttle was to his right and he put the engine in neutral and began to turn the key but stopped when he realized that the boat was still tethered to the dock. He jumped off the boat and as he undid the line, he heard the squeak of the door opening.

"So predictable," a voice said.

Shaun turned to see the business end of an oar coming hard and fast at his face. He ducked, and the oar passed harmlessly over his head but as he moved backward, he tripped over the line that tethered the boat to its berth. He fell hard, the breath knocked from his body. He jumped up quickly and ducked another blow that again missed his head but struck his shoulder a glancing blow that caused him to stumble backwards. Flailing wildly for balance, his hand found the material of his attacker's shirt and they stumbled back together, splashing into the dark water, going under as the terrified Tanya screamed for her father.

CHAPTER 2

Two months earlier

Shaun peeked through the curtains at the audience, trying hard to stifle his amusement at the standing room only crowd that had come to the Willows Reading Club to hear him speak. The audience was predominantly white, expensively dressed, and firmly ensconced in the one percent. Ironic, since the Willows Reading Club was formed almost two hundred years ago by former slaves with the express purpose of teaching their escaped brethren how to read and write. The original purpose of the club was largely forgotten, its legacy hijacked by the wives of investment bankers and Wall Street financiers.

"Can I get you anything Mr. Harmon?" The chipper young girl, whose name Shaun couldn't believe actually was Muffy, asked. She'd been hovering around for a few minutes, tasked with taking care of him while he prepared for his talk.

He closed the curtain. "No thank you, I'm good," he said with a forced smile.

The truth was he wasn't good, far from it. He hated these events. In the minutes before he spoke his stage fright kicked in and his stomach became one big knot. He usually found someplace to hide before he went on but the Willows Reading Club, although elegant and obviously exclusive, was small and didn't offer much in the way of hiding places. People probably thought the great author was being quiet to collect his deep thoughts but in actuality it was all he could do not to vomit his lunch up on their ancient hardwood floors. The nervousness usually passed as soon as he stepped onto the stage but the minutes before were no kind of fun.

His mind began to race and he heard Claire in his mind. “Take a deep breath,” she said. “Just breathe honey.” She’d given him the same advice thousands of times when the words wouldn’t come to him, or when he received yet another rejection letter from another publisher.

He breathed deeply, wishing with everything in him that she were here with him. He closed his eyes and tried hard to channel memories of her. It was at times like this that he missed Claire the most. She would have gotten a huge thrill out of seeing him talk to an enraptured audience about his work. He saw her in his mind’s eye, smiling and holding his hand, he could almost smell her perfume feel her hand in his…

“Mr. Harmon,” Muffy said, breaking the spell. The young woman was hovering around him, obviously trying to work up the courage to say something.

“I hope you don’t mind me saying so but Oh-Emm-Gee you are my favorite author in the whole world, and I can’t believe we live in the same town, I mean, it’s such an honor to meet you, I love everything you write, you’re amazing.” She held Shaun’s newest hardcover in her hands. “I was wondering if you would…”

“Muffy, why don’t we give Mr. Harmon a chance to gather his thoughts before his speech,” a voice said from behind the wide-eyed young woman. The voice was cultured, low and very sexy. Jessica Rabbit with a finishing school education.

Trudy Willows-Brown stepped out from behind Muffy and gave Shaun a dazzling smile.

“Oh. You're right. I’m sorry Mr. Harmon, I really didn't mean to...”

It’s okay... um, Muffy,” Shaun said. He could barely say her name without wanting to laugh. “You weren’t bothering me at all. Tell you what, catch me after the speech and I’ll sign your book, okay?”

"Muffy could you go get Mr. Harmon a Cherry Coke please, I left some in the refrigerator especially for him.

"I'm so sorry Mr. Harmon," Trudy said after Muffy eagerly ran off to get his soft drink. "I hope she didn't bother you too much, it's just that she admires your work so. We don't get many celebrities in our small town, much less one that lives here."

"I'm hardly a celebrity," he said. "And please call me Shaun," he said. "And anyway, how did you know I liked Cherry Coke?"

"And I'm Trudy," she said with a smile. "I think I'll have to disagree with you about the celebrity part. You're one of the most famous writers in the world. The President of the United States said you're his favorite author, your books have been on every best-seller list there is and the movie they made of your first book broke all kinds of box-office records. I'd say that grants you celebrity status, so I made it my business to find out everything I could about you. Including that you love Cherry Coke."

She extended a hand and he took it, expecting well-manicured, soft fingers but her nails were short and the hand was hard and calloused with a strong grip. His surprise must have shown because she laughed and pulled her hand back.

"Horses."

"Excuse me?"

"Horses. I've worked with horses since I was old enough to walk. You have to have a strong grip, and manicures don't really survive too long when you're on horseback most of the time."

"Have you been around horses much Mr. Harm... Shaun?"

"Not much. My mother took me for a horseback ride once for my birthday when I was about six, but that's about the only experience I've had."

"That's a shame; all children should get a chance to be around horses."

"Maybe, but there wasn't much chance of that in the South Bronx."

"Well, now you're here in Willows where there are plenty of chances. This is your open invitation to bring your family by our farm anytime."

"It's just me and my daughter," Shaun said.

"How old is she?"

"She's four. She just started preschool over at Candyland."

At the mention of the prestigious local school, Trudy's face darkened but she regained her composure quickly.

"Four? What a great age! I have the perfect horse for her, his name is Puddles, he's perfectly gentle and..."

Trudy caught herself and laughed.

"Look at me Shaun, I chased poor Muffy away from you and now I'm here doing the same thing."

Shaun smiled.

"I don't mind at all," he said, and meant it.

There was something about Trudy, despite her obviously expensive clothes and patrician air that calmed him. He hadn't been living long among the wealthy, a class that he was now a part of thanks to the massive success of his books and the resulting hit movie, and he felt constantly off balance among them.

"That's very gracious of you," Trudy said. "But I think I'll leave you to gather your thoughts. She turned to go but turned back to look at him.

"They told me you had a way of making a lady feel... at ease. They were right. Good luck with your talk."

She smiled and walked away before Shaun could ask her what she meant. "They" said? Who were "they"? Before he could speculate any further she was gone.

A moment later footsteps approached and his agent, Sara Diamond, appeared with a Cherry Coke.

"I intercepted some teeny bopper back there with this," she said, handing him the soft drink.

He greeted Sara with a kiss on the cheek before accepting the soft drink from her.

"I see you met the local gentry," she said, as Shaun sipped

the soda.

"Who? Trudy?"

"Trudy? My God. She even has a snooty name," Sara said, rolling her eyes.

Shaun said nothing. He loved Sara; if it weren't for her none of the success he'd had over the past two years would have occurred. She was the only agent out of the fifty or so he'd sent his manuscript to who had bothered to even respond to his query. Since his success plenty of other larger and more established agencies had contacted him, trying to woo him away from Sara, but she'd believed in him when no one else did and that earned her a loyalty that would never waver. She got him. More importantly, she got his work. She believed in it and fought for his manuscripts like a mother tiger defending her cubs.

Shaun took another sip of his soda and glanced at his agent. As usual, her curves were prominent in her tight skirt accentuated by the insanely expensive heels she was addicted to. Her top was equally as tight and her enhanced cleavage tried its best to bust out of it. She fit in perfectly in New York City where she was another hard-driving, fifty-something with store bought breasts and dyed roots. Here in Willows, among the tasteful pearls and Prada, she stood out like a roach on a wedding cake. She didn't care. Sara had nothing but contempt for the wealthy women of Willows and did absolutely nothing to hide it.

She parted the curtain and looked out onto the growing audience.

"My God, it's like shark week out there."

"What are you talking about?"

"Just look at them. Predators in tasteful pearls. All here to get a look at the big, handsome, Bronx import."

"Sara, please..."

"I don't see why you couldn't just stay in the city. If you wanted the suburbs, you could have moved to Westchester. What's wrong with Scarsdale? Chappaqua even. There are plenty of rich people there and I wouldn't have to drive for three damn hours and pay a hundred dollars in tolls to see you."

"It's only an hour from New York and not anywhere close to a hundred bucks in tolls. Stop exaggerating."

"Whatever. It's far."

She took the Coke from him and sipped.

"I do appreciate the pool though," she said.

"Are you saying that you're staying the night and taking advantage of my pool?"

"Fuck no. I'm saying I'm staying the entire weekend and taking advantage of your pool AND your hot tub. Plus, we have some business to go over, so get used to this face buddy, you're putting me up for a few days."

Sara smiled at him, and he smiled back. He enjoyed having her around and his daughter Tanya loved her too. He was about to reply to Sara when he heard the microphone come alive and the hostess begin the introduction. He squeezed Sara's hand, plastered a smile on his face, and walked onto the stage.

CHAPTER 3

"Daddy can I ask you a question?"

Shaun knew this was coming. All through her bath time the normally talkative Tanya had remained silent. He didn't press the issue, he knew her well enough to know something was on her mind and she would come out with it in her own good time.

"Sure hon, you can ask me anything."

"Why doesn't Sara stay with us all the time?"

"Because this isn't her home, honey. She lives in New York. C'mon, arms up."

Tanya held her arms up and Shaun slipped her Hello Kitty nightshirt over her head and onto her tiny frame.

"I know that Daddy." She used the tone that all daughters used when they thought their Daddies were being silly. "But she can move here, right? Just like we did."

"I don't think so, Princess, her home is in New York. She would miss her friends."

"But I miss my friends in the Bronx and we moved here anyway. I miss Nylah and Anna and Jordyn and Madison and Ava and Juliette and..."

"I know you do hon, but let's talk about it tomorrow okay. It's time to go to sleep."

Tanya yawned as Shaun put her in her bed and pulled the covers up to her chin. Normally, the let's talk about it tomorrow ploy would never have worked but she was exhausted. Tanya loved when Sara came over and the two of them had run all over the house playing until they wore themselves out. Shaun had let her stay up a little bit past her bedtime but now she was dead tired and more than ready for sleep, but she kept on trying to fight it.

He kissed her on her forehead as stroked her hair.

"Have a good night; I'll see you in the morning. I love you."

"I love you too Daddy," Tanya said, yawning.

Her eyes were already closing as Shaun gently pulled the door halfway closed, making sure, as he always did, that light from the hallway entered her room. He lingered for a moment, feeling a pang of guilt at his daughter's question about their former home. It'd been only a few months since they'd left the Bronx, but Tanya still asked about it from time to time. Hell, her new bedroom was almost as big as their old apartment, he thought. The school she now attended was only about one thousand times better than her old one, but none of that mattered to a young kid missing her friends.

After his third novel had hit the bestseller list and was quickly snapped up by Hollywood, his first and his second, which no one had paid any mind to before, quickly followed suit. Much success and even more money had quickly followed, and Shaun saw no reason to stay in the Bronx. The idyllic neighborhood he'd grown up in had changed for the worse. Landlords refused to make any repairs to the buildings, the gangs were more and more of a presence every day, and Shaun shuddered every time he passed the ramshackle building that housed the school that Tanya would soon attend. As soon as he was able, he looked for a better place to raise his daughter and quickly found the small but affluent town of Willows about an hour away in New Jersey.

Shaun walked down the gigantic staircase and into the kitchen where Sara sat at the table drinking from his bottle of twenty-five-year-old single malt.

"Found the good stuff, I see?"

"No sweetheart, it found me," she said.

She picked up her glass and took another sip, then poured him a shot and pushed the glass over to him.

"Now it found you too."

Shaun rarely drank but he picked up the glass and drained the contents, then pushed the glass back over to her for another.

Sara raised an eyebrow in surprise but poured him another and pushed the glass back.

"You all right?"

He drained the glass again, wincing as the harsh liquid hit his stomach.

"I'm fine."

"Yea, I can see that."

Shaun sat down opposite her and poured himself another drink.

"She asked me about the Bronx again. About her friends..."

"Shaun, we've gone through this, you know that..."

"I know Sara but try and explain that to a four-year-old kid who misses the only home she ever knew."

Sara took a drink, then set her glass down.

"Did I ever tell you why I accepted you as a client?"

He shook his head.

"I did it because I knew you were just like me. You would do whatever the fuck you had to do to make your dreams come true. You came into my office that day with your manuscript in your hand, remember? You could have easily e-mailed it, but you wouldn't leave until you put it in my hands personally. You had that fire in your belly. You had ambition! I knew you were going to do big things. You couldn't do those things if you stayed where you were."

"I know, but maybe I should have stayed closer to ho... to the Bronx, so she could visit her mother once in a while."

"Claire lives in her heart, Shaun, and in yours. It's only her body that's in Woodlawn Cemetery. I break your chops about this Stepford town but moving was the right thing to do. Of course, you don't exactly fit the Brooks Brothers, suburban mold," she said, smiling.

Shaun laughed. "You're one to talk; you don't fit in here either."

"Maybe. But the difference is I don't give a fuck. I don't have to live here and play nice with the Stepford wives." Sara rose and put her arm around Shaun. "Speaking of Stepford wives," she whispered in his ear. "How many of them have you... um, you know?"

"Uh... well there is someone I've been seeing..."

Sara smiled. "I was kidding, Shaun. I don't care."

Shaun said nothing.

"Is the Princess asleep?" Sara asked.

"Yea, she's knocked out. Playing with you always wears her out."

"What a coincidence," Sara said. "I have the same effect on her father."

She picked up the bottle of Scotch and poured herself another drink. She drained half of it, then handed him the glass and he drank the other half as she removed her panties and put them on the table next to the bottle.

Shaun felt a twinge of guilt as Sara sat on his lap, but quickly put that aside as she kissed him. Sara was thinner than Claire had been, she was curvy, but tall and long-limbed unlike the shorter and more full-figured Claire. But, like Claire, she was passionate and strong. He closed his eyes and, in his mind, willed Sara to become his dead wife. The fantasy became so real that he almost felt Sara grow heavier on his lap; her hips grew wider as he caressed them and her breasts became fuller and pushed against his chest. He pressed his face into her skin and smelled Joy, the perfume Claire had worn every day since her father had bought her a bottle for her sixteenth birthday. Soon, it was Claire on top of him, Claire's breasts that his face was buried in; Claire's scent, Claire's voice in his ear, urging him on. His writer's imagination filled in the blanks, and he was transported back to their tiny Bronx apartment, their lovemaking causing their cheap furniture to squeak and protest, laughing at their inability to stifle their sounds of pleasure so their neighbors wouldn't hear. He smelled the roast she'd cooked for dinner earlier and the fresh laundry they'd picked up from the laundromat together. He heard the familiar, comforting clanking of the aged refrigerator that the super refused to replace and the drip-drip of the kitchen faucet. He held Claire's face in his hands and kissed her hard, then buried his face in her breasts, kissing and licking as her body bucked with the force of her climax. He smiled to himself as he always did, happy that he could satisfy this woman that he loved with all his soul. As Claire's orgasm subsided, his own was upon him and he buried his face deeper into her breasts and let himself go, losing himself even deeper in the make-believe.

Afterward, he opened his eyes and his fantasy abandoned him. They were in Willows, in his huge house. Sara was on top of him, not Claire.

Claire was dead.

He put his head on Sara's chest once again, hoping that she would mistake his tears for the perspiration that dripped from them both.

CHAPTER 4

Shaun's alarm went off at 5:00am and he quickly reached over and shut it off, not wanting to wake Sara who slept naked next to him. She had kicked off the covers and he put them back on her then dressed in sweats and a t-shirt and trudged downstairs.

He flicked a switch in the kitchen, the lights came on and he squinted, his sleep-dimmed eyes unused to the lights glinting off the kitchen's many stainless-steel surfaces. The room was huge, looking more like the kitchen of a small upscale restaurant than one for only two people.

The half-finished bottle of scotch, the glasses, and Sara's panties were still on the table. He put the bottle away, washed the glasses, and looked around for somewhere to put the underwear, finally sticking them in his pocket.

His cell phone still sat on the table where he'd left it. The battery was at two percent and barely holding on but there was enough juice left for him to see the text messages and phone calls he'd missed. He checked the messages and read the texts then plugged the phone into the wall to charge.

His coffeemaker beeped softly, obeying its preset program, and the kitchen filled with the aroma of Colombian Roast. Shaun poured himself a cup then trudged to his den to get his laptop.

Ever since he could remember, the space to the right of whatever computer he used to write was reserved for neat stacks of the pages he'd written the day before. To the left were outlines and notes. For months, the space to the right of his computer had been empty. He wasn't worried at first, putting it down to the pressures of moving and then the new environment. But as the months passed, the words showed no sign of coming back. He awoke at the same time every morning, poured his coffee, sat down before his computer, and stared at the empty screen for hours. The publishers were clamoring for pages, but Sara had managed to keep them at bay, but now even she had begun to question him.

He took the laptop out by his pool and turned it on. Same as yesterday, the empty page waited for him to fill it. He put his fingers on the keyboard but hesitated, thinking back to the night before with Sara. It was an unspoken pact between them, they'd slept together a few times before and neither of them would ever talk about it, each knowing the other was owed nothing except orgasms and the courtesy of not bringing it up once it was over. He'd been on tour, his first, the first time they slept together. It was only about a year since Claire had died but he still felt her loss as if it were yesterday. His sadness, combined with missing his daughter and a good bit of expensive Scotch had conspired to drive him into bed with Sara. He'd wept afterwards then too, he always did. Partly because he wished with all his soul it was Claire he'd made love to and partly because of the guilt he felt in using Sara in that way. He'd vowed to himself it wouldn't happen again, but despite his vow it happened in city after city. He'd grown better at hiding the pain and the guilt he felt afterwards but it was no less intense for his hiding it.

The blinking cursor drew him back to reality, but he ignored it and looked out at the thin sliver of pink on the horizon over Willows Lake where the sun was just making up its mind to rise.

When they first moved to Willows, just sitting by the pool would make Shaun happy. It was HIS pool. His. He'd earned it. No one in his family had even owned an above-ground pool before, much less one large enough to host Olympic events. It represented everything he'd worked years to attain. While in the Bronx struggling to make ends meet not a day had gone by when he didn't dream of owning a home like this. He'd fantasized about the pool, the kitchen, the massive acreage on which his daughter would run and play. Shaun sighed. Things were easier then. He'd rise at 4:00am, throw on his old sweatpants and a tee and go running on Mosholu Parkway. Then, on the way home he'd buy a coffee and a buttered roll from Papi's bodega then return home and take his breakfast on the fire escape with a pad and a pen. As the sun rose over the Bronx Botanical Gardens, the words would inevitably come in a flood; it was all his hand could do to keep up with the torrent. He became a familiar sight to his neighbors walking up Bedford Park Boulevard to the D train, the big man sitting on the fire escape with a pen and a pad, lost in worlds of his own making.

Later that evening after work he'd type out the pages he'd written that morning and stack them carefully with the others on his wobbly old Fingerhut desk. He'd written four books in this way, and submitted them to more publishers and agents than he could count; only receiving rejections for his efforts. Undaunted, every single day after writing he would visualize the fruits of his efforts. The book signings, the big home, the movies made from his books. He knew it all was coming; it was only a matter of time. Now it was here. Everything he had... they had dreamed of had all come to pass and he was miserable. With a sigh, he returned to the blank page and the blinking cursor and began to try to pull the words out of his head and onto the page.

Two hours later the MacBook's low battery alert warned him that it would shut down soon and he saved his work and read it over. He'd only written five pages and the few words had not come easily. He read them over and sighed with disgust. His work was best when the words flowed easily from him. When he struggled to get them down, they read like the pained rambling of some delusional stranger who was trying hard to convince himself that he had a story to tell. He knew he would delete the pages eventually but for now he clicked save, then shut the computer down and gazed out at Willows Lake.

"Communing with nature?" Sara asked from behind him.

"Something like that."

She took a sip of the coffee she'd poured herself and sat across from him. She was dressed in a two-piece bathing suit and the shirt he'd worn last night. He glanced at her body then looked away quickly.

"So, how many pages did you write this morning?"

"A few," he lied.

She grinned and sipped more coffee as she sat.

"You lie."

"What?"

"You heard me. You lie. Like a rug."

Shaun said nothing.

"So how long have you been blocked? And why didn't you tell me?"

"I'm not blocked," he lied. "I'm just having a... creative crisis right now."

"How long?"

He said nothing.

"How long, Shaun?"

"A few months."

She at upright in her chair. "A few... Jesus Christ, why didn't you say something?"

"Sara, don't break my balls okay, I'm fucked up enough as it is."

Sara leaned back in the chair and took an angry sip of her coffee, then took a calming breath.

"Okay, okay, fine. It's not as if you're the first writer to go through this. What's the problem anyway?"

Shaun rose from his chair and paced along the side of the pool.

"That's just it, I have no idea. I mean, in the Bronx I sat on that old rusty fire escape and breathed fumes from the Bx31 bus and wrote my ass off." He gestured toward the pool and the lake. "Now look where I am and I can't write a fucking word."

"Is it about Claire?"

"What did you say?"

"You heard me Shaun. Is it about Claire?"

"Leave her out of this."

"How can I?" She gestured around at the house and the pool. "This was the dream you had for your lives, wasn't it? She was the first person who encouraged you to write, she knew you could make it, she..."

"I said leave her out of this, Sara. I mean it!"

"There's no shame in admitting you miss her, Shaun."

"Of course I miss her, Sara. I miss her every minute of every day, but that's not the problem. She's been gone for a long time, and I've written three books since then, that's not my problem."

"So then what is it?"

He said nothing.

"Does it have something to do with last night?" She asked.

"What about last night?"

"What about it?"

"You, me, in the kitchen? In bed?"

"What does that have to do with anything? We fucked, we had fun, no big deal. It wasn't the first time. That's got nothing to do with writing."

"But that's just it, Shaun, we didn't fuck. We never just... fuck. It might start out that way, but we always end up making love. You make love. That's what you do. You're not a hit it and quit it, booty call kinda guy. You lose yourself in the person you're with. You kiss, you hold, you caress, and you're all passion. And that's not fair."

"Not fair? I thought that's what women wanted."

"Sure we do. I know I do. But I want that when it's me that you're passionate about. But every time you and I sleep together I'm not Sara, I was Someone Else. You close your eyes and kiss Someone Else and you hold Someone Else, and you made love to Someone Else. You weren't present last night, or all the other times we slept together for that matter. You were here but your mind was somewhere else."

"That's bullshit," he said weakly.

"It isn't, and you know it."

"That's not true," he roared, slamming his fist on the table, causing his coffee cup to go flying and his laptop to levitate briefly. He rose and flung his chair into the pool where it floated for a moment before sinking into the clear blue water.

Sara didn't flinch.

"You want something that you had, but it's gone," she said gently. "Claire is gone. She's gone forever and you try to resurrect her with every woman you're with."

"Jesus Chris, Sara, that's a bit dramatic don't you think?"

Sara chuckled.

"Really? Remember London?"

"Of course I remember London we went there on my book tour. What about it?"

"What about it he says? The woman you met in the hotel, the Dutch chick, what the hell was her name..."

"Helena."

"Helena. That's it. That poor woman will never get over you. She wept when you left. Wept, Shaun, and she only knew you two days. How about Christine in L.A.? Or the singer in Atlanta, the real pretty one, Nadine?"

"Nadia."

"Whatever. You left her heartbroken, and not because you're a bad guy, it's just the way you relate. You talk to them, you really listen to them, and you're sensitive to their needs. Same way you were with Claire. Then the panties drop, and boy, that's when you really go to work. They don't have a chance."

Shaun paced by the side of the pool.

"So what's your point?" He said angrily.

"You're not a bad guy," Sara said again, "I know you don't mean to do that, but they have no way of knowing that you're looking for something that you don't have anymore. They don't know that they can never give it to you. No one can. It's not fair. Not fair to you, and definitely not fair to the women you do it to."

"I get the point. Is the lecture over, professor?"

"That was mean, Shaun. And no, it isn't. I'm talking to you as your friend so enough with the Goddamn wisecracks. I saw those women at the event last night. Half of them were in there drooling over the big black stud from the Bronx and scheming to get a crack at you."

"Oh please. Now you're really going..."

"Listen to me," Sara snapped. "Just listen to me. I know you're lonely, I know you miss her, and I know the temptation to jump into bed with these women is hard to resist but trust me, nothing good is going to happen if you do."

"I guess I should save it all for you, huh?" He said with a smirk.

Sara's face fell. "Fuck you. That was cruel. You know what Shaun? I think I'm going to shut up now before you say something else that's going to make me forget that we're friends."

"I'm a big boy, Sara, I can..."

"Daddy, why is the chair in the water?"

Tanya stood behind them in her PJ's rubbing her eyes.

"Your silly daddy knocked it over by mistake," Sara said quickly.

"That's right," Shaun said. "Silly."

He picked his daughter up and gave her a kiss. "C'mon, Princess, let's get you ready for school."

He picked Tanya up and walked inside, already feeling horrible about what he'd said to Sara. He stopped and put his daughter down, intending to go apologize but stopped when he saw her dive gracefully into the pool and begin swimming slow laps over the sunken chair.

Thank you for reading.

Click the link below to get ***CANDYLAND*** from Amazon.

GET CANDYLAND!

ALSO BY HUGH O. SMITH

SOCCER MOM

Also set in the drama hotbed of Willows, New Jersey.
Read on for a synopsis and to find out how to
get a copy of ***Soccer Mom*** for **FREE.**

When Valerie's husband loses his job, a mysterious woman makes her an offer that will keep her family from losing everything. Valerie soon finds that what seemed like a Godsend is a curse, and now, this suburban Soccer Mom wants out of the dark world she finds herself in, but is it too late?

Get ***Soccer Mom*** now. Read this riveting story of a good woman slowly getting in touch with her dark side, then ask yourself the question...

What would **YOU** do to save your family?

Want to read this riveting novella for **FREE**?

Clike **HERE** to get join Hugh's mailing list and get ***Soccer Mom*** now.

WILLOWS

living in the past is easy when your future has been stolen.

Marcus has life figured out. Love + marriage = happiness. He's got big plans that include gold rings, white picket fences, and the pitter patter of little feet. But what he doesn't know is that the love of his life, his fiancé Tami, has other plans. Plans that don't include him...

...he'll soon learn the hard way that sometime love just isn't enough.

Tami knows Marcus is a good man, but good men are boring. She has secret desires that need an outlet, desires that

Marcus could never understand, much less fulfill. She doesn't want to be treated like a queen... she wants someone who will take the gloves off... she NEEDS, a bad boy...

A **VERY** bad boy

And she found one in the last place she thought she would... behind the pulpit!

The Reverend Justin Oliver loves his calling. The Lord has given him this opportunity to minister to the good people of the town of Willows, and he is happy to serve. But he's not perfect... he's still a man... and men have needs...

...and Lord knows he has more needs than most.

His flock – men and women alike – are finding out that the Pastor has many, many, ways for them to come to the light.

Ways that include pleasure... and pain!

Maria is broken. She knows this. Things have happened in her past that make her unfixable, unwanted, unlovable. Time and again men have used her and thrown her away. She was certain that was her destiny, until she found a man filled with Spirit who could make her whole.

She had hope for a new life... until her best friend Tami did the unthinkable.

Now she knows the truth. The man she loves cannot, will not, ever love her back...

Her life is ruined. Now someone has to pay.

Can Marcus Make sense of his new reality after his dreams have been taken from him, or does he have to get revenge in order to reclaim what is his?

Will Tami find happiness with her choices or will her dark desires eventually consume her?

Can Maria heal or will she give Tami a taste of her own medicine? After all, Marcus is all alone now... and vulnerable!

Will the Reverend continue to "minister" in his own unique way or will he finally be exposed for what he is?

If you love DRAMA, a SCANDALOUS villain and HOT, steamy scenes that will leave you unable to sleep, get Willows now!

Be warned reader! This is no sweet love story.

Sometimes there is no happy ending.

"This book is amazing! It has everything you look for. Love, sex, betrayal, violence, and the unexpected. There were so many twists and turns. I gasped half a dozen times. So good."

"Unique perspective of a relationship gone horribly awry."

"A gripping tale of mistrust and betrayal."

"Love, Heartache, Lies, Scandal, Low down dirty unspeakable behavior and that's just to name a taste of what you get from this awesome story line. "

"By the end, this well written dramatic novel left me emotionally spent but looking forward to future novels."

"This is a great book! It held my interest and kept me turning the pages to find out what was going to happen next."

WILLOWS

HUGH O. SMITH

About the Author

Hugh O. Smith is the author of ***WILLOWS, GREEN EYES AND GOOD HAIR***, the novella ***SOCCER MOM, CANDYLAND,*** and his newest novel ***PLEASURE PARTY***.

Originally from Jamaica, Hugh credits his Jamaican upbringing and its rich storytelling tradition for his writing inspiration.

Website - HughOSmith.com

Email - hugh@hughosmith.com

Facebook - /hughosmithofficial

Twitter - /hughosmith

Instagram - /hughosmith

Edited by Dot and Dash LLC

Cover Design by 100covers.com

Pleasure Party / Hugh O. Smith

Made in the USA
Middletown, DE
02 April 2022